He was asleep, sprawled on his stomach on the double bed under the window, snoring quietly.

But when one has made his name as the greatest thief in the world, true sleep is a habit you lose quickly, which was the only reason he heard the sound at all. The noise was soft, almost lost in the crash of the distant waves, yet unmistakable to anyone who'd heard it before. A sword snickering in anticipation isn't a sound you forget.

Eli threw himself out of bed as the blade stabbed into the mattress where his bare back had been a split second earlier. He landed on the floor in a tangle of sheets as the man, head to foot in dark clothing, yanked his sword free. Eli didn't waste any more time looking. He turned and bolted for the door.

"Josef!" he shouted, scrambling over the rag rug. "*JOSEF!*"

The assassin caught him on the second yell.

———————

Praise for *The Spirit Thief*

"*The Spirit Thief* is a delightfully giddy romp of a novel."
—**KAREN MILLER**

By Rachel Aaron

The Legend of Eli Monpress

The Spirit Thief
The Spirit Rebellion
The Spirit Eater

THE SPIRIT EATER

The Legend of Eli Monpress Book 3

RACHEL AARON

orbit

www.orbitbooks.net

This book is a work of fiction. Names, characters, places, and incidents are the product of the author's imagination or are used fictitiously. Any resemblance to actual events, locales, or persons, living or dead, is coincidental.

Copyright © 2010 by Rachel Aaron
Excerpt from *The Spirit War* copyright © 2010 by Rachel Aaron

Orbit
Hachette Book Group
237 Park Avenue
New York, NY 10017
Visit our website at www.orbitbooks.net.

Orbit is an imprint of Hachette Book Group. The Orbit name and logo are trademarks of Little, Brown Book Group Limited.

Printed in the United States of America

First edition: December 2010

10 9 8 7 6 5 4 3 2 1

For Nate, who made it.

THE SPIRIT EATER

PROLOGUE

The great hall of the Shapers had been flung open to let in the wounded. Shaper wizards, their hands still covered in soot from their work, ran out into the blowing snow to help the men who came stumbling onto the frosted terrace through a white-lined hole in the air. Some fell and did not rise again, their long, black coats torn beyond recognition. These the Shapers rolled onto stretchers that, after a sharp order, stood on their own and scrambled off on spindly wooden legs, some toward the waiting doctors, others more slowly toward the cold rooms, their unlucky burdens already silent and stiff.

Alric, Deputy Commander of the League of Storms, lay on the icy floor near the center of the hall, gritting his teeth against the pain as a Shaper physician directed the matched team of six needles sewing his chest back together. His body seized when the needles hit a nerve, and the Shaper grabbed his shoulders, slamming him back against the stone with surprising strength.

"You must not move," she said.

"I'm trying not to," Alric replied through gritted teeth.

The old physician arched an eyebrow and started the needles again with a crooked finger. "You're lucky," she said, holding him still. "I've seen others with those wounds going down to the cold rooms." She nodded at the three long claw marks that ran down his chest from neck to hip. "You must be hard to kill."

"Very," Alric breathed. "It's my gift."

She gave him a strange look, but kept her hands firmly on his shoulders until the needles finished. Once the wounds were closed, the doctor gave him a bandage and left to find her next patient. Alric sat up with a ragged breath, holding his arms out as the bandage rolled around his torso of its own accord and tied itself over his left shoulder. After the gauze had pulled itself tight, Alric sat a moment longer with his eyes closed, mastering the pain. When he was sure he had it under control, he grabbed what was left of his coat, buckled his golden sword to his hip, and got up to find his commander.

The Lord of Storms was standing in the snow beside the great gate he had opened for their retreat. Through the shimmering hole in the world, Alric could see what was left of the valley, the smoking craters rimmed with dead stone, the great gashes in the mountains. But worse than the visible destruction were the low, terrified cries of the mountains. Their weeping went straight to his bones in a way nothing else ever had and, he hoped, nothing ever would again.

The Lord of Storms had his back to Alric. As always, his coat was pristine, his sword clean and sheathed at his side. He alone of all of them bore no sign of what had just occurred, but a glance at the enormous black clouds overhead was all Alric needed to know his commander's mood. Alric took a quiet, calming breath. He would need to handle this delicately.

The moment he stepped into position, the Lord of Storms barked, "Report."

"Twenty-four confirmed casualties," Alric said. "Eighteen wounded, eight still unaccounted for."

"They're dead," the Lord of Storms said. "No one else will be coming through." He jerked his hand down and the gate beside him vanished, cutting off the mountains' cries. Despite himself, Alric sighed in relief.

"Thirty-two dead out of a force of fifty," the Lord of Storms said coldly. "That's a rout by any definition."

"But the objective was achieved," Alric said. "The demon was destroyed."

The Lord of Storms shook his head. "She's not dead."

"Impossible," Alric said. "I saw you take her head off. Nothing could survive that."

The Lord of Storms sneered. "A demon is never defeated until you've got the seed in your hand." He walked to the edge of the high, icy terrace, staring down at the snow-covered peaks below. "We tore her up a bit, diminished her, but she'll be back. Mark me, Alric, this isn't over."

Alric pulled himself straight. "Even if you are right, even if the creature is still alive somewhere, we stopped the Dead Mountain's assault. The Shepherdess can have no—"

"*Do not speak to me about that woman!*" the Lord of Storms roared. His hand shot to the blue-wrapped hilt of his sword, and the smell of ozone crept into the air as little tongues of lightning crackled along his grip. "What we faced tonight should never have been allowed to come about." He looked at Alric from the corner of his eye. "Do you know what we fought in that valley?"

Alric shuddered, remembering the black wings that blotted out the sky, the screaming cry that turned his bones to water and made mountains weep in terror, the hideous, black shape that his brain refused to remember in detail because something that horrible should never be seen more than once. "A demon."

The Lord of Storms laughed. "A demon? A demon is what we get when we neglect a seed too long. A demon can be taken out by a single League member. We kill *demons* every day. What we faced tonight, Alric, was a fully grown seed." The Lord of Storms took a deep breath. "If I hadn't taken its head when I did, we could have witnessed the birth of another Dead Mountain."

"Another..." Alric swallowed against the dryness in his throat. "But the Dead Mountain is under the Lady's own seal. Tiny slivers may escape, but nothing big enough to let the demon actually replicate itself could get through. It's impossible; the whole containment system would be undermined."

"Impossible?" The Lord of Storms shook his head. "You keep telling yourself that. But it is the Lady's will that keeps the seal in place, and when her attention wanders, we're the ones who have to clean up."

The Lord of Storms clenched his sword hilt, and the smell of ozone intensified. Alric held his breath, wondering if he should go for cover. When the Lord of Storms was this angry, nothing was safe. "It's not just a large seed," the commander said at last. "That would be too simple. What we saw tonight was as much a product of the soil as the seed. The Master got his claws in a strong one, this time. Thirty-two League members and a ruined valley are *nothing* compared to what this could end up costing us. We have to find the creature and finish her."

Alric was looking for a way to answer that when the soft sound of a throat clearing saved him the trouble. He turned to see a group of old men and women in fine heavy coats standing in the doorway to the great hall. Alric nodded graciously, but the Lord of Storms just sneered and turned back to the mountains, crossing his arms over his chest. Undeterred by the League commander's rudeness, the figure at the group's head, a tall, stern man with a white beard down to his chest, stepped forward.

"My Lord of Storms," he said, bowing to the enormous man's back. "I am Ferdinand Slorn, Head Shaper and Guildmaster of the Shaper Clans."

"I know who you are," the Lord of Storms said. "We'll be out of here soon enough, old man."

"You are welcome to stay as long as you need," Slorn said, smiling benignly. "However, we sought you out to offer assistance of a different nature."

The Lord of Storms looked over his shoulder. "Speak."

Slorn remained unruffled. "We have heard of your battle with the great demon, as well as its unfortunate escape. As Master of the Shapers, I would like to offer our aid in its capture."

"Guildmaster," Alric said, "you have already helped so much, providing aid and—"

"How do you know about that?" The sudden anger in the Lord of Storms' voice stopped Alric cold.

"These mountains are Shaper lands, my lord," the

Guildmaster replied calmly. "You can hardly expect to fight a battle such as you just fought without attracting our attention. Our great teacher, the Shaper Mountain, on whose slopes we now stand, is enraged and grieving. His brother mountains were among those injured by the demon, many beyond repair. As his students, we feel his pain as our own. We cannot bring back what was destroyed, but we do ask that we be allowed to assist in the capture of the one responsible."

"What help could you be to us?" the Lord of Storms scoffed. "Demons are League business. You may be good at slapping spirits together, but what do Shapers know of catching spirit eaters?"

"More than you would think." The old man's eyes narrowed, but his calm tone never broke. "After all, we Shapers live our lives in the shadow of the demon's mountain. You and your ruffians may be good at tracking down the demon's wayward seeds when they escape into the world, but it is my people, and the great mountains we honor, who suffer the demon daily. Tonight, several beautiful, powerful spirits, ancient mountains and allies of my people, were eaten alive. Even for us, who are used to bearing sorrow, this loss is too much. We cannot rest until the one responsible is destroyed."

"That's too bad," the Lord of Storms said, turning to face the old Guildmaster at last. "I'll say this one more time. Demons are League business. So, until I put a black coat on your shoulders, you will stay out of our way."

The Guildmaster stared calmly up at the Lord of Storms. "I can assure you, my dear Lord of Storms, we will avoid your way entirely. All I ask is the opportunity to pursue our own lines of inquiry."

The Lord of Storms leaned forward, bending down until he was inches away from the old man's face. "Listen," he said, very low, "and listen well. We both know that you're going to do what you're going to do, so before you go and do it, take my advice: Do not cross me. If you or your people get in my way on the hunt for the creature, I will roll right over you without looking back. Yours wouldn't be the first city I've razed to kill a demon. Do you understand me, Shaper?"

Slorn narrowed his eyes. "Quite clearly, demon hunter."

The Lord of Storms gave him one final, crackling glare before pushing his way through the small crowd of Shaper elders and stomping back across the frozen terrace toward the brightly lit hall.

Alric thanked the Shaper elders before running after his commander. "Honestly," he said, keeping his voice low, "it would make my life easier if you learned a little tact. They were just trying to help."

"Help?" the Lord of Storms scoffed. "There's nothing someone outside the League could do to help. Let them do whatever they like. It'll end the same. No seed sleeps forever, Alric. Sooner or later, she's going to crack, and when that happens, I'll be there. The next time I corner her, there will be no escape. I don't care if I have to cut through every spirit in the sphere, I won't stop until I have her seed in my hand." He clenched his fists. "Now, get everyone out of here, including corpses. We burn the dead tonight at headquarters. I want nothing of ours left in this mountain."

And with that he vanished, just disappeared into thin air, leaving Alric walking alone through the center of the

Shaper hall. Alric skidded to a stop. It was always like this when things were bad, but the only thing to do was obey. Gritting his teeth, he walked over to the best mended of the walking wounded and began giving orders to move out. His words were met with grim stares. Most of the League were too wounded to make a safe portal back to the fortress, but they were soldiers, and they obeyed without grumbling, working quietly under Alric to bring home the dead through the long, bloody night.

Ferdinand Slorn, Head Shaper and Guildmaster of the Shaper Clans, watched the Lord of Storms' exit with heavy-lidded eyes. The other heads of the Shaper disciplines were already dispersing, whispering to one another as they walked into the crowded hall. Only one stayed behind. Etgar, the Master Weaver, youngest of the elders, remained at the edge of the terrace, the embroidered hem of his elegant coat twitching nervously against his shins.

The old Shaper smiled. "Go on, Etgar."

Etgar paled. "Master Shaper," he said, his deep voice strangely timid. "Yours is the voice of all Shapers. I do not oppose your judgment, but—"

"But you do not agree," the Master Shaper finished.

"We're all upset," Etgar said, his words coming in long, angry puffs of white vapor in the cold night. "What happened in that valley is tragedy enough to fill our laments for the next dozen years, but demons are the League's responsibility. Even if we could do something, if the demon is still alive as the League thinks, it's probably gone back to the Dead Mountain by now."

"No," Slorn said. "Once awakened, a seed can never return to the mountain. The seal works both ways, repelling awakened demons from the outside as surely as it pins their Master below the mountain's stone. My son told me that much before he vanished." The old man smiled a long, sad smile and turned his eyes to the snow-covered mountains. "No, Etgar, if the creature is still alive, it's out there, somewhere, and if it wishes to survive the League's wrath long enough to recover its power, it will have to hide. If that is indeed the case, the best place for it is under the only cover the creature has left, its human skin. Demons may be League business, but humans are another matter."

"What difference does that make?" Etgar shook his head in frustration. "Even if she does take a human form to escape the League's justice, what are we to do about it? I want justice served as much as any, but we are crafters, Guildmaster, not bounty hunters. How are we even to search for her?"

"We will not," Slorn said. "We shall allow others to search for us." The Guildmaster reached into his robes and pulled out a small notebook. "She may be a daughter of the Dead Mountain, but so long as she takes refuge in a human form, she will be vulnerable to human greed." He pulled an ink pencil from his shirt pocket and began to write furiously. After a few moments he smiled, ripped the page from his book, and handed it to Etgar. "Take this to the Council of Thrones."

Etgar stared dumbly at the paper. "What is it?"

"A bounty pledge," Slorn said. "The girl, alive, for two hundred thousand gold standards."

Etgar's eyes went wide. "Two hundred thousand gold standards?" he cried, looking at the paper again as though it had suddenly grown fangs. Sure enough, there was the figure, written out in the Guildmaster's nearly illegible hand across the very bottom of the note.

"A small sum compared to what we have lost tonight," Slorn said, his voice cold and terrible. "This world is not so large that we can afford to be placid, Etgar. Too long we Shapers have left these things to the League, and look where it has gotten us. There are more seeds than ever, and now a fully awakened demon slaughters our ancient allies while we do nothing but wring our hands. I don't know what game the Shepherdess is playing letting things get this bad, but we cannot afford to play along anymore. This may all be for nothing, but no matter the outcome, I will not be the Guildmaster who shuts his hall against what he does not wish to see." He reached out, folding the younger man's hands over the paper. "See that that gets to Zarin."

For a moment Etgar just stood there, staring dumbly at the note in his fist. Finally, he bowed. "As you will, Master Shaper."

The old man clapped Etgar on the shoulder and set off for the great hall, the ice on the stones creeping away to make a clear path for him across the wide terrace. Etgar stayed put, looking down at the torn page in his hand, reading it again, just to be sure. Two hundred thousand gold council standards to be paid out on proof of death for the daughter of the Dead Mountain. That was it, no mention of the crime, no personal details, just the amount and a short description of a thin, pale girl with dark hair and dark eyes taken from what one of the wounded League men had been able to get out before he died.

"The Weaver's will be done," Etgar muttered. Frowning, he thrust the bounty request into his pocket and set

off across the terrace to find a messenger to take the order
to Zarin.

In the hills at the foot of the mountains, just above the
tree line where the snow was still thin, something black
fell from the sky. Ice and dirt flew up in an explosion
where it hit, leaving a rounded crater on the silent mountainside. Eventually, the dust settled, but inside the crater,
nothing moved. The mountain slope returned to its previous stillness, until, when the sky was turning gray with
the predawn light, something reached up and clutched
the crater's edge. Black and bleeding, it pulled itself up,
leaving a trail in the dirt. It climbed over the crater's lip
and tumbled down the mountainside, sliding down the
slope until it hit the first of the scraggly trees. The creature rasped in pain, clutching itself with long black limbs.
It stayed like that for a long while, lying still against the
scrubby pines.

As the sky grew lighter, the darkness clinging around
the slumped figure burned away, leaving the small, broken body of a girl. She was pale and naked, lying doubled
over on her side, clutching her stomach. There was snow
on the ground around her, but her body scarcely seemed to
feel it. She lay on the frozen ground, never shivering, eyes
open wider than any human eyes should, staring up at the
mountains above, or, rather, past them, toward something
only she could see. Her skeletal body twitched, and she
took a shallow, ragged breath.

Why are you still here? The voice was colder than the
snow.

The girl on the ground closed her eyes in shame and
took another breath.

Stop that, the voice said. *You failed. You lost. What right do you have to go on living? Why do you waste my time?*

The girl shook her head and curled her body tighter. "Please," she whispered, her voice little more than a hoarse vibration in her throat. "Please don't leave me, Master."

The voice made a disgusted sound. *Shut up. You don't get to speak. You don't even deserve my attention. Just die in a place that's easy to find so my seed doesn't go to waste.*

The girl gave a sobbing cry, but the voice was already gone. Her head throbbed at the sudden emptiness, and she realized she was alone. Truly alone, for the first time since she could remember. She would have wept then, but she had no strength left even to break down. She could only lie there in the shade of the tree, hoping the slope was close enough to fulfill the Master's final request. After losing so completely, it was the least she could do.

It wouldn't be long, at least. Her blood was red again, mixing with the dirt to dye the snow a dull burgundy in a circle around her. Soon, all her failures would be behind her. All her weakness, everything, it would all be gone. She was so focused on this she didn't notice the man coming across the mountain slope toward her until his shadow blotted out the sun in her eyes. She looked up in surprise. He was very tall, dressed like a poor farmer in a ragged wool coat, but his body was that of a fighter, with blades strapped up and down his torso and a monstrous iron sword on his back.

He stood a step away from her, his face shadowed and unreadable with the sun behind him. Then, in one smooth motion, he drew a short sword from the sheath at his hip. This much, at least, she could understand, and the girl closed her eyes, ready for the blow.

It never came. The man simply stood there, staring at her with the blade in his hand. When she opened her eyes again, he spoke.

"Do you want to die?"

The girl nodded.

Overhead, the sword whistled through the cold air, then stopped. The man's voice spoke again. "Look at me and say you want to die."

The girl lifted her head and stared up at him. The morning sun glinted off the sharp blade he held in the air, ready to come down. How easy it would be to let this stranger end it, how simple. And yet, when she tried to tell him to go on, finish what the demon hunters had started, her voice would not come. She tried again, but all she managed was a squeak. The dull red circle on the snow around her was very wide now. Soon, she wouldn't even have a choice. She knew she should take his offer, end it quickly, but her mouth would not move, because it was not true.

She did not want to die. The realization came as a surprise, but the truth of it rang in her, vibrating against the inner corners of herself she'd long forgotten. She had been defeated, abandoned, wounded beyond repair. She owed it to the Master to die, owed it to herself to save the horrible shame of living on when she was not wanted, but still, despite all reason...

"I want to live." The words came out in a croak, and she only recognized the voice as her own from the pain in her dry throat.

Above her, the man nodded and sheathed his sword. "Then take another breath."

She met his eyes and slowly, shuddering with pain, did as he said.

He grinned wide and reached down, grabbing her arms in his hands. He lifted her like she weighed nothing and tossed her over his shoulder. "Come on, then," he said. "I had a long walk up here to see what that crash was, and we've got a long walk back. If you've chosen to live, you'll have to keep your end and keep breathing. Just focus on that and I'll get us back down to camp to see to your wounds. Then we'll see where we go from there. What's your name?"

"Nico," the girl said, wincing against his shoulder. The Master had given her that name.

"Nico, then," the man said, setting off down the mountain. "I'm Josef."

Nico pushed away from his shoulder, trying not to get blood on his shirt, but he just shrugged her back on and kept going. Eventually she gave up, resting her head on his back to focus all of her energy on breathing, letting her breaths fill the emptiness the Master had left inside her. As she focused her mind on the feel of her lungs expanding and contracting, she felt something close at the back of her mind, like a door gently swinging shut. But even as she became aware of the sensation, she realized she could no longer remember how she'd come to be on that mountain slope, or where her wounds came from, and just as quickly, she realized she didn't care. The one thing she could remember was that before the man Josef appeared, she'd been ready to die. Now, clinging to his shoulder, death was her enemy. Something deep had changed, and Nico was content to let it stay that way. Reveling in a strange feeling of freedom, she went limp on Josef's shoulder, focusing only on savoring each gasp of air she caught between jolts as Josef jogged down the steep slope to the valley below.

CHAPTER
1

Two years later.

The house on chicken legs crouched between two steep hills, its claws digging deep into the leaf litter to keep the building from sliding farther down into the small ravine. If Heinricht Slorn had any worries about the precarious position he'd put his walking house in, his face didn't show it. He sat in his workroom, his brown fur glowing in the strong lamplight. His dark, round eyes glittered as they focused on the object taking up most of the large worktable. It was about four feet long, white as a dried bone, and shaped somewhat like a sword, or like a stick a child had carved into a sword. Despite its crude form, Slorn hovered over the object, his enormous hands running over its smooth surface with the painful, meticulous slowness of one master appreciating the work of another.

Pele sat at his elbow, also staring at the white sword.

She was trying her best to match her father's focus, but they'd been doing this for two days now and she was getting awful sick of staring and seeing nothing. Sitting in the dark room, her mind began to wander back to the other, more interesting projects she'd been working on before Slorn had put her to work on the Fenzetti blade.

"Pele." Slorn's gruff voice snapped her back to attention. His eyes hadn't left the sword, but that didn't matter. Her father seemed to have a supernatural ability to tell when her attention began to drift. "What is the first thing we determine when examining an unknown spirit?"

"Its nature," Pele answered at once, sitting up on the hard workbench. "A Shaper must know the nature of her materials. Only when a spirit's true nature is known will the Shaper be able to bend it to her purpose."

"Good," Slorn said, reaching out to take her hand and press it against the smooth surface of the Fenzetti. "And what is the nature of this spirit?"

Pele flinched when she touched the sword. It was unnaturally smooth and strangely warm, yet she knew from experience that its surface could not be scratched even by an awakened blade. They'd tried half a dozen blades the morning it had arrived, and none of them had been able to make so much as a nick in the sword's white face.

Slorn was looking at her now, and she shrank under his intense gaze, her brain spinning to come up with an answer. "It's not wood," she said uncertainly. "Not stone either. It could be a metal not yet known, one of a different nature than iron or the mountain metals, perhaps a—"

"Stop," Slorn said. "You're not answering the question. I did not ask what it wasn't."

Pele sighed in frustration. "But—"

"Look again."

Slorn picked up the sword and set it point down on the floor between them. "Look at it as if you'd never seen it before and tell me what you think it is."

Pele bit her lip, looking the sword up and down. "A bone," she said at last.

Slorn grinned wide, showing all his yellow teeth. "All right, let's say, for the moment, it's a bone."

"But that's impossible," Pele said. "Bone metal is ancient. If it was actually bone, it would have rotted away ages ago. And why haven't we found any two pieces together? Surely if it was bone we'd have found a skeleton or…"

She stopped. Slorn was shaking his head.

"You're doing it again," he said. "If you're ever going to be more than a common wizard tinkerer, you need to stop trying to make the spirits fit into your expectations." He returned the blade to the table. "This is the spirits' world, Pele, not ours. We may command them, but they see the nature of things that we cannot. As Shapers, it is our job to fit into the spirits' order, not the other way around. Fenzetti understood this, and that's how he was able to shape what everyone else called unshapable."

He reached out and took the sword, not by its handle but by its point. "A Shaper must remember," he said, wrapping his fingers around the blade, "trust what you see, not what you know. Human knowledge is fragmented, but the spirit always knows its own nature."

With that, he began to tilt his hand up. The table creaked as he pressed against it, the muscles in his arms straining from the pressure. The sword, however, remained unchanged, but then, slowly, subtly, it began to bend. The white point curled with his hand, bending over on itself with a creak unlike anything Pele had heard before. Sweat started to soak through Slorn's shirt, but his face remained calm and determined. His hands were steady, bending the strange metal in a slow roll until, at last, he'd bent it over completely so that the tip of the sword brushed the blade.

He stopped, panting, and slumped over the bench, an enormous grin on his face. Despite the pressure of Slorn's bending, the curve was smooth, like an ox's curved horn. Pele touched it with murmured wonder and then snatched her hand back again. The sword was warm as a living thing.

"It *is* bone," she whispered, eyes wide. "But bone from what?"

"That's a mystery I cannot answer," Slorn said, sitting down on the bench. "But I think it's time we tested the rumor that drove me to send Monpress after it in the first place." Still smiling at the curled tip, he picked up the sword. "Fenzetti wrote that bone metal is indestructible, even by demons. It's the one spirit they can't eat." He paused. "Do you know why I make manacles for your mother?"

Pele shook her head, silent. Slorn never talked about her mother.

"They give the demon something to chew on other than the demonseed herself," he said. "Before she had to be isolated, Nivel and I did many experiments on the subject. She was the one who came up with using restraints. A demon, you see, will always attack spirits outside the demonseed first, since the seed relies on the host's strength until it is ready to awaken. This need to be constantly eating can be exploited by placing a strong-willed material along the host's body. Even though the demon knows better, knows it's a trick, it can't help its nature. It will attack those spirits endlessly, focusing its attention on the manacles instead of the host. This division of attention slows its growth phenomenally. Of course, it's not a perfect solution. Manacles are still spirits, and even the most stubborn awakened steel can only hold out for so long before it gets eaten down. But"—he tapped the bone metal against the table—"let's see how the demon does with a manacle it can chew on forever. If this bone metal is truly inedible by demons, it may slow Nivel's degradation to almost nothing, buying us a few more years to work on a cure."

"But Father," Pele said slowly. "You always say there is no cure."

Slorn's smile faded. "It is good to think that way," he said, laying the bent sword down again. "We must be realists. Still"—he looked at her, and his dark eyes were almost like the human eyes of the father she remembered from her childhood—"your mother has not given up. Not yet. And I would be a poor husband indeed if I let her fight alone."

Pele shook her head, blinking back tears. Slorn put his arm around her shoulders, pulling her to lean against him. "None of that," he whispered.

Pele sniffed and scrubbed her eyes, trying to compose herself. They had work to do. Now was not the time to go crying. But as she tried to pull away, she realized her father had gone stiff. She looked up at him, but he was staring out the window, his round bear ears swiveling.

"Father?" she whispered.

He didn't answer. Then she heard it too. Outside,

something thumped in the dark. It was big, and loud, far too loud to be one of the mountain cats, and the bears never came near Slorn's house.

"Pele," Slorn said, "get your knife. We have company."

She did as he told her, grabbing her knife from its hook. While she was belting it on, Slorn whispered something to the wall. She couldn't hear what he said, but the wall's answer was plain.

"I don't know," it said apologetically, timbers creaking. "He's no wizard, and that makes him very hard to keep track of. This one's especially bad. His soul is like a dull spot. He'd never have been able to slip by the Awakened Wood otherwise."

"I am well aware of the wood's weaknesses," Slorn said, giving the wall a pat. "You'd better wake the house."

"Yes, Slorn," the wall whispered, but Slorn was already gone, marching down the narrow hall. He threw open the front door and stepped out onto the rickety stairs. Pele pushed right up behind him, gripping the hilt of her knife as she peeked over his shoulder. There, standing at the edge of the rectangle of yellow light cast from the doorway, clinging to the steep slope with one arm, was a man she never wanted to see again.

Slorn glared down from his steps, crossing his arms over his chest. "Berek Sted."

The man sneered and moved into the light. He looked very different from when Pele had seen him last. His bald head was covered in several weeks' growth of stubbly hair, all except the top, where true baldness had left him bare. His scarred face was overgrown as well and streaked with dirt. His black coat was gone, as was his sash with its grotesque collection of severed hands and broken swords.

Instead, his bare chest was wrapped in bandages, most of which were dark with old, dried blood. But the greatest change of all was his left arm. His shoulder and the first half of bicep looked the same as ever, but then, his arm simply stopped. He had no elbow, no hand, just a badly bandaged lump that he kept pressed against his side.

"Found you at last," Sted panted. "Swordsmith."

"What do you want?" Slorn asked, his voice dry.

Sted shifted his weight, pushing off the steep hillside with his one good arm to hurl something straight at them. It landed with a clatter at Slorn's feet, biting into the weather-stained wood. Slorn looked down, arching a furry eye ridge at what was left of Sted's black-toothed awakened blade. The top half of the sword was gone, leaving a ragged, twisted edge, as though the metal had been ripped apart.

"You sold me a faulty sword," Sted said. "I want another, a real one this time. One that won't break when I need it."

Slorn reached down and picked up the broken blade. He turned it over in his hands, and Pele winced. This close, she could hear the metal whimpering.

"Your sword was a quality piece of work," Slorn said. "Even if there was a flaw, the League is the only body entitled to demand my services, and I doubt very much they sent you here looking like that."

"Don't talk to me about the League," Sted growled.

"Ah," Slorn said, his voice cold. "Now I see. You've been drummed out."

"That's none of your business."

"It is indeed my business," Slorn said. "I made that sword for the League, not for you. What was it, Sted? Insubordination? Dereliction of duty?"

"Little of everything," Sted said with a shrug. "To hear that bastard Alric talk, choosing a good fight over a quick demon kill was the end of the world. After all I gave up to join the League, he kicked me out, took away my gifts. But I wouldn't be in this position if your sword had been up to the task, bear man."

Slorn crossed his arms over his aproned chest. "And how did my sword fail you?"

"It was weak!" Sted shouted. "Too weak to take a blow from that blunt bat Liechten uses. I said as much in my defense, but Alric couldn't stand to hear the truth about his precious swordsmith."

Slorn bared his teeth just a fraction. "If that's how you feel, why did you come here?"

"To get what I'm due," Sted said. "After all, it's only fair. You're the one whose failure got me kicked out, so you're the one who's going to have to make it right."

Slorn turned the broken sword over. "I can see from the dents that your sword took several blows from Josef Liechten's 'blunt bat.' An impressive achievement, standing up to the greatest awakened sword in the world. I'd hardly call that deficient." His eyes narrowed. "Though I can't say the same for its wielder."

"Don't blame this on me!" Sted shouted. "I was winning until your sword broke! It's not my fault I lost! I don't lose! Your sword failed me, and now you're going to make up for it. Make me a proper sword, swordsmith! Make me a blade that can take the Heart of War!"

"Impossible," Slorn said, handing the broken blade to Pele. "The Heart of War is the first and greatest awakened blade, forged at the beginning of the world. Even if I could somehow make a blade to rival it, it would be pointless." He glared at Sted. "A blade is only as powerful as the swordsman behind it. I've never seen you fight, but I can tell from how you're acting now that you are no match for Josef Liechten."

Sted sprang forward with astonishing speed and grabbed Slorn by the collar. Slorn was a large man, but Sted towered over him, his face scarlet with rage.

"Mind your snout before I take it off your face!" he roared, jerking Slorn off his feet. "You're going to make me that sword, and then I'm going to kill Liechten and everyone else who's made a fool of me. Starting with you, if you don't watch yourself."

Pele fumbled for her blade, her hands trembling in panic, but Slorn's calm never faltered, even with Sted's screaming mouth an inch from his black nose.

"You will unhand me," he said.

"Or what?" Sted growled.

Slorn smiled, and the fibers of his collar where Sted was holding him suddenly unraveled. Sted was left gripping air as Slorn dropped down. The Shaper landed neatly, and he had just enough time to give Sted a toothy smile before the stair beneath the swordsman's feet snapped like a green branch, launching the larger man into the night. Sted was too surprised to make a sound. He flew through the air, landing with a bone-snapping crack on the opposite slope. He bounced once and then began to slide into the ravine as the leaves that might have stopped his fall skittered away from the source of Slorn's displeasure.

Sted slid all the way to the bottom of the little gorge, landing with a splash in the icy stream. Twenty feet up, Slorn stared down from his stairs, a smirk on his muzzle as his torn collar began to mend itself. "This is my land, Sted," he said calmly. "You don't get to make demands here. Any tacit welcome you had as a League member is now gone, and I suggest you go as well. The forest is unkind to those who threaten me."

As he spoke, a large outcropping of rocks on the slope above Sted began to creak menacingly, but Sted heard none of it. "This isn't over!" he screamed. "You owe me!"

Slorn gave him a final long, disgusted look before turning and marching silently back into the house, pushing Pele ahead of him. The moment the door closed, the house began to move, climbing expertly along the ravine edge on its wooden chicken legs. From the window, Pele could see Sted flailing through the creek after them, but the trees along the water were barring his way, tripping him with their roots and tangling him in their branches. The last thing Pele saw before Sted vanished into the dark was Sted falling into the water, his one arm still reaching out for the retreating house.

"Will he come after us?" she whispered.

"He'll try," Slorn said, easing Sted's broken blade to sleep before tossing it into a barrel full of damaged parts. "The League doesn't take men who give up easily. But don't be afraid; the woods are a dangerous enemy and he's no wizard."

He gave her a yellow-toothed smile and disappeared into his workroom. Pele looked out the window one last time. The dark woods sped by outside as the house crawled north faster than a man could run, farther into the mountains, leaving no footprints behind.

In the dull light just before morning, Nivel sat as she always sat, straight on her rock with her hands folded across her lap. High overhead, the treetops, flat, black shapes against the gray sky, rocked in the wind, but here in her dry ravine it was silent, except for her manacles. As always, the metal cuffs buzzed against her skin. Their silver outsides were gnawed away in places, revealing the dense steel core. Nivel shifted. The decay was unsettling. Slorn had made the manacles for her just a month ago, but each new set seemed to wear out quicker than the one before. Nivel's lips tightened. She knew what that meant, even if she'd never seen it happen. She knew.

Of course you know. The voice sounded almost bored. *You always knew you would lose in the end.*

Nivel folded her hands tighter.

I don't see why you're putting your family through this, it said. *How selfish, fighting a losing battle on their time. You should just let go, let me have you, and set them free. Do you think your husband likes having a bear's head?*

An image flashed before her eyes, Slorn as he'd looked fifteen years ago when they were first married. But the memory had that strange crispness to it that told her it was the demon's sending, and not her own. It liked to riffle through her mind for weapons, but this was a battle they'd been fighting for a long time now, and Nivel was too wise for these old tricks. She closed her eyes against the image and kept her silence. Speaking to the voice only gave it more power, and she had no more to give.

She was finding something else to think about when a strange shadow appeared at the edge of her ravine. Nivel snapped her head up. It was far too early for Slorn or Pele, and no spirit would come near the warding. It could be a phantom. The demon had been making her see things that weren't there for years. Yet, from the confusion in her head, she felt that this was as much a surprise to it as to her. That terrified Nivel more than any false vision. She couldn't afford surprises.

The figure leaned over the edge of the ravine, peering down, and she saw it was a man. A large man with a bald head and a missing left arm. He had bandages across his torso and scars everywhere else. His skin was filthy and scratched all over, as though he'd been wrestling with a thornbush, and his eyes were the eyes of a madman.

He jumped down without a word, landing in a crouch on the sandy bed of the dead creek. He stayed in that crouch, looking around until he spotted her a few feet in front of him.

"There you are," he said, a crooked grin spreading across his face. "Took me awhile to find this place, but I knew the bear man wouldn't take his house too far from his big secret." He took a step forward, his boots dragging through the dry sand. "They tried to keep it away from us, back at headquarters, but the Lord of Storms has a loud voice and no love for you. To hear him talk, I thought you were some sort of monster, a barely controlled disaster waiting to happen, but you're just a woman."

Nivel glared at him. Her eyes were burning, a sure sign they were glowing, but for once she was glad. The large man didn't look so confident anymore. "Who are you?" she said. "Are you League?" Had her time come at last?

"Berek Sted," the man answered, eyeing her more carefully. "And no, not League. You're a demonseed, aren't you? The one Slorn's been experimenting on, trying to find a cure?"

"We have been experimenting together," Nivel said testily.

The man shrugged. "But you have a demon inside you, right? I want to talk to it."

Nivel recoiled. "Where is Slorn? How did you get here through the trees?"

"Trees can be bashed down like everything else," Sted said. "As for the bear man, he's not my problem anymore. Are you going to let me talk to the demon, or am I going to have to force it out?" He looked her up and down. "I may not be League anymore, but even I can tell it wouldn't take much. You're so close to the change I'm surprised you can keep a human form."

"Being close to the edge doesn't mean jumping over," Nivel said. "You League types never appreciated the difference, but then, your lot never was any good at subtleties."

"Don't talk to me about the League!" Sted growled, stepping closer. "I'm here on my own. You see, I have a fight to win, and that thing inside you is going to help me." He took another step. "I've seen the kind of power it can give. If it makes a little girl into a monster who can break my arm, how much stronger will it make me?" His hand shot out and grabbed her wrist. "Let me talk to the demon!"

Before she knew what was happening, Nivel lashed out. She kicked him, hard, and Sted flew backward, crashing into the wall of the ravine with enough force to crack the stone. For a moment Nivel just stood there, panting, and then she realized what she'd done.

"No," she whispered, falling to her knees as the demon-given power roared through her. Her wrists, ankles, and neck burned as the last bits of her manacles dissolved. "No no no no."

Yes.

The voice was roaring in her mind, louder even than her terror. But even as it laughed in triumph, Nivel was not beaten. With a wordless cry of rage, she threw open her spirit. For the first time in a decade, power surged through her, filling her until she thought she would burst. Her own soul felt dark and slimy against her mind, polluted by the creature who had lived in it for so long. Even so, she grabbed her power with the intense focus Shaper wizards train for years to master. Grabbed it and turned it inward.

The laughter stopped. *What are you doing?*

"I didn't fight this long to lose now," Nivel whispered around a mouth that was no longer fully human. "I didn't put my family through this to lose to you."

You answered me at last, the voice crowed triumphantly. *Now I really have won. Rest, Nivel, you fought long and hard. Give up; you deserve it.*

Nivel opened her soul wider still, forcing her will stronger and stronger until she almost matched the demon. "No," she said. "Never." Just a little further. Just a little further.

A hand closed on her throat.

Nivel's eyes shot open. Sted was standing over her, his fingers on her neck, bearing down. She began to choke, beating against him with her fists, but her blows were as weak as a child's. Her demon strength was gone.

Of course, dear. Why would I give you anything you so clearly do not want?

Nivel choked again. She couldn't tell if the voice had been in her head or if she had spoken the words herself. The demon drenched her, flooding through her open soul even as it collapsed. All she could see was Sted above her, laughing as he crushed her throat.

I can kill him for you. The words were a whisper in her ear. *All you have to do is let me.*

Nivel's chest began to convulse, and she realized she was laughing.

"You should know by now," she whispered as she dangled from Sted's hand, "I'd rather die to a stranger than give in to you."

Her breath was gone now, and she could feel her body growing heavy. Still, she wasn't afraid. After ten years of fighting, death felt like a release. She could feel the demon's frustration as her consciousness dimmed, feel it struggling to grab final control of her mind and force the awakening. But it was too late. She was dying, but she was dying as a human. Nivel felt her lips curl into a smile. She may have lost, but so had the demon, and that was as great a victory as she could hope for. Clinging to that final, happy thought, Nivel let the demon, and the last shreds of her life, go. Her last thought was a fuzzy image of her husband, fully human and happy, holding their newborn daughter. She ran to him, arms out and free, as a final, welcome silence fell over her mind.

Sted stood panting in the dark ravine, clutching the neck of the dead demonseed. He could have dropped her at any time, and his muscles begged him to, but Sted ignored them. The bitch was dead—he was sure of it—but she'd died smiling. That was never good. Worse, she was still human. He may have been in the League of Storms for only half a year, but even he'd paid enough attention to know that any demonseed past its first week of gestation should change on death. So why was the thin body hanging from his hand still human?

He was mulling this over when he felt a familiar burning sensation against his fingers. He cursed and jumped back, dropping the body. The woman crumpled to the ground. Then, like a puppet with its strings caught, she jerked. Sted sucked in his breath. The body jerked again, sitting up stiffly. Its back was to Sted, and he briefly considered running before dismissing the idea with a sneer. Men didn't run. So he stood firm in the sand, watching as the corpse turned slowly to look at him.

It was only when he saw its eyes that he was truly afraid. The woman's eyes were enormous, and bright as lanterns. They fixed on him like snake eyes on a mouse, and the creature, for he knew for certain there was nothing human left in the body before him, gave him a small, cold smile. "You wanted to speak with me, yes?"

Sted flinched. The voice coming out of the woman's body was nothing like the voice she had used in life. It was low, strong, masculine, and extremely wrong sounding. Something in it made him want to run, to hide, to cower like a rabbit before a predator. It was a deep, primal need, and for a long moment he had to fight himself to stay still. In the end, however, he stood firm in the sand as the creature in the woman's body examined him.

"You expected something grander," it said bitterly. "So did I. But that woman trapped me at the very end, and if I hadn't taken a bit of you just now, this seed would have died with her." It sighed with a hiss. "Such a waste. This is one of my oldest surviving seeds. If it could have completed the awakening, this cursed trap of a valley would be a very different place right now, and you, dear sheep, would be on your way to the mists."

Sted swallowed. He was barely following this, but the threat in the creature's words was clear enough for a deaf man. Every instinct he had was screaming at him to run, but Sted held fast. After all, he'd come here for a reason, and he wasn't leaving until he got what he wanted.

"You're the demon, then?" he said, standing up straight. "Good, I wanted to talk to you. Seeing how you admitted just now that you wouldn't be here without me, I think you should listen carefully."

The creature chuckled. "Don't think too highly of yourself, Berek Sted. I would have beaten this girl in a few months anyway had you not interfered, *and* had a proper awakening." The woman's head tilted, and the creature's voice grew smooth. "Still, let's not fret on particulars. I know why you came here. I saw it just now"—it tapped its head with one of Nivel's long, pale fingers—"in your mind. You want the power to pay back the Heart of War and its wielder, plus one of my own errant children, for your rather pathetic defeat."

"I wasn't defeated!" Sted shouted. "The League sent me in unprepared with a faulty weapon. If I'd had the power to match that bastard's sword, I would have slaughtered them both! Instead, the coward took my arm, humiliated me, denied me a warrior's death! I won't rest until I pay him back in full!"

The creature gave him a long look. "Under usual circumstances, I'm afraid I wouldn't be able to help you. It takes just the right kind of soul to provide what my seeds need to blossom, souls inevitably belonging to those members of your species who are less deaf than the rest, whom you call wizards. Sadly, you're deafer than most and too old as well, so I cannot give you a seed."

Sted's eyes narrowed. "You're hardly in a position to refuse me, corpse dweller. I may be a one-armed cripple, but I can still bash that body in and reduce your precious seed to a dead nub, so you'd best reconsider."

The creature in the corpse laughed. "Your ignorance is both astounding and refreshing. I can see why they kicked you out. However, while I can't give you a seed, perhaps we can come to an arrangement."

Sted leaned back. "What do you mean?"

The creature gestured at Nivel's chest. "The woman, Nivel, tended her seed for years, far, far longer than any of my others, holding it back through sheer will. A formidable trick, but it had quite the unintended effect. While a seed's awakening can be prevented by the host's will, nothing can stop its growth. Through Nivel's stubborn refusal to give in, she inadvertently created inside herself a seed more powerful than anything I could otherwise get through my formidable prison. Indeed, she has become, almost through accident, the second-most-powerful shard of myself I have ever created." It tapped Nivel's lips. "I am speaking to you through a full-grown seed, steeped in power, yet unawakened. Your meager soul may not be fit to bear a new seed, but it *can* keep this one alive. So, Berek Sted, let me make you a deal. I will give you Nivel's seed and all the power she put into it over ten years of fighting. The seed will give you strength, quickness, and all the gifts I graciously bestow upon my children who do my work in the world. I will set it up so that the Heart of War will come to you. You will have power, eternal life, so long as you can keep it, and the opportunity to thrash

Josef Liechten into the ground. I'll even give you your arm back. Is that not generous?"

Berek Sted swallowed and clutched his bandaged stump. "And what price do you charge for this?"

The creature smiled. "Obedience."

"I'm no one's slave," Sted spat out.

"Who said anything about slaves?" the demon said. "You will be my weapon. An unbeatable weapon, greater even than the Heart of War itself. What do you say, do we have a deal?"

Sted stroked the stub of his arm. He'd sworn never to take another order, but he could not beat Liechten as a cripple. His League powers were gone. His skin was as cuttable and weak as any man's. If he was going to beat the Heart, he needed an edge at any cost.

"And you swear I'll get to fight Liechten?" Sted said. "Man to man, fair and square?"

The demon shrugged. "If fair is what you like, certainly."

Sted nodded. "Then you have your deal."

The creature grinned inhumanly wide, showing a full mouth of teeth and gums. "Welcome to the mountain," it said, its voice a hissing whisper. "Berek Sted."

As the creature spoke his name, the corpse of Nivel jumped forward. It moved impossibly fast, slamming its hands into Sted's bandaged stomach. Sted grunted and fell back as the wounds opened, and he felt something crawl into him. *Crawl* was the only word to describe it. A shadow fell from the dead woman's hands into his stomach, galloping into him on waves of fear, revulsion, and bitter cold. Then, as quickly as it had started, it was over. The woman's corpse flopped to the ground, lifeless again. Sted stood panting, grasping his stomach, but even as he clutched his injured flesh, he felt the skin knitting together under his fingers. Suddenly, the dark shadows of the ravine were clear. The dark was still there, but he could see perfectly. He felt ten years younger, stronger than ever, whole. He had just a moment to revel in this feeling before a crippling pain in his arm sent him to his knees. He turned in horror just in time to see the stump at the end of his shoulder burst open as a hand pushed its way out of his flesh.

Sted cried out in terror. It was no human hand. It was black and shiny, like a bug's shell, and tipped with five long fingers, human looking but wrong. The hand clenched and grasped, pulling itself out of his arm inch by agonizing inch. An eternity of pain later, it stopped, and a new, black arm slightly longer than his own hung from his shoulder, meeting his body in a mash of flesh that hurt to look at.

Sted stumbled back in horror, but the black arm caught him before he could fall. He stopped and stared at the new limb, wiggling each long, sharp claw just as he would his normal fingers. The more he moved the arm, the more he felt its power. The claws were sharp enough to cut bone, and the black skin was as hard as obsidian. He stood there a moment longer, clenching and unclenching his new fist as a smile began to spread over his face.

There, do I not keep my word?

Sted froze in terror. It was the voice from before, but it had not come from the crumpled corpse of the woman on the ground. It had come from inside his head. The creature was in his head.

I told you. He could almost hear it smirking. *You're my weapon now. We're going to be very close, you and I.*

Now, the bear-headed man is coming. It's time to go home and get your first assignment.

"Where?" Sted's voice was barely a whisper.

You know where.

And, Sted realized with a creeping horror, he did. Without quite knowing what he was doing, he bent his legs and jumped. The leap sent him flying over the trees, and Sted began to flail as he shot through the morning air.

So much fear, the demon sneered. *Get rid of it. Fear is for spirits, not my creatures. You asked for this, Berek Sted. You came to me seeking power, and power I have given you. Don't tell me you're too weak to grasp it now that it's yours.*

Sted winced. The creature was right. He could feel the power, an incredible force so much greater than his own. His jump just now, the lack of pain from his injuries, even the black arm was starting to feel like part of himself. It was all power, power he'd paid for, power he'd use to pay back his humiliation.

With this firmly in his mind, Sted hit the ground in a shower of leaves and began to run, skipping northward toward the snowcapped mountains through the long morning shadows. He'd show the demon how a real man used power. Already he could feel the fear fading, and the longer he went, the easier it became. Soon, he was grinning at the sheer strength of his motion, the incredible rush of his power.

Deep in his soul, far deeper than Sted's poor, deaf mind could go, the demon began to laugh.

CHAPTER
2

It was early morning in the port city of Mering on the southern coast of the Council Kingdoms. Down in the bay, the fishing boats were preparing to leave the harbor, the fishermen stringing up their nets by lantern light, for the sun was still just a gray ghost below the horizon. High on the bluffs above the docks, the city lay dark and quiet. Weathered board houses clustered in a nest of narrow, sandy streets, their dark windows open to the warm ocean breeze. Toward the rear of town, where the sandy ground was more solid, stood the Fisherman's Rest, Mering's only inn and the only building with an upper story in the entire town, a feature of which its owner, who was also Mering's mayor, was exceedingly proud.

This night was an exceptionally rare event, for all three of the inn's upper rooms were occupied, despite the relatively exorbitant price their prestige and views demanded. But the strange pair of men and the silent girl who followed them had been throwing gold around like chicken feed from the moment they'd walked into town, and so the innkeeper had no qualms about putting them up in the best rooms Mering had to offer, especially since, as outsiders, he could charge them triple. He'd even cracked open his best cask of wine in hopes of getting them drunk for even more money, but all he'd gotten was a rowdy party from his regular customers and terrifying glares from the taller stranger with the arsenal strapped to his chest. By morning, however, everything was quiet, even the seabirds, and it was this strange, chancy silence that saved Eli's life.

He was asleep, sprawled on his stomach on the double bed under the window, snoring quietly. But when one has made his name as the greatest thief in the world, true sleep is a habit you lose quickly, which was the only reason he heard the sound at all. The noise was soft, almost lost in the crash of the distant waves, yet unmistakable to anyone who'd heard it before. A sword snickering in anticipation isn't a sound you forget.

Eli threw himself out of bed as the blade stabbed into the mattress where his bare back had been a split second earlier. He landed on the floor in a tangle of sheets as the man, head to foot in dark clothing, yanked his sword free. Eli didn't waste any more time looking. He turned and bolted for the door.

"Josef!" he shouted, scrambling over the rag rug. "*JOSEF!*"

The assassin caught him on the second yell. The gloved hand closed on Eli's shoulder, pulling him back with an iron grip as the sword, still snickering, flashed overhead. Eli dodged with an undignified yelp, rolling out of the way as the sword whooshed past him to land with a deadly thunk in the floor. The man ripped it free instantly

and tried to give Eli a kick in the process, but the thief
was already behind him, going for the window. The man
whirled around and raised his sword again, grabbing Eli's
bare foot in his gloved hand to hold the squirming thief
still. But then, just as he was about to bring the sword
down on Eli's shoulder, the blade fell from his grasp, and
the intruder cried out in pain.

With a lightning-quick motion, Eli caught the falling
sword and flipped around, turning the blade on its former
master, who was doubled over on the carpet, clutching his
sword hand, which now had a throwing knife lodged halfway through its palm. That was all Eli saw before Josef
barreled out of the darkness, tackling the man as he went.
They landed against the room's wall in a brawling tangle.
The man in black was shorter than Josef by a foot, not to
mention lighter and injured, but he had a long knife in his
unbloodied hand and Josef, for once, was unarmed. For
a frantic moment, the man had the advantage. Using the
wall for leverage, he pushed the knife toward Josef, going
for the swordsman's naked throat. Josef leaned away, but
he couldn't get out of reach entirely without letting the
man go. When the knife was less than an inch from his
throat, Josef had had enough. Faster than Eli could see,
Josef ducked inside the man's reach and, with a rolling
turn, flipped their positions.

Or he tried to. But rather than turning along the wall, the
assassin's shoulder slammed into the unlatched window.
With a great bang, the shutters flew open, leaving Josef
and the man struggling against thin air. They began to fall,
each flailing in the air, reaching in vain for the window
frame. Just as they started to tumble out of reach, a thin
hand shot out of the darkness and grabbed Josef's wrist.

It was Nico. She was halfway out the window, bracing with both legs against the wide frame, her coat flying around her as she struggled to hold Josef's weight. Struggled and failed. Even braced, Josef's weight was too much, and she was rapidly toppling after him. Just before she lost her footing, Eli's hand grabbed Josef's wrist just below hers, and together they yanked the swordsman back into the room, landing in a heap on the rag carpet.

"Powers," Eli gasped, dropping the assassin's sword, which was no longer snickering. "What about the—"

A sickening crunch finished his sentence for him, and all three of them winced. They sat for a moment in silence before Josef pushed himself up. "I'll check the body," he said, his voice calm, as though he did this every night. "Nico, you're with me. Eli, take the innkeeper."

Eli and Nico nodded and the group split, Josef and Nico slinking down the stairs, quiet as cats, Eli somewhat more loudly, shouting for the innkeeper. Fortunately, the old man was already rushing across the common room in his night cap and dressing gown, a fluttering lamp in his shaking hands.

"Oh, sir!" Eli cried, jumping away from the stairs to cut him off. "Something *dreadful* has just occurred!" And with that Eli launched into a terrible story of robbery, foul play, and tragic ends. By the time he finished, the innkeeper, the night staff, the guests, and every neighbor within earshot was gathered in the inn's common room wearing unified expressions of horror. Eli kept going until he saw Nico wave at him from the front door, signaling that Josef had finished whatever he'd needed to finish. Eli wrapped up his hysterics just as the night watch appeared. Claiming exhaustion, Eli retired to Josef's room, stopping first at his own to retrieve the large stash of coins he'd hidden beneath a loose board. All evidence safely loaded onto his person, he went next door to Josef's somewhat smaller room and locked the door behind him.

"That," he said, "was not how I intended to spend my evening."

Josef didn't even look up from the basin where he was washing his hands. "I think your evening came out better than his, if it makes you feel better."

"It certainly does not," Eli said, flopping down on the bed beside Nico. "Josef, what is going on? We came to this... wherever we are, to get *away* from the hunters for a few days. They're worse than mosquitoes lately. I can count on one hand the number of incident-free days we've had in the last two weeks. Did bounty hunting suddenly become the stylish profession? Have we stumbled into a hunter boom, or do I have a 'Please Ambush' sign on my back that you haven't told me about?"

Josef chuckled, wiping his now clean hands on the towel. "Nothing so complicated. Check out the poster on the table."

Eli glanced over at the end table in surprise, and then reached out to snatch the oversized square of folded parchment, shaking it open as he did so. "It's just my poster," he said, frowning. "Wait, this isn't right." He looked at Josef. "It has to be a joke. Where did you get this?"

"From the inside pocket of our visitor's coat," Josef answered, tossing the towel into the linen bin. "Not that he'll miss it. And it's no joke. That's an official Council bounty notice."

"Impossible," Eli scoffed. "I know my own bounty! Counting what Gaol just threw in, I should be at an even seventy-five thousand, eighty thousand if Miranda would ever do as she promised and combine the Spirit Court's bounty. But even if she accidentally combined it twice over, it wouldn't explain this." He flipped the poster around and held it up. There, below the usual picture of Eli's smiling face, was a number written in tall, blocky strokes: 98,000 gold standards.

"This is a breakdown of government," Eli said. "What's the Council of Thrones coming to if it can't even keep something as important as my bounty straight?"

"Whatever the reason," Josef said, "we may need to lie low for a bit."

"I thought we were lying low," Eli said, still frowning at his poster.

"Lower, then," Josef snapped back. "All this attention is causing problems, like the one that just fell out of your window. That man wasn't your standard thug chasing the Eli lottery. He was a professional. He didn't wake you up or brag or try to take you alive. No, he did it exactly how I would have, clean and quick in the night. If you hadn't woken up when you did, you never would have felt a thing."

Eli gave him a dirty look. "Just how you would have? Have you thought about this before?"

"Only when you're being a jerk," Josef said dryly. "Listen, I don't know why the number is so high, but attacks like this one are only going to happen more often. And once your bounty breaks a hundred thousand, we're going to start seeing armies coming after us. We need our trail to be ice cold when they do."

Eli heaved a defeated sigh. "Fine, fine, where would be low enough for you? And don't say the mountains.

I've had more than enough wandering through the wilderness."

Josef leaned against the washstand. "I was thinking we could go home."

Eli froze. That was not the answer he'd expected. Nico, on the other hand, lifted her head. "Home?"

Josef nodded. "It's as low as we get. No one will find us there."

"But home is so boring," Eli said. "Nothing happens."

Josef crossed his arms over his chest. "Nothing's supposed to happen. Do you not understand the concept of lying low?"

"Fine, fine," Eli said, shaking his head. "We'll slip out tomorrow morning before whatever passes as the guard in this boring depression of a town gets too close and decides I look familiar."

"I'm surprised it hasn't happened already," Josef said. "Since you didn't even bother with disguises."

"My disguises are for my jobs," Eli said with a sniff. "I wouldn't waste them on places like this."

Josef just shook his head.

"Anyway," Eli said, lying back on the bed, "if we're going to be cutting out early, let's get some sleep at least. It would be a horrible shame to waste a rare night of sleep in a bed."

"Right," Josef said. "So get out of mine."

Eli looked at him innocently. "But my room still has people poking around in it."

"Too bad," Josef said, glaring. "Floor or hallway, pick one."

After some argument, Eli ended up on the floor with one of Josef's pillows and an extra quilt from the chest.

Nico excused herself halfway through the bickering, trailing back to her room with a weary look that stuck with Eli long after Josef put out the light.

"Josef," Eli said in the dark, "what's going on with Nico?"

The swordsman's quiet breathing continued without interruption, but somehow he knew Josef was listening.

"What happened in Gaol?" Eli asked, more quietly this time. "I've seen her lift you over her head like you weighed nothing, so why couldn't she pull you out of the window by herself? There's something going on with her demon, isn't there?"

His question hung in the silence. Then, at last, Josef answered. "Leave it alone."

Eli took a deep breath. "I *have* left it alone. We haven't pulled any thefts since leaving Gaol. I've been waiting to see if she'd snap out of it, or at least say what's happening. But she doesn't tell me anything!" He crossed his arms over his chest. "Everyone's got secrets, but this could get dangerous for us if I can't trust her on a job anymore. Her not telling me she was a wizard was bad enough, but I can get over that. I can understand. This?" He shook his head. "I don't even know anymore."

He heard the bed creak as Josef rolled over. "I don't know what's wrong either," the swordsman said. "And I'm not going to push it. Whatever's going on with Nico, it's a battle she has to fight herself. If she needs us, she'll ask."

Eli frowned. "Are you sure about that?"

Josef's long breaths were his only answer, and Eli knew the conversation was over. He tried to think of a way to bring the topic up again from a different angle, but all he got were more dead ends until, at last, he drifted off to sleep as well, curled up in a ball on the rug in the middle of Josef's floor.

Nico sat on the floor in the dark, her coat wrapped around her, her bony knees clutched to her chest. She sat perfectly still, listening through the wall until Eli's breaths evened out into sleep at last. Only then did she let out the long, shuddering sigh she'd been keeping in. Of all the demon-enhanced senses the seed could have left, why did it have to be hearing?

It's for your own good, the voice whispered, smooth and confident as ever. *I help you hear the truth.*

"Shut up," Nico grumbled, pulling herself toward the narrow bed.

You can't shut the truth out, the voice said. *Ignoring the problem won't change how the thief feels. He's a clever, efficient man. It's only a matter of time before he decides to cut the dead weight. I wouldn't be surprised if he left you here. After all, you're nothing but a weak girl who couldn't even pull Josef through a window. Why would they ever want—*

"SHUT UP."

Nico's words roared through her head, but the voice just chuckled and began to hum a song from Nico's child-hood, one of the only things she could remember from before the morning she woke up on the mountain. Unbidden and without reason, tears sprang to her eyes. She wiped them on her coat and bundled herself into a tiny ball in the center of her bed.

You can always come back. The voice's whisper was like a cool wind on her mind. *Why waste your time with people who don't trust you? Come home, Nico. Come home to where you're wanted.*

She took a deep, shuddering breath. "Never listen to the voice." Her words were a harsh whisper, but she could almost hear Nivel speaking them with her. "Never listen. Never listen."

She kept repeating the words until, at last, exhaustion took over and she fell into a deep, dreamless sleep.

And in her mind, the voice waited.

CHAPTER
3

The sun had barely peeked over the ridge above Zarin when Miranda Lyonette, newly reappointed Spiritualist of the Spirit Court, arrived at the gate of the Whitefall Citadel, home of the Council of Thrones. She hopped carefully off the hired buggy and paid the driver, overtipping him just to be sure she had it right. Hired transportation wasn't something she was used to, but she hadn't wanted Gin on this trip. For one, the ghosthound was easily bored, and she had a feeling this visit would be full of waiting. Trips to the Council always were, and a bored ghosthound in the Council of Thrones stables sounded like an invitation for disaster. Second, she hadn't wanted to mess up her outfit riding through the busy streets. She had dressed her best for this, a white silk jacket and matching wide trousers with short-heeled blue slippers instead of her usual boots. She wore her hair bound back in a tight braid that was a bit severe for her face, but she hadn't wanted to take chances with it frizzing on her. After all, it wasn't every day one got a handwritten invitation to the Council from a member of the Whitefall family itself.

The invitation was carefully tucked into her jacket's inside pocket, and though she'd read it through a dozen times since it arrived at the Spirit Court's tower by special courier yesterday, she still wasn't exactly sure why she'd been called to the Council. One thing, however, was certain, the invitation had come from Lord Phillipe Whitefall, Chief Domestic Enforcement Officer to the Council of Thrones and first cousin to Alber Whitefall, the current Merchant Prince of Zarin. There'd been no request for reply, but the letter didn't need one. Miranda had lived in Zarin long enough to know that when a Whitefall asked you to be somewhere, Spiritualist or common townsfolk, you didn't say no.

The guards opened the gate when she gave her name, and as she stepped into the courtyard a white-liveried page appeared seemingly from thin air to escort her into the citadel. Miranda followed the boy across the white-paved yard, under the long shadows of the famous seven towers, and into one of the graceful arching doors. The interior of the citadel was as lovely as the exterior, and positively dripping with wealth. Everything, from the paper-thin porcelain vases nestled in carved nooks between the windows to the thick, golden carpet underfoot, was exquisite, tasteful, and quietly expensive. If Miranda had not been here once before, accompanying Master Banage when she was still his apprentice, she would have gawked openly.

The page led her down half a dozen halls before opening a set of heavy double doors into a long gallery filled with tables. Miranda blinked in surprise. Each table was covered with stacks of paper and tended by a small army of well-dressed men and women. They worked furiously, sorting the piles into smaller piles before passing them along to others who bound the papers and stacked them on the shelves that ran along both sides of the gallery. No one spoke as the page led Miranda between the tables. Indeed, no one seemed to notice her at all. Their focus was entirely on their work, and the only sound in the large room was the rustle of paper. Miranda was still staring when the page stopped suddenly, turning to stand beside a tall door at the end of the gallery.

"Lord Whitefall will see you now," he said, bowing low. "Just through the door, if you please."

"Thank you," Miranda said.

The boy hurried off, walking silently back through the long gallery. Feeling a little abandoned, Miranda turned and opened the door. Like every door in the citadel, it opened silently, and she found herself standing at one end of a large, overfull office.

Overflowing would have been a better description. There was paper everywhere, stacked on tables, rolled up in bins, bursting from the shelves that lined the walls. It was all piled as neatly as possible, but there was simply too much for the room to contain. It clung to every piece of furniture like white blubber, and Miranda had to press herself against the door simply to have room to stand. The only wall of the office not covered with shelves was still covered in paper. Maps of the Council Kingdoms, to be specific, every one of which was blanketed with a forest of colored stickpins.

Directly ahead of her, down the little clear aisle that ran like a valley between the mountains of paper, was a sight that made her pause. At the far end of the room was a large desk covered with the same piled paper that infested the rest of the office, but otherwise it was empty. No one sat in the worn, high-back chair set behind it or on the wooden stool beside it. Still, what caught Miranda's attention was what hung above the desk. There, filling almost the entire back wall of the office, was an enormous piece of corkboard. It ran from just behind the chair all the way up to the room's soaring ceiling, nearly ten feet from start to finish. Miranda had never seen anything like it, but even more amazing was what was pinned to the board— bounty posters, hundreds of them. They were pinned with military precision, marching in a neat grid from the very top of the board to just above the empty chair's headrest.

The collection must have been long going, for the posters at the top were an entirely different color from the ones toward the bottom. Miranda leaned forward, trying to make out the names on the lower line, when a sudden voice made her jump.

"Knocking is customary before entering someone's office, you know."

Miranda stifled an undignified squeal of surprise, composing her features in an instant before turning to face the voice. Standing in a little alcove set just behind the door was a small, balding man with a large gray mustache. He wore a somber but expensive jacket that he somehow managed to make frumpy, and he was carrying a large stack of papers that he had obviously been going through when she had come in.

He gave her a final glare before tossing the papers on the shelf beside him, nearly causing an avalanche in the process.

"Phillipe Whitefall," he said. "I assume you are Spiritualist Lyonette?"

"Yes," Miranda said, dropping a polite bow. "An honor to meet you, sir."

"Quite," Lord Whitefall said, turning to walk briskly to his desk. "Apologies if I don't dawdle on formality, Miss Lyonette. I'm a very busy man." He sat down with a huff that made his mustache bristle. "I've heard much of your exploits from my agents in the field, especially involving Mellinor and this late unpleasantness in the duchy of Gaol. Quite an impressive display for someone so young."

"I was only doing my job as a Spiritualist," Miranda said, smiling despite herself. "The Spirit Court takes all infractions against the spirits very—"

"Yes, yes," Lord Whitefall interrupted. "The Spirit Court's dedication is not what I'm after. I called you here today to talk about your experience with Eli Monpress."

Miranda went stiff. "Well—"

"My primary duty as Chief Domestic Enforcement Officer is the maintenance and enforcement of the Council's bounties," he said, cutting her off again. "I receive the pledges, set the figures, track the criminals, oversee poster production and distribution, so on and so forth. That's how you came to my attention." He reached into the nest of papers on his desk and plucked out a formal letter bearing the Spirit Court's seal. "Several weeks ago, our office received this rather strange request from you, Spiritualist Miranda. You wrote on behalf of your Court asking that I combine the Spirit Court's private bounty with the Council's offering. Is that correct?"

He waved the letter in front of her until she nodded.

"Hardly a common thing," Lord Whitefall went on, tossing the letter back into the piles. "So I did a little digging and discovered some rather interesting facts about

your recent exploits." He paused, giving her a long, probing look. "It seems you are something of an expert on Eli
Monpress."

"I wouldn't say expert, my lord," Miranda put in
quickly. "It's true I've been involved with Eli Monpress
on several occasions, but I'm hardly in the position to
tell you anything you don't already know. My bounty
request was simply a fulfillment of a previous promise to
Monpress."

"If you're anxious about your past failures to catch
him, don't bother." Lord Whitefall sat back in his chair
with a heavy creak of leather. "I'm not here to judge you,
my dear. Quite the opposite, in fact. What I'm interested
in is your experience."

Lord Whitefall put his feet up on his desk, resting his
glossy leather boots on a stack of bound ledgers. "Monpress is a bit of a thorny problem, you se . His fame greatly
outstrips his threat, to the point where it's becoming fashionable to be his victim. Why, in the last two weeks I've
gotten four separate bounty pledges from kingdoms all
across the Council, all for crimes I'm certain Monpress
did not commit. Not that it matters to the nobles who
placed the bounty." He snorted. "The silver goes missing
and they send me a letter screaming Monpress."

"You mean people are placing false bounties?" Miranda
said. "But why?"

Lord Whitefall shrugged. "Notoriety. Excitement. The
Council has made this a smaller continent. It's no longer
enough to be the richest and most fashionable person in
your kingdom. You now have to compete on a Council-
wide scale. For some, this means being on the fashionable
end of everything, even if it's a fashionable theft. It's well

known that Monpress only steals the best, so if he robs you, that means you had something worth stealing. The higher Monpress's bounty goes, the worse the problem gets. I have to send officers to investigate every crime, but even if I find no proof of Monpress whatsoever, even if the object they claim was stolen is still sitting in the middle of their treasury, I can't do anything about the bounty pledge. It's their money. I can't stop them from spending it on stupid things."

"But that's ridiculous!" Miranda said. "If false reports become rampant, how will the Council track Eli's actual crimes?"

"Ah," Lord Whitefall said with a grin. "That's where you come in."

He stood and walked around to the front of his desk, looking Miranda square in the eye. "I'd like to make you an offer, Spiritualist Lyonette. As you are no doubt more aware than most, tracking Monpress is a very difficult prospect. The man moves like smoke, and leaves less of a trace. Reaching the scene of his crimes before what little clues there are have vanished is nearly impossible. Catching him in the act, completely so. But you, you're different. You have observed the thief at his work—even, if the reports are right, worked with him on two separate occasions."

Miranda went pale. "Those were—"

"Highly mitigating circumstances, I know," Lord Whitefall said. "Powers, girl, I don't care about *why* you were there, just that you *were*. Your experience with Eli Monpress is unprecedented. It makes you far too valuable to leave with the Spirit Court, which is why I'm offering you a job."

"Really, sir, I—" Miranda stopped cold. "Wait, what?"

"A job," Lord Whitefall said slowly. "To address your combined bounty request, I'm creating a new position within my department, and I'd like you to fill it. You would be head of the Eli Monpress joint investigation for the Council of Thrones and the Spirit Court. The position comes with full access to Council resources, complete autonomy on all matters involving Monpress, and the ability to call upon the aid of any kingdom in the Council without question. What do you say to that?"

"It's . . ." Miranda struggled for words. This was far beyond anything she could have dreamed of. "It's a very generous offer, sir. But"—better to get this out now—"why me? I would of course be happy to offer my knowledge and services to assist the Council in bringing Monpress to justice, but investigation head? Surely you have your own people who are vastly more experienced."

"That I do," Lord Whitefall said. "But I'm not about to waste them on Monpress." He ignored Miranda's insulted look and pointed up at the bounty posters on the board behind him. "Monpress is a thief, nothing but a two-bit con man with a flare for the dramatic. He's not a threat to the Council. The only reason his bounty is nearing the hundred-thousand mark is because he steals from people who can afford to put a large price on his head. This, combined with his propensity for grandstanding, has inflated his importance to the point where we at the bounty office can no longer ignore him. But look here."

Lord Whitefall walked over to the corner of his office, beckoning for Miranda to follow. He stopped in front of a second, smaller corkboard decorated with ten bounty posters pinned in two neat rows. Miranda frowned, wondering why these posters were singled out. Then she saw it. Every single poster displayed had a bounty of more than one hundred thousand.

"Look here," Lord Whitefall said. "These are the faces of true threats to the Council. Criminals who earned their bounties with blood, not flamboyance. Take this one"—he tapped a poster toward the bottom with the sketched face of a middle-aged man with a hook nose and an impatient sneer—"Izo, the Bandit King." Lord Whitefall's voice was almost reverent. "Over the last five years, he's banded together all the small bandit groups that prey on the trade routes through the northern kingdoms into his own private military. We had to send an army up last year to keep him from taking over the kingdom of Chessy all together, and we still didn't catch him. The northern kingdoms have always been the poorest in the Council, yet they got together and posted one hundred and fifty thousand gold standards to Izo's capture. And if that's not enough, look here."

He tapped the poster beside it, which had no picture at all, only a number, 200,000, and a name.

"The Daughter of the Dead Mountain," Lord Whitefall read quietly. "The only bounty request we've ever received from the Shaper Wizards. No one knows who she is, or exactly what she did, but if it was bad enough for the Shapers to come to us, I don't think I want to know. She has the second-highest bounty ever offered. As for the first..."

His finger moved to the poster at the far end, the oldest of all the posters. The picture was of a man with slicked-back dark hair and a grin that made Miranda's blood run cold. His face, neck, and shoulders were riddled with

scars, and his eyes told why. Even from the crude drawing, the killing gleam in them was undeniably terrifying,
as was the number written below.

"Five hundred thousand gold standards," Miranda read
in a hushed voice. "What did he do?"

"More than a man should," Lord Whitefall replied.
"That's Den the Warlord. He first appeared during the
Council's war with the Immortal Empress, selling his services as a soldier for hire. The Council hired him first,
and he slaughtered the Empress's forces like a butcher in
a pen of lambs. But then she offered him double what we
could and Den switched sides, single-handedly wiping
out an entire Council legion in one night."

Miranda shook her head. "Surely that's an
exaggeration."

"Not enough of one," Lord Whitefall said. "He disappeared after that. Powers grant that he met a bloody end,
but we don't know for certain. The Council considers five
hundred thousand a fair price to make sure the traitor's
dead."

Lord Whitefall sighed. "As you see, my dear, my office
has far more serious problems on our hands than a flam-
boyant thief. But his bounty demands we do something,
and so I am giving him to you. Banage assures me you're
a competent, clever sort of girl, and your experience with
Monpress is certainly unparalleled. That said, I'm completely confident placing the job in your hands. Assuming
you take the job, of course."

He looked at her, and Miranda swallowed. "It's a great
honor, but I'd have to get permission from the—"

"Oh, I got Banage's blessing this morning," Lord
Whitefall said with a flippant wave of his hand. "He's

keen on seeing you broaden your horizons. Do you have any other objections?"

"Well, I . . ." Miranda trailed off. "Not at all. I would be honored, Lord Whitefall."

"Excellent," the balding man said, smiling. "I'll have them set up an office for you in town and move all the Eli files over. Now, since Monpress is a wizard, you won't be reporting to me. You'll be under Sara."

"Sara . . . ?" Miranda prompted, waiting for a last name, or at least a title.

"Yes," Lord Whitefall said, completely missing the cue. "Sara's in charge of everything magical for the Council. She's been bothering me about Monpress since he first popped onto the bounty rolls, so I just let her have him. I've far too much to do handling the real criminals, anyway."

"Yes, my lord," Miranda said, trying not to be insulted. "When do I start work?"

"Tomorrow," Lord Whitefall said. "I'll tell Sara to send someone round to fetch you." He looked down at his papers. "That's all. You can go. The page will show you out."

And just like that, the meeting was over. Lord Whitefall seemed to have shut out her presence entirely, going through the endless papers and muttering to himself. After a few awkward moments, Miranda bowed, excused herself, and made her way as quickly as possible to the door. As Lord Whitefall had promised, a page was waiting for her when she opened it. The boy escorted her back through the opulent hallways to a waiting buggy and, after politely refusing Miranda's tip, left her to go on her way.

Miranda rode in silence all the way to the Spirit Court's

tower, wishing more than ever, as the buggy crept through the crowded streets, that she'd brought Gin. She had to talk to Master Banage, had to figure out what it really was she'd just agreed to. But the traffic had no respect for her urgency, and so she sat slumped in the cushioned seat, fuming while the morning sun beat down on the white walls of the Council capital.

CHAPTER
4

Josef, Eli, and Nico settled their bill and left the port of Mering in a bit of a hurry the morning after their unfortunate incident. They took a good chunk of the inn's larder with them, for, as Eli pointed out numerous times, a thief could hardly be expected to pay for *everything*. Thus resupplied, they set off west and a little south along the coastal plain. Eli kept them to the back roads, cutting across the rolling hills on cart tracks that were little more than dents in the grass. Josef grumbled about more walking, but Nico rather liked it. Picking her way over rough roads kept her mind occupied just enough to push the voice back, and the exercise made her feel invigorated and human, a sensation she was learning to cherish. The whole experience was so pleasant, she didn't even notice Eli's strange path until they started seeing signs for the great port at Axley.

"No," Josef said, stopping right below the signpost. "No major cities."

"Relax," Eli said. "We won't have any trouble. I'm just going in for a pickup."

Josef gave him a skeptical look. "A pickup?"

Eli nodded. "You'll see."

And he was right. When they reached the city walls, Eli went in alone, coming out less than an hour later with a cart, a mule, and an extremely smug expression.

"A cart?" Josef said, glaring. "You came here to pick up a cart? We could have gotten that anywhere."

"I highly doubt it," Eli said, beaming down from his perch on the cart's seat. "Come around and have a look."

Nico and Josef walked around to the edge of the cart, Nico hopping up on the little wall that ran along the road so she could see. The cart was covered with a thick oiled sheet, and underneath were large bags, each marked with a tag.

"Mr. Miller?" Nico said, reading one.

Josef just shook his head. "You'd think I'd be used to this by now." He opened one of the bags, revealing a sparkling stack of loose diamonds in a variety of cuts and sizes. "You're as bad as a squirrel, burying stashes all over the continent."

"Ah," Eli said. "But unlike a squirrel, I remember where I leave things. Reliable storage is vital to a thief, and the good merchants of Axley do most of their business with pirates and smugglers, so they're very kind about not asking too many questions. They even threw in the cart for free."

Josef looked sideways at the mule, which was standing perfectly still, glaring at him. "How generous," he mumbled, taking a step back. "Is this it then?"

"Powers, no," Eli said with a laugh. "I haven't been

home in a while. We've got three more stops to make. Hop on."

He scooted over to make room, and Josef jumped up onto the seat beside him. Nico climbed into the back, holding her coat close. She kept clear of the mule. Animals were better than most spirits at sniffing out a demonseed.

Of course. They know a predator when they see one.

"Shut up," Nico muttered.

"What?"

Her head shot up. Eli was looking back at her, his face concerned. "What did you say?"

Nico shook her head and scooted down among the bags, biting her tongue. She didn't speak again until it was time to stop for the night.

They made four more pickups, two at smaller towns, one at a crossroads tavern, and one in the middle of an otherwise perfectly normal field. That one had looked like just a rest break to admire the scenery until Eli had a chat with one of the large stones. After a short exchange, the stone rolled away to reveal a small treasury of valuables, including two midsized statues and a large painting wrapped in waxed cloth.

"I don't get it," Josef huffed, lifting one of the statues into their straining cart. "When did you find the time to hide all of this stuff? I never see you do any work after a robbery."

"You should pay more attention," Eli said, carrying a wooden chest fixed with a broken exquisite gold lock. "I'm always working. There." He shoved the chest into the final bit of open space left in the cart. "That should be it."

"Can the mule carry it all?" Josef asked, looking doubtfully at the overloaded cart.

"Of course," Eli said, hopping into the driver's seat. "I asked the cart to help." He winked at Josef. "I told you. I'm always working."

"So I see," Josef grumbled, helping Nico into the back of the overloaded cart before climbing up himself.

Nico settled herself as well as she could on the lumpy bags of treasure, pulling her knees in to avoid bumping them on the painting's sharp edges. "Where now?" she said.

"Homeward bound," Eli answered. He tapped the reins, and the cart lurched forward, down the field and back onto the dirt road, where Eli turned it north and west, toward the plains.

They rode for two days straight. They would have made better time, but Eli insisted on stopping in every village with a bounty board to see if his bounty had taken another spontaneous jump upward. It hadn't, though Eli couldn't figure out if that was because the number had ceased its strange inflation or if the towns they passed through were simply too small to receive timely bounty updates. Either way, he spent most of his spare breath coming up with theories.

"It's probably an impostor," he decided for the second time in as many hours. "Someone banking on my fame."

Josef chuckled. "Don't you mean robbing on your infamy?"

Eli gave him a sour look. "I would write the bounty office myself and ask if I thought I'd get an answer this year. Bunch of paper-pushers, they probably have five approved explanations and they still don't know what's going on."

The farther they went up into the great plains at the

heart of the continent, the more desolate the landscape became. Each village they passed was smaller and farther out than the one before until, at last, they gave out all together, leaving only the rolling hills of endless grass. Neither Josef nor Eli seemed concerned by the sudden nothingness, but Nico crouched down in the cart as far as she could get from the enormous empty space that stretched out all around her.

"It has been awhile," Josef said as the mule trudged through the tall, yellow grass. "I can't even make out the road anymore."

"I don't see how you would know," Eli said. "Considering the last time I brought you here, you were unconscious."

Josef grunted and Eli turned to grin at Nico. "This was before we had you to drag him around when he goes down. I had to use a wheelbarrow."

Nico smiled back faintly, but his words drove a sharp barb into her mind, reinforcing how useful she'd been and, in contrast, how useless she was now. She held her breath, waiting for the voice to make a comment, but nothing came. Still, she could feel it, a cold, clammy blackness just behind her conscious mind, watching smugly, letting her draw her own bleak conclusions.

The sun was just beginning to set over the rolling hills when the cart came to a creaking halt. Nico dragged herself up to see why Eli had stopped them and saw the thief standing on the driver's bench.

"There you are," he shouted over the wind as Josef and Nico stood up to look as well. "Home."

They were on the edge of a wide, shallow valley, and below them was a village. At first glance, it looked very much like the other villages they had passed, a small cluster of stone houses arranged in a square around a well. But the more one looked at the village, the stranger it became. For one thing, each of the stone houses was at least two stories, well kept, and prosperous looking. There was glass in every window, all the shutters were painted in bright colors, and every door sported a cheery lamp with a colored-glass shade. The square between the houses, which in the other towns had invariably been little more than a stretch of hard-packed dirt, was a carpet of bright green grass. Little fields, just as green as the grass in the square, dotted the slopes all around the village. There were gardens behind the houses as well, each boasting an amazing variety of plants, from common plains wheat to tropical fruit trees. Large herds of fat cattle, fluffy sheep, and dancing goats grazed on the hills above the fields, tended by woolly dogs and boys on horseback. The whole picture was, in short, beautiful, pastoral, prosperous, and amazingly out of place on the empty, rolling plains.

"Come on," Eli said, jumping out to lead the mule down the hill. "We should be in time for dinner."

A crowd had gathered by the time they reached the edge of town. Villagers flowed out of houses, some young, many old, but all plump, well dressed, and healthy looking. They gathered around the well, and a cheer rose up as Eli walked the cart into the square.

"Welcome back, Mr. Mayor!" A great man with a bushy red beard pushed his way through the crowd to grab Eli's hand, shaking it fiercely. "It's been too long."

"Good to be home, Derrik," Eli said and grinned back. He turned and grabbed Nico, pulling her forward. "You all met my swordsman on my last visit. Now I've added another hand to the game. This is Nico. Make her feel welcome."

Another round of applause went up. Nico tried to pull back, away from the attention, but Eli's hand on her shoulder held her firm, and she could only look down at her feet as the people began to chatter.

With a final squeeze, Eli left her to mingle with the crowd, all of whom seemed to be falling over themselves to shake his hand. Josef stepped up to take Eli's place beside her, and they watched in silent fascination.

"What is this place?" Nico whispered as the people began to fawn over Eli. "They're as bad as spirits around him."

"Of course," Josef replied quietly, shifting the enormous sword on his back. "Eli owns this town."

Nico frowned. "Owns it? Even the people?"

"Especially the people," Josef said, stepping away from the cart as a horde of people swarmed over it, opening bags and sorting through the various priceless treasures inside.

Nico didn't follow him. She stood where she was, watching with a mixture of horror and amazement as the townsfolk ravaged the cart. They opened bags and spilled the treasures out onto the grass, sorting the coins, gems, rings, bracelets, crowns, and so forth into piles. Each villager gathered up a collection, and then went to the man with the red beard who made a note in his ledger of what each person had taken. Once it had been accounted for, the people carried their armfuls of treasure, Eli's treasure, things Nico had helped him steal, into their houses, and all with Eli not five feet away, still chatting and shaking hands while Josef stood solemnly beside him, neither of them doing anything about it.

All across town, doors were being thrown open so the people could move the goods into their houses, and what Nico saw inside made her eyes go wide. Every house in the square was absolutely full of treasure. There were tables set with golden plates and gem-encrusted cutlery, ready for dinner. Famous paintings that belonged in king's halls hung over stone fireplaces, protected from the soot by makeshift wooden mantels. She saw young children sitting on silk carpets playing with rubies the size of their fists. One house even had a lamp inlaid with gold coins instead of mirrored reflectors nailed to its front entry, the round coins turning the light butter yellow. Everywhere she looked, the wealth of nations had been reduced to simple home furnishings, and Nico, who didn't say much under the best of circumstances, was at a complete loss for words.

"Amazing, isn't it?" said a soft female voice beside her. Nico whirled around to find a woman not much taller than herself standing beside her. She was very pretty, in a demure sort of way, with dark blond hair and delicate features. She smiled at Nico and gestured toward the cart, which was almost empty.

"I had the same reaction you did when I first saw it," she said. "But that's how the mayor likes it, and so that's what we do." She turned and held out her hand. "I'm Angeline. I run the school here. Derrik is my husband." She nodded at the man with the red beard who was still taking inventory from a line of people with armfuls of treasure. "He's the deputy here. He keeps Home running when the mayor is out."

"The mayor?" Nico said, taking her offered hand shyly. She wasn't offered handshakes much. "You mean Eli?"

Angeline put a slender finger to her lips. "Don't use that name here. It's bad luck. Even in the middle of the plains surrounded by friends, we don't want to take any chances."

"I don't understand," Nico said, lowering her voice. "What is this place?"

"It's Home," Angeline said simply. When it was obvious this explanation didn't make things any clearer for Nico, Angeline took a breath and tried again. "You saw how there was no road into town, right?"

Nico nodded.

"Well," Angeline continued, "there used to be a dirt trade track going across the plains, and that was what supported this village. Then, eighteen years ago, the Council of Thrones completed the Great Road, its first large building project. The Great Road connected the southern kingdoms with the northern half of the Council, becoming the world's longest trade highway and, in turn, completely eliminating the need for the little dirt track that ran by the village.

"The village deteriorated. The land here is hard, and with no money from traders, the young people left. Eventually, there were only a handful of families still living here, and it looked like the village would vanish altogether, like so many others on the plains. But then a miracle happened." Angeline's face grew wistful. "One day, or so my husband tells it, the mayor walked in from the plains. Just appeared from nowhere, leading a cart almost exactly like the one he brought today. The mayor brought everyone together in the square and made the village an offer. He would buy everything, our houses, our land, our well, everything. He wanted to buy the town."

Nico nodded. It sounded exactly like something Eli would do.

"Several of the people were angry, of course. It was all family land. Where would they live if this stranger bought it? The mayor answered that he would buy them too. Everyone in the village, old, young, whole, or crippled, was to be put on his payroll. In return for his money, all he wanted was our secrecy, a safe place to rest every time he was in town, and the pledge that we would keep all outsiders away. Of course, this just made people more skeptical than ever, but that's when he unveiled the gold." Angeline chuckled. "After that, there were no more objections. He was voted mayor that night, and he renamed the town Home. We've flourished ever since, and not just with money. Our fields have produced with hardly any work on our part, doubly so after one of the mayor's visits. The well stays full even in drought, and we don't have trouble with storms or wild animals. We live a blessed life here, and it's all because of the mayor."

Nico squinched her eyebrows together. "And how often does he—"

"He brings in a cart like this once, maybe twice, a year," Angeline finished for her. "Until two years ago, he was always alone. But then the swordsman joined, and now you." She gave Nico a very serious look. "I know you're one of his trusted companions. Please know that everyone in this village would die before betraying the mayor. No one wants to go back to how things were, or risk our great fortune. We spend only the coined gold, and only far away. We never trade any of the unique treasures. We follow his orders to the letter, always, so don't worry, you're all safe and welcome here."

Nico wanted to tell the woman that she hadn't been

worried, but Angeline seemed so concerned that Nico think well of them, she had no choice but to smile and nod. Satisfied, Angeline gave Nico's hand a final squeeze and walked over to her husband, handing him a fresh ledger just as his was about to be filled up. The cart was almost empty at this point, and Eli, having shaken hands at least four times with every one of the two dozen villagers, wandered over to stand beside Nico again.

"Well," he said, "what do you think?"

She gave him a sideways look. "It's quite an extravagant setup."

"I would settle for nothing less," Eli answered, and then he sighed. "I'm only sad the Duke of Gaol is dead and can't see this. He would have turned purple."

Nico didn't understand that statement at all. She was trying to think of something to say when her stomach gurgled loudly.

Eli laughed. "Hungry already? Josef's rubbing off on you. Come, let's go ask about dinner."

He grabbed Nico by the shoulder and walked her toward the red-bearded man with the ledger who was deep in conversation with Josef. Angeline was nowhere to be seen, and both men looked very grim.

"Ah, Mr. Mayor," the deputy said. "I'm afraid—"

"We've got a problem," Josef finished for him. "Seems last night a stranger came into town asking for Eli Monpress."

Eli's smile faded. "A stranger? *Here?* What kind of stranger?"

"A girl, Mr. Mayor," the deputy said. "None of us had seen her before. We took her into custody at once. I must assure you that Home is as safe and secret as—"

"It's all right, Derrik," Eli said. "I'm sure everyone here has been playing by the rules. Did this girl say where she was from or why she was here?"

"No, Mr. Mayor," the deputy said, shaking his head. "She wouldn't say anything, other than that her name was Pele."

Eli's smile faded instantly. "Powers," he hissed under his breath. "All right, where is she?"

Derrik motioned for them to follow him. "This way, sir. I've got her at my house."

He led them across the grass and toward a large house at the far end of the square. Nico expected him to stop at the steps, but he walked past the front door and around to the back of the house, where a pair of double doors was set into the ground.

"You've got her in the cellar?" Eli said. "You haven't been treating her badly, I hope."

"Of course not," Derrik said, unbolting the large lock. "I've got a nice little room down here I use for storing grain. It's dry and comfortable, but this door's the only way out. I thought it would be best, considering...Anyway, she hasn't complained, just sits and waits for you."

Eli nodded and, as soon as the doors were open, started down the stairs. "Wait here," he said when the deputy began to follow him. "We won't be long."

Looking a little taken aback, the man nodded and stepped aside, letting Eli, Josef, and Nico climb down into the cellar.

It was just as the man had said, a small, dry room in the cellar with a lamp and a bed and a stack of books that had obviously been brought down from the house above. Sitting on the edge of the bed was a familiar girl in hunter's leathers with a long, lovely knife at her hip and dark circles under her eyes, as though she'd been crying.

Eli stopped at the foot of the stairs and gave her a long, serious look. "Hello, Pele."

The girl nodded. "Eli."

Eli grabbed a stool from the corner and set it down beside her. "You chose a difficult way of getting in touch, you know," he said, sitting down with a long sigh. "Why not just get your father to reach me? Slorn has more tricks than any three bears put together."

"If I could do that, I wouldn't need you in the first place," Pele said, her voice going a bit ragged. "My father's... Slorn's gone missing."

There was a long silence.

"Missing?" Eli said at last. "Men like Slorn don't just go missing." He leaned forward and grasped Pele's hand. "What happened?"

Pele didn't try to take her hand back. Instead, she leaned forward, blinking back tears, and began to tell her story.

By the time she finished, Eli was looking grim indeed, and Pele was sobbing openly.

"After what Sted did to my mother, Father was inconsolable," she said, her voice quivering. "He locked himself in his workroom and wouldn't come out for two days no matter how I beat on the door. Then, on the third morning, he came out dressed in traveling gear and said he was going after Sted." Pele took a deep breath. "I wanted to go with him, but he said someone had to stay and take care of the house. He said he had to go, that he'd made a promise to the League of Storms to keep the seed secret and safe. That it was the only reason the League had let him keep Mother alive in the first place. So he left and I stayed behind. He said he'd contact me when he knew something, but that was three weeks ago. Since then, I've heard nothing. Please." She gripped Eli's hand. "Please, Eli, you're one of his oldest friends. You have to help me find him."

Eli calmly began extricating his fingers from her grasp. "Pele," he said gently. "I'm a thief, all right? This isn't really my area of expertise. Surely there's someone else—"

Pele refused to let go. "But you go everywhere. You know all sorts of things. And there is no one else. Father took all his contacts with him. I only knew where you were because this village is listed as your delivery address in our records."

"You're panicking," Eli said, his voice calm. "It's been only three weeks. He probably hasn't even found where he's going. Slorn's a powerful wizard. He can take care of himself."

"But he's not a fighter!" Pele said fiercely. She turned to Josef. "I know you beat Sted in Gaol. That was why he came to us, to get a new sword that could beat yours. He took my mother's seed when we wouldn't give him a sword. Please, I don't know what else to do. The man is a monster. I can't let my father face him alone. If you won't help me, then tell me where to go, or tell me where to find Sted and I'll help my father myself, just—"

She cut off when Eli stood up suddenly. "All right," he said, running his hands through his hair. "I'll help you. Just calm down."

Pele's eyes lit up. "Thank you!"

Eli waved his hand. For all her gratitude, he didn't look

happy at all. "Come up and have some dinner, and we'll
see about moving you into a real room."

Pele shot up from the bed, grabbing Eli and hugging
him tightly. "Thank you, thank you!"

"Yes," Eli said, extricating himself from her grip. "Let's
go on up. We've been on the road all day and we're tired.
Let us get some food and rest and then we'll see what's to
be done about our missing bear, all right?"

Pele nodded and, after embracing him one last time,
ran up the stairs with a smile on her face. Eli followed
more slowly, his smile quickly fading to a grimace. Nico
and Josef exchanged a look as they followed Pele and the
thief out of the cellar and into the deputy's house, where
he and Angeline were just getting supper on the table.

Dinner was a grand spread. There was pork and braised
potatoes; some sort of pea soup, which was green, creamy,
and delicious; roasted squash; and a large basket of fresh
biscuits, golden and flaky and dripping with honeyed butter. Everyone ate with gusto, even Nico. Normally she
despised eating. It felt too much like what the demon did,
but her stomach was growling and she dove into the very
human pleasure of stuffing herself full of delicious food.

Pele was stuffing herself too. The second Eli had
agreed to help her she'd started to look better and was now
eating her dark circles and pale cheeks away with a vigor
only teenagers can achieve. Josef ate as he always did,
efficiently and enormously, much to Angeline's delight.
The only person who wasn't stuffing himself was Eli. He
ate and made conversation, letting the deputy fill him in on
what he'd missed being away from Home. Still, to Nico,
who spent much of her time watching, it was clear Eli's
mind was somewhere else. He ate his food perfunctorily,

not with the energy he usually showed toward a good meal after days of living off hardtack and whatever animal was unlucky enough to get caught in Josef's traps. Though Eli appeared to be actively engaged in the deputy's reports, Nico could see the slight glaze in his expression that meant he was really thinking of something else entirely, and whatever it was, he wasn't happy about it.

After dinner, Pele wanted to discuss plans to rescue Slorn, but Eli gently turned her around and sent her to bed. She put up a fight, but not much of one. It was obvious she'd been sleeping even worse than she'd been eating. Angeline took her off to a bed that wasn't in the basement while Eli said his good-nights to the deputy. Then, motioning for Josef and Nico to follow, he slipped out the door and into the night.

"Come on," Josef said, standing up from his chair with a long-suffering sigh. "He's planning something. Let's find out what before he just goes and does it."

Nico nodded and followed the swordsman out the door. They walked across the grassy square, following the dark outline of Eli's gangly figure away from the bright houses and up toward the hills. When they reached the edge of the valley, he stopped suddenly and flopped down in the scruffy grass. Now that they were away from the town lights, the full moon was brighter than ever. Even without her demon-enhanced vision, Nico had no problem finding a flat spot of ground near Eli. Josef flopped down on the other side, dropping the Heart on the ground with a dull thunk.

Almost before they were seated, Eli began to speak.

"Well," he said, his voice dripping with bile. "Some trip Home this has been. Can't I even relax for one day without something coming up?"

"Don't whine," Josef said. "You could have said no."

"Easy for you to say," Eli snapped. "You don't have a compassionate bone in your body. I've known the girl since she was ten, Josef. What was I supposed to say? 'Sorry about your dad, but I'm on holiday. Good luck, chop chop'?" He flopped back on the grass with a disgusted sigh. "So much for lying low."

For a while, no one said anything. Then, at last, Eli sat up again with a frustrated groan. "Anyway, this is all beside the point. Even if Pele hadn't asked me, I'd have to go investigate. No matter how insufferable he can get, Slorn's an old, old friend. We have to help him. He'll never make us toys again if we don't." Eli tilted his head skyward, staring at the bright moon hanging alone in the black sky. "I only wish Slorn'd asked me himself. Then I could have at least gotten a huge favor out of the deal, maybe even free work. Now I'm stuck doing a sob job pro bono."

"Can't make money all the time," Josef said with a shrug.

Eli's only answer to that was a loud harrumph.

"Well," Eli said after a long silence, "done is done. First thing now is to find Slorn."

"Considering we're talking about a man with a bear's head, I don't think it'll be too hard," Josef said. "It's not like he can just blend in."

"Don't underestimate him," Eli said, lying back on the grass again. "If it were that easy, Pele wouldn't have come here. Slorn's surprisingly skilled at not being noticed."

"What about a broker?" Josef said. "Could we just pay one of them to find him like you did with the Fenzetti blade?"

Eli shook his head. "Brokers are great for finding inanimate objects but lousy at finding people. Also, we're trying to stay low, remember? The last thing I need is a broker getting suspicious. Goin was way out on the borderlands, so it was worth the chance, but we're in the middle of the Council Kingdoms. Any broker we could visit would probably have my poster on the wall. The moment I walked in I'd become a new commodity to sell."

"So, what?" Josef said. "Do we start asking in the usual channels? Spreading money around?"

"No, no, no," Eli said. "Far too risky, and I'm not spending cash on a job with no payout. Also, this is *Slorn* we're talking about. If the usual tactics worked, the Shapers would have gotten him years ago. What we need is a new angle." Eli began to grin. "Remember, we're not just looking for a *man*. We're also looking for a *bear*, and fortunately I know just who to ask when it comes to bears."

Josef looked skeptical. "You never struck me as the bear hunter type."

"I'm not," Eli said, standing up with an extremely self-pleased smile. "And I didn't say anything about hunters. Trust me, this is much better, and the best part is I won't even have to use a favor. I'll just cash in one of Slorn's. It's only fair that he should pay for his own rescue."

"You seem awful confident," Josef said, staring up at him. "Are you sure this is going to work?"

"Of course it will work," Eli scoffed. "My plans always work." His voice shifted at Josef's oh-come-on look. "Well, perhaps not always as I'd first intended, but they *do* work. Anyway, it's the only plan we've got." Nico jumped as Eli's hand settled on her hooded head. "I'm sure I don't need to remind you of the consequences of letting the only man in the world capable of creating coats and manacles that can hold a demon captive vanish into the night."

Josef gave him a dirty look. "Don't use her to make your points."

"Ah," Eli said. "But the point has been made." He gave Nico's head one last pat before turning back toward town. "Come on, we need to get packed. We've got a long trip ahead of us."

Josef didn't move. He sat glaring at Eli's back as the thief trotted down the hill. Finally, when Eli's long shadow disappeared inside the house, Josef pushed himself off the ground with a sigh.

"He can be a real ass sometimes," he grumbled, offering his hand to Nico.

"He is doing this for me," Nico said. "At least partially."

"Don't be fooled," Josef growled, pulling her up. "He's doing it for himself. He lives for favor swapping as much as fame and thievery. This is just another move in whatever game he plays. Don't let him trick you into thinking otherwise."

"I know," Nico said, but her words didn't sound convincing, even to her. Josef could label and dismiss Eli's reasons, but Nico couldn't. After all, that whole business with the Fenzetti had been for her, same with the trip up to Slorn's in the first place. It hadn't bothered her then because she'd been a participating, worthwhile member of the team, doing her share and helping as she had been helped. Now . . .

Now you're deadweight.

Nico closed her eyes.

Worse. The voice was low and laughing. *You're a*

liability without payoff, a bad piece of meat. The thief is no idiot. How long until he leaves you somewhere? He only uses you to keep the swordsman in tow, but even a muscle-brained lug like Josef will realize what a bad deal you've become sooner or later. What happens then, little Nico? What will you do?

Nico didn't reply, though she wasn't sure if that was because she knew better than to talk to the voice or because she didn't have an answer.

Come, little girl. The voice was honey dripping down her throat. *You already know how to help, don't you?*

But I don't know. Nico winced and slammed her lips tight; the answering thought had been automatic.

Yes, you do. Think, if you can. Who is Slorn after?

This time Nico refused to let her mind go forward. It did her no good. The voice rolled right over her wall of silence.

He's after Sted, the man who killed his wife and took the subject of their life's work, Nivel's precious seed. Sted is in my realm now, and you should know better than any that I always keep an eye on what belongs to me.

The memory overwhelmed her as the voice faded. She was standing in a room underground. She was older, powerful, standing beside a figure made out of darkness that meant more to her than any life. The figure took her hand, the long, cold fingers sliding across her palm, and a rush of loyalty, security, power, and safety sent her to her knees. The figure, the source of all her fealty, did not help her up. Instead, the cold hands reached and took her head, turning it toward the far end of the room. There, cut into the stone, was a map. A great map showing all the world, from the Council Kingdoms to the Immortal Empress's lands and the great frozen country far to the north. It was carved in relief, the mountains standing up from the stone as sharp and cold as the real thing, and crouched on this tiny, perfect model were little black creatures with wispy beetle legs.

The figure made a small, beautiful gesture, and she understood. The black creatures were markers for something greater, their slow, crawling movements reflections of a larger scale.

My seeds, the figure's voice hummed in her bones, masculine and resonant with a dark beauty that filled her with a terrible longing for home. *Every single one of them, all across the world.*

Nico swallowed.

Just ask. The cold hand reached up to stroke her cheek. *Ask and all shall be given to you, my dearest daughter, seed of my own heart.*

She clutched the long, cold fingers, tears flowing down her cheeks. "Yes, Master."

"Nico!"

Her eyes shot open. She was sitting on the grassy slope by Eli's town. Josef was leaning over her, his concerned face inches from her own. This close, she could see the pale scars running below his stubble. Nico flinched away, squeezing her eyes shut before he could see the tears in them.

"Are you all right?" He ran his hands over her limbs. "You fell down. What happened?"

"Nothing," she said, ashamed at the dreamy lilt in her voice. The haze of the memory still clung to her mind, fogging her thoughts with overwhelming loss for the safety she'd felt standing beside the figure. Her body grew heavy as the memory of power faded, leaving her small and helpless as a blind grub on the grass. She wasn't even sure if what she'd just seen was her own memory or a sent one, but the wetness on her face was real, and she wondered, not for the first time, if she was losing her mind.

You can't lose what isn't yours, the voice whispered. *Every bit of you belongs to me, willingly given. Why do you hold back now?*

"Leave me alone," Nico whispered.

"What?" Josef leaned closer. "Did you say something?"

Tell him, the voice said. *Just speak the truth. Tell him you can ask me to find Sted at any time, and through him, Slorn. Make them happy, or lie here and be a burden. Your choice, dearest.*

Nico sat up, her coat twitching over her hands as she scrubbed her face. "I'm sorry," she whispered. "I'm just tired."

"Understandably," Josef said, helping her up. "Let's get to bed before Eli decides he needs to leave tonight."

Nico nodded and started down the hill again, this time with Josef walking beside her, watching. His face was blank, but she knew him well enough to know he was worried. Well, she decided as she straightened up, he didn't need to be. She wouldn't lose, and she wouldn't let them down. She'd find a way to be useful without the demon. She'd do everything she could to make sure Eli's plan worked. She didn't know what that was, but she'd do it. She didn't need the voice.

But even as the thought spun through her head, she could feel the weakness coming back, the feeling of being lessened, of being lost, and with it, the echoing memory of the power she'd had in the memory. The power and security she could have again, if she would only ask. That feeling was the only answer the voice made, but it was an answer for which she had no retort. Tiny and beaten, she followed Josef into the house and shut the door on the night.

CHAPTER 5

The mist was still thick on the plains when three figures slipped out of the deputy's house and into the sleeping town of Home. There was no one in the square to see them creep out through the window, or to see the large bag of foodstuffs they helped themselves to from the baker's larder. Once they had shoved as much as they could carry into a flour sack, also pilfered, they vanished into the ghostly fog, slipping silently into the hills without a sound.

Across the grassy square, a young man slid down from his window and stretched the hours of waiting out of his joints. Finally, the thief had made his move. Shaking with excitement, he crept across his bedroom to the ostentatious writing desk his father had made for him out of a pair of matched thrones the mayor had brought in last year. He reached behind the desk's left leg and felt around until his trembling fingers found the bit of extravagant carving he was looking for. Grinning, he pressed down, hard. There was a little *clack* of a latch, and a small, wooden compartment popped out by the desk's foot, just above what had been the larger throne's clawed armrest. His hands went greedily for the tiny compartment. He'd discovered it by accident a few months ago, and even his father didn't know about it. He'd always wondered what a king would store in that secret place. Poison maybe, or state secrets. Whatever it had been, surely not even the secret stash of a king had ever held a treasure like this.

He raised his hand, bringing up a marble-sized sky-blue globe of crystal bound by silver wires to a silver chain. Gentle as a new father, he rolled the globe in a circle around his palm as he had been told. As it moved, the blue globe began to change color, shifting from clear, calm sky to the deeper, turbulent blue of the north sea. As the color shifted, something inside the globe began to move as well, showing the sphere was ready. After looking over his shoulder one last time, the young man crouched and cupped the globe to his mouth. Then, as softly as he could, he whispered, "Sara."

The response was immediate. The globe flashed between his fingers, and a woman's voice, cross, clipped, and vaguely scratchy, answered. "Has he moved?"

"Yes," the boy whispered. "All three of them left at dawn. They took a bunch of food with them."

"A long trip then." The woman's voice paused, and he heard her let out a long breath. "What about the stranger girl?"

"The mayor met with her." The young man was whispering quickly now, for the dawn was beginning to slip through his window, a sure sign that his mother would come looking for him soon. "Turns out he did know her.

She's staying at the deputy's house now. Only name I could get for her was Pele."

"Pele?" The woman's voice was sharp as razors. "You're *sure* it was Pele?"

"Yes," the boy said, grinning. When she cut in like that, it meant she was pleased. "Pele, tall girl, very upset. She had this crazy knife on her, never seen one like it before."

There was a pause from the other end, and then, "All right, good work." He heard the scratching of a pen. "Thank you. Keep me posted if the mayor reappears or the girl tries to leave."

"And my reward?" the boy said quickly.

The woman made an irritated sound. "Your reward is the same as ever. Three years of service, and then I will bring you to Zarin. All you have to do is keep reporting and not blow your cover and it's a done deal. That is, unless you keep bothering me about it."

"Yes, Sara," the boy whispered, his voice shaking. "I'm sorry."

"Just keep me informed," she said. "And don't do anything stupid. Remember, idiocy is its own cure in time."

"Yes, Sara," he said again, but the globe in his palm was already fading back to light blue, a sure sign that she was already gone.

He sneered at the globe. The woman might be his only chance at getting out of this nowhere backwater, but Powers, was she high-handed. One day, when he was in Zarin living like a lord with followers and women and a big city house, he'd make her swallow that sharp tongue.

A clatter from downstairs disrupted that happy line of thought, and the boy lunged toward the desk, dumping the orb on the chain back into the secret compartment just as his mother's footsteps sounded on the stairs. He dove for his bed, still made up from the night before, and jumped between the sheets right as his mother banged on the door, yelling for him to get up and come do his chores before breakfast. He made a noncommittal sound and waited under the covers as she climbed back down. Only when her footsteps vanished did he let out his breath.

In the town of Home, betraying the mayor was an unthinkable crime. Sometimes even he couldn't believe what he was doing, but he had to do it. It was his only way out of this tiny, isolated, prison of a town. Keeping that thought front and center in his mind, the young man threw open his door and clattered down the stairs. Under his window, hidden in the dark of the secret compartment of a wronged king, the orb lay quiet and still, listening.

"You have a spy in Monpress's town?" Alric, Deputy Commander of the League of Storms, smiled thinly as the blue orb in the woman's hands faded from stormy sea to calm blue. "Why am I not surprised, Sara?"

The woman sitting at the cluttered desk beside him leaned back in her leather chair and took a draw from her long-handled pipe. "Because you are a man incapable of surprise, Alric," she said, blowing a line of smoke in his direction. "Though you seem to delight in surprising others. Now, did you stop by just to eavesdrop on my private correspondence, or do you have a matter you actually came to discuss? If so, you'd better get on with it. I'm very busy right now."

With any other member of the Council of Thrones, Alric would have called that a bluff, but with Sara it was the absolute truth. Despite the Council's supposed indifference to magic, the office of its chief official on the subject was a hive of activity at all hours of the day. Actually, he didn't know when Sara slept. He'd never seen her leave her labyrinthine compound deep below the Council keep. Even so, he took his time answering. Busy she might be, but her implied threat was an empty one. She would never kick him out before learning why he'd come. No reason he couldn't use that edge to get a few answers of his own.

"Even the League isn't exactly sure where Monpress goes to lick his wounds," Alric said, taking a seat on the worn couch beside her desk. "Yet here you are, not only with knowledge of the village's location but with a spy already set up inside. Very impressive; how did you do it?"

"Quite simple," Sara said, putting her booted feet up on the desk in front of her and obviously trying not to look like she was bragging. "When Eli's stolen goods failed to show up for resale, we knew he was hoarding them somewhere. With his flair for the dramatic, I was sure he wasn't stuffing his treasures under some rock. That left stashing the property, probably in a town. So I put out a general search with the Council tax bureau for any unexpected prosperity, and sure enough I found an interesting report of a little town in the middle of nowhere that, mysteriously, despite losing its place on the central trade route thanks to the Council's completion of the Great Road, has continued to pay its annual taxes every year, even while all the towns around it were defaulting."

"You found him through tax fraud?" Alric was impressed despite himself.

"Just the opposite," Sara said. "Eli's a clever boy, far

cleverer than those idiots at the bounty office give him credit for. He knew there's no faster way to get the Council's attention than to skip on your taxes. Unfortunately, in his anxiety to slip under the audits, he neglected to take into account that the only thing more suspicious than defaulting on your taxes is to be the one town in a failing area that doesn't." She paused, giving Alric a smoke-wreathed glare. "But you didn't appear in my office unannounced to talk about Eli. Why are you here, Alric?"

Alric leaned forward. "You are a great friend of Heinricht Slorn, are you not?"

Sara's mouth twitched. "Heinricht is a colleague of mine. There's no greater mind for Spirit Theory on the continent. We often work on problems together. But I don't know why you're coming to me. He's *your* pet Shaper."

"He is indeed very important to our interests," Alric said benignly, refusing to rise to the bait. "However, a short while ago, he vanished. I had hoped that, as his friend, you would have some clue to his whereabouts. We're very concerned, you see."

"Yes, I'm sure you are," Sara said, smiling as she cast a pointed look at the golden sword at Alric's hip. "Swordsmith slipped the leash, did he?"

"Call it what you like," Alric said, casually adjusting his coat to cover his sword's hilt. "I'm only asking if he's contacted you. Slorn is a proud man, but he's in a desperate situation. Desperate enough that I wouldn't be surprised if he's tried to reach you through his own relay point." His eyes flicked to the blue orb on its silver chain, still lying on Sara's desk where she'd put it down. "The information and resources at your disposal are quite considerable, and Slorn's not a man to pass up opportunities."

"What makes you think I gave Slorn a relay link?" Sara said, quietly picking up the blue orb and dropping it into the strongbox on her desk, where it landed on top of a dozen other orbs just like it. "Each link is a monument of wizardry, the product of months of work by myself and my team." She snapped the strongbox lid shut. "They are for Council use only."

"Really?" Alric said. "How interesting, then, that you planted something so valuable in the hands of a boy spy just to keep an eye on Monpress."

"Not at all," Sara said. "Eli is of great interest to the Council."

"Really?" Alric's smile sharpened. "If that's the case, then it's even more interesting that you don't share your information, or the town's location, with the Council Bounty Office."

"If you're here to talk Council politics, Alric, I suggest you move on," Sara said crossly. "I have quite enough of it without your nosing about. Now, the answer to your question is no. I have received no communication from Slorn for weeks. Is there anything else I can do for the League?"

"Just let us know if anything comes up," Alric said, pushing himself off the couch. "The League's interests rarely overlap with those of the Council, but we've worked together enough for you to know that our word is good. You can believe me when I say that we will not forget your cooperation in this matter."

"Quite," Sara said. "You don't need me to see you out, I'm sure."

"No, thank you." Alric held his hand out in front of him and closed his eyes, concentrating on his office back at League headquarters. His neat desk, the dark stone, the heavy book piled with paperwork that had undoubtedly multiplied in his absence. It took less than a second before the air shimmered in front of him, opening a long, narrow slit that glowed bright white at the edges. Through it was his office just as he had envisioned it. It was a very neat opening: no sound, no flash, just a slight breeze, but then, Alric had been a League member for a very long time.

He put one foot through, stepping down on the cold stone of the League fortress, then he paused, standing halfway between two places, and looked over his shoulder. "Oh, Sara," he said, almost as an afterthought. "The girl who appeared in Eli's town, your spy said her name was Pele, correct?"

"You heard it as well as I did," Sara said stiffly, looking at him around a plume of pipe smoke.

"Slorn has a daughter with the same name," Alric said. "Isn't that interesting?"

"Does he?" Sara said. "I don't keep up with his family."

"A pity," Alric said, smiling. "Good day, Sara, and don't forget to keep me informed. The League is a good friend to those who help us."

"And a bitter enemy to those who don't," Sarah finished. "Point made, now get out."

Alric gave her one final, gracious smile before stepping completely into his office, the cut in reality vanishing with a dim flicker behind him.

Sara sat in her office for a while after he was gone, smoking furiously. Then, with a long sigh, she reached over and yanked the bell pull in the corner. It made no sound when she pulled it, but a second later, a lovely, long-haired man in a garish red coat, green britches, and a tall pair of polished black boots entered her office with a flourish.

"Forget our discussion this morning," Sara said as soon as he closed the door behind him. "We're going bear hunting after all."

"Oh?" The man arched one perfectly manicured eyebrow. "Why the change of heart?"

"It's the stakes that have changed," Sara said. "Not the heart. We might have a very rare opportunity to catch two wayward talents in one swoop, but we're going to need a strong grip."

"So send Tesset," the man said. "He's the strongest grip we've got. And I'll go along to make sure he doesn't have one of his fits of morality."

Sara shook her head. "No, for this we need the biggest hammer we can get, Sparrow." She leaned back in her chair. "I want you to get me Mellinor."

For the first time since he'd entered, Sparrow's smug expression faltered. "Banage's girl? But she's the head of the Monpress investigation. The particulars of our deal with the Spirit Court involving her employment with the Council are very strict."

"As I said," Sara said, grinning, "the stakes have changed. If Slorn sent his daughter to Eli, then we can only assume the thief is in this race as well. Banage's pet has a strange connection with Monpress, and that's exactly the kind of leverage we're going to need to pull this off. I must have her. No one else will do."

Sparrow ran a long hand through his glossy hair. "Banage won't like it."

"Hang Banage," Sara said, blowing a ring of smoke at

him. "Just   find the girl and convince her to come along.
That's wh   I pay you for."

"As you wish," Sparrow said, turning back toward the
door.

"Have her here tomorrow morning," Sara called as he
left. "First appointment."

The door closed without an answer, but she knew Sparrow had heard. Even if he hadn't, she didn't care. There
were larger games afoot. Sara turned back to her desk and
reached under the piles of drafting parchment scribbled
with designs and notes. After a little fumbling, she pulled
out the long, narrow slip of paper she'd hidden when Alric
had stepped unannounced into her room, right before the
badly timed call from her spy in Eli's village had come in.
It rankled her that Alric had been there to yank that bit of
information, but she pushed her annoyance aside. He was
the sort of man who it was better to assume knew everything already anyway. That way you were never caught
off-guard.

She smoothed the strip of paper between her fingers. It
had arrived this morning, dropped through her window by a
large bird she didn't recognize. That much wasn't unusual.
She often received messages that way, but the contents of
this paper were something else entirely. It was a short letter, barely more than a paragraph, asking for assistance in
a chase. The letter was not signed, but there was no need
for a name. It was a hand she knew well. After years spent
poring over whatever of his documents she could get her
hands on, Slorn's writing was as familiar as her own.

"Well, well, Heinricht," she murmured, feeding the
note into the little furnace in her office. "Looks like you'll
get your help after all."

She smiled as the paper curled into ash. As it burned, she looked up at the wall above her desk. There, pasted to the metal, were two rows of nearly identical wanted posters. They were arranged chronologically, each bearing the same name above a portrait of the same smiling, boyish face. The only differences between them were the list of crimes, which grew longer and denser with each printing, and the number below the portrait. It was the number that was truly impressive, climbing exponentially from its start on the first poster at three hundred standards to the newest entry, a freshly printed sheet at the end bearing a number large enough to be a national budget: ninety-eight thousand gold standards.

Sara reached up to touch the closest poster, tracing her finger along the boy's intricately shaded jawline. "High stakes indeed," she whispered, her face breaking into a smile. "Let's see whom luck favors this time around, my little Eliton."

On the wall, the poster's unchanging face smiled back, just as it always did.

CHAPTER
6

Miranda Lyonette squinted at the tiny script of the report in her hands, wishing, for the hundredth time that hour, that the Council had decided to save money in some way other than teaching its scribes to write in microscopic strokes. It would also help if the investigators could somehow manage to be thorough *and* interesting in their reports. It might be asking a bit much, but how anyone could make Eli Monpress's theft of the Queen of Verdun's diamond crown and his subsequent getaway through the burning canals *boring* was beyond her comprehension.

Miranda threw the report on the table and leaned back in her chair, rubbing her tired eyes. It had been three weeks since Lord Whitefall had made her head of the joint Spirit Court and Council of Thrones Monpress investigation. True to his word, he'd arranged an office for her the next day, and Miranda found herself operating out of a Council warehouse by the river that was uncomfortably warm during the day and damp at night. This was tolerable, however, for the space was large enough for Gin with plenty of room left for the enormous stacks of filing shelves Lord Whitefall had sent over from the main Council offices. She had also been provided with a staff, consisting of a runner, a scribe, and a file clerk. This had struck her as odd at first. She'd thought she'd be getting a Council investigator, or at least someone familiar with Monpress, but that was before she'd discovered exactly how much paperwork was involved in her new position.

One week into her new job and she understood why Lord Whitefall's office looked the way it did. The Council produced paper at a spectacular rate. Every afternoon a cart brought boxes of reports, observations, and strategies from the central office. Each was copied in triplicate, one for her to sign and send back as proof that she had read it, one for her active use, and one for her records. Worse, nearly all of it was useless—commentary on past crimes and idiotic suggestions from Council members who seemed to get all their information on Monpress from the gossip sheets, where he was a regular and much followed figure, even when he hadn't pulled a crime in over a month.

"Especially when he hasn't pulled a crime in over a month," Miranda muttered, looking balefully over at the other stack of papers on her desk. Shorter than the Council reports but still an impressive pile, these were great sheets of cheap yellow paper folded in half and printed with enormous lettering. The top one proclaimed MONPRESS STILL AT LARGE!!! above a dramatized engraving of a jaunty Monpress carrying a fat man with a crown, presumably the king of Mellinor, over his shoulder while

a tall man with rings on his fingers and another figure in
the white uniform of the Council guards looked around
cluelessly in the background.

Miranda rubbed her throbbing temples. If the Council
reports were dull and overresearched, the gossip sheets
were the exact opposite. Below the picture were para-
graphs full of exclamations and bold claims with the
important points underlined for maximum impact. Where
was Monpress now? Why hadn't he been active? Was it a
cover-up? Why wasn't the Spirit Court doing anything?
Where are the bounty hunters?

The speculations ran all the way to the fold, which was
a bit long even for cheap sensationalism. Still, with Eli
gone to ground, the public was hungry for more cover-
age, even when it was a simple rehashing of known information. Miranda reached out and flipped the paper open,
grimacing as the cheap ink smudged onto her fingers. The
feature on Monpress continued below the fold, ending
with an editorial piece from an anonymous Concerned
Council Member titled OUR GREATEST THREAT.

*"Who is the greatest threat to our security today?
Besides the ever-present threat of the Immortal Empress
from across the sea, a look down the Council's bounty list
provides a feast of villainy. Yet ask the man on the street,
the farmer in the field, and the answer is always the same:
wizards. We all know of the events in Mellinor, where a
wizard nearly took control of a kingdom single-handedly
through force of his magic. The so-called Spirit Court has
told us this was the doing of Eli Monpress, but if that's
so, then why does Monpress go uncaught? How does an
organization that can talk to the wind itself fail to capture
a man so notorious? The answer is simple enough for a*

child: Because they are in allegiance with the thief! How many more disasters will we allow the wizards to blame on Monpress, their 'supposed' rogue? How much higher must Monpress's bounty get before we wake up and realize that our anger should be focused not on the thief, but on his masters, the so-called Spirit Court and its king, Etmon Banage!"

There was more, but Miranda didn't bother to read it. She balled up the paper and threw it as hard as she could across the room. It landed beside Gin, who woke with a snort, glaring at the paper before turning his orange eyes on his mistress. "I told you not to waste your time with that trash."

"It gets worse every day!" Miranda shouted, slamming her hands on the table.

"It's always been like this," Gin said. "It just seems worse because you're paying attention to it now."

"Look." She grabbed a fistfull of yellow sheets from the stack and shook them at the hound. "Every one of these sorry excuses for print sings the same tune: 'The Spirit Court is a bunch of bungling idiots who can't catch a thief,' 'Eli Monpress is working for the wizards!' And it's *always* us. You never see one of these anonymous letters criticizing the Council."

"That's because the Council outsources all its catching to bounty hunters rather than sending its own people," Gin said, yawning. "Easier to blame someone when you know their name."

"That's not it and you know it." Miranda glared at him. "It's just what Master Banage said would happen. That thief is ruining the reputation of the Spirit Court! Master Banage's name, *all* our names are being dragged through the mud on the front page of the Zarin gossip sheets and it's *all Monpress's fault*!"

"So why are we sitting around here?" Gin said, standing up. "You're head of the Eli investigation. Let's go catch him."

"Catch him doing *what*?" Miranda cried, gesturing at the snowdrift of paper on her desk. "Eli hasn't robbed so much as a roadside charity box in a *month*."

"At least we'd be out there doing something," Gin snapped back. "Better than being in here, pushing paper and getting angry at gossip sheets. Who ever heard of catching a thief by reading reports?"

"No," Miranda said fiercely, shoving her reports into order. "This is where I need to be. The Council has the best information network on the continent. If Eli pulls anything, I'll be the first to know. And this time it won't be like Mellinor or Gaol. This time I'll have the full backing of the Council. No more going after him alone, no more playing up to local officials. We'll come down on that thief with the combined forces of the Council of Thrones and the Spirit Court. Bam!" She slammed her hands on the table. "I'd like to see him wiggle out of that."

Gin flicked his ears back at the crash. "Why are you getting so worked up? I thought we kind of liked Eli now."

Miranda stuck her nose in the air. "Thinking he's not evil isn't the same as liking him. He's a scoundrel and a lawbreaker and a thief, not to mention a liar, and though I will admit he's not a bad sort of guy underneath all that, it hardly makes up for the rest." She clenched her fists. "I'm going to catch that thief, Gin. I'll bring him trussed up like a hog before Master Banage and clear the Spirit Court's name once and for all. And then I'm going to use the bounty money to put these *liars*"—she swatted the stack of gossip sheets—"out of business for good."

"Don't waste your gold," said a lilting, unfamiliar voice. "More would just spring up."

Miranda and Gin both jumped and whirled around to face the sound. There, five steps inside the locked and bolted door, was a man. He was very tall and dressed extremely oddly. He wore red snakeskin boots with pointed toes, black trousers that were far too tight and were embellished with lemon-yellow thread, and a green velvet jacket the color of new grass over a bright pink shirt and a maroon vest. His long hair was ice blond shot with black (an obvious dye job, though she couldn't say which, if either, had been his original color), and his head was crowned with a large red hat trimmed with gold that he wore swooped down over his eyes.

"Anyway," he continued, traipsing into the room as if he'd been invited. "There's no point in getting angry at the gossips. If it wasn't the Court, they'd be after someone else."

"Who are you?" Miranda shouted, jumping up, her rings flashing as her chair toppled over behind her. But Gin was even faster. By the time the words were out of her mouth, he had launched himself off the floor and pounced on the man, pinning him to the ground.

"How did you sneak in here?" Gin snarled, his orange eyes blinking rapidly, as though he was having trouble focusing. "How do you make no sound? Why do you flicker like that?"

The man smiled up at the large, sharp teeth hovering inches above his head. "Easy, doggie," he said, his eyes darting toward Miranda. "I'm afraid I'm not a wizard. So if your guard dog is addressing me, he's wasting his rather terrible-smelling breath. If you wouldn't mind?" He wiggled helplessly.

Miranda made no move to call Gin off. Instead, she walked across the room to stand over the man as well. "You haven't answered my question," she said. "And I'll add Gin's to it, since you can't hear. Who are you? How did you get in here? What are you doing?"

"You left out the part about the flickering," Gin growled, leaning harder on the stranger's shoulders until the man's face turned pasty against the garish backdrop of his hat. "Can't you see it?"

Miranda shook her head. Other than questionable color choices, the man looked normal to her.

The stranger wiggled one hand into his pocket and flipped out a card, which he tossed toward Miranda's feet.

"The name's Sparrow," he said as she picked it up. "I got in through the door, and I do almost anything. Tonight, I'm an errand boy. I've been sent by our mutual employer to request your presence at a meeting tomorrow morning."

"Employer?" Miranda said, holding the card by its edges. "Lord Whitefall?"

"That windbag?" The man laughed. "No, dear, I'm no paper-pusher. I'm talking about Sara, the lady running the show."

Miranda looked at the card in her hand. It was surprisingly plain, considering the man it belonged to, just a white rectangle on heavy stock with a small engraving of a sparrow in flight in the lower left-hand corner. She flipped it over. The back was as blank as the front, save for a small notation written in slanting script: *8:40.*

"Eight forty?" Miranda read, brows furrowed.

"Yes, and don't be late," Sparrow said. "Sara keeps an extremely tight schedule. She'll be intolerable if you throw it off."

She gave him a suspicious look. "Where am I going?"

"The Council citadel, of course," Sparrow said, tilting his head sideways so that he wasn't directly under Gin's bared teeth. "Just show up and I'll bring you down. I play doorman as well as messenger."

Miranda slipped the card into her pocket. "Is that all you have to tell me?"

"Yes," Sparrow said. "Can you get this dog off of me? I'm having trouble feeling my legs."

Miranda looked at Gin and jerked her head to the side. With a final growl, Gin pulled back, circling around to stand beside Miranda as Sparrow sat up and wiped his face with an orange handkerchief.

"I can see you'll be a delightful addition to our team," he said, standing up stiffly. "I'll see you tomorrow, yes?"

"Eight forty." Miranda nodded. "I'll be early, and your Sara had better have a good explanation."

"Oh, she has dozens," Sparrow said. "Getting one out of her is the challenge." He straightened his coat and turned to face her, tipping his extravagant hat politely. "Until tomorrow, Miss Miranda."

He flashed her a wide smile and then, spinning on his tall heel, walked out the previously locked door. Gin watched him intently, ears swiveling, but Sparrow made a perfectly normal amount of noise as he left, and the dog seemed disappointed. He stared at the door as it swung shut, growling low in his throat. "I don't trust that man."

Miranda could only laugh at that. "What was your first clue?"

"No," Gin said sharply. "There's something really wrong about him."

Miranda stopped laughing. "What do you mean?"

"He flickers," the dog said. "He's hard to look at, like he's there but not."

"Flickers how?"

Gin made a frustrated sound. "I can't explain it. It's just wrong. I had to look at him with my eyes to see him clearly. I've never had to do that before." He looked at her intently. "You should be careful tomorrow."

"I always am," Miranda said. "Still, I don't care what's wrong with the man. There's something going on and I want to know what. Whitefall said this Sara person was in charge of wizard affairs for the Council. If she's calling me in, it could mean she has some information about Eli. Anyway, whatever this meeting is about, it has to be better than paperwork."

Gin gave her a firm look. "I'm going with you."

Miranda shook her head, reaching out to scratch his long nose. "I wouldn't have it any other way."

Gin leaned into the scratch, but he stayed put as Miranda gathered her things and closed up the office for the night. Only when she blew out the lamp did he rise and pad through the doorway, going ahead of her into the rowdy Zarin night.

The next morning, thirty minutes after the eight o'clock bell, Miranda and Gin trotted up to the front of the Council fortress. As the Council's offices didn't open for formal business until ten (since no Court official worth his silks would be up before then), the gates were still closed, but Miranda was able to get past the guards with her official title and a well-placed growl from her ghosthound.

The growl was, perhaps, a little harsher than it needed to be. Gin was in a foul mood this morning. He'd spent the whole ride over trying to convince her to turn around, but Miranda would hear none of it. Truth be told, Sparrow's sudden appearance last night was the most exciting thing that had happened since Lord Whitefall's letter arrived, and she wasn't about to waste her chance, even if Gin's hunches had a bad habit of being right.

They waited in the courtyard, out of the way of the few carriages that came and went. Miranda spent the time checking her rings. She woke each spirit, soothing and nudging it until each ring glowed with its own light. Mellinor was already awake and waiting at the base of her soul, his cool presence dark and cautious.

After about ten minutes (ten minutes exactly, Miranda would wager), Sparrow appeared from a small door on the far side of the yard. He was dressed this morning in a long fuchsia coat that dropped to his knees with gold buttons and cream lace spilling out of the cuffs. His pants were orange and covered with some sort of black beadwork that clacked as he walked. They were wide-legged, and their ends were stuffed into the tops of his low black boots, which boasted silver heels and toes. He wore no hat, and his hair was all blond now, but a different shade from last night, more honey than white blond, and tousled in a way that suggested he'd spent an hour arranging it to fall just so.

Miranda winced at the clashing colors and leaned in close to Gin. "Is he still flickering?"

"Worse than ever," Gin growled.

"It's more like he's fading," Mellinor put in. "I don't like it."

"No one seems to," Miranda muttered. "Keep watch; let me know if it changes."

"Why?" Gin said. "You won't be able to see it."

"That's why you're the ones watching," Miranda hissed, and then smiled graciously as Sparrow stopped before her.

Sparrow dropped a flourished bow. "Miranda," he said. "Right on schedule. I'll take you in directly." He paused. "Will you be bringing your pet as well?"

Gin snarled at that, and Miranda put her hand on his nose in a warning gesture. "Gin goes where I do," she said.

Sparrow shrugged. "We'll have to take the back way, then. Follow me."

He led them through an arched breezeway and out onto a side path that had been cleverly hidden behind the ornamental trees. It was narrow going. They were walking down an alley with the outer wall of the Council fortress towering over them on one side and the side of the fortress itself going up on the other. There was room for the three of them to walk single file comfortably enough, but Miranda couldn't help feeling trapped as the road circled downward and the walls grew higher and higher around them.

At last, when the morning sky was a thin strip far overhead, the steep road stopped at an enormous pair of double doors set deep in the citadel's base.

"Apologies for taking you in through the service entrance," Sparrow said, fishing a ring of keys out of his monstrosity of a coat. "But I doubt your puppy would fit down the tunnels."

"This is fine," Miranda said over Gin's growling. "I had more than enough of Council finery on my previous visit to last me awhile."

Sparrow unlocked the door and held it open for her, motioning for Miranda to go first. Miranda stepped inside with a curt nod of thanks, then stopped again, her mouth dropping open. She was standing inside the largest room she'd ever seen. It was twice the size of the throne room in Mellinor and easily half again as tall as the Spirit Court's hearing chamber. Or that's what she guessed, since she couldn't actually see the ceiling. The chamber was huge and hollow, with pillars sprouting from the stone floor at regular intervals, climbing up into the darkness. Between the pillars, set in rows like the giant, gray eggs of some enormous insect, stood tall, fat, cylindrical towers. The towers stretched off forever in all directions, a forest of identical gray metal ovals suspended on an iron framework that kept their ends off the floor. Miranda was still gawking at the sheer number and size of ... whatever they were when Sparrow shut the door behind them and locked it again.

"This way," he said, starting off into the darkness.

Miranda followed, craning her neck as they walked between the metal cylinders and up a set of wooden stairs that had been built into the framework. Gin followed more slowly, delicately picking his way along the narrow path. The stairs led to a wide wooden scaffolding that ran like a suspended road between the strange metal cylinders. Tiny glass lanterns lined the metal railing that separated the walkway from the straight drop down to the stone floor, their collective soft glow casting large, ominous shadows behind the iron towers.

"What are they?" Miranda whispered as they walked down the scaffold, gawking at the endless forest of metal silos just out of arm's reach.

"Tanks," Sparrow said, picking up the pace. "This is the Relay Room. Don't touch anything, please."

Miranda's eyes widened. "You mean the Ollor Relay?"

"You know any other relay the Council cares about?" Sparrow said. "Watch your step; we're turning."

Miranda followed him blindly. Her mind was entirely on the metal cylinders around him, the tanks. The Ollor Relay was the backbone of the Council of Thrones. The precise way it worked was a closely guarded secret, but it had something to do with water, which explained the tanks. She wasn't exactly sure how it was used, but common knowledge was that a person with a Relay point could speak to a person at the base Relay from any distance, and the person at the base could speak back, or pass the message on to another Relay point somewhere else entirely. It was this ability to communicate instantly across the kingdoms that had allowed the Council armies, which had included only a handful of countries at the time, to beat back the much larger invading army of the Immortal Empress twenty-five years ago. That impossible victory had sealed the Council of Thrones as the foremost power on the continent, an achievement Merchant Prince Whitefall had leveraged to form the greatest coalition of nations in the world.

The Council would have grown even faster if access to the Relay had been more widespread, but Relay points were famously rare. However, looking out over the endless rows of tanks, Miranda suddenly had a hard time believing the Relay was as small as people claimed. True, she had no idea how it worked, but there must be hundreds of tanks down here. How could such a huge infrastructure support only a tiny number of Relay points?

She was puzzling over this when Sparrow's rapid pace suddenly slowed. They were approaching a brightly lit crossroads of several scaffoldings, the center of which seemed to be a single, enormous tank. As they got closer, however, Miranda realized the giant thing in the center wasn't a tank at all. It was a building. A great, metal building inside the larger room, complete with a rounded roof and a half dozen little chimneys spewing steam. The building was several stories tall, but the main story seemed to be the one level with the scaffolding. The building was at an intersection of walkways, and the suspended scaffolding joined together to form a wide platform. On the platform, men and women in plain white jackets and trousers clustered around long tables, their work lit by enormous hanging lanterns that burned steady and bright. Metal doors opened and closed without sound as workers entered and left the metal building, which looked to have more workstations inside.

The workers shuffled out of the way as Sparrow, Miranda, and Gin stepped onto the ring of wooden scaffolding. Sparrow ignored them completely and walked straight across the wooden boards toward the building's largest door. He pushed it with a grunt, and the heavy metal slab swung inward, revealing a dimly lit room.

"Go on," Sparrow said, standing aside. "It's a bit cramped, but Sara wanted to see you in her office so this visit wouldn't interrupt her work too much. You understand, of course."

"What work does she do?" Miranda said, stepping inside.

"Everything that matters," a brisk voice answered.

Miranda's head snapped up, and she found herself looking into the blue eyes of a small, formidable woman. She was sitting on a leather chair set directly between three large desks covered with . . . Miranda wasn't quite sure. The farthest was swamped in Council papers, which Miranda could recognize too well these days. Most of these were dusty and untouched, however. The other two desks were far neater. One supported a large, bright lamp and a stunning variety of jars filled with various amounts of a clear liquid and a small book open to a page filled with neat, tight handwriting. The other desk was covered in what looked to be pages of lists and drawings, all laid out neatly, with arrows drawn across the edges connecting one page to another.

The large office was otherwise sparse. There was a bookcase filled with leather notebooks and a threadbare couch set against one wall, but otherwise, nothing. None of the niceties Miranda would have expected from a Council member with such obvious authority. Her walls, however, were far from bare. The metal was covered with notes and drawings on all sides, including diagrams of the tanks outside covered in the same tight, neat handwriting as the papers on the desk.

But all of these were to be expected in an office at the heart of the Relay. What caught Miranda off-guard were the posters papering the space above the largest desk. There, laid out in a neat grid, was a complete collection of Eli Monpress bounty posters. They started when his bounty had been a mere three hundred and went up all the way to the current ninety-eight thousand with a good bit of room at the bottom for new additions. Seen all together, the effect was quite impressive, and Miranda couldn't help smiling at the thought of how Eli would react if he saw it. Probably insufferably.

The woman herself was dressed in the same plain white coat and trousers as the other workers, but any plainness ended there. Her hair was pale ginger streaked with gray, tied up in a coil of braids at the top of her head. Her face was lined, especially between her eyebrows where she scowled, but otherwise she didn't look very old. She mostly looked serious, harried, and already out of patience. A long pipe dangled from her lips, which accounted for the spicy reek of smoke that permeated the room, and a pair of spectacles hung on a gold chain around her neck. Otherwise she wore no decoration, not even rings. However, from the way Miranda's spirits were buzzing, she knew without a doubt that this woman was a wizard, and powerful one.

The woman looked Miranda over, starting with the feet and working her way up. Next, she switched her gaze to Gin, who had somehow managed to squeeze himself through the door and was now sitting nearly doubled over behind Miranda, his eyes narrow and sharp despite the indignity of his cramped position, and ended on Sparrow, who was pushing Gin's tail out of the way in an attempt to shut the door.

"You must be Miranda Lyonette," she said when she'd finished her inspection. "You're not as pretty as I'd thought you'd be, considering your family. Nice hair, though, and strong spirits. I can see why Banage made you his favorite."

Miranda bristled. "I assure you, madam," she said through gritted teeth, "neither my looks nor my family has anything to do with my position."

Sara rolled her eyes. "Don't get your hackles up, girl. I was only making an observation." She took a drag off her pipe and blew a long line of smoke into the air. "This is why I don't usually work with Spiritualists. You're all so prickly and bound in. Terrible waste of wizards. Though I suppose the world must have you."

Miranda's rage must have been clear on her face for Sara laughed. "Feel free to disagree all you like. I welcome constructive argument. But if you're just going to be miffish, you'd better get over it quickly. Those who can't take an honest opinion don't last long down here. Right, Sparrow?"

Sparrow, who'd given up on Gin's tail and taken a seat on the couch, merely smiled. "No one lasts long with you, Sara."

"Not so," Sara said curtly. "You've been with me five years."

"That's because I care more for your money than my ego," Sparrow said. "Get to the point before the Spiritualist girl becomes terminally insulted and my trip becomes a waste."

Sara turned to Miranda. "Right. Then let's see it."

Miranda stared at her. "See what?"

"Your Great Spirit," Sara said, giving her a look that said this should have been obvious. "If you're going to be working for me, I have to see what I'm dealing with."

Miranda started to object, but stopped. It wasn't actually an unreasonable request. Swallowing her temper, she closed her eyes and gave Mellinor a little mental nudge.

A nudge was all it took. With that curious, skin-crawling feeling of being a faucet, the water spirit poured out of her. When Miranda opened her eyes again, Mellinor was floating beside her, a ball of pure, blue, strangely smug-looking water, spinning slowly before Sara's obviously rapt attention.

"A Great Spirit," she whispered, stepping forward, smiling and as bright eyed as a child. "I've met several, but I've never seen one come out of a person."

"Nor will you," Mellinor said. "So far as I know, my circumstances are unique."

Sara reached out, tracing her fingers across the water's surface. "Absolutely marvelous."

Mellinor puffed up a little at that, and Miranda covertly rolled her eyes. Her sea could be as bad as her dog some-times.

Sara didn't notice. She was busy walking around Mel-linor, stepping high over Gin's paws where there wasn't room. "Do you still have tides?" she asked. "Currents? What about your salinity?"

"No tides," Mellinor said. "Not enough water. My currents were always my own. I changed my salinity to match Miranda's blood. It seemed the easiest thing to do, and I don't care for much salt, anyway."

There was something dark in his voice as he spoke that last bit, but Sara just nodded and jotted several notes on a pad that she fished from her pocket. Miranda, however, was busy staring at her water spirit. She'd never even thought to ask questions like that, and she was starting to feel ashamed. Mellinor was her spirit. She should know all there was to know about him, not leave it to some stranger.

Sara looked as though she had more questions, but a whistle outside made her put away her pad.

"Well," she said, "if the sea's on your side, the tide may wait, but time never will." She gestured at Miranda as she went back to her chair. "You can pull him back now. You've made the team."

"Team?" Miranda said, stretching out her arm. "What do you mean?"

Mellinor took his time coming back, obviously appreciating the attention from Sara. Miranda resisted the urge to nudge him along.

"I'm the Head Wizard for the Council of Thrones," Sara said, sitting back down at her desk. "Officially, I'm in charge of all wizards working for the Council, though I don't bother with most of them. They're dull dropouts from the Spirit Court mostly, with no will to speak of. They're better left in the copy rooms ordering ink spirits around. But you," she said, grinning. "You, Miranda, with your shining sea and your dog and whatever else you've got on your fingers, are different. I thought you would be. That's why I had Phillipe Whitefall send you that letter."

Miranda frowned. "I thought I was appointed as head of the Eli Monpress investigation on account of my experience with the thief."

"Yes, well, that was the reason I fed the bounty office." Sara took a long splinter from a box on her desk and held it near her lamp. At once, a spark jumped from the lamp flame to the splinter's end. "Only way I could get you away from Banage, really. He doesn't have much patience for me," she said, touching the burning splinter to her pipe. "It wasn't hard. Phillipe jumped at the chance to make the thief someone else's problem. Of course," she said between puffs, "it would be wonderful if you *could* catch Eli for me. I'm even more keen to meet him than I was to meet you. I'm very interested in the way this world works, you see, the different aspects of wizardry and spirits and how they interact. Things like how a Great Spirit could shrink himself down small enough to fit into a human while maintaining his essence as a Great Spirit. These are the curiosities I love to surround myself with. It keeps the mind young. But Eli's the greatest mystery of them all. A wizard whom every spirit obeys." Her voice grew almost wistful. "Now *that* is something I'd love to examine for myself."

"You'd have to get in line," Miranda said, crossing her arms over her chest. "There are a lot of people who want a piece of Eli Monpress." Sara gave her a sharp look, and Miranda glared right back. "Perhaps I haven't made this clear, but I am a Spiritualist first, foremost, and forever. I agreed to work for the Council to get support and information in my hunt for Monpress. With all due respect, Lady Sara, that doesn't include being one of your 'curiosities.' If I'm only here so you could have a look at Mellinor, I'll be on my way."

Sara gave her a smoky smile. "Direct," she said. "I like that. Very well, Spiritualist Lyonette, I will answer in kind. I pulled the strings to bring you here because we have a delicate matter on our hands. One of my dear friends, a Shaper and a great scholar of wizardry, has vanished. Though he's not formally involved with the Council, it would be a great loss for all of us if Heinricht Slorn were to remain missing. Therefore, I am putting a group together to find him and bring him safely back to Zarin under the Council's protection."

"Slorn?" Miranda frowned. The name was desperately familiar, but it wasn't the one she'd been waiting for. "I'm sorry to hear about your missing friend," she said. "But I don't have time to—"

"Slorn has many friends from all walks of life." Sara's voice rolled right over her. "Including a certain thief."

She paused, and Miranda had to swallow her words, motioning for the woman to get on with it. Sara did no such thing. She merely sat there and smoked, watching Miranda squirm. Finally, when she obviously felt Miranda had stewed enough, Sara continued.

"We have a good tip that Slorn has asked for Eli's help as well as mine. However, Eli doesn't know where Slorn is." Sara smiled. "I do."

Miranda's eyes widened as Sara's implications hit her. The idea of getting somewhere before Eli did was almost intoxicating. "Where?"

Sara arched her eyebrows at Miranda's abandoned aloofness. "You'll go on the mission then?"

Miranda stopped cold. Powers, she'd stepped right into that one. She took a moment to think, keeping her eyes away from Sara's cool, sure expression. If she left Zarin and Sara was wrong about Eli going after Slorn, she could miss his next theft altogether. Besides, one look at Sara and the company she kept was enough to set off a whole tower full of warning bells. Miranda's eyes slid over to the couch where Sparrow was sitting with his legs crossed, watching her. Just being in the same room with him put her on edge. But if Sara was right...

She felt a warmth against her back as Gin leaned in behind her. "You should take it," he growled low in his throat. "Even if Eli robbed Lord Whitefall's mansion tomorrow, we'd still be eating his dust. A trap is always better than a chase."

Miranda nodded. You could always trust a predator about these things. Still, she decided as she glanced at Sara, no need for the old lady to know her intentions just yet.

"If I went," she said slowly, "where would I be going?"

"No, no, no," Sara said, shaking her head. "That's not how this works. You don't get confidential information for free. I asked you, are you joining us? Answer, yes or no, and I'll decide what to tell you after."

Miranda took an angry breath and nearly marched out right then and there. It was her need to catch Eli that kept her in place. Could she really throw her chance at catching him away over rankled pride? After all, she had no other leads, and just the thought of going back to paperwork nearly made her ill. Miranda grimaced and looked over her shoulder at Gin, who flicked his ears as if to say it was her choice. Miranda bit her lip. Well, she'd already come this far. She might as well go in all the way.

"All right," she said, looking Sara directly in the eyes. "I'm in."

Sara grinned in triumph. "Are you familiar with Izo the Bandit King?"

Miranda nodded.

Sara waved her pipe in a grand gesture. "That's your answer."

Miranda stared at her. "What?"

"Be here tomorrow at dawn, packed for a long journey," Sara said, sticking her pipe back in her mouth. "I'll give you the rest when I explain the plan to everyone."

"Everyone?" Miranda said.

"Yes," Sara said, looking at her as though she were stupid. "Dawn tomorrow, don't be late."

And that was all the answer Miranda could get.

Hours later, Sara was still in her office. She sat at her least cluttered desk, reading through the day's stack of observations while distractedly eating a bowl of fish soup that one of her assistants had brought down hours ago. The soup was congealed and cold, but Sara didn't seem to notice, shoving a spoonful around her pipe and into her mouth whenever the thought of eating could get past the dozen other issues demanding her attention. She was just scraping the bottom of the bowl when the door to her office slammed open.

She dropped her spoon with a frustrated huff. "If this is about tank seven," she said, spinning around in her chair, "I already know. There's no reason..."

Her words trailed to a stop as she got a look at the man who'd barged into her room. He stood in the doorway, tall and impossibly imposing in his severe red robes. His black hair was touched with gray at the temples while his clenched fingers, wrists, and neck were laden with enough gems to make a king jealous. He looked angry enough to spit nails, and his blue eyes were flashing murder, but Sara couldn't help smiling as she leaned back to take him in.

"Hello, Etmon," she said, blowing a thin line of blue pipe smoke into the air between them. "It's been too long."

If possible, his fists clenched tighter still. "Not long enough."

Sara's smile widened. The sight of him was nostalgic enough, but the sound of Etmon Banage's furious voice made her feel twenty years younger. "This seems to be my week for unexpected visitors," she said. "To what do I owe the pleasure?"

"You never change, do you?" Banage said. "Still asking questions you already know the answers to just to make me say it. I'm here to tell you that my apprentice will not be accompanying your goons on whatever scheme you're plotting. I lent her to the Council at the request of Lord Whitefall to assist in the capture of Eli Monpress, not so that you could use her as spiritual muscle whenever you had a problem your undertrained, impotent Council wizards couldn't handle."

Sara bit down on her pipe. "Don't get angry, Etmon. It's bad enough seeing you in those ridiculous red bed-sheets your little social club requires without your face changing to match. And for your information," she added quickly, cutting off Banage's furious retort, "I am doing nothing improper. Your little Miranda is going to help my people set a trap for the thief, among other things."

"It's the 'other things' that concern me," Banage said through gritted teeth. "I knew I was taking a risk letting Miranda get anywhere near the Council, but Whitefall assured me you would keep your claws out of her affairs. Miranda is a strong wizard and a fine Spiritualist who's been through a great deal in the last year. I won't have you abusing her sense of duty to trick her into doing your dirty work."

"As if I could," Sara snapped, her anger rising to meet his. "She's as moral and dutiful and closed-minded as any of your flock. You don't have to worry about her."

"Don't tell me what to do with my own people!" Banage roared. "You're sending her to the edge of the Council to make some kind of deal with Izo the Bandit

King. Have you finally lost what little grip on reality you ever possessed?"

"You're one to talk about reality," Sara said. "Seeing as you live in some black-and-white fantasy where we catch thieves without dealing with the underworld."

Banage sneered, and Sara blew out a long huff of bitter smoke. "Anyway," she said, "the deal is done. The girl already agreed to go, and as a servant of the Council, she's legally obligated to see the job through. So if that was the only reason you had for honoring me with your presence this evening, I'm afraid you're out of luck, old man. Run on home to your tower and let me get back to my work. You know, the stuff that's actually important."

"Oh, yes," Banage scoffed. "I forgot. Your work is more important than anything else." He thrust a jeweled finger at her. "I'm taking this to Merchant Prince Whitefall."

"Go ahead," Sara said. "He'll just side with me. Council matters are my playground, Etmon. Go back to your tower and your fawning, self-righteous Spiritualists. Tell you what, when we catch Eli, I'll bring him by and you can preach him to death."

Banage whirled around, his fists clenching in rage, and Sara heaved a frustrated sigh.

"Why did you even come?" she muttered. "You knew it would be like this."

Banage didn't look at her. "Because," he said quietly. "Fool that I am, I still believe that, someday, you will remember your oaths."

"What, to the Spirit Court?" Sara's eyes narrowed. "Or to you?"

Banage didn't answer. He walked out of her office without another word, slamming the door behind him with a crash that made Sara wince. She glared at the closed door for a long time, furiously puffing on her pipe until the bowl was nothing but dead ash. Shaking her head at the wasted time, she emptied her pipe into the dregs of her cold soup and got back to work.

CHAPTER 7

Nico gasped at the thin, cold air and pulled her coat tighter across her shoulders. She walked with her face down, her boots crunching over the crust of ice on the rocky slope. They were far north, beyond the Council Borders, farther even than Slorn's Awakened Wood, on the cold, high slopes of the Sleeping Mountains. An impressive distance, considering it had been only three weeks since Eli had driven them out of Home before dawn. That much wasn't unusual. Eli was always in a rush when he had a job in mind, but this time keeping up had been much harder.

It doesn't have to be.

Nico grimaced. The farther north they went, the stronger the voice became.

Why do you do this to yourself? The voice echoed loud and clear through her head, as though the speaker were standing behind her eyeballs. *All I ask is honesty, Nico. Embrace what you are and you can have everything back, your strength, your senses, everything.*

Nico stomped her aching legs down and focused on the sound of frozen pine needles as they crunched under her boots. "How much farther?"

"Not far," Eli said. He was well ahead of her, walking lightly between the scrubby evergreens like he didn't know what tiredness was.

"So you keep saying," Josef grumbled, keeping pace with Nico. "Is this another of your moving houses?"

"No," Eli said. "Or I don't think so. I've never actually been here before."

Josef stopped and stared at him. "Then how do you know where we're going?"

"I don't," Eli said cheerfully. "Not many do, past this point. It's not exactly on a map."

Josef sneered up at the mountains surrounding them. "Fantastic. Three weeks on a death march just to get lost in the mountains."

"I'm not lost," Eli said sharply, turning around to face them. "We are exactly where we should be. And if the stories I've heard are correct, we shouldn't be able to go much farther before our hosts find us."

Josef opened his mouth to ask another question, but stopped midbreath. He dropped to a crouch, his hand flying to the hilt of the massive sword on his back. A second later, Nico heard it too, the faint crunch of something moving in the woods. Something large. She dropped to a crouch beside Josef, ignoring the protests of her aching legs. Looking around, she could see nothing but trees and stones and empty country, the same as she had seen for the past two days. But she knew something was there, a darker shadow beneath the shaggy pines, watching them. Beside her, she heard Josef draw the Heart. Off to her left, something growled.

"Ah," Eli said brightly. "That would be them now."

Nico watched wide-eyed as Eli trotted back down the hill and stopped with a grand bow, flourishing his hands dramatically. "Greetings, ancient guardians of the heights! I am Eli Monpress, and—"

"We know who you are," a voice rumbled. "Get out. This is no place for humans."

Nico swallowed as several more growls went up in agreement. She felt Josef shift, his muscles clenching. He might not be able to hear the voice, but the obvious threat in the rumbling sound from the shadows required no interpretation.

"Don't be so hasty," Eli said, putting up his hands. "I'm here on behalf of a mutual acquaintance, Heinricht Slorn." A great round of growls went up at this, and Nico winced at the sound of claws scraping on frozen ground. Eli didn't even blink. "I ask an audience with Gredit."

For a moment, nothing happened, and then the trees around them began to rustle, and Nico pulled back as the source of the growls stepped into view. All around them, stepping out of trees and from behind stones, were enormous mountain bears. They moved in, yellow teeth bared and ready, shaking the snow off brown, furry shoulders that stood taller than Nico's head. The bears stopped at the edge of the trees, growling and pawing the ground. Only one bear came closer, striding across the frozen stones until he was a few feet from Eli. When he was close enough to reach out and bat Eli across the face with his massive paw, the bear stopped and, far more gracefully than Nico could have imagined, stood up on his hind legs. Nico swallowed. The bear was ten feet tall at least, and from the way he glared down his silver-streaked muzzle at the thief, she didn't doubt for a moment that he could crush Eli like a ripe berry if he wanted, and they all, especially the bears, knew it.

"You have a lot of nerve coming up here and saying that name," the bear growled, brown eyes darting between Eli and Josef. "Tell the deaf one to put up his weapon."

"It won't matter if I tell him," Eli said. "Josef does what he wants. However"—he leaned forward conspiratorially—"maybe if you weren't giving him such reason to use it, he might put it up on his own."

The large bear glared at Eli and then jerked his head. All around the circle, the bears backed away. Josef, well used to one-sided conversations, got the point and slowly slid the Heart back into its sheath.

Eli smiled at the bears. "Now," he said, "about that audience?"

The lead bear dropped back on all fours. "If you want to talk with Gredit, we'll take you there, but don't expect to like what you hear. He doesn't care much for your kind."

"So I've heard," Eli said. "But one takes the chances one must. Lead on."

The bear gave him a final poison look and turned around, trotting off into the trees. As the other bears did the same, Eli turned to Josef and Nico. "Stay close," he whispered.

"Right," Josef said, easing his daggers in and out of his sleeves. "Close to the pack of enormous bears."

"Never a boring moment," Eli said with a grin before turning and jogging after the bear. Shaking his head, Josef followed. Nico stayed close behind, holding her coat tighter than ever.

The bears followed no path. They trundled straight across the mountainside, hopping easily over rocks and fallen trees. Nico had the suspicion that they did this on purpose, to make it hard for their human followers, but they had another thing coming if they thought they could slow down people who traveled with Eli Monpress with a little hazardous countryside. Nico, Josef, and Eli kept the pace, following the bears along the mountain ridge until they reached a narrow valley ringed on all sides by old, dark firs.

The bears slowed, picking their way down to the narrow, swift stream at the valley's base. The air here was different than the slopes. It clung in the throat, wet and thick with the wild smell of pine and fur. The damp cold went straight through Nico's coat, making her movements slow and clumsy. Fortunately, the bears stopped when they reached the water and turned upstream.

"There," the largest bear said, looking over his shoulder at Eli.

They didn't have to ask what he meant. Down by the water they could see what had been hidden by trees from above. Ten feet up the slope, nestled back in the gray stone of the mountain face, was a cave, and all around the cave were bears. Even Eli pulled back when he saw them. The bears were all different sizes and colors. Some were enormous and black, while others were smaller and honey brown. They sat in clusters, watching the intruders with cold, dark eyes.

"I didn't bring you here to stare," their guide rumbled. "Go and be done, or leave now."

Eli gave the bear a smile, but even Nico could tell it wasn't one of his best. The bear just turned away with a huff. Thoroughly dismissed, Eli started up the hill, Josef and Nico close behind him. The bears at the cave mouth didn't move. They just watched as the humans scrambled up the muddy slope toward the cavern's entrance. It was a large opening, three times Josef's height and wide enough for four carts to drive abreast with space to spare, but the musty smell that drifted out of the dark, a potent mix of wild animal and old blood, was enough to give even Eli pause.

The moment they stopped, all the bears began to growl. Eli jumped at the sound and gave himself a shake. Then, with a dazzling smile at the rumbling bears, he marched into the cave as though he were entering a banquet where he was the guest of honor. Nico and Josef followed more cautiously. Once they were inside, the gray light faded. The cave only seemed to get bigger the deeper they went, and in the shadows Nico could make out more bears watching them as they stumbled across the uneven floor in the dark.

Fifty feet from its entrance, the cave ended abruptly in a slope of broken rocks, and sitting on the rocks like a king on his throne was the largest bear Nico had ever seen. He towered in the dark, lounging with his back against the broken stone. Even lying back, the bear was nearly fifteen feet tall, and almost as broad. His enormous paws, each large enough to crush Nico's head like a walnut, rested on his monstrous stomach, the black claws moving slowly back and forth through his black, coarse fur.

As her eyes adjusted to the dark, Nico realized that the bear's fur was actually more gray than black. His pelt was crisscrossed with thin patches where scars interrupted the growth of his coat, and one of his black eyes was silver with cataracts. But any illusion of age and weakness was dispelled when he bared his massive jaw full of yellow teeth in an expression that could have been a grin had it been less terrifying.

Undaunted, Eli stopped at the foot of the great bear's slope and dropped a deep, formal bow. "Greetings, Gredit, eldest of all bears," he said solemnly. "I am Eli Monpress, and I come before you to beg a boon for one of your—"

"I know who you are."

Nico winced at the bear's voice. It was deep enough to shake the stone below her feet, and full of anger.

Eli glanced up from his bow, and the bear gave him a nasty sneer.

"So," Gredit rumbled. "The white bitch's favorite has come to ask a boon from me. This is quite the turn."

"Not for myself," Eli said quickly. "I would never dream of troubling you for my own benefit. I'm here on behalf of our dear, mutual friend, Heinricht Slorn."

The bear's eyes, black and cloudy silver, narrowed. "And what would Slorn want of a lapdog like you?"

"He hasn't had the chance to tell me," Eli said, straightening up. "He's gone missing."

The bear made a horrible sound, like a growling cough, and it took Nico a terrifying moment to realize he was laughing.

"Now it comes together," the bear said, still chuckling. "You want me to tell you where he is."

"You are the Great Spirit of the northern bears," Eli said simply. "It *is* within your power."

"And what would a human know of my power?" the bear said. "We bears have been here as long as the mountains themselves, as long as the winds in the sky. What would you know of that?"

"Nothing at all," Eli said. "But I'm not here for history. I'm here to learn what I need to know to save a friend. A *mutual* friend, unless I am sadly mistaken."

Gredit gave him a long look. "We honor Slorn. Of all your kind, he was the only one who used your unnatural power over spirits to help us. But"—the bear growled at Eli's growing smile—"that gratitude does not extend to you, little favorite." The bear leaned back on his throne of crumbled boulders. "If you want our help, you'll first have to prove what you are."

"But you already know me," Eli said. "You interrupted me to make that much clear."

"Oh, I know you," the bear said. "I'm no blind fool like your lot. But I want to see the proof for myself." Gredit bared his teeth. "Show me her mark, or get out."

Eli took a deep, frustrated breath. "Surely there's another—"

A chorus of deep growls from all over the cave cut him off. Eli looked around with a grimace. "All right," he said, shaking his head. "Get a good look. I'm only doing this once."

Eli closed his eyes, and Nico gasped as a tremendous pressure swept over her, making every hair on her body stand on end. She wasn't alone. All around them, the bears began to shuffle, grumbling and keening. The thief, however, stood perfectly still, feet spread, eyes closed, his face calm and untroubled as the pressure mounted. After a few seconds Nico could barely move, and yet, for some reason, she wasn't afraid. There was something comforting about the pressure, something warm and familiar. And then she realized what was happening. Eli had opened his spirit. The pressure, the hot feel of familiarity pressing on her skin; it was Eli's soul flung wide. Now that she knew what it was, she could almost feel its shape in the air. Eli's soul filled the room, spreading in all directions, and everywhere it touched, spirits woke.

Even Josef saw it. He stood beside her, blades in hand, watching in amazement as the bears trembled. Trembled, and began to bow. And it wasn't just the bears. All around them, the world was paying homage. The breeze from the mouth of the cave stilled. The stones rearranged themselves, tilting down and whispering obedience. Everything, from the lichen on the cave roof to the dirt on the floor, bowed down when Eli's spirit touched it, and though Nico did not understand why, she could feel it too. Deep inside, deeper even than the demonseed, something called for her to show obedience. The urge was so strong that she found her eyes had lowered without her knowing, and try as she might, she could not raise them again.

Of every spirit in the room, only the great bear seemed unaffected. He watched from his throne, his massive head rested on one oversized paw, perfectly still, even as the stone he sat on fought to bow down. Just before the force became unbearable, he raised his head. "Enough."

Eli's eyes opened and the pressure vanished. All around the cave, bears pushed back to their feet. A few began to growl, but most stayed silent, their dark eyes fixed on Eli, their haunches lowered reverently.

Up on his seat, the great bear sighed. "I see the mark of the favorite is as powerful as ever. The Shepherdess's touch is laid strong on you. How strange, then, that she would let such a bright treasure run around loose."

"I'm no treasure," Eli said. "I am myself and no other.

Now"—he folded his arms over his chest—"I've done as you asked. Tell me where Slorn is."

The bear laughed. "Your display may have awed my children. They are too young to see past the Shepherdess's glamors. I, however, am too old to be much impressed with such theatrics. I have seen many favorites, after all."

"Then why did you make me do it?" Eli's voice was angrier than Nico had heard it in a long time.

"To get her attention," the bear answered, growling so low the stone vibrated under their feet. "She may let you run wild through her creation, but I'd bet my fur she's always got an eye on you. After that display, I know for certain she's watching very closely. Good. I want her to hear what I have to say."

He eyed Eli hungrily. "I am the lord of bears, favorite. It is my purpose to protect my children. I feel every creature of my blood as though they were my own flesh, and I protect them with tooth and claw. So it has always been since before the Powers were born. Before the Shepherdess or the Weaver or the Hunter. Yet, look at me." He ran his paw across his silvered coat. "For the first time since the beginning of creation, I grow old and weak. My sight dims and my claws grow dull. I fear I am dying." The bear drew a deep breath. "I do not expect a human to understand. Your kind die like flies. But I am no mere flesh creature. Of all Great Spirits, I am one of the oldest. I was created by the Creator to be the guardian of all bears. So long as they thrive, I thrive. Yet here I am, old and weak. What does this mean for my children?"

Eli started to say something, but the bear kept going. "Every year my bears grow smaller, stupider, and weaker," he growled. "The mountains, our neighbors and friends since time began, sleep and do not wake while the dark hunger they were assigned to guard sends its seeds into the world unhindered and unchecked."

Nico swallowed and pulled herself deeper than ever into her coat.

"But I am a Great Spirit," the bear went on. "I do my duty. All of this I brought to the Lady's attention again and again, but I never heard a word back from her. For years this went on, and not knowing what to do, we kept living as we always had. Then the darkness took one of my greatest sons."

All around the room, the bears bowed their heads in sadness. "Gredeth," they rumbled.

"Yes, Gredeth." The great bear's voice was thick with loss. "Greatest bear of his generation. It was Gredeth who found the human wandering in our woods, its soul already half eaten by a seed of the thing that lives below the Dead Mountain." The bear made a disgusted sound. "Blindness and power are a reckless combination, and putting them together in one creature was the Shepherdess's greatest folly. The blind human, infected and mad, wandered into our territory, and brave Gredeth did what needed to be done. He fought the monster and won, devouring it so the black seed would not destroy our lands. But his bravery was his undoing. The seed survived the devouring and took root in Gredeth himself."

The great bear's good eye grew sad and distant. "I could do nothing," he rumbled. "I tried. I sent word to the Shepherdess. I threw away my pride. I *begged*, human. Begged her for aid as I have never done before, and received *nothing*. Gredeth continued to decline. The seed ate him until he was only a shell. That was when Slorn appeared. He was wise for a human, and very knowledge-able about the ways of the demon. We put our trust in him, but Gredeth was too far gone, and in the end, all Slorn managed was to slow the seed's growth."

The bear heaved a great sigh. "I was grateful that the human had tried and bade him go with my thanks. But Slorn had not given up. He proposed a radical plan. He would take what was left of Gredeth into himself. Just as he mixed metals, he would meld human and bear spir-its into a new soul. I would have forbade it, but Gredeth asked me to change my mind. He wanted to live, proud bear, not die to the hungry dark. With no answer still from the White Lady, I did what I deemed best. I helped Slorn take Gredeth's soul and body into his own. The result was neither man nor bear, but he was Gredeth just as much as he was Slorn, and my dear son still to this day."

The bear's voice faded to a low rumble as the story ended, and the cave fell silent. In the stillness, Eli stepped forward. "If that's how you feel," he said softly, "help me help him. Tell me where he is."

The great bear's glare grew cold as iced stone. "I will help you on one condition. You, the favorite, must call Benehime down. The great Shepherdess was deaf to my begging. Now let's see if her deafness extends to you. Call her and ask, favorite, why, if she is guardian of all spirits, does she not kill the thing under the mountain? Why does she allow her world to stagnate unattended while she wastes her time with favorites? Why did she create humans and give them power over every true spirit, yet make them so blind they can do nothing but fight and enslave the world around them?"

With a great creaking of bones, the lord of bears stood

up, towering over them. "Bring her down to finally answer for her negligence!" he roared. "I will not cower before her as all the others do! Call her down, favorite! Bring her before me and I will make her answer!"

His booming voice rang through the cave, and all the bears began to cower. Nico felt like cowering as well. She could feel the ancient Great Spirit's anger in her bones. Yet Eli did not step back. He just stood there, looking the raging bear straight in the face as he spoke one word.

"No."

The great bear's snarl shook the stone, but Eli did not move.

"I am no one's dog," Eli said. "I'm the greatest thief in the world. Benehime may call me her favorite, but that was her choice. My life is my own, not hers, and not yours. I sympathize with your plight, I really do, and I hope you get the chance to call her out for every spirit she's ignored. But you'll have to find someone else to tempt her down because I won't ask her for anything ever again."

The bear sat down again with a great crash. "Then find Slorn yourself."

"Come on," Eli said, a little more desperately. "You just said Slorn was like your son. How—"

"He is my son, as much as any bear," Gredit growled. "If he wished for my help, he would have asked for it, not sent you. But no message have I received, no cry for aid. You are the one asking, not Slorn, so you must pay the price." He tilted his enormous head. "I will tell you that Slorn is far from here. If he's in as much danger as you seem to think, he will certainly die before you can find him on your own. I'm your only chance."

"Surely we can come to some other arrangement,"

Eli said. "I have many other talents besides being the favorite."

The great bear tossed his head. "This is not a negotiation, human. The only reason you are still alive right now is because you are the favorite."

Eli took another step forward. "But—"

"Call down the White Lady or get out."

Nico shrank back at the menace in Gredit's voice. All through the cave, bears were growling through clenched teeth. The open menace was clear enough that even spirit-deaf Josef went for his sword, but Eli's hand stopped him before he could draw.

"It seems we are at an impasse," Eli said, stepping back again. "Thank you for your hospitality, Lord Bear, but your price is too rich for my blood. We'll find Slorn on our own."

"So you say." The great bear was grinning now. "But you'll be back. I'm your only path to saving Slorn, and you don't seem like a human who takes failure on the chin." The other bears laughed at that, which only made Gredit grin wider. "See you soon, favorite of the Shepherdess."

Eli gave him a polite smile and a half bow before turning on his heel and marching toward the cave mouth. Josef and Nico fell in behind him, keeping right on his heels as the sound of laughing bears followed them out into the sunlight.

Eli marched down the valley, fists clenched. When he reached the bottom, he jumped over the stream and started up the other side, climbing with a singleness of focus that was hard to keep up with. Nico was covered in sweat by the time they cleared the valley's edge, and even Josef was breathing hard. Eli took no notice. He simply flung himself down on a sunny bit of crumbled stone and glared as hard as he could down the valley at the cave now hidden by thick trees.

"Stupid, presumptuous, stubborn bears."

Josef crossed his arms over his chest. "You want to translate all that growling for me so I know what you're talking about?"

"Oh"—Eli flung his hands out in frustration—"spirit politics. He knows where Slorn is, but he won't tell me unless I do something I swore never to do again."

"Uh-huh." Josef scowled down at him. "And what is that?"

"Something I'm not going to talk about," Eli said. "My plan didn't work out, all right? Let's just leave it at that."

"No," Josef said, and Nico cowered at the anger in his voice. "Don't treat me like an idiot just because I could only hear half the conversation. The bear wanted something and you wouldn't give it. Why? What's more important than finding Slorn?"

"You care a lot about Slorn all of a sudden," Eli said, glaring at the swordsman.

"Don't change the subject," Josef snarled, leaning menacingly forward. "Besides the fact that he's always been a stand-up sort of guy by us, Slorn is the only man who can make Nico the tools she needs to fight off the seed inside her. If that bear knows where he is, then we need to give that bear what he wants."

"You think it's that simple?" Eli yelled. "How long have we been working together, Josef? Two years? Three? And how many times in those years have I passed up an opportunity to do things the easy way?"

"Every time," Josef said.

"Never," Eli snapped back. "If I could just give the bear what he wants and walk off happy, I would, but I *can't*. Not this time. So let's just move on."

"No," Josef said again, louder than before. "How can I trust you to do the right thing when you won't even tell me why? For all I know this *is* the easy way out for you. You tried to find Slorn, it didn't work out, oh well, back to thievery." He stared at Eli's suddenly downcast eyes. "That's it, isn't it? You're just going to let him go, aren't you?"

"What else am I supposed to do?" Eli shouted. "The bears won't help me. I can't find Slorn on my own, and in any case, Heinricht didn't even directly ask for my help. For all I know Pele's overreacting and Slorn has the situation well in hand. I tried my best, all right? We've spent three muddy, profitless, fameless weeks on this nonsense. I think even Slorn would agree we gave it our best shot. But it's over. We lost. Slorn could be anywhere. He could be on the other side of the world and we wouldn't know. We'd have a better chance of convincing the Spirit Court to give me Spiritualist of the Year than of finding our bear man at this point."

Eli was flailing his arms by the end, but Josef didn't even flinch. "That's still not an answer," he said. "As I see it, you're the one making this difficult. Why won't you give them what they want?"

"What part of 'I can't' don't you understand?" Eli shouted.

Josef crossed his arms. "Maybe it would be easier to understand if you told me what it was?"

"So that's it," Eli scoffed. "You don't trust me."

"Oh, I trust you," Josef said. "I trust you to be a con

man, a liar, and a thief. That's why I put up with you, because you're the best at what you do. But that same stellar reputation makes it hard to take what you say at face value."

Eli gave him a nasty look. "Do I ever ask you about your past, Josef? Do I ever pry? No, I respect and trust you to handle your affairs and do your job." He whirled to face Nico, and she shrank back farther still. "Do I ever ask you how you got your seed? Have I pressed you at all about what happened in Gaol, or why you've suddenly become the weak little girl you always appeared to be?"

"That's out of line!" Josef shouted, stepping between Nico and Eli.

"Is it?" Eli shouted back. "She's just as much a part of this as either of us. Despite your mother-hen routine, she can speak for herself. We're all thieves together in this."

"This isn't a heist, Eli!" Josef roared. "If Slorn dies because of your pride or whatever idiocy keeps you from going back in that cave and finding out what we need to know, we're not losing some gold or risking imprisonment. If we can't get Slorn, Nico's the one who's going to lose." Josef reached out and grabbed Nico's arm, dragging her between him and Eli. "Coats wear out," he said, pulling her coat back to reveal her wrist, where the silver cuff danced against her thin arm. "So do manacles. If there's no one there to replace them, then you're sending her into battle naked. How could you do that to someone you claim to trust as one of your own?"

Eli glared at him around Nico's upthrust hand. "I won't call Benehime," he said, his voice so quiet the words were more breath than sound.

Josef's glare was cold and sharp. "So you won't do what

it takes to save Slorn?" he said. "You'll break your trust with Nico, your trust with me, and you won't even tell us why."

"No," Eli whispered. "But I will tell you this." He leaned in until his cheek brushed Nico's arm. "I will break every oath I have before I give up my freedom."

Josef's muscles tensed, and Nico could feel his fist closing, his fingers tightening on her arm. Eli went stiff as well, his blue eyes cold and guarded. Nico could barely breathe from the tension in the air. She'd seen them fight many times, but never like this. Never seriously.

And it's all your fault. The voice in her head was closer than ever, barbed and laughing. *Josef wouldn't even care about the bear if it wasn't for you. Now you're about to break up one of the most enduring friendships of our age, and all because you're too weak to live without props from your little missing Shaper bear.*

A terrible chill went through Nico's body. Eli and Josef were the only people who mattered to her, and they were fighting, destroying years of trust, all because of *her*. She had to stop it, but how?

You know how. An image filled Nico's mind, a great black mountain where snow never fell and wind never blew. It was there for only an instant, but the old terror at seeing it nearly made her brain go numb.

You know how to find Sted, the voice said as the image faded. *I showed you before. Find Sted and you find Slorn. This is your chance to be the solution instead of the problem. All you have to do is stop being a coward. But do it quickly, while you still have people left to worry about.*

Another image flashed across her mind. It was there less than a second, but it was sharp enough to burn into her brain. Eli walking one way, Josef walking another, both of them looking over their shoulders at her in accusing hatred as they left her behind. Alone.

"Stop!" Nico shouted.

Her voice echoed across the valley, and both men jumped. Nico stared at them, horribly aware of the tears rolling down her face. She could still see the hatred in their eyes.

"Stop," she said again, quietly now. Josef, alarmed and looking a bit surprised, carefully released her wrist and stepped back. Eli did as well.

"I know how to find Slorn," she said, the words tumbling over one another in her rush to get them out. "All we have to do is find Sted. He's the one Slorn's after."

"Find Sted?" Eli said, mulling it over. "How?"

Nico took a deep breath. After this, there was no turning back. "Sted has Nivel's demonseed inside him. We can find it easily if we go to the place where all demonseed are connected."

Josef gave her a guarded look. "Where?"

"The Dead Mountain."

Josef sucked in a breath, but Eli's eyes flashed at the possibility.

"Step into the demon hive itself," he said thoughtfully. "Find the bear by finding the bait." His eyebrows arched. "Sounds brilliant."

"Sounds dangerous," Josef said, staring at Nico. "Can you even go there?"

"No," Nico said, her voice thick and halting. It had never been spoken, but she knew deep in her soul that if she ever set foot on that black slope, she would never leave it again. "But I can take you to the edge."

"And we can take it from there," Eli said, grinning.

"I've always wanted to know what was on the demon's mountain. If even a tenth of the stories are true, it's bound to be a macabre wonder of the world. And let's not forget the thrill of breaking into a place even the League won't go."

"That had better not be what this is about," Josef growled.

"Of course not!" Eli looked hurt. "But you can't fault me for seeing the many side benefits of Nico's delightful plan, which solves our problem at no cost to ourselves."

"Don't be so sure," Josef said. "I don't know much about these things, but I don't think the Dead Mountain is a place you just walk into."

"Neither was the fortress of Gaol," Eli said with a smile. "That's the whole point of walking in."

The swordsman gave him a dirty look. "Don't turn this into one of your stunts. You're still not off the hook."

Eli's face grew deathly serious. "I didn't imagine I would be. Are you in on this, or are you going to be difficult?"

Josef put a hand on the Heart of War's hilt. "That depends on her," he said, and turned his stony glare to Nico. "If you want to do this, Nico, I'm behind you, but only if you really want to. Don't let Eli make this about him."

Eli harrumphed at that. Nico and Josef ignored him. "I want to help," Nico said. "I owe Slorn a greater debt than any of us."

Josef nodded. "Then lead on."

Nico closed her eyes, opening her soul to the nagging pull in her bones she'd been ignoring all the way north. Her feet turned of their own accord, and when she opened her eyes again, she was facing north and west. Though she could not see it yet, and wouldn't for a long time, she knew she was pointed directly at the Dead Mountain.

As she stepped forward, she tried to marshal the feeling that she was doing the right thing. That she was helping Eli and Josef instead of being a burden for once. But every step left an ashy taste on her tongue and a dull pain in her legs. Deep inside her mind, scraping the bottom of her thoughts, she could feel the voice smiling. That alone chilled her more than the cold wind, and no matter how tight she pulled her coat, she could not get warm again.

CHAPTER 8

They climbed for three days, moving ever higher into the sharp, gray mountains. The trees vanished on the second day, replaced by thorny shrubs, and then nothing, just endless slopes of bare stone and snow. At night, great gusts blew in icy sheets across their meager campsite, leaving tracks of frost on the path that Josef had to break up with his boots before they could move on. Still, despite none of them being dressed for mountain weather, they made good time, mostly thanks to Karon, Eli's lava spirit.

As soon as the cold became uncomfortable, Eli had opened his shirt and had a nice long chat with the burn on his chest. Karon was happy to help them stick it to the ice and wind spirits, and he cheerfully kept the air around Eli as warm and dry as a smokehouse.

"I only wish it didn't reek of sulfur," Josef said, pressing up the mountainside. "I'd almost rather deal with the cold."

"Well, don't let me stop you," Eli huffed, though even

he looked a little green. "Who am I to stand between a man and his frostbite?"

Nico would have chuckled at that, but even a smile felt out of place on the gray slopes. They were getting close. Though she kept her hood down and her eyes on the path, it did little good. She could see the mountain all the time now, even when she closed her eyes, which she did as little as possible. It only made her more aware that she was never alone. The voice sat like a lump in her mind, rarely speaking but ever present, a constant weight that could not be removed or ignored.

"Nico?"

She jumped at her name and looked to see Eli staring at her.

"You stopped. Are you all right?"

Nico swallowed. She didn't remember stopping. "I'm fine," she said softly.

Eli gave her a look of superb disbelief, and she hurried forward, scurrying up the mountain until she was at the edge of Karon's warmth.

If you embraced what you were there would be no need for these charades, the voice tsked. *If the thief and the swordsman are so important to you, why bother fighting this fight we both know you're going to lose? What do you hope to gain? Admit it, everyone would be so much happier if you just accepted your fate.*

Nico clenched her jaw and focused on pulling herself up the slope. Eli followed behind her, watching her back with a cautious, closed expression.

Josef reached the top of the slope first. He'd taken to pushing forward, plowing through the snow to make a path for the others before falling back to the circle of

Karon's heat to warm up again. This time he waited for them, standing impatiently at the peak while Nico and Eli trudged the last fifty icy feet. The top of the slope was not the top of the mountain, however. Instead, they came out in a short, narrow pass between two peaks. It was a forbidding place, a wide alley of stone paved with sharp, icy rocks and crusted snow, but it was sheltered from the wind and that was enough to make it feel almost homey.

"At last," Eli said. "I thought we'd be climbing forever."

"We may not be done yet," Josef answered, picking his way down the pass. "Don't get too cozy."

Eli's mouth twitched, but he said nothing. Though they were speaking mostly as usual, Nico was keenly aware that Josef and Eli still weren't looking directly at each other. It made sense, of course. No matter how close the friendship, the things they'd said outside the bear's cave couldn't be forgotten as easily as that. Still, Nico couldn't even look at them together without feeling a horrible pang of guilt. She had to find Slorn as soon as possible, she thought, hurrying down the pass after Josef. The sooner the pressure was lifted and the problem was resolved, the sooner they could all go back to how they were before.

She caught up to Josef quickly, not because she was moving so quickly but because the swordsman had stopped. He was standing at the other end of the sheltered pass, staring out at the white landscape beyond with a hard look on his face. She didn't have to ask him what he saw; she could feel it waiting out there, beyond the snow.

"We're here, aren't we?" Josef said softly.

Nico could only nod, forcing her foot to take the last, terrified step to stand beside him and look out on their final destination.

The pass between the mountains let out on a steep, snow-covered slope that plunged down into a little valley. Snow blew in sheets across it, hiding everything else behind a blanket of pure white, but here and there the wall of snow thinned, allowing a fleeting glimpse of the mountain at the other end of the valley. It towered above the other peaks, twice as high as any of the lesser mountains that ringed it, its cold, black stone showing through the blowing snow like dark water under ice.

"There's no snow on its slopes," Josef said, squinting against the white storm.

"No," Eli said, stepping up to join them and bringing the welcome sphere of warmth with him. "No snow, no water, just dry, dusty stone, and the cold, of course." He glanced at Nico. "Or so I've heard."

Nico looked away. She didn't know how to answer that. All the way here she'd been probing her mind, trying to dig up memories about her time on the mountain. The closer they came, the more familiar things had felt, but a black haze hung over her mind, drawing a curtain between the morning Josef found her from everything before it. Nico frowned. Perhaps the demon ate her memories as well as her soul. Perhaps she really was starting to lose her mind.

You can't blame everything on me, the voice purred. *You locked those memories away yourself. Pity, you were so much stronger then. It sickens me when I think of what you threw away.*

Nico firmly turned her attention toward the valley floor. She did not want to hear it.

"All right," Eli said, dropping his bag on the ice at his feet. "Since you can't go to the mountain, Nico, Josef

and I will sneak in ourselves and find that map you mentioned. We'll have to take Karon with us. Will you be all
right without heat?"

Nico considered. "I should be. I'm sheltered here, and
I've got my coat. I'll be good until nightfall."

"Plenty of time," Eli said, glancing at Josef.
"Let's go."

Josef nodded, and the pair of them started down the
steep slope toward the black mountain. Eli skidded a little
on icy snow and half ran, half slid down the first slope.
Josef, however, took one step and stopped cold.

Nico thought he was testing the ground, but the seconds
ticked by and still he didn't move. Eli recovered his footing
and, realizing he was alone, glanced up at his swordsman.

"Are you all right?" he called.

Josef didn't answer. He had a look on his face Nico
had never seen on him before. On anyone else, she would
have called it bewilderment. For a long minute he just
stood there, the wind blowing snow into his short blond
hair. Then, very slowly, as though he were pushing against
enormous pressure, Josef lifted his arm, raised his hand
to his shoulder, and, with a flip of the buckle, undid the
strap that held the Heart of War to his back. The sword
fell to the ground with a crash that echoed off the mountain walls, sending the snow sliding down the slopes. The
second he was free, Josef staggered forward, panting and
red-faced like he'd just run a mile in full armor.

Eli looked from sword to swordsman. "What just
happened?"

"I don't know," Josef said, struggling to stand upright.
He turned to face his fallen sword, which was lying on
the ice just inside the ravine. Scowling, he leaned forward

and grabbed the handle with both hands, pulling as hard as he could.

The sword did not move.

Josef braced his legs and pulled again, but the sword stuck to the icy stone as though it had grown there, and nothing Josef did could move it. After the third pull, he fell backward into the snow. Josef sat up again with a flurry of thrown snow, gasping and glaring at his sword. But the Heart just sat there, black and silent as ever.

Eli climbed back up the slope and leaned over the sword until his nose was almost level with the leather-wrapped hilt, staring intently. When he had examined it from every angle, he stood up with a shrug. "I guess it doesn't want to go to the Dead Mountain either."

"That's too bad," Josef said, breathing hard. "Because I'm not going in there without it, so it'll just have to come along."

He grabbed the hilt to pull again, but this time he stopped, his face going ghostly pale.

"What?" Eli said.

Josef shook his head, like he was trying to clear it. "It can't go," he said.

Eli stared at him. "*What?*"

"The Heart just told me it can't go to the Dead Mountain," Josef said again.

"Since when do you talk to your sword?" Eli scoffed.

Josef gave him a murderous look. "It's more like a feeling, but I know what it said. It told me it has to stay here."

Eli sighed. "Well, did it give a reason?"

Josef crossed his arms. "Sure, it explained all its motivations to me in great detail. And then we sat down and had tea."

"Okay, okay," Eli said, putting his hands up. "The Heart stays. But if it's not going, then you shouldn't either."

Josef arched an eyebrow, and Eli shook his head. "I'm not saying anything about your fighting prowess, but if you can't bring your big weapon I'd probably have an easier time sneaking in alone."

"How does that make sense?" Josef growled.

"It's the first rule of thievery," Eli said with a shrug. "One person makes less noise than two. And I'd much rather you be here with Nico and the Heart than stuck on some mountain with just me and your pot-metal normal blades."

Josef's hands flicked to the blades on his hip, as though he was about to show Eli just how dangerous those pot-metal blades could be, but Eli was already walking over to the cranny where he'd dropped his bag.

"If I go solo then I can do things I can't do with you two," he said, pulling a folded bundle of black clothing out of his sack. "Anyway"—he began to take off his jacket—"it's not like I'm planning on fighting. I'll have a much easier time giving trouble the slip if I don't have to worry about you and your bash-happy ways."

Josef frowned but didn't argue the point. Satisfied, Eli leaned on the wall and began pulling off his boots. He placed them carefully beside his pack, followed by his jacket. Then, standing in the snow in his shirtsleeves and socks, Eli shook out the folded black cloth and started to pull it over his head. It was a tight fit. The fabric was obviously meant to go over the skin, not other clothes, but Nico didn't blame Eli for layering. Even with Karon there to keep him warm, the cold was bitter. When the black cloth was wrapped all the way down to his feet, Eli slid on a pair of padded black boots, completing the ensemble. When he straightened up, he was dressed toe to chin in a black catsuit not unlike the one Giuseppe Monpress had worn back in Gaol.

"Don't ever tell the old man I actually wore this," Eli said, pulling the last bit, the black mask, over his head. "I'd never hear the end. Of course"—he grinned behind the thin cloth—"mine has improvements."

"I hope they make you demonproof," Josef said. "You've got four hours before dark; don't dawdle."

"Yes, Mother."

Josef snorted indignantly. Eli gave them a final wave and started down the slope, half walking, half sliding over the ice-crusted snow. Despite being a black dot on a field of white, he vanished almost instantly. Still, Nico and Josef watched for several minutes more, just in case.

Finally, Josef turned around. "Come on," he said. "Let's see if we can find something that will burn before I turn blue."

Nico nodded and hurried after him. For the next half hour they scoured the ravine and the slope they'd come from, eventually gathering enough burnables to make a fire. It was a small, pathetic thing, but at least it was bright and warm, and they huddled together beside it.

Now that it was clear they weren't going to the Dead Mountain, the Heart let Josef pick it up again. He sat with the black blade in his lap, idly running his fingers across its pitted surface. This close, Nico could smell the bite of cold iron and the fearsome, bloody scent of the sword itself. Even so, it was a comforting, familiar smell, and for the first time since they'd seen the bears, she began to think things might turn out all right.

That was when the sunlight began to fade.

"Powers," Josef grumbled, looking up at the fast-moving clouds. "A storm. As if we didn't have enough to deal with."

He lowered his head and crouched tighter over his sword, but Nico could only stare wide-eyed as the swift, gray clouds were pushed aside by black, angry thunderheads moving against the wind. "Josef," she whispered. "I don't think that's a normal storm."

He looked at her, and then looked up again. By this point, the storm clouds blotted out every inch of sky. They tumbled overhead, enormous and midnight black, lit up from the inside by flashes of blue lightning. Thunder crashed, drowning out even the howling of the wind outside the pass. Josef muttered a curse and stood up, the Heart of War in his hand. It was as dark as night in the ravine now, their pathetic little fire the only sputter of light.

All at once the world flashed bright blue as lightning struck, and in the lightning, a tall man appeared before them. His long black hair fell over the shoulders of a long black coat edged with silver. A long sword with a blue-wrapped hilt sat on his hip, and his long, ageless face was transformed by a triumphant smile.

The lightning faded, but the image of the man was burned into Nico's eyes. In the second before the thunder crashed, a harsh, laughing voice spoke over the howling wind.

"Alone at last."

Nico went cold as the stone behind her. She knew that voice. It came roaring from the memories she'd locked away, from the place in her mind she could never go.

Instinctively, she dropped into a fighting stance, feeling stupid even as she lifted her tiny fists. But she didn't back down. So long as Josef stood beside her, she could not ever run away.

As her eyes adjusted to the returned darkness, she saw that the man in the black coat was looking at her. His blue-silver eyes flashed like the lightning in the sky, and his victorious smile grew even colder as he opened his mouth to speak.

"Don't move."

The command fell on her like an avalanche, slamming Nico to the icy rock. Her breath flew out of her lungs as she crashed into the stone, and she felt a sharp pain as her arm, caught beneath her by the sudden fall, snapped like a twig. Gasping, she tried to roll over, to save her injured arm from her weight, but she could not move. She couldn't even twitch. It was just like what Sted had done in Gaol, only a thousand times stronger, a million times. That time at least she had been able to shift a little; now it took every ounce of her will just to take another breath.

Not for much longer. The voice filled her mind, louder than even the blood pounding in her ears. *You know who this is, Nico. You know how he works. He's letting you breathe, playing with you, savoring his victory. Soon, when he decides or when the pain becomes too much, you'll suffocate under the weight of the spirit's hatred for our kind. But there's no need to suffer. No need to be weak. After all, you've broken his hold before.*

Nico took a desperate breath and closed her eyes, but something inside her head reached out and pried them open again, forcing her to look as Josef stepped forward, his mouth moving in words she could not hear over the pain.

Tears running from eyes she could no longer close, Nico watched Josef reach back and draw the Heart of War. A moment later, the horrid man in the black coat drew his own blade. Her breaths were coming in shallow little gasps now as the swordsmen faced each other, and though she would have gladly broken her own neck to do it, she could not look away.

Watch closely. This time the voice was a bare whisper over her mind. *Everything that's about to happen is your fault.* The voice grew fainter with every word. *When you're ready to do what's necessary, when you're ready to fight again, I'll be here.*

With that, the voice trailed off, leaving Nico to gasp in the sudden, enormous silence of her own head.

Less than five feet from her crumpled body, the two swordsmen lunged.

Out of the corner of his eye Josef saw Nico crumple, but he put it out of his mind before she hit the ground. Nico could take care of herself. She was a survivor, and she'd keep surviving, so long as he protected her chance to fight. To do that, he needed all his attention on his opponent. Across the stone ravine, the man in the coat smiled and drew his sword with a blue-silver flash. The blade shone in the heartbeat of light, long and gently curved, cutting the air with a thin whistle. The man in the coat took a step toward Nico and Josef matched him, sidestepping to block his path, the cold, dull blade of the Heart of War ready in his hands.

The man stopped and stared, his pale face almost amused. "Do not try me, human," he said. "Step aside. This is none of your concern."

"Nico and I are comrades," Josef said simply. "Her concerns are my concerns."

"Is that so?" The man arched a thin eyebrow. "Are you so eager to die, then, comrade of a demon?"

"Death comes when it comes," Josef said. "I won't step aside for it."

The tall man's eyes narrowed. "Have it your way, Josef Liechten, Master of the Heart of War."

"That's unfair," Josef said. "You know our names, but we don't know yours."

The tall man swung his sword up, resting the flat against his shoulder. "I am called the Lord of Storms. So I was named when I was pulled from the sky and given my purpose, the eradication of the creature who stands behind you and all others of her kind. I cannot be killed and I do not give up. Now do you understand the position you are in?"

"More than before," Josef said, tightening his grip on the Heart. From the moment he saw the clouds overhead, the Heart had been almost vibrating in anticipation. He could feel its excitement even now, and it made his own pulse quicken. The only thing that roused the sword was the possibility of a good fight. Josef smiled, remembering that night in Gaol. From the way the Lord of Storms was talking, a fight seemed inevitable, and this time, Josef was determined to honor his sword. This time, he wouldn't hold back.

"I've found that men of purpose are the best fighters," Josef said, looking the taller man straight in the eye. "Tell me, Lord of Storms"—Josef's face broke into a wide smile—"are you a good swordsman?"

"What does it matter?" The Lord of Storms gave him a

bored look. "I told you, I can't be killed. No matter what you do, the end will be the same. I will kill the demon. You can either die with it, or step aside."

Josef didn't move. "It may be you can't be killed," he said. "But never did you say you couldn't be defeated." He reached up and undid the buckle on the belt of knives across his chest. The heavy belt of blades fell to the ground with a thud, followed by the swords at his waist. Piece by piece, Josef shed his weapons. When he dropped the last knife from his boot, he stepped toward the Lord of Storms, completely unencumbered. "I'll ask you again. Are you a good swordsman?"

"I am the first swordsman," the Lord of Storms answered. "And the best."

"Then I will not move," Josef said, pointing the Heart's dull, dark blade at the Lord of Storms' chest. "I am Josef Liechten, and I will become the greatest swordsman in the world. So come and fight me, Lord of Storms. Give me a challenge worth dying for."

The Lord of Storms looked at him for a long time. "I won't spare you once I begin," he said. "If you step down this path, there's no turning back."

Josef braced his feet on the icy rock, the Heart sure and heavy in his hands. "I've never needed a path I could turn back from."

The Lord of Storms laughed. "You are bold to the point of stupidity," he said, swinging his sword so that it matched tip to tip with the Heart. "I find that refreshing. Very well, Josef Liechten, your life has bought you a lesson in the difference in power between you and me. It will be quick, so learn it well."

Josef's answer was to lunge, swinging the Heart of War

with both hands. The black blade whistled through the air, carrying the weight of a mountain as it swung under the Lord of Storms' sword and up toward his unprotected chest. What happened next happened too fast for Josef to see. One second the Lord of Storms' guard was broken, the next, the long, blue-white sword was in front of him, poised to meet the Heart's charge. The two swords met in a blinding clash, and the Heart stopped cold.

Josef grunted as the breath slammed out of his lungs. Hitting the Lord of Storms' parry was like running into a stone wall at full speed. He bore down with a roar, pushing with all his strength. The Lord of Storms stood before him, a bored look on his sharp face, holding the blue-silver sword against the Heart of War's straining blade with one, bored hand. The will of the Heart pounded through Josef's muscles, clearing his vision and sharpening his senses to a level he'd reached only once before, and it was only thanks to that painful clarity that he perceived what was about to happen.

He caught the gleam in the taller man's eyes just in time before the blue-white blade swung, cutting through the air where Josef's head had been a split second earlier. Josef danced back, panting, bringing the Heart up again. But the Lord of Storms lowered his blade, looking at Josef as though he were seeing him for the first time.

"If you're good enough to dodge my attack, then you're too good to die like a dog here," the Lord of Storms said calmly. "The Heart chooses its wielders with great care. It must see great potential in you. Don't waste its time on a battle you can never win."

The Heart of War quivered in Josef's hands, rejecting the idea, and the Lord of Storms looked surprised.

"You always did love lost causes," he said, shaking his head. "But facing me with a deaf boy for a wielder is foolish even for you. The Lady will not be happy when she hears how you're using the freedom she gave you."

The Heart burned against Josef's hands, and a surge of strength flowed up his arms, urging him forward. Josef didn't need to be told twice. He charged, but this time he was watching for the Lord of Storms' lightning-fast block. Sure enough, it moved into position with a silver flash, but with the Heart's rage singing through him, Josef moved even faster. He dropped and rolled under the Lord of Storms' sword, coming up inside the taller man's guard with a triumphant cry as the Heart of War's black blade bit into the Lord of Storms' unprotected ribs.

The Heart slid into the Lord of Storms' side, cutting flesh for a split second before a flash of lightning blinded Josef, and the Lord of Storms vanished. Josef reeled as the resistance disappeared, flying through the air on the force of his blow, which was now lodged in thin air. He was still trying to make sense of what had happened when something hard and impossibly sharp struck his back directly between his shoulder blades. Josef slammed into the ground, gasping and choking on the blood that was suddenly everywhere. The Heart of War clattered from his hand, but Josef couldn't see where it had landed. Flashing spots danced across his eyes, but as he struggled to push himself up, something cold and dull slammed into his ribs, flipping him over onto his back.

The Lord of Storms towered over him, taller and darker than before, his long black hair dancing in a wind that blew only for him. His lightning-colored sword was dark with blood, but what caught Josef's eye was the man's left side, where the Heart of War had stuck. There, where the wound should have been, black clouds were billowing. There was no blood, no bone, just black thunderheads swirling in and out of the gap in the Lord of Storms' black coat. Josef blinked in disbelief as lightning arced across the wound, and the hole in the man's side began to shrink. The clouds pulled together until there was only the smooth fabric of the Lord of Storms' coat, leaving no sign that he had been breached at all.

Josef's horror must have been plain, for the Lord of Storms' face broke into a wide grin.

"Ah," he said and chuckled. "The arrogant boy begins to understand his situation." He held out his sword, pressing the flat against Josef's cheek. "And I was so impressed. To think, someone as spirit deaf as you was able to feel the Heart's will. I haven't seen such a thing in centuries, yet here you are, on your back like all the others, not even realizing you're dead."

Josef tried to answer, but his retort turned into a hacking cough. He spat out the hot blood in his mouth and tried to focus, but his back was burning against the freezing stone, and he could feel the slick, hot blood melting the ice below him. It hurt to breathe. It hurt to move. Above him, the Lord of Storms was blurring, becoming just another shape in the red dark, and Josef realized with a start that he was dying. Truly dying, from a single blow.

The Lord of Storms watched sadly as Josef struggled to breathe, and then he turned in a swift motion.

"I am not without honor," he said, walking to the far end of the narrow pass. "You fought well for what you are, so I shall give you a warrior's death." He turned again when he reached his destination, sword held delicately in his long hands. "Stand up," he called, fixing his eyes on Josef's. "Stand and die as the swordsman of the Heart of War should."

The pass fell silent. Even the endless winds outside ceased their blowing, leaving the narrow space between the cliffs dark and still, save for Josef's ragged breathing. With a low groan, Josef's hand reached out from his chest and began to feel for his sword. He found it at once, the rough-wrapped hilt jumping into his grip. He expected the Heart to say something. He was certainly gone enough to hear it, but the black blade stayed silent.

A great, clear sound rang out between the mountains as Josef plunged the Heart of War into the stone. He took a long, shuddering breath and, using the Heart as a crutch, pulled himself up. The moment he was no longer horizontal, blood began to rush down his back. The pain between his shoulders grew so intense he had to stop a moment, halfway between sitting and standing, just to bear it. But a second later he was moving again, uncurling inch by inch until he was standing straight, facing the Lord of Storms with his sword clasped in both hands. He would not die. He would not fail Nico. He would not fail Eli. He would not fail his sword. He hadn't thrown everything away to die like this. He would stand and meet the monster, the man whose body was made of storms, and he would not go down.

The Heart of War radiated its approval, and he felt its strength flowing back into him, clearing his vision, dimming his pain. This was it, the final blow, and they would make it together. But as he stepped into the ready position, a piercing cry stopped him cold. It was high and keening, and it came from behind him. Even the Lord of Storms looked startled, and they both turned to find the source of the sound. What Josef saw next turned his blood to ice water.

"Powers," he whispered. "Not now."

CHAPTER
9

Eli climbed down the snow-covered slope until the pass hiding Josef and Nico from the wind was itself hidden by the blowing snow. This turned out to be a shorter distance than he'd anticipated, thanks to the rather spectacular blizzard howling on this side of the peak. The flurries were so thick he could barely see his own feet as he picked his way down the cliff, but the white storm did little to hide the mountain rising across the valley ahead, enormous and sharp against the endless snow.

Eli let out a low whistle. The mountain was an inkblot on the white landscape. Impossibly tall, it towered over the surrounding peaks, its black slopes rocky and bare without a flake of snow or twig for cover. Eli stared in wonder at the mountain a moment longer before he sat down in the snow to wake up his suit. Sneaking into castles and treasuries was one thing. To sneak into the home of the demonseeds, he was going to need all his tricks.

"Eli." Karon's whisper was like smoke in his ear. "Are you sure about this?"

"Getting cold feet?" Eli asked, laughing as he rubbed his hands on his sleeves. "I didn't think it was possible in a lava spirit."

The burn in his chest began to tingle, a sign that the lava spirit was not in a joking mood.

"I'm positive," Eli said, his voice steady and certain. "This is our best chance of helping Slorn, and the *only* chance to get around Josef's stubbornness." He heaved an annoyed sigh. "The man is thick as his sword, sometimes. If I hadn't taken Nico's offer I might have ended up on the wrong end of that iron pigsticker. A famous death to be sure, but not the kind I want."

"Josef wouldn't raise his hand against you," Karon said. "It's not his way. As for Slorn, he's a better friend to you than most, but to go willingly onto forbidden ground? The very home of the demon? That's too much, even for him. So why are we here? For real, this time."

Eli closed his eyes. "Nothing gets by you, does it?"

The lava spirit chuckled. "I've lived in your chest for four years now. If I can't call your bluffs, then your tongue really will have turned to silver."

"Fair enough," Eli said. "I am here to find information on Slorn, but also because Nico suggested it. I always suspected she knew more than she was letting on, and now's a good time to show I trust her advice."

"Do you?" Karon sounded surprised.

"Well, I certainly want her to think so," Eli said. "I don't know what's going on with that girl most of the time. If she feels I trust her, maybe she'll open up a little more, especially about her powers, or the lack thereof.

But"—he lowered his voice to a whisper—"that's just extra, sugar on the pie. Really, I'm here because it is forbidden." Eli leaned back and stared up at the shadow of the mountain. "It's the only place in creation Benehime forbade me to go."

"Naturally," Karon said. "You're her darling. She didn't want you to become a bed for a demonseed."

"No, I don't think that's it," Eli said. "Not all of it, anyway." He squinted through the snow. "Living with her, I always felt like I was a doll in her perfect white dollhouse. Nothing there existed unless she willed it, even me. Everything I did, I did because she wanted me to do it. So while she always said I had everything I wanted, what I really had was everything *she* wanted. But I always knew, even then, that somewhere beyond the white world there had to be places she didn't control. Places where the spirits didn't fall all over themselves to answer her every beck and call. I think the Dead Mountain may be one of them."

"But it was the Shepherdess who trapped the demon under the mountain," Karon whispered. "Her will that keeps it pinned." A tremor ran through Eli's chest, and he realized the lava spirit was terrified. "This isn't something we want to mess with, Eli."

"Maybe so," the thief said, grinning. "But we're already here. We need to find Slorn, and there's no harm in just taking a look. Besides, last time I checked, even demons weren't omniscient. If we play our cards right, they'll never know we were here."

The burn tingled again, painfully this time, and Eli gave his chest a pat. "We'll leave at the first sign of trouble," he promised. "Fast as we can, trust me."

"First sign, don't forget."

"I swear," Eli said.

The burning sensation faded, and Eli rubbed his chest with a long, painful breath. Now, to business. He looked down at his suit. It was a simple cat burglar suit, all muted grays and blacks tied close to keep his limbs limber. This particular suit was a little worn. It had been given to him by the original Monpress, back when the old man still thought his adopted son would make a respectable cat burglar one day. He'd learned better, of course, but Eli had kept the suit. Not for sentimental reasons, but because he'd remade it with some improvements.

Eli moved his long fingers over his padded shoes, drying them out with Karon's heat and talking constantly about what he needed them to do in the low, excited voice that smaller spirits found irresistible. They woke easily, the woven fibers turning like snakes under his fingers. Once his feet were awake, he moved up his legs to his chest, then his arms, talking constantly in that same low voice. He did his mask last, unwrapping and holding it up between his hands as he gave an extremely energized pep talk about what they were all about to do together.

Altogether the process took about fifteen minutes. Of course, if his suit had been made from Shaper cloth it would always be awake and he wouldn't have to go through this every time, but Shapers were nosy, and Eli preferred to keep the true nature of his thieving clothes a secret. If the old Monpress had taught Eli anything, it was that you never showed all your cards. Besides, Shaper cloth was horridly expensive.

Now that it was properly awake, Eli's cat burglar suit began to show its true value. Every thread had seven colors, a spectacular bit of dye work that had taken Eli five tries and one very angry cloth merchant to get right. Once awakened, these threads had one job: turn in unison so that the color on the suit's surface best matched the color of whatever Eli was hiding against. Now that every piece was awake, the effect was instant. The moment Eli tied his mask back around his face, his suit went dapple gray-white, a perfect match for the snow he crouched in.

Eli grinned behind his mask. It wasn't perfect, of course. Even when he could blend them together by alternating threads, seven colors was hardly enough to camouflage him from someone who was really looking. Someday, when he had favors to burn, he'd have Slorn make him a suit with a hundred different colors. Assuming, he thought bleakly, they found the bear in time. For now, though, he was satisfied to creep through the snow, keeping Karon's heat just at his body as he made his way across the valley until, at last, he stood at the foot of the mountain where piled snow met bare stone in a razor-sharp line.

Eli stopped, staring at the division between the normal world and the forbidden. Finally, he took a deep breath and, bracing himself one last time, lifted his foot out of the snow and placed it carefully on the mountain's dry slope.

Nothing happened. Eli blinked, confused. He'd always imagined that setting foot on the Dead Mountain would feel different, forbidden, or at least dangerous. But standing there, with one foot on the stone and one in the snow, he didn't feel anything special. In fact, he felt absolutely nothing. It was like stepping into a void. He could hear the wind screaming behind him, the wet of the snow pressing against his back, but ahead there was nothing but cold, empty silence. Even so, it took him a solid minute to put his other foot on the slope. It was the emptiness. Stepping into something that silent, that bare, made him feel tiny and weak, like a rabbit stepping into an open field when there were hawks overhead. Eli swallowed. He wasn't used to feeling like prey.

His suit dutifully switched from dapple white to dull black as he began his creep up the mountain. It was rough going. Other than being coal black and completely bare of snow, it was much like any of the other mountains in the range, only taller and sharper, unshaped by wind for who knew how long. The air on the slope was still and heavy, yet even as he took great gasps of it, there wasn't enough. He felt light-headed and weak, and it only got worse the farther up he went. He clung to the slope, a tiny black spot moving up the great black spike of the mountain's peak, until, at last, he reached a ledge.

Eli threw himself onto the flat surface with a relieved gasp and lay there on his back for several minutes, catching what breath he could from the strange, heavy air. When he felt somewhat himself again he lifted his head and looked around. He was lying on the lip of a long, level rise tucked between the sharp cliffs of the mountain's face, cutting between the impossible slopes almost like a path. But that wasn't all. Eli tilted his head, staring at the ground beside him. The ledge was covered in fine black dust, proof that, even separated from the elements, the Dead Mountain was decaying. Well, Eli thought, no surprise there. No physical body, not even a mountain, could keep itself together without its spirit. But it was what he saw in the dust that caught his eye. There, not an inch from his head, was a small scuff in the blanket of powdered stone, a long depression in the unmistakable shape of a human foot.

Eli sat up, careful not to touch the footprint. There was another one not far from it, and another by the cliff's edge, following the slope of the ledge behind the cliffs and up the mountain.

"Well, well," Eli said, standing. "Not so lifeless after all."

Karon's only answer was a deep, terrified shudder as Eli dusted himself off, turned his suit a duller black with a wave of his hand, and began to follow the footprints up the mountain. The path, for it was unmistakably a path now, wound up the mountainside, cutting back and forth to avoid the steep drops between the cliffs. Eli climbed it slowly, partly because he was being careful and partly because he couldn't go any faster. The air was nearly unbreathable now, thin and dank and icy cold. Every breath burned his lungs, yet he couldn't stop gasping. He sucked in the air as best he could, moving at a slow shamble until the path he was following suddenly and unceremoniously ended at the lip of a little hidden valley. Eli cursed and dropped, pressing himself against the ground as he stared wide-eyed over the valley's edge.

"I don't believe it," he whispered.

Just below him, nestled in a hidden valley on the Dead Mountain, was a town. It was a small town, two dozen stone shacks arranged in a semicircle around a stone cistern half filled with greasy water. Still, that was two dozen more shacks than Eli had expected to find on the forbidden mountain. All around the shacks, people in threadbare black robes moved with their heads down, carrying boxes from a horseless wagon into a small cave at the other end of the valley under the supervision of two large men in matching black leather armor.

"Who sets up shop on the Dead Mountain?" Eli whispered. When Karon didn't reply, Eli answered his own question. "They must be cult members. I remember hearing the League saying something about the cult of the Dead Mountain, misguided idiots who actually want a demonseed inside them."

"How can they live here?" Karon said, trembling. "Can't they see it?"

"Of course not," Eli said, waving his hand in front of his face. "Blind, remember?" He paused. "Out of curiosity, what does it look like?"

"Like something that should never be seen," Karon whispered. "We should leave."

"Not before we get what we came for," Eli said, scooting forward. "Nico described a map room, but I bet we won't find one in those shacks. My money is on that." He pointed at the low cave entrance across the little village where the people in the robes were carrying the boxes down into the mountain itself.

Karon grumbled, but Eli ignored it. He pushed himself up into a crouch and began to inch his way down into the valley. The mountain was silent around him, the dead silence of a land without spirits, and every movement he made sounded like a crash in his ears. But the people down in the valley didn't seem to notice him at all. They just kept hurrying back and forth, their faces as blank as corpses' as they ferried the boxes from the cart to the cave. Eli reached the outermost shack without incident, and he stayed there, back pressed against the loose stone, until the cart was empty.

Once the last box had been unloaded, one of the armored guards reached down behind the wagon seat and pulled out a small bundle. The bundle struggled as the guard set it on the ground, and Eli realized with a horrified shock that it was a child. A little boy, no older than four, wrapped in a dirty cloth and tied with ragged ropes, his smudged face downcast and streaked with dried tears. The boy's thin neck was angry and red, as though something had rubbed it raw, and Eli clenched his jaw. He'd seen those injuries on children before, down in the southern islands where Council law was thin. He couldn't see from where he was, but he would bet the boy had similar marks on his wrists, ankles, and waist. Slavers liked to keep their merchandise secure.

One of the pale, robed figures came forward to take the boy, grabbing him by the shoulders. The child tried to struggle, but it was clear he had no more strength to fight. The robed figure led him away, pulling him to a stone hut that was set off from the others. The cultist opened the gray door with one hand, and Eli shrank back at what he saw inside. There, tied in the dirt like animals, were five more children, boys and girls. They were all tiny, skeletal things. None of them looked up when the newcomer was shoved inside. The boy fell with a sad, light thud as the cultist slammed the door behind him, plunging the children back into the dark.

"They're all wizards," Karon whispered.

"I'd guessed that already," Eli whispered back.

"Don't you see? Those are the beds of future demon-seeds." Karon's voice shook with rage. "Aren't we going to do something?"

"What can we do?" Eli said, taking a deep breath. "We're here for information, not to play hero. Even if I wanted to, we've got no backup. First rule of thievery, if you must fight, only fight the fights you can win."

Back at the center of town, the cultists were bowing before the cart guards, bending to scrape their heads against the stone. The two large men sneered in unison at the display and turned away, each grabbing one pole of the cart's empty harness. Then, with a sickening and familiar twisting of shadows, they vanished, taking the cart with them.

Eli rolled his eyes. "Of course this place would be crawling with demonseeds."

"We should move while they're gone," Karon said. "Before anything worse shows up."

Eli nodded and crept between the shacks toward the cave, keeping an eye on the local inhabitants. He might as well not have bothered. Now that the demonseeds were gone, the people slumped to the ground, exhausted. They didn't speak, didn't touch one another. They just sat there, staring at the ground, their frail hands clutching the dusty stone. Just looking at them gave Eli the creeps, and he shuffled faster than he should have toward the cave.

The moment he stepped inside, the sunlight winked out. It was as though the cave's mouth was a line the sunlight could not cross. Eli blinked in the dark, letting his eyes adjust. Slowly, he saw that the cave was piled with boxes, all made of the same gray, flimsy wood, and all of them unmarked. There was one right by Eli's feet, and he nudged it experimentally. Whatever was in the box, it was horribly heavy, for the crate didn't even budge, but the wood on the outside fell away in flakes, completely dead. Eli would have investigated further, but Karon was burning in his chest, reminding him to keep moving.

Careful not to touch the fragile boxes, Eli edged his way past the stacks and started deeper into the cave. He walked for some time, stumbling in the thick, heavy dark. The cave floor was uneven and tilted upward, climbing toward the mountain's peak. Eli crept low in the dark, keeping as silent as he could, but they didn't see anyone, or anything, until suddenly, after nearly an hour of climbing, the cave opened up again. Eli blinked in the sudden brightness. The cave let out onto a cliff high above where they'd entered. He'd crossed the mountain as well, and as best as Eli could tell he was now on the opposite face from where he had entered, looking north. The view was spectacular. He could look down for miles on the peaks of the lesser mountains, snowcapped and silent in the afternoon sunshine. It was actually quite pretty, and Eli stood a moment, enjoying the scenery, until Karon made a little, terrified noise. Eli whirled around, arms up, ready to take on whatever demonseed or cult thrall was surely about to jump them. But there was no one. Just another view.

Eli stood and stared, trying to make sense of what he was seeing. He was looking down on a valley, a long, straight stretch between mountains just like the approach he'd taken to the Dead Mountain, only this valley obviously should not have been there. No natural formation of stone could have made a valley that straight. It ran like a road from the foot of the Dead Mountain due northwest, and wherever a mountain got in its way, that mountain was sundered, ripped apart in long, terrible gouges until only sheer cliffs remained.

"What happened here?" Eli's voice was barely a whisper.

"I don't want to know," Karon whispered back. "But one thing is certain. Something ate those mountains."

"Ate?" Eli said. "What do you mean, 'ate'?"

"Look at the valley floor."

Eli looked, squinting to make sense of the tumbled impressions beneath the drifts of snow. Slowly, the random shapes came together to form enormous craters. He could see the great ripped-up places where mountains had been, but now nothing was left except piles of boulders, their faces as black and dead as the slope Eli stood on.

Eli swallowed. "What eats a mountain?"

"I already said I don't want to know," Karon rumbled, pulling farther back inside Eli's body. "It's like the demon of the mountain itself escaped and made a run for it, eating everything in its path."

"Come on," Eli said. "If that had happened we'd all be dead. But you're right; something came out." He crept closer to the cliff edge, his eyes following the trail of destruction north and west toward the horizon. "I wonder where it was going. The only thing north of here is the Shaper Mountain." He frowned, contemplating. "*And* I wonder what stopped it, and why I haven't heard about it. I would like to think I'd know about something that eats mountains."

Karon's burn began to singe. "Let's just go."

Eli tore his eyes away from the destruction and set back to the task at hand. The path between the two cliffs was steep, narrow, and open. Had there been wind, the crossing would have been impossible, but this being the Dead Mountain, Eli was able to pick his way along the narrow going with little trouble. After a hundred feet, the path began to jackknife, taking them steeply upward toward the

Dead Mountain's knife-sharp peak. They saw no one as they went, not a guard, not a cultist, not a seed, nothing but dead stone and air. They walked so long Eli began to wonder if he'd missed something, for they were quickly running out of mountain. But just as he was about to suggest they turn around, the path ended abruptly at the mouth of a cave.

Eli stopped in his tracks. This was not like the cave they'd come in through. That at least had been somewhat normal, just an opening in the stone. This was like looking into a pool of ink. No light penetrated past the stone's edge. Instead, the cave's darkness seemed to press outward like a living thing, moving subtly just beyond what Eli could see. He stared into the blackness, waiting for Karon to say something, but the lava spirit was silent. For a moment, Eli seriously considered turning back, but the idea of having to explain to Josef that he'd chickened out gave Eli the burst of courage he needed. With a final breath of the cold, thin air, Eli lurched forward and stepped into the dark.

The blackness swallowed him as soon as he moved. All light vanished, and for a moment Eli stood there groping like a blind man. He was on the edge of turning back around when he realized that, despite this, he could still see. The dark was total, and yet it did not obscure his surroundings. He was standing at the apex of a large, circular cave. Perfectly circular, he realized, as though it had been cut into the stone with inhuman precision. The floor was smooth underfoot, the black stone polished to a slick edge except for the pattern cut deep into its surface. Eli followed the grooves with his eyes through the strange not-dark, biting his lip as the familiar symbol came into focus. It was Benehime's mark.

Eli swallowed. Now that he knew what he was looking at, what he saw directly ahead of him suddenly became much more terrifying. At the center of the room, standing at the place where the lines of the Lady's mark came together, was a man. He was dressed in the same dark robes as the cultists of the valley below, but unlike them, this man was not stooped or downtrodden. He stood straight and haughty, his arms crossed over his chest in a way that only emphasized how skeletally thin he was, and his eyes glowed with a cold light that illuminated nothing.

For a long, long moment, no one spoke. Eli stood frozen at the edge of the circle, his boots just touching its outer border. Karon's mad fear was burning through him, mixing with his own until the urge to run was so strong it was physically painful to remain still. But Eli did not move. He stood his ground, clamping down as hard as he could on the terror while Slorn's voice played over and over again through his head.

Demons feed on fear.

After almost a minute of silence, the man at the center of the circle began to chuckle. "Very brave, little favorite."

Eli winced. There was something horribly wrong with the man's voice. It was far too deep for his thin frame, and there was something wrong with the tone. It was like an inner harmonic was missing, leaving only the shell of a voice. But even the strangeness could not mask the power that reverberated through it.

"You did an excellent job getting past my servants," the man said. "Of course, since I knew weeks ago that you were coming, you needn't have bothered. They had orders to escort you up."

"How hospitable," Eli said slowly. "And who are you?"

"Come, now," the man said, laughing. "You know who I am. Your little lava spirit certainly does."

Eli crossed his arms over Karon's burn, shielding the terrified spirit. "Humor me."

"My kind do not indulge in the conceit of names," the man said, walking forward. "But my children call me the Master of the Dead Mountain."

There was something horribly wrong with the way the man walked. It was jerky, unnatural, like there was something inside his skin moving just a hair faster than his flesh.

"Of course," the man said, stopping a bare inch from the edge of the circle, so close Eli could smell his flesh rotting. "Your mistress gave me another name."

"Yes," Eli said, making sure he was firmly outside the circle of the Shepherdess's seal. "Demon."

"There." The strange, horrible voice hummed with satisfaction. "Was that so hard?"

The demon smiled at Eli's sour look and turned on his heel, marching back across the seal with that horrible jerky walk until he was at the opposite side of the cavern. "As I said, I knew you were coming, and I know why you're here." The demon put out his hand, brushing the wall where it touched the circle's edge. All at once, the stone began to change. It sank away from his touch in places and rose to meet it at others, forming an intricate carving of tiny mountains, valleys, and seabeds across the curve of the wall. Eli watched in amazement as a perfect map of the world emerged from the dark stone, and not just the Council Kingdoms, but the Frozen Lands of the far north and the great realm of the Immortal Empress herself, far across the Barrier Sea. As the land took shape, other things appeared as well. Small, black shapes seeped from the black stone. Round, multilegged buglike things with shells like liquid tar. They rose from the stone and crouched on the continents, tiny antennae quivering whenever the demon's hand passed near.

"Here," the demon said, stretching up to point at one particularly large black beetle crawling far to the east of the great black point marking the Dead Mountain, somewhere in the coastal foothills of the Sleeping Mountains. "This is where you'll find Sted. If you hurry, you might even catch him before that bear-headed friend of yours does." He looked at Eli, his face all concern. "And I would hurry. Between the two of us, Slorn doesn't stand a chance."

Eli just stared at him, utterly speechless for once in his life. This encounter had taken a sharp turn from horrifying to bizarre. "Wait," he said. "Wait, wait, wait, what are you doing?"

The demon looked hurt. "I'm helping you."

"Yes," Eli said. "Why?" He pointed at the map, so confused he almost stretched his arms over the seal before he caught himself. "Why show me this? Why tell me where Sted is? You know I can't possibly trust you."

"You came here specifically to see this map," the demon said, dropping his arms. "If you can't trust me, why did you even bother?"

Eli snapped his jaw shut. He couldn't tell the demon that spying on the map would have made the information much more trustworthy than having the thing presented to him. But what was really getting under his skin was how much the creature knew. How did the demon know they were after Slorn? How had it known he was coming? It was a powerful, powerful creature with a wide network of spies, so he was willing to accept a certain amount of omniscience, but this was getting downright uncomfortable.

"Come now, Eli," the demon said when the thief's silence had stretched on too long. "You and I both know I'm your last shot. Old Gredit won't tell you anything without payment. I'm giving you this for free. You can either take it and save your friend or go back to stealing kings and stocking that charming little museum of a town you keep as a monument to your own audacity."

"How do you know all this?" Eli shouted. He regretted the words as soon as they were out. If there was anything he knew about demons, it was that you never showed them a weakness. But if all his secrets were hanging in the open air, he had to know *how*.

Across the blackness, the creature inside the puppet suit of flesh grinned wide. "My dear thief," he said. "A father sees everything through the eyes of his children, and my children are very, very watchful."

Eli's stomach dropped to his feet as everything fell into place. "Nico."

The creature smiled wider still. "First rule of thievery," he quoted. "The last place a man looks is under his own feet."

Eli took a step back. "I'm going now," he said, keeping his voice carefully flat. "You'll forgive me if I don't thank you for your help."

"I never expected you to," the demon said with a toothy smile. "Good-bye, Eli Monpress. I'll be watching."

Eli's mouth twitched, but he kept his face blank. He walked backward, his eyes locked on the demon's glowing gaze until, at last, he reached the cave mouth. The afternoon sunlight hit him like a hammer, and Eli stumbled, blinking in the brightness. As soon as he could see again, he was off, sprinting down the mountain as fast as his legs could carry him with no care at all for how much noise he made.

"I don't believe it," he hissed. "She's been playing us for fools this whole time. How could I have been so stupid? Awakening and going back? Skipping through shadows like it's nothing? She's been his little creature this whole time, and I ate it up. I believed that *drivel* about fighting for her humanity. She's nothing but a little *spy*."

"Eli," Karon said in a warning tone. "Remember that the demon is a trickster. You can't trust anything he says."

"Trust has nothing to do with it," Eli snarled. "He made his case clear enough."

Karon's heat flickered under his skin. "What are you going to do?"

"First, I'm getting off this mountain," Eli said, slowing down to navigate the thin strip of path between the cliffs where he'd stopped before to gawk at the horrible destruction left by the thing that ate mountains. "Then, I don't know. Nothing at first. Josef is going to be the linchpin in all of this. I'll have to break it to him slowly."

"I still don't understand *why*," Karon said. "Why would the demon put all this energy into spying on you?"

"Because I'm the favorite," Eli said bitterly. "Because I'm the greatest thief in the world. Because spirits listen to me whether I want them to or not. Because I'm the key to Benehime, who locked him up in the first place."

"Then why would he let you know he was watching?"

"I don't know!" Eli shouted. "There are so many angles going on, I don't know which way is up anymore. But trust me, I'm going to find out."

"Just watch out you don't break your team when you do," Karon muttered.

Eli had no answer to that. He plunged ahead, racing for the tunnel he'd taken up here from the cultists' encampment. He was so intent on getting off the demon's land, he didn't even notice the enormous storm clouds on the other side of the mountain, blackening the entire mountain range where he'd left Josef and Nico.

CHAPTER
10

When the Lord of Storms' sword cut into Josef's back, Nico lost control. She raged against the pressure holding her down, muscles burning as she fought to stand and attack the smug man made of storms who stood over Josef. She wanted to rip him open, to eat him whole, to punch that smug look off his face.

All she managed was to lift her head a fraction off the stone before the Lord of Storms' command slammed it down again.

She turned her cheek against the ground with a frustrated sob. She was so worthless. Across the ravine there was a soft, wet thump as the Lord of Storms turned Josef's body over with his boot. She heard the hateful sound of his haughty voice, followed by Josef's hacking cough. Nico began to shake. She couldn't even lift her head to see him, but she knew, completely and instantly, that Josef was dying. He was dying, and she couldn't save him. Couldn't do *anything*.

She stopped, holding her breath. This was where the

voice would speak, offer her power. But her head was silent. The waiting stretched on. She could hear the Lord of Storms telling Josef to stand. Stand and face his death. She heard Josef moving, the great ringing sound of the Heart as he thrust it into the stone to pull himself up. The horrible shallowness of his breath as his life bled out of him.

And still, the voice stayed silent. All she could hear was the pathetic, doomed sound of Josef's breathing as he stood to face his death. A death she couldn't even turn her head to see.

Suddenly and without warning, a rage like she'd never felt ripped through her. If this was how it ended, why was she holding out? What did any of her sacrifices mean if Josef died? The Lord of Storms would kill her as soon as he finished Josef. Why was she even trying?

A good question.

Nico gritted her teeth. Fine. She didn't care anymore.

"You win," she whispered against the stone. "Give it back."

The words hung in the air, heavy and irretrievable. Slowly, languidly, the voice answered.

No.

Nico choked. "But you said—"

You want power? Power to save your swordsman?

She nodded.

Then prove it. Beg.

Something inside Nico began to tremble. "What?"

Beg for Josef's life. The voice spoke each word slowly, pointedly. *My gifts are for obedient children. You've been quite the pain in my side, little lost seed. If you want my help, beg for my forgiveness.*

Nico's breath came in shallow, tiny gasps. Across

the silent pass, she could hear the crackle of the Lord of Storms as he raised his sword, hear the soft drip of Josef's blood as it hit the stone. She had no more time.

She squeezed her eyes shut with a sob and pressed her forehead into the ground.

"Please," she whispered, dragging the word out like a vital organ. "Give my power back. Let me save him."

Deep in her soul, she felt the voice smile. *Say it.*

"Please," Nico whispered again. "Master."

Pain and power hit her like a wall, and the world went black. Nico screamed as her body wrenched itself from the stone, a high, keening sound that grew less and less human with each passing second. Inside her, the seed rose like bile, clawing its way to the front of her mind as deep, triumphant laughter filled her ears.

The Master's voice wiped out all other sound. *Welcome home, little slave.*

The last thing Nico saw was Josef's face, pale and horrified, before the blackness ate everything.

Nico's scream echoed off the icy walls, repeating over and over in the frozen silence. For a long moment the three of them, Josef, Nico, and the Lord of Storms, stood frozen, and then Nico began to change. Her shaking stopped. She grew taller, her skeletal body rounding out, muscles forming under skin that was no longer pale but growing dusky and hard. With a horrible crack, her broken bone reset itself as her arms stretched out, her fingers lengthening and sharpening until they barely looked human at all. But the worst by far was her eyes. It nearly made Josef sick to watch. Her eyes were stretched wider than any human's should be, the dark irises fading behind an eerie yellow glow.

She fell to a crouch, her arms and legs spread out around her like a spider about to spring. When she opened her mouth, now horribly stretched to accommodate a growing set of jagged, razor teeth, the sound that came out wasn't human at all.

"You came to catch a demon, Lord of Storms," the creature hissed. "Not butcher a man. I am your opponent now."

As she spoke, something else rode beneath the words, spreading through the canyon in an invisible wave. It struck Josef's mind like a night terror, a primal fear that went to his core. He was not alone. Above him, the mountains began to shake, the stone squirming and sliding over itself in terror. Josef stumbled as the ground beneath his feet turned to jelly, and it was only with the Heart's help that he saved his back from another slam as he went down. The whole pass was shaking now, forcing Josef to scramble for cover as boulders began to slide down from the cliffs. Within seconds, the whole ravine was thrashing in terror, all except for the place where Nico stood.

The ground below Nico was no longer dull gray stone streaked with ice, but coal black and bone dry. Even in the dark it stood out from the surrounding, panicking stone. It was a blot, a circle of dead, quiet nothing spreading from her feet, and as it grew, so did Nico.

She's eating the mountain. The Heart's voice boomed in Josef's head. *You have to stop her.*

Josef flinched at the edge on the Heart's voice. If he hadn't known better, he would have said the sword was afraid. He started to ask how he was supposed to do that when another voice crashed through his mind, crushing every other sound.

Don't move.

The ravine froze. The mountains froze. Nico froze. Even Josef went perfectly still. Stones hung frozen in midfall and dust stood suspended in the air. Nothing dared to move. On the opposite edge of the pass, the Lord of Storms lowered his hands with a grim smile. His body was going fuzzy at the edges, little bits of his clothes fading back and forth from cloud to flesh while his sword flickered in his hand, the blade flashing between metal and a curved bolt of lightning.

Josef's eyes widened. He tried frantically to get his sword up, but he could no more move than he could hear the spirits' voices. However, the Lord of Storms seemed to have forgotten him entirely. His attention was only for Nico.

"You," he said, his voice thick with something very close to joy. "It is you, isn't it? I always knew. I *always knew* you weren't dead. I had no proof, but I knew." He threw out his empty hand and another sword, a perfect twin of the blade he grasped in his right, flashed into existence. "Now"—his face broke into a monstrous grin—"now we finish what we started." He raised his swords for the charge. "Daughter of the Dead Mountain!"

Across the frozen pass Nico screamed, a horrible sound of loss and mad anger woven through hundreds of voices, and vanished. She exploded from the shadows behind the Lord of Storms an instant later, her claws going for his back, just as he had struck Josef. The Lord of Storms turned without moving. One second his back was to her, and then his body flickered and he was facing her, meeting her blow with both blades, his face mad with joy as they crashed in a shower of sparks.

• • •

The Lord of Storms swept his swords with a roar, cutting a great gash in the mountainside. Nico dodged easily, flitting up through the shadows to the cliff top before launching herself down again, claws going straight for his unguarded head. She laughed as she flew, reveling in the intoxicating freedom of her power. Everything was so easy, so fast. Strength pounded through her limbs, banishing the pain, the fear, the constant worry. With all the power flowing through her there was simply no room for thought, no time for it. All that existed was her, the power, and the threat who must be killed. What did it matter if she couldn't stop to remember why?

She landed on the Lord of Storms with a gleeful scream, rending him from shoulder to ankle before he managed to flash away. For an intoxicating moment she could taste him on her fingers, a sharp mix of electricity and compressed power. Oh, what she could do with that power if only she could get more.

"You'll find me hard to chew, monster." The Lord of Storms' voice echoed through the ravine, and Nico turned just in time to see him blink back into existence, whole and uninjured as always.

Nico frowned. Had she spoken out loud? Well, no matter. He'd chosen a bad place to reform; his back was full to the shadows. She grinned wide and prepared for another jump.

The Lord of Storms lowered his swords. "How much longer will this farce go on?"

Nico shifted, unsure at this new ruse.

"The years you spent in starvation with the thief must have damaged you," he said, thrusting his sword at her. "This is barely worth my time. Look at you, nearly human, too weak to even damage my human shade. Any of my League could cut you down as you are now."

Nico answered by slipping through the shadows behind him, leaping at his open back. He spun and met her halfway, lightning swords cutting deep into her wrists. She screamed in pain and danced back while the Lord of Storms looked on with disgust.

"I have seen you hover in the sky on impossible wings," he sneered. "Blacker than night and larger than the mountain that spawned you. I have seen you eat Great Spirits like a wolf eats rabbits. Do not insult me by pretending at this *weakness*!"

He vanished only to reappear behind Nico, his long swords pressed against her throat. "Let go," he hissed in her ear. "Let go and we shall fight as never before. I have been hobbled and bored these past years, a slave to that woman's fancies. Give me something to feel alive again or I will kill you here."

Really, my Lord of Storms? You would sacrifice the lives of innocent spirits for a good fight?

"Really, my Lord of Storms?" Nico whispered, her throat fluttering against the swords as she breathed. "You would sacrifice the lives of innocent spirits for a good fight?"

The blades at her neck drew closer. "Spirits are sheep," he said bitterly. "Stupid, panicky creatures. I am the Shepherdess's dog, sworn to keep predators from the flock. If a few sheep are killed in the wolf catching, what does it matter? So long as the wolf is killed, the dog is free to do what it likes. And it's been so long since I had a real challenge." The blades drew closer still.

Nico flitted away, emerging from the shadows at the other end of the ravine clutching her bleeding throat. Deep in her mind, a feeling of wrongness nagged at her. She shouldn't be doing this, but why? It was so hard to concentrate.

Forget it. The Master's voice flooded her mind, cold and dark and reassuringly strong. *You're home, Nico. You don't have to think anymore. You don't have to try. Go to sleep. Put yourself in my hands and I will awaken you to your full potential. Then we'll see if our dear Lord of Storms stays so cocky.*

Nico almost cried as the relief washed over her. She'd been fighting for so long, what or how she couldn't remember, but she felt the tiredness in her bones. But everything was different now. The Master was with her. She could give in. Already she was relaxing into the welcome dark. As she sank, she could hear a girl's voice screaming, crying. It sounded so familiar, but Nico couldn't be bothered to turn and see. She was so tired.

There's a good girl.

Just as the last bits of her mind began to sink into the dark at the heart of her soul, something extraordinary happened. All at once, the mountain silence was broken by a deep, ringing gong. The sound of it shook the ground below her feet and forced her eyes open. Across the ravine, the Lord of Storms stood against the cliff, a surprised expression on his face and the great iron length of the Heart of War sticking out of his chest, pinning him to the stone like a butterfly on a board. For a second, all was still, and then, with a great rumbling roar, the Heart's spirit burst open, and the weight of a mountain slammed down.

Nico went down flat on her back, pinned to the icy stone, unable to move. Even the Lord of Storms was still, crushed by the mountain's weight. A few feet from her, at the edge of the ravine, a man pushed himself to his knees, then to his feet. She watched him get up, amazed that he was moving, for he was covered in blood. He stood a moment, steadying his large frame on his shaky feet, and started to hobble toward her, his scarred face terrifying in its determination.

"Nico." His voice was as bloody as the rest of him. "You told me you would never give up."

Nico hissed and struggled, but the mountain's weight held her flat. The man didn't seem hindered at all. He limped over and fell to his knees beside her. "What you're doing isn't fighting," he said softly. "It isn't moving forward. It isn't making anyone stronger. So long as you want to keep trying, keep fighting, I'll fight beside you. But if you've truly given up, then I'll save the Lord of Storms the trouble and kill you myself." He sat back and met her eyes with a calm, serious gaze. "Are you still with us, Nico?"

Somewhere inside her, deeper than the dark she longed to escape into, deeper than the Master's iron, undefeatable power, a tiny, sobbing voice answered, "Yes."

"Then take another breath," said Josef. "And come back."

Don't listen, the Master said. *He's sabotaging you. He doesn't want you to be stronger than him.*

Nico pushed the voice down with a firm mental hand. "No," she said.

She spoke with her own voice now, the small, pathetic thing crawling up from the depths it had been pushed into, and all at once, her spirit poured open. She ripped the darkness that had claimed her mind, shredding it to nothing, pushing free. Her body convulsed against her, clinging to the strength, the power, but she threw the demon gifts away. The second she cast them aside, the pain flooded back, and she screamed in agony as her body withered back to its true, bony shape. Her vision went dark as the nightsight left her, and her eyes burned as the demon light faded. But even as she transformed from powerful being to shuddering wreck, Nico began to sob with relief. Despite all odds, despite the terrible pain, she had not lost herself. She was still human.

Well, mostly.

When she could open her eyes again, she looked down at her once broken left arm, squinting in the dark. What she saw didn't surprise her, but knowing made it no less terrifying. There, growing out of her shoulder where her left arm should have been, was a demon claw. Its skin was as black as the Dead Mountain, and the curled hand had claws instead of fingers. The limb was awkward and ugly, far too long for her small body. Experimentally, she tried moving it, and the pain that followed sent spots dancing over her vision. When she could breathe again she clutched the arm to her side as best she could under the Heart's enormous pressure, belatedly trying to hide the hideous thing from Josef.

But Josef just looked at her with dry interest. "Can't change it back?"

Nico shook her head.

A reminder—the Master's voice was hard and cutting—*of what you threw away. When will you learn, idiot girl? You can't stop being what you are just because you say so. You're mine. You've always been mine, and I will have you in the end.*

"Not if I can help it," Nico grumbled, less sure than she would have liked.

We'll see. The Master's voice sweetened. *Just remember, I didn't force this on you. You begged to have your power back. It's only a matter of time before you beg again. When that happens, Nico, there will be no turning back.*

To make the point, her demon arm began to burn. Nico clutched it to her side, closing her eyes against the sudden tears of pain. Josef stayed on his knees beside her, waiting patiently until she opened them again.

"I'm sorry I can't let you up yet," he said, his voice straining. "The Heart's the only thing keeping the Lord of Storms from ripping us both apart."

Nico nodded, glad that she had an excuse to stay on her back. "What are we going to do?"

"I haven't decided yet," Josef said, grabbing her coat and tossing it over her.

The coat began trying to wrap itself around her as soon as it landed, but Nico paid no attention. "We have to treat your wounds," she said, eyeing the blood on the ground with growing fear.

"I'm fine for now," Josef said. "The Heart is helping me. It's been carrying me this whole time."

Nico shook her head. "Still, you have to do something before—"

Josef raised his hand sharply and she snapped her mouth shut, confused. Then she felt it as well. Deep below the crushing weight that held her down, something was pushing back. Overhead, the dark clouds churned in a great vortex, flashing with lightning as a howling wind blew ice in horizontal sheets across the ravine's top. The stone cliffs began to groan as the Heart fought back, but the storm was quickly growing into a hurricane, and the Heart, powerful as it was, was still just a sword.

With a scrape of metal, the black blade slid out of the stone, landing with a resounding clang at the Lord of Storms' feet. As it fell, the mountainous weight vanished, and the Lord of Storms stepped forward, his face pale as lightning and contorted with rage. He walked toward them, growing larger with every step as entire pieces of his body swirled between solid flesh and looming storm. His swords were no longer even a semblance of mundane weapons, but two controlled bolts of hissing blue lightning clutched in his hands.

"I'm through playing," he said, his voice true rumbling thunder as he raised the lightning in his hands. "This ends now."

Nico could only stare at the bright death coming toward them, but beside her, she felt Josef start to stand. *Of course*, she thought, *he would never sit for his death.* Jaw clenching, Nico started to stand as well, clutching her useless black arm as she struggled to her feet.

The Lord of Storms began to charge, raising his lightning swords with a shout of pure rage as he barreled toward them. Standing beside Josef, Nico squeezed her eyes shut, ready for the strike.

But the blow never came.

She waited, confused, before slowly opening her eyes. Then she blinked them again, not sure of what they showed her.

Eli stood between them and the Lord of Storms. He was still in his black thief suit, and he was standing with his arms out, perfectly still. The Lord of Storms was still as well, his lightning blades a scarce half inch from Eli's forehead.

At first Nico didn't understand why the Lord of Storms

had stopped, or *how* he could have stopped a blow with such momentum. Then she saw it. Just above Eli's head, sticking out through a white line in reality, was a pure white hand. It reached through the air, the long, shapely fingers clutched around the Lord of Storms' lightning swords. The ravine was deathly silent. Nothing made a sound. Even the Lord of Storms was still, a horrified expression on his white face. In the stillness, a second line appeared beside the Lord of Storms, and another white hand shot out to grab him around the throat. The Lord of Storms made a frantic, choking sound, and then, in the space it took to blink, he was gone. The Lord of Storms had simply vanished. The white hands were gone too; so were the dark clouds overhead and the howling wind, leaving them alone in the now silent ravine.

Eli turned around, taking off his mask. "You all right, Josef?"

Josef looked at him a second and started to say something, but before he could get out a sound his eyes rolled back in his head and he toppled over, landing on the stone with a horrible, folding crunch.

"Josef!" Nico and Eli cried together, dropping to their knees beside the swordsman.

"Powers," Eli muttered, looking around. "I didn't know he had this much blood in him." He reached down and grabbed Josef's shoulder, grunting with effort as he lifted the swordsman to get a look at the wound on his back. When he saw it, his face went white.

"His back is filleted," he said, turning to Nico. "How long did he fight like this?"

"I—" Nico stopped, shuddering as she remembered the dark haze that had consumed her mind for part of the fight. "I'm not sure. Things happened quickly."

Eli looked at her, but not like he usually did. Not slyly or openly or with one of his too congenial smiles. No, he looked at her like he was seeing her for the first time, and Nico felt something clench inside her.

He knew.

He knows everything, the voice whispered.

At her side, the black, monstrous arm began to burn, and Nico clenched it closer under the drape of her coat, glad that this at least was hidden from Eli's piercing glare.

Finally, Eli turned his eyes back to Josef. "We need to get him medical attention," he said softly. "And we're not going to find that here. Let's start with getting him to the Heart. Where is it?"

Nico pointed across the ravine to the great crater in the wall where the Lord of Storms had been pinned. It was so dark now she couldn't even see the Heart's shape on the ground, but she could feel it, a large, angry presence in the dark.

Eli nodded and slid his arms under Josef's. "Help me. He's a lug, but we've a better chance of moving him than the Heart."

Nico nodded and moved to Josef's feet, grabbing one with her good arm and one with her demon claw through her coat. If Eli noticed the strange arrangement, he gave no sign. Together, grunting with effort, they lifted Josef off the ground and shuffled him over to his sword. They nearly dropped him when they reached it, but found the final bit of strength to put the swordsman down gently before flopping on the ground beside him, panting.

"I like the muscles more when he's the one carrying them," Eli groaned, leaning back against the shattered cliff face. He reached out and wrapped Josef's hand around the Heart's hilt. The unconscious grimace on the swordsman's face eased at the contact, and his breathing grew less shallow, but he still looked deathly pale.

"We have to get him to help," Nico said.

"I know that," Eli snapped, whipping his head to look at her. "Where are your manacles?"

Nico flinched. "Over there. I had to—"

Eli waved his hand dismissively. "If you're still human it couldn't have gone that badly. Get them; we're leaving in just a moment."

Nico nodded and hurried across the bloody stone with a horrible sinking feeling in her stomach. Eli had never been this sharp toward her.

He's using you because he can't move the swordsman alone, the Master said calmly. *How practical.*

Nico closed her mind to the sound and walked over to where her manacles were lying in the center of the black circle of stone. She hesitated. She could feel the absence of the stone's spirit here like a hot brand across her body. With a deep breath, she closed her eyes and grabbed her manacles, slapping them on as fast as she could. They began to buzz like insects the moment they touched her, and she felt some of the pressure ease from her mind. When they were all in place, two on her wrists, two on her ankles, and the large ring around her neck, she put her coat on properly, keeping the demon arm inside beside her rather than chance putting it through the sleeve. Throwing her hood up so her face was hidden, she turned away from the circle of dead stone and ran to where Josef had dropped his weapons. These she picked up lovingly, gathering the bandoliers of throwing knives, the sheathed swords, and the long-handled daggers he wore in his boots into her arms before hurrying back to Eli.

The thief nodded when she approached, but he didn't look at her. He was staring down the ravine they'd climbed to get here, his face invisible in the dark.

"There's no chance we can get him down that, is there?"

Nico looked down at the steep mountainside they'd scrambled up only hours ago, before everything went wrong. "No."

Eli sighed. "Desperate times, desperate measures, and all that." He stopped and looked at her, eyes flashing in the dark. "What I'm about to do, you will tell no one." His voice was quiet and deadly serious. "Swear to me on Josef himself you won't."

Nico stepped back. "What are you going to do?"

"Just swear," Eli said.

"I swear," Nico answered quickly. If it would save Josef, she didn't care if Eli turned into the Master of the Dead Mountain himself.

"Right." Eli turned away. "I'd say don't look, but there's really no point anymore. Just don't say anything. I haven't done this in a while."

Nico nodded, but Eli wasn't paying attention to her anymore. He walked to stand at Josef's feet and, after a deep breath, closed his eyes. Nico leaned forward, expecting to feel the hot rush of his open spirit crash over her like it had before, back with the bears, but she felt nothing but the cold wind. So far as she could tell, Eli was just standing there. Then, without warning, the air rippled in the dark in front of him, and a thin, white line appeared. It grew as Nico watched, cutting soundlessly through the empty space until it was as tall as Eli himself. When it reached the ground, it turned slightly, and a hole opened. Nico blinked in amazement. Hanging in the air in front of them was a door in the world. Through it she could see what looked like the inside of a small cabin, complete with a cold stone fireplace and green trees dancing outside the tiny window. She stared unbelieving even as a warm breeze floated through to brush her skin. Nico breathed it in, smelling pine and the musty scent of unused furniture. It was real, but where it was Nico had no idea.

Eli nodded and turned to grab Josef's arms again. His movement snapped Nico out of her gawking, and she scrambled to get the swordsman's legs. Using Josef's arm to move the Heart, for there was no other way to move it, they placed the black blade on his chest. Then, grunting with effort, they lifted sword and swordsman and carried them through the hole in the air.

Nico gasped as she stepped through. The biting cold of the pass vanished instantly, replaced with crisp air that felt almost balmy by comparison. Their boots clomped on the wooden floorboards, tracking in dirty snow that melted quickly as they lugged Josef through the gap in the world. The second Eli was through, the opening vanished, fading into the air with only the lingering smell of ice and stone to prove that it had ever been.

They were standing at the center of a large, well-appointed cabin filled with evening sunlight. Paintings of rustic scenes hung on the rough timber walls above dusty racks of wine bottles and sheet-covered furniture. There were even gold candlestick holders on the mantel above the large stone fireplace.

"Stop gawking and help me get him on the bed," Eli

gasped, pulling Josef's shoulders toward a narrow bed in the corner. Nico scrambled to help, and together they set the swordsman down on the heavy blankets.

"We have to stop his bleeding," Eli said, pushing past Nico toward a chest at the other end of the room. He dug into it, pulling out a jug of clear liquor, bandages, and a surgeon's thread and needle. "You'll have to sew him up," he said. "Help me turn him over."

"No," said Josef's breathy, pained voice.

Eli and Nico were at his side in an instant.

"Don't be stupid," Eli said. "And don't talk. We're going to get you patched up."

"No," Josef said again, shaking his head. "The Heart is telling me it's going to handle things."

"What?" Eli cried. "Is the pain making you delusional? You can't even hear spirits and you're telling me your sword is promising to un-fillet your back?"

"Something like that," Josef whispered. "The Heart also says that it has a lot more experience in keeping swordsmen alive than you do, and that you should mind your own business."

Eli jerked back. "And does it have anything else to add?"

"Yes." Josef's voice began to slur and fade. "Don't move me for two days."

"Two days?" Eli shouted. "We're supposed to sit here and watch you bleed for two days?"

But Josef didn't answer. He lay on the bed, eyes closed, his chest moving in long, shallow breaths beneath the Heart of War, which lay across his chest from chin to knees with his white-knuckled hands still clutching the hilt. With a long, angry sigh, Eli pushed away from the bed and began shoving the first-aid supplies back into the trunk. Nico watched, biting her lip as Eli walked over to the dusty wine stand, grabbed a bottle at random, and flopped down on the floor.

When it was clear he was more interested in digging the old cork out with one of Josef's throwing knives than giving her vital information, Nico asked the burning question. "Where are we?"

"Safe," Eli said, popping the cork at last. "Well, safer. We're still in the Sleeping Mountains, though not as far north as we were, and much farther east, about fifty miles from the coast. This is one of Giuseppe Monpress's many hideouts. The old fox set them up years ago as refuges of last resort in case things got too hot, which explains the extravagant furnishings." He cast a disapproving eye at the richly appointed wine rack. "He could never stand to be without his luxuries. We're still technically inside Council lands, but no patrols come up here."

Something about the way he said that made Nico distinctly uncomfortable. "Why not?"

Eli took a long drink from the bottle. "Because this is bandit land," he said, wiping his mouth on his sleeve. "The Council can claim it all they want, but without influence in the area, it's all talk. Izo is the real power here." He took another swig. "Bastard has a bounty higher than mine."

"Will he be a problem?" Nico said.

"Shouldn't be," Eli answered, leaning back against the cabin wall. "Not unless we make trouble for him, which we might have to." A strange expression passed over his face. "I didn't just choose this place because it was safe and far away. This is also the closest spot I knew to where Sted is."

Nico's eyes widened. "It worked then! You learned where Sted is!" She couldn't believe it. Her plan had worked! But Eli didn't look happy.

"Yes," he said slowly. "Among other things."

Nico flinched at the bitterness in his voice. The black arm began to ache beneath her coat, and Nico clutched it as subtly as she could. It didn't matter, though. Eli was staring into his bottle with a focus so intense, she got the feeling he was not looking at the wine so much as avoiding looking at her. A cold, heavy feeling settled at the base of Nico's stomach, and she scooted closer to Josef, tilting her head down so she didn't have to watch Eli staring anywhere but her.

You always knew he would turn on you. The Master's voice was soft and coy. *It was only a matter of time.*

Nico put her head on her knees. Outside, the sun sank lower. It was going to be a long two days.

Benehime stood in her white nothing, a furious scowl on her perfect white face as she stared at the man hanging suspended by his thumbs in the air before her.

You presume too much! she hissed, her voice like cut glass as she paced back and forth in front of the Lord of Storms' dangling body. *I told you to stay away. I told you to let it be. And still you disobey!*

On her last word, she slapped him across the face. Wherever she touched him, his body broke apart into black, flashing clouds. The Lord of Storms cried out, his voice more gale than scream.

You are my creation! she roared. *Mine to do with as I see fit! To use in what work I choose! A tool does not act without its master, or have you forgotten what you are?*

She lowered her hand, and the Lord of Storms slowly pulled himself back together. But when his face reformed from the thunderheads, his murderous expression was even harsher than hers.

"It is you who has forgotten, Shepherdess," he growled through gritted teeth. "You knew the Daughter of the Dead Mountain was still alive. You knew, and you let her wander free, all because of your shameful intoxication with that thief! Have you forgotten what happened the last time she awoke? Have you forgotten your duty?"

I forget nothing! Benehime began to stalk back and forth in front of him. *Do you think I fear the demon? The little worm trapped under a rock he can never lift? In the five thousand years since I tore the spirit from the mountain and flung the dead stone on top of him, the creature has never managed to get so much as a tendril over the edge of my seal. The seeds he sends out are a nuisance, nothing more. And even if he succeeded, even if a seed managed to grow large enough to be a real threat, I would just trap the new demon as I trapped its father.*

"And at what cost?" the Lord of Storms yelled, straining against the unbreakable force of the Lady's will that held him in place. "I don't know if you've taken time from your little one-sided love affair to notice, but this world isn't what it was, Shepherdess! This isn't some nuisance seed grown too big. If the Daughter of the Dead Mountain were to fully awaken and start feeding in earnest, we would need another great mountain to keep her down, and we both know you no longer have one to spare. Have you forgotten what's at *stake*?"

He jerked against his bonds like he was trying to throw his arms out, but all he managed was to set himself swinging slightly in her hold. Still, from the way her eyes narrowed, it was clear Benehime didn't need the gesture to know what he meant.

All around them, at the edges of her white world where she did not look, something was moving. Everything was still perfect, still flawless white, but beyond the white perfection, something pressed against the walls of her world. Long claws scraped at the barrier like knives against a sheet stretched taut, probing and searching for weakness. The movements were small, faint, gray shadows, but they were everywhere, pressing in on every inch of the Shepherdess's domain.

"They never get tired, do they?" the Lord of Storms whispered. "That is the fate that awaits all of us if you forget your duty."

I forget nothing, the Lady said, layering cold power into the words until he writhed beneath her voice, his body flashing between flesh and storm. But even her displeasure was not enough to keep the Lord of Storms from raising his head to met her eyes again.

"Everything I do." He spat the words at her. "Everything I've ever done has been in your service. If you will not let me do my job, then dissolve me back into wind and water right now, because I won't stop until all demonseeds, all threats to your domain, are crushed, even those who hide in your favorite's shadow."

Enough! The Lady's voice echoed through the white nothing, and the Lord of Storm's body dissolved into cloud, his cry of pain becoming a low rumble of thunder.

You would be so lucky if I dissolved you, she said, glaring at the thunderhead floating where the Lord of Storms' suspended body had been only a second before. *But you*

*belong to me, and I have no desire to toss you aside just
yet. I have been too soft with you for too long. Go and
blow out your anger over the sea. We'll see if some time
as a mindless storm will help you remember the obedience you owe me.*

She waved her hand and the thunderhead vanished.
Baring her teeth at the place where he had been, the Lady
whirled around and stalked back to her sphere.

In all her white world, the sphere alone was vibrant
and colorful. Inside that perfect bubble, the world, her
world, hung in suspended beauty. Continents floated on
a flat, glassy sea, their wrinkled faces covered with tiny
forests, golden deserts, and rolling plains dotted with tiny
grazing creatures. White-capped mountains rose from the
forested hills, their snow-covered peaks cutting through
the clouds like islands on a second, sky-bound sea. Deep
beneath the oceans, sea trenches scored the heavy layers
of stone that filled the lower half of the sphere, cutting
down to the glittering red flow of the magma that pooled
at the sphere's lowest point.

Benehime's eyes flicked past all this with the contempt
born of long familiarity, darting past the mountains and
the glittering rivers to a wild stretch of sea. The moment
she focused on the sea, the Lord of Storms appeared
above it. In his true form, he was the size of a small continent and utterly mad, a roving war of wind and water. As
she watched, the storm spun in circles, eating the lesser
clouds, whipping the sea into a froth. Storm surges forty
feet high began to wash over the southern tip of the eastern continent, soaking the desert beneath a brine of terrified water. Benehime watched as a medium-sized city
was washed under, and then she turned away in disgust.

Who was he to think he could tell her things she did not already know? She was the Shepherdess, had been the Shepherdess since the beginning. Everything within the sphere was hers alone to direct, to control. In the balance of power between her and her brothers, this was her domain. She turned back to the sphere, looking not at the growing storm, but north to the wooded foothills of the white-capped mountains.

She laid her hands lovingly along the curve of the sky. Angry as she was, there was opportunity here. The Lord of Storms had disobeyed her, raised his sword to her favorite, but he had also forced Eli to use the power she'd given him to travel her sphere freely for the first time in years. He'd shown he was willing to use gifts he'd sworn to her face he would never touch again in order to save his swordsman. What other slips might he be willing to make if pressed hard enough?

A smile spread across her white lips. Now that her darling had decided to play with things she'd warned him against, life was going to be a great deal more difficult for him. Usually, this would be the point where she stepped in to help, but not this time. This time, the Lady decided, she would make Eli come to her. This time, she'd let him stay on the hook, let things get as bad as they could get. Only when he was broken and defeated would he realize what he had thrown away. That, when he begged for her help, was when she would save him and bring him home at last to her side.

Benehime sank down beside her sphere, watching the northern forest where, somewhere, her favorite was sleeping. Behind her, ignored, the claws continued to slide over the edge of her white world while far, far away, too distant for any ears except her own, something screamed in endless hunger. Benehime turned her head and leaned forward farther still, deftly focusing her attention on the tiny world inside the sphere until it was all she knew.

CHAPTER
11

Gin was growling deep in his throat. Miranda reached down and pinched him, hard, but that only sent the growl deeper into the dog's chest and did nothing at all for the predatory glare the ghosthound fixed on the over-dressed man riding in front of them. She pinched him one more time, then gave up, flopping forward against the prickly fur of the dog's neck. The growling had been going on for nearly two weeks, but she couldn't really blame Gin. She would growl at Sparrow too if she had the throat for it. Traveling with the man was insufferable.

"He's too slow," Gin mumbled through his long, clenched teeth. "He packs like an idiot, can barely set up a camp, wakes up too late, and he eats too much."

"Why are you still complaining?" Miranda said. "It didn't help yesterday; it didn't help two weeks ago. What makes you think it'll help now?"

"We'd have been there last week if that fool didn't take two hours every morning getting his clothes right." Gin's fur bristled. "We're in the middle of nowhere and that idiot acts like he's going to a party every night. And he won't stop *flickering*." The dog shook himself. "If looking at him didn't make me feel ill I'd eat him just to make it stop."

Miranda rolled her eyes. That again. She'd stopped pressing the dog for an explanation of Sparrow's "flickering" days ago, but getting him to stop complaining about it was like asking him to stop growling—impossible. She sat up again, looking over Gin's ears at the path they'd been following since yesterday. Sparrow was well ahead of them, guiding his nervous horse between the thick trees like a Zarin dandy leading a shy partner through a new and intricate dance. He was certainly dressed the part. His plumed hat, orange silk coat, and chocolate-brown trousers tucked into gold-tooled boots would have been at home in any Zarin ballroom. Here in the ragged woods of the mountain foothills he looked like a misplaced tropical bird.

Gin shook his head, and the growling was back, stronger than ever. "Tell me again why we can't just leave him in the woods."

"Because as Sara's second, he's the highest-ranking Council official we've got," Miranda said. "And he has all the papers we need to bribe Izo. Trust me, I would have left him at the Zarin gate if I'd thought we could get away with it."

"Sara would have done better to send more like the other man," Gin said. "Save us all some time."

Miranda agreed. The morning they left Zarin Miranda had been met at the gate by Sparrow and another, a man who called himself Tesset. She had no idea if that was his last name or his first, maybe neither. Sara's goons seemed to be one-name-only kind of people. Unlike Sparrow, however, Tesset had shown up in sturdy travel clothes, a long, brown coat and worn-in boots, and carrying a small pack. She'd been a little concerned that he had arrived with no horse, but she'd found out quickly that the lack of a mount didn't hinder him. The man could run forever, and Sparrow's pace wasn't exactly breathtaking.

Right now, however, he was nowhere to be seen. That wasn't unusual. Tesset tended to disappear for hours, running ahead to scout the area and keep them on track. Miranda appreciated his skill, but his excursions meant she was alone with Sparrow and the inane conversations he started every few hours. If Tesset didn't vanish without a word every morning, Miranda would have insisted on scouting with him just for a break.

Gin's growling hitched, and Miranda looked up to see that Sparrow had stopped. A moment later, she saw why. Tesset was standing beside him, his dull, brown clothes and short, brown hair blending in with the undergrowth. Miranda smiled and nudged Gin forward. She didn't care if he'd come back to report they were about to be eaten by cannibals; any break in the monotony was welcome.

The two men stopped talking as she approached, and Sparrow's horse began its terrified dancing that always occurred whenever Gin was closer than ten feet.

"Ah, Miranda," Sparrow said, getting his horse under control with some difficulty. "Splendid timing. Tesset here was just informing me that we're closing in on our destination."

"Two miles straight ahead," Tesset said, reaching out with a calm, strong hand to grab Sparrow's horse before it threw him. "We've been passing his watchposts for the last two days, so we should be getting a welcome soon."

"Two days?" Miranda said, glancing around at the deep woods. "I haven't seen anything."

"You wouldn't," Tesset said. "Unless you knew where to look."

"Spoken like a true expert," Sparrow said, leaning over his now subdued horse's neck. "Tesset here is the closest legal thing you'll find to a guide for this area."

Miranda gave Tesset a curious look, and he shrugged his broad shoulders. "I grew up around here," he said simply. "Of course, that was back when these hills were nothing but a patchwork of ragged gangs, before Izo pulled them all together. In a strange way, Izo's made it easier for us. If things were still the way they were in the old days, we would have had to bribe half a dozen petty bandit lords by now."

"The benefits of unified government are myriad for all walks of life," Sparrow said with a sigh.

Miranda ignored him. "How did Izo do it?" she asked. "Pull the gangs together, I mean. Have there been other bandit kings?"

"None like Izo," Tesset said, shaking his head. "There've been a few leaders whose gangs got pretty big, but nothing on Izo's level. Right from the start, Izo was smart as well as strong, very charismatic, and, most important, ruthless. He raided other bandits as much as he raided the Council, and eventually there was no one left strong enough to stand up to him. No one knows exactly how many men he controls, but considering the reports from the border towns, I'd say at least five thousand fighting troops, maybe more. Anyway"—he turned and started walking again—"we'll see for ourselves in a moment. He's already sent a welcoming party."

Miranda scowled. "How do you—"

"He's right," Gin said, pricking his ears up. "Men and horses approaching from the north." He gave Tesset a respectful look. "That man must have ghosthound ears to hear that."

"Or advanced knowledge," Miranda murmured. "Keep on guard."

Gin nodded and they began to follow Tesset, who was still dragging Sparrow's horse by the reins, down the path. Miranda sat high on Gin's neck, straining to catch the jingle of approaching horses, but all she heard were birdcalls and the wind in the trees overhead. After several hundred feet, Tesset stopped again and stood in the center of the path, waiting. Gin's ears were swiveling madly, but to Miranda the forest was achingly silent. She was about to lean down and ask the hound what he heard when the men stepped out from behind the trees.

There were too many to count. The forest was suddenly full of men dressed in drab colors, sitting on their horses like they'd been waiting. Though no glint of metal showed at their hips or boots or anywhere else knives were generally kept, Miranda was sure they were armed to the teeth and would show it well enough if provoked, and she kept a firm hand on Gin's fur. Tesset and Sparrow, however, looked perfectly calm, even a little bored by the men's sudden appearance. They waited patiently until the oldest of the bandits, a tall, lanky man with prematurely gray hair, nudged his horse forward.

"Welcome, strangers," the man said, his voice thick with a coarse, mountain accent that turned words into gravel. "What brings you so bold into King Izo's trees?"

"Diplomacy, good sir," Sparrow said, his words

dripping with politeness. "We seek an audience with your master, and his trees seemed a good place to start."

"Audience, eh?" The bandit scratched his scarred chin. "And what does a peacock like you want from the king of bandits? We already got a fool."

This raised a huge laugh from the men, but Sparrow's smile only deepened. "It's Sparrow, actually, and I come on behalf of the Council of Thrones to make your master a very generous offer."

"Generous?" The bandit's eyebrows shot up. "Now I know you're lying. The Council don't know the meaning of the word, not without a hook wrapped inside. Why don't you save our time and your skin and just tell us the catch now, before we string you up for the crows?"

"Nothing would delight me more," Sparrow said. "But my offer is for Izo's ears alone."

The bandit gave him a long, hard look, then shrugged. "Your death wish, pretty bird. Follow us."

The bandits turned and started into the woods, falling into a loose circle around Miranda, Sparrow, and Tesset. Their formation was ragged, and Miranda got the feeling they were used to riding much closer around prisoners, but several of the horses were already wide-eyed being so close to Gin, and the bandits weren't taking any chances. As they rode, Miranda could see how the bandits had snuck up on them. Every bit of their tack, from the bridles to the stirrups and even their horses' hooves, was wrapped in wool cloth to make no sound. They rode in absolute silence, communicating through hand movements when they talked at all. In answer, Gin began to creep as well, matching their silence as though it were a competition. Tesset was also silent, his boots soundless on the leaf-strewn ground. By contrast, Sparrow was garishly noisy, his heavy bags and flashy tack creaking and jingling like a circus cart.

They made their way through the woods and onto a well-maintained road leading up a hill between two cliffs. Though she saw no one, Miranda could hear the creak of bowstrings on the rocks overhead. Their guide whistled, and the creaking bowstrings fell silent. Grinning wide, the bandits started up the hill again, motioning for their guests to follow. The narrow path forced them to walk single file, and Miranda was cursing her luck at being forced to stay behind Sparrow yet again, especially since he kept stopping. But a few steps later, she understood why. There, just beyond the pass, lay what Miranda could only describe as a bandit capital.

It was a box canyon cut out between two rocky hills and ringed with large conifers that hid it from the surrounding woods. Inside the canyon, wooden buildings of all sizes, from one-room log huts to enormous timber halls, covered every inch of the sandy ground. Wooden lookout towers sprouted like weeds from every other rooftop, often connected to other towers by rickety rope bridges, and every one of them flew the same red banner: a crudely painted black fist floating in the air above a mountain, ready to slam down.

People came out to watch as the bandits escorted their guests into the city, and Miranda was shocked to see women and young children peering down from curtained windows. The roads between the houses were hard-packed dirt, but there were torches at every intersection, each stocked and ready for the evening lighting as in any civilized city. There were shops with their doors open to the fine weather, restaurants with the day's offerings drawn in chalk on wooden boards, and even glass windows in a few of the larger buildings. Looking down the roads as they passed, she saw a mule-driven mill beside a bursting grain silo. Another road led to a slaughterhouse with a pen full of pigs and chickens and a sign advertising fresh meat, and somewhere just beyond that she could hear a smithy working, the banging hammers accompanied by the acid smell of steelworking.

Miranda gripped Gin's fur. Steel usually meant swords, good ones. As they rode toward the center of the canyon town, she saw more and more men openly wearing weapons. Their swords were not the mismatched collection of stolen goods she would have expected, but standardized blades from the same smithy. Likewise, the drab clothes the men wore weren't actually ragtag, but uniform sets cut from the same cloth. Subtly, her fingers crept over her rings, gently waking her spirits. What kind of a bandit camp was this?

At the center of the canyon the buildings opened up, and they entered what looked like a town square. Only here, the square was more like a great, sandy lot, and at its center, rather than the fountains or wells or community halls generally found at the heart of towns, an enormous pit had been dug down into the floor of the canyon. The pit was about eight feet deep and circular, braced along the edges with wooden beams to keep the soil from sliding. At one end, a raised platform stuck out over the pit's edge, forming a small stage. The other was dominated by a large tower with a covered pavilion at the top. Red and black banners hung from every available ledge, surrounding the pit in a blaze of crimson. Miranda stared out the corner of her eye as they rode by, trying to figure out the pit's purpose. They had almost reached the other side of the square before she realized it was an arena.

She'd heard about places where men fought to the death for the crowd's entertainment, but seeing one in person made her feel ill. Of course, she shouldn't have been surprised. This was Izo's city. What more could one expect from a man who called himself the Bandit King? She'd let the town's unexpected civility lure her into a sense of false security, but the large, brown stains on the pit's sandy floor were enough to cure her of any further delusion. Miranda shuddered at the barbarity.

As they left the central square, the buildings changed. If this were a normal town, she would have said they were entering the government district. The construction was more stone than wood now, the buildings taller and wider, with red banners spilling from their windows like bloody waterfalls. Several buildings had their doors flung open to let in daylight, and Miranda could see the front rooms of barracks, training halls, tack stores, and weapon stocks, all well supplied. A block away, acrid forge smoke belched from a set of tall chimneys. These were matched by another set farther down the road, and Miranda began to wonder just how many forges this city had.

That thought was put out of her mind when their guide led them around a blind corner and stopped at the entrance of the most intimidating building Miranda had ever seen. Unlike the others, it was all stone and iron, built directly into the cliff face. There were no windows, only doors that led out onto archer galleries with red banners the size of Gin hanging from their ramparts. The fortress was fronted by a great gatehouse with a barbed portcullis raised halfway so that its jagged spikes hung over the entry like hideous teeth ready to snap. Inside the gatehouse, the tiny paved yard was full of armed men sharpening their swords, obviously bored. They did not look up as the new arrivals filed past, but Miranda could feel their eyes on her as their bandit guide led them through the yard to the iron-bound doors of the hall itself.

Here they dismounted, the bandits holding Sparrow's horse as he jumped down. No one offered to hold Gin, and that made Miranda smile. Outnumbered and surrounded as they were, it was comforting to remember she still had power on her side.

The citadel doors were thrown open to let in the afternoon light, revealing what was clearly not so much a room as a natural cave improved for human habitation. The stone floor had been chiseled flat and the walls braced with wooden beams to keep the stone from collapsing. It was quite dark, and the sparse torches seemed to make it only darker. From where she stood in the sunlight, Miranda could see only about twenty feet inside to where the hall had been split in half by a wrought-metal gate marked with the same fist and mountain as the banners outside.

Sparrow squinted into the dark hall. "Very impressive," he said, sounding decidedly unimpressed. "But we didn't come all this way to see a cave. Where is Izo?"

The bandit grinned and pointed at the gate. "Through there. You can leave your horse with the boys. They'll take care of your things."

"Which is why I'm taking them with me," Sparrow said, unhitching his bags and flinging them over his shoulder with surprising ease.

The bandits laughed at that, and their guide gave Sparrow a knowing wink before waving for them to follow him into the dark hall. The iron gate opened before they reached it, and a man stepped forward to greet them. The moment she saw him, Miranda began to shiver. She didn't know how she knew, but she knew all the way to her core that something was terribly wrong with the man in front of her. He wore no weapon she could see, and he was skeletally thin. His face was pale and hollow, and though his clothes were fine, they hung strangely limp on his body, like rags on a scarecrow. Behind her, Gin began to growl deep in his throat.

Even their bandit guide seemed a little put off by the man. He went through the gate without looking at him, motioning for his guests to follow. The strange man just watched them pass, his eyes eerily bright in the dark as he shut the gate behind them.

On the other side of the iron gate was a smaller but far grander chamber. Fat torches hung on the walls, their smoky light painting everything in flickering reds and oranges. Rich rugs lined the stone floor and gold glittered from the ornate wooden cabinets that lined both walls. But all of it—the silks, the rare metals, the chandelier of antlers hanging from the high cave ceiling—was just a guide for the eyes, leading them toward the back of the cave. There, on a raised stage lined with an impressive display of weaponry, below a great red banner marked with the same icon of the closed fist and mountain she'd seen all through the city, was an enormous iron chair covered with furs, and seated on the furs was a man.

Miranda blinked. For all the buildup, he was not particularly impressive. Though he was sitting, it was clear he was not remarkably tall, his shoulders not particularly broad. His black hair was streaked with white, and his face, though perhaps handsome once, was now old before his time, worn by years of hard living and bad food. His eyes, however, were sharp as daggers as they watched the newcomers enter his hall. His gaze jumped from one to the next without even a raised eyebrow for Gin. He wore no jewels, no weapons, but plain as he looked, Miranda would have known who he was even without the throne. She'd seen his picture on Whitefall's wall. This was Izo the Bandit King, the third-most-wanted criminal in Council history.

"Well, well, Garret," Izo said in a deep, rich voice as the skeletally thin man climbed up to stand beside him. "What do you bring?"

Their bandit guide bowed. "Messengers, my king. They say they're from the Council."

Izo began to chuckle. "Well, well, fifteen years of getting the cold shoulder from Zarin, and here you are. To what do I owe the honor?"

Sparrow stepped forward with a flourish, his voice booming theatrically through the cave. "Greetings, great Izo, lord of bandits. My name is Sparrow, assistant to Sara, Head Wizard of the Council. This"—he gestured toward Miranda—"is Miranda Lyonette of the Spirit Court, and"—his hand shifted again—"Tesset, our guard and guide. We have been sent here by the Council of Thrones to make you an offer."

"An offer?" Izo grinned at his bandit. "If the Council wants me to stop raiding their borders, you're a pretty sorry showing, little bird."

"Please," Sparrow said. "Such matters are between you

and the northern kingdoms. We are here to find a missing wizard, a man named Heinricht Slorn, who we believe has come to your lands."

"Ah," Izo said. "I see. You want to know if I have him."

"Or the freedom to search for him in your woods without having to worry about waking up with a slit throat," Sparrow said.

"The woods are fraught with danger," Izo said with a shrug. "I'm not a charity house, Mr. Sparrow, but I could perhaps see my way toward helping you, if the price was fair."

"I have been given the authority to be very fair in this matter," Sparrow assured him.

"Is that so?" Izo sat back, stroking the stubble on his chin. "Give me an example."

"Well," Sparrow said. "Take your latest incursion into Council lands. Your men burned and pillaged the city of West Clef, and Markel of Sorran, the rightful lord of West Clef, is understandably upset. He's been pushing the Council to formally declare war on your little operation for years. Now he's got a few hundred dead tradesmen and a burned Council tax office to add to his complaint. He may be a small border lord, but his words are falling on very sympathetic ears at the moment. I wouldn't be surprised if the Council voted to take action within the year. However"—Sparrow raised a long finger—"should your help guide us to our man, alive and well, I can promise you that no declaration of aggression will ever get past committee. A great promise indeed for such a small inconvenience on your part, don't you agree?"

The thin man leaned over and whispered something in Izo's ear. The bandit nodded and began to smile.

"Great indeed," he said, sitting forward. "But why are you wasting my time with talk of missing wizards? Why not get straight to why you're really here?"

For a moment, Sparrow looked surprised, but the expression was gone so quickly Miranda thought she'd imagined it. Izo, however, missed nothing.

"I'm no backward mountain horse thief," he said slowly, shifting his eyes to Miranda. "I make it my business to know everything I can about what goes on in the Council Kingdoms, but even if I were ignorant as you seem to think me, I would know the name Miranda Lyonette, the poor Spiritualist who keeps bungling the capture of Eli Monpress."

Miranda stepped forward, red-faced, but stopped when she felt a hard grip on her wrist. She looked over to see Tesset shaking his head.

"Did you think you could just slip her past me?" Izo scoffed. "Did you think I would not know? You said yourself, this is my land. I know everything that happens here, and I would never miss something as splendidly convenient as the three of you just happening to show up in my town the day after Monpress himself mysteriously appears inside my borders."

This time even Sparrow looked shocked, and Izo grinned so wide Miranda could count his gold-capped teeth.

"Oh, I knew," he said. "I was thinking of how to catch him myself. Ninety-eight thousand gold standards will catch any man's attention. Though, now that you're here, things are more interesting than simple money." He turned his smile to Sparrow. "I may be a bandit, messenger bird, but I'm not stupid. I know what kind of power your mistress Sara can throw around in the Council when her mind is set."

Sparrow made a good show of looking abashed. "I would never imply—"

Izo waved his hand. "Save the flowery talk. Truth be told, I don't really care why you came into my lands, be it hunting missing wizards or thief catching. But if you want to do whatever it is you came here to do, then here are my terms." He leaned forward on his throne. "First, I want all charges and bounties against me dropped. Second, I want full recognition of my sovereign right to the northlands, from the Sorran border to the mountain peaks and from the edge of the Shaper lands all the way to the eastern sea."

He sat back when he was finished, enjoying the stunned silence.

It was Miranda who recovered first. "Impossible!" she cried. "Sorran to the peaks? From the Shaper lands to the sea? That would make you the largest kingdom in the Council! It's never going to happen. You're a bandit and a murderer, not a king. You have no sovereign right to anything."

Izo gave her a hard look. "Is this the Council's answer?"

"Not at all," Sparrow said, cutting in front of Miranda before she could say anything else. "*If* you help us find Heinricht Slorn, and get us Monpress alive, *and* we are able to bring both safely back to Zarin, Sara will see to it that you become a king in full."

"Done!" Izo said, standing up. He marched down from his throne and took Sparrow's hand, shaking it hard. "Garret, make our guests comfortable. Tonight, we plan a trap even the famous Monpress can't weasel out of."

Their bandit guide saluted and waved for them to

follow. Miranda was still trying to get a word in edgewise, but Sparrow's sharp heel was digging into her foot. She gave him a murderous glare as the bandit led them out through the iron gate and back into the hall. They walked in silence down the steps and under the gatehouse. When they reached the main road, their guide ducked almost immediately into a small alley, stopping at a wooden guesthouse right beside the keep. Garret left them with promises they'd be called when Izo wanted to see them again, and Sparrow tipped their guide well before dumping his bags on the largest of the soft beds downstairs.

"Well," he said. "I don't see how that could have gone better."

"Really?" Miranda said. "Because I don't see how it could have gone worse. Izo? A king? You just sold a crown to the most violent criminal in Council history."

"It's not like he's getting his crown on the cheap," Sparrow said. "He *is* sacrificing a ninety-eight-thousand gold-standard bounty."

"Men like Izo don't deserve crowns," she grumbled. "Do you honestly think Sara will be all right with this?"

"Sara will be delighted." Sparrow's voice grew very dry. "Remember, sweetheart, I've worked with her far longer than you, and I've seen her make men kings for less. Monpress is something special to her, more than Slorn, and far more than you or I. If letting some bandit play king is all it takes, she'll consider him cheaply bought."

"But it's not right," Miranda said.

"Who cares?" Sparrow answered. "If you get a chance to nab Eli and clean off the dirt he kicked all over your shiny white tower, what do you care about how he was caught? So a bad man gets away with his crimes, so what?

It happens every day. That's how the real world works, sweetheart. Bad people doing bad things and getting rich off it. Powers, girl, for all we know, this may be the best thing that could happen to this situation. At least if Izo's a king under the Council of Thrones, he can't go raiding his neighbors anymore. Did you think about that?"

Miranda bit her lip.

"Didn't think so," Sparrow said. "We need you here, Miranda. You're the one who knows Eli. Don't get all moral on us about things you can't change. Focus on the good. Catch Eli, go home a hero, and let us deal with Izo. Okay?"

"Okay," Miranda said, stomping up the stairs toward the loft bedroom.

There was no way Gin could fit into the small house. So the moment she got upstairs, Miranda threw open the window only to find the ghosthound had anticipated her, jumping up and making himself comfortable on the roof of the neighboring building, much to the alarm of the current inhabitants. He crawled over when he saw her open the shutters and stuck his head in.

"I hate to say it," he growled, "but the bird boy has a point."

"I know," Miranda snapped, flopping down on the bed. "I don't want to talk about it. I'm done with Council politics. Let's catch the thief and go home."

Gin rested his jaw on the windowsill. "How are you going to catch him?"

"I've got a plan," Miranda said, burying her face in the pillow. "This time, he'll be the one who's surprised."

Gin gave her a suspicious look before pulling his head out again and setting about the serious business of cleaning the road grime off his silver, shifting coat.

• • •

Izo sat on his throne for a long time after his guests left, taking in the feeling. After so many years of scrabbling at the edges, fighting like dogs with other bandits over every inch of backward woodland, he was almost there. He would be Izo the King.

"Just as the Master promised."

Izo flinched at the cold voice and turned to find Sezri standing over him, a skeletal horror draped in a mockery of flesh, his dark eyes glowing in the sunken shadows of his sockets. Izo turned away. He had no intention of tainting his moment of triumph with the thin man's creepiness.

"The Master is with us always," Sezri continued. "Watching, listening; nothing is hidden from him. Truly, you could ask for no better ally."

"Aye," Izo said, standing up. "And I've paid for it. Your 'Master' had first pick of every captive we've taken over the last three years, not to mention all our wizard children. There's not a soul in this camp who can hear the winds anymore, thanks to you. Your master said he'd make me king."

"And you're well on your way to being one."

"By a lucky guess, and none of your doing," Izo sneered, walking over to his weapon wall. "This Monpress tip was just a lucky break for you. How could you know he'd be up here? Or that the Council dogs would be on his trail? I was the one who put two and two together and made the deal, so don't act like I should be falling down on my knees to your boss. I pay my tribute and I'll reap my reward, but don't think you can lord a lucky strike over me and call it a plan."

Sezri stared at him, his too-wide eyes brighter than ever.

"You should be more careful with your assumptions," he said slowly. "The Master has hands everywhere, and he plays a game on a higher stratum than any of us can comprehend. The arrival of Sara's monsters, the appearance of Monpress, your own position at the nexus, it was all laid out by the Master, and it will all fall apart without his continued goodwill. You would do well to remember that."

Izo sneered. "We'll see."

Sezri just smiled, a strange baring of teeth that was more unsettling than his glare. "That reminds me," he said. "In order to make sure the capture of Monpress goes smoothly, our Master has sent another of his children to help us."

He made a beckoning motion with his skeletal hand, and Izo's guard went up. Sure enough, though his room was ordered empty and locked at all times, a figure stepped out of the shadows beside the wrought-iron door. Izo gritted his teeth. He hated how they could do that, slip through shadows like fish through water.

Izo felt even less happy about this new arrival when the man stepped into the torchlight. He wasn't sure what he'd been expecting, another skeleton like Sezri, perhaps. Whatever it was, this man was not it. He stomped out of the shadows, a giant, taller than Izo's best bruisers and built like a bull. Scars ran across his body, some pale and ancient, others red and angry, crisscrossing his muscles like deep-dug canals. His clothes were filthy and they hung from him with the same shapeless weight as Sezri's dark rags. He stood crooked, with his left shoulder higher than his right, as though his left arm pained him. Izo understood that any man with scars like those could be expected to carry a serious injury, but whatever was wrong with the man's arm was hidden by the long, dirty cape he wore flung over one shoulder.

Sezri waited until the man was fully in the light before continuing. "Izo," he said, "may I introduce Berek Sted."

Izo's eyes went wide, and he began to grin in spite of himself. "Berek Sted?" he said, all anger forgotten. "*The* Berek Sted? The famous pit fighter? Powers, man, you're a legend!" He grabbed Sted's uncovered hand and shook it hard. "The boys here love you. I tried to find you to invite you to join us a year ago, but you'd disappeared." His voice trailed off. A foot and a half above him, Sted was glaring down, his eyes shining with the same unsettling light as Sezri's.

Izo dropped his hand and stepped back. "I guess I know why, now," he muttered. "Still, it's an honor to have a legendary fighter in my camp."

"I didn't come here to put on a show for bandits," Sted growled, his scarred face pulling up in a sneer. "I came because this is where Josef Liechten will come."

Izo paused. "Josef Liechten?"

"Monpress's pet swordsman," Sezri said. "Sted is here to deal with him. With Josef out of the way, Monpress's party should be no trouble at all." He smiled wider, forcing Izo to look away from the hideous sight of a human face pulled in ways it was never meant to go. "Is not the Master thoughtful?"

"Very," Izo muttered.

"You will call the Council dogs tonight," Sezri went on as though Izo had not spoken. "Let them take the thief and the girl he keeps with him while Sted handles Liechten. Monpress is fickle, so we may not have long to act. Set it up quickly and you will be king before the month is out."

Izo couldn't help grinning at that thought. "There, at least, we agree," he said, stomping down the stairs from his throne. "I'm going to make the rounds. We meet at sundown. I want both of you there."

Neither of the men answered, but Izo just kept walking. He was king here, not them, and he would not stoop so low as to look back to see if they would follow. Instead, he pushed his way through the iron gate and stomped into the yard, yelling for his guard. Tonight, everything needed to be perfect, for tomorrow he was going to make himself king.

Sted watched the iron gate swing closed with a deafening clang. "He's older than I expected," he said when the sound of Izo's shouting had faded. "Shorter, too."

"Izo has been the Master's servant for many years," Sezri said. "Our numbers are greatly increased by his ambitions."

"Who cares about your numbers?" Sted snorted, shifting his arm beneath his cape. "When do I get to face Liechten?"

"That depends on you." Sezri's voice was decidedly colder this time. "Follow the plan and you will have everything you desire. Be an idiot and I'll rip the seed right out of you and give it to someone more worthy."

Sted gave the skeletal man a sneering smile. "Is that what the voice tells you to do?"

Sezri's eyes glowed brighter than ever. "He doesn't have to," he said, his voice carrying a hint of the strange double harmonic Sted had come to associate with well-entrenched seeds. "Unlike you, or the girl who had that seed before you, I am an obedient servant of the Mountain.

In the end, the Master's desires will be fulfilled. I suggest you make sure you're on the right side."

"I've only got one side," Sted said, shifting his arm below the cloak again. "Mine."

"So I've heard," Sezri said. "You should watch yourself, Sted."

"I do," Sted said, turning away. "Better than anyone." He stepped sideways, slipping into the shadows. "See you at the briefing."

He gave the thin demonseed one last smirk before vanishing into the shadows. Sezri glared a moment at the empty space where he had been, and then vanished as well, disappearing like a puff of smoke on the wind, leaving the great hall empty and dark as the sun began to set behind the mountains.

CHAPTER
12

Josef woke up to horrible, blinding pain. His back felt like someone had removed his spine and replaced it with a hot iron rod, and the rest of him didn't feel much better. On the off chance his lungs worked, he took an experimental breath. It hurt. Powers, did it hurt, but not more than anything else. That gave him hope, and, very slowly, he opened his eyes.

He was lying in a bed in a cabin. Dappled sunlight streamed in through the open window, bringing with it the smell of mountains and trees. Josef frowned. He dimly remembered Eli and Nico moving him. After that, things went blank. He could tell from the light that they were no longer high in the mountains, but where?

Taking another deep breath in an attempt to clear his foggy mind, Josef began the serious business of finding his sword. He unclenched his aching hands and began to feel along the bed frame, careful not to make a sound.

"It's on top of you," said a familiar voice.

Josef's head shot up, sending waves of pain down his back, and he cursed loudly as Eli's smug face appeared in the air above him.

"Good morning, sunshine," Eli said. "Glad to see you up."

Josef glared murder at the thief and moved his hands to his chest. Sure enough, the Heart was resting directly on top of him. At least that explained the feeling of having a boulder on his ribs. He relaxed down into the bed with a long breath. "How long have I been out?"

"About three days," Eli answered, pulling his chair closer to the bed. "And I've got the crick in my neck to prove it. You've been hogging the only bed. I've had to make do with a spare cushion on the floor."

Josef was not sympathetic. "What about Nico? Where is she?"

"Who knows," Eli said. "Out."

Josef was startled by the hostility in his voice. "What happened?"

Eli shrugged. "The usual. You went down, Nico went crazy, I got us out. We thought you were going to die on us for a while, but the Heart did an excellent job patching you up. You look like you usually do after one of your fights now, which is miles better than the bloody mess you were when we laid you down."

"And what about Nico?"

"Powers, Josef!" Eli cried. "Can you think about something besides the girl for two seconds? I go out on a limb, not even a limb, a *twig*, to save your hide, and when you wake up all I hear is Nico this, Nico that. I don't even get a thank-you."

"Thank you," Josef said. "Don't get angry about it. You

can take care of yourself, but Nico has a hard time with that right now. So when you say she's 'out,' like you don't even care—"

"Maybe I don't," Eli snapped. "Maybe you shouldn't either."

Josef stared at his friend. In the four years he'd known Eli, he'd never seen the thief this upset.

Eli looked away and took a deep breath. "Josef," he said, more quietly. "When you found Nico, did you ever wonder why she was out there naked on the mountain?"

"Of course," Josef answered. "But I figured she would tell me when I needed to know. I'm not concerned with people's pasts, Eli."

"Maybe you should be," Eli said, running his hands through his dark hair, which was getting long and scruffy. "You know how oddly she's been acting, right?"

Josef nodded.

"When I was in the mountain, I heard things," Eli said. "I'm not someone to trust everything I hear, but this made too much sense to ignore. You've heard of the Daughter of the Dead Mountain?"

"I've seen the posters."

"Who hasn't?" Eli said with a shrug. "Two hundred thousand gold standards, the second-highest bounty ever posted. It's twice as high as *mine*." Eli scowled. "I think that's what bothers me most. All this time, and she didn't even have the courtesy to—"

"Stop," Josef said. "Just stop. I know where you're going. Nico is the Daughter of the Dead Mountain. So what? The Lord of Storms told me as much, but you can't hold it against her. She lost her memory, remember? Maybe she didn't even know."

Eli rolled his eyes. "Come on, Josef. You're stubborn, not stupid. Do you really believe all that garbage? Memory loss," Eli said and snorted. "She remembered well enough how to get back to the mountain."

"Yes," Josef said. "To help us."

"She lied to us."

"She kept a secret," Josef corrected. "You're hardly in a position to blame others for keeping secrets, Monpress."

Eli said sullenly, "This is too big. She should have told us."

"And what would you have done?" Josef said.

"Not what I did," Eli said. "She *lied* to us, Josef. We let her take off her manacles. I took her to Slorn's *house*, to *Nivel*. Do you know what she could have *done*?"

"I never heard of her doing anything," Josef said. "And I never heard her lie. I never heard her say anything about the Daughter of the Dead Mountain, that is, when she could say anything at all without you taking up all the breathable air." He glared at Eli. "Whoever she is, whatever name you give her, it doesn't change the last year. She's still the same Nico who put her life on the line dozens of times for your stupid thefts, who risked exposing her past to help you find your bear-headed friend, which was more than you did, I could add. So if you have something to say about that Nico, unless it's how you're going to go find her and tell her I'm all right, then I don't want to hear it."

Eli looked away. "It's not like that," he grumbled.

"Then don't make it like that," Josef snapped back. "I don't ask about your past, I don't ask about Nico's, and I haven't told you about mine because the past doesn't matter, Eli. What we did and who we were are just dregs compared to who we are now and how we act when the sword is coming down. Think about that while you go out to find Nico."

Eli started to say something, but then he snapped his mouth shut and stood up, sweeping the chair back with a clatter. He grabbed his blue coat from the peg on the wall and stomped out the door, letting it slam shut behind him. Josef listened until the thief's angry footsteps faded into the forest, then lay back with a long sigh.

"He's gone," he said. "You can come in now."

Something rustled below the window, and Nico quietly climbed into the cabin. Her hood was down, but it did little to hide her puffy eyes and wet cheeks. Josef held out his arm and she ran to him, burying her face in his hand.

"He hates me now." Josef felt the words more than heard them.

"He may," Josef said. "Eli doesn't like surprises, but he'll get over this. He can be a selfish idiot on occasion, but he's rarely deliberately unfair. He'll come around soon enough and things will move on. We're all survivors. We'll be all right."

Nico didn't move, but her breathing was slowing. Josef cupped her cheek gently. They sat like that for a while, Nico on her knees beside the bed, her head in Josef's hand. Then, without warning, Josef went stiff.

Nico looked up immediately, but Josef put his finger to his lips, listening. Gently but firmly, he pushed her aside and sat up. Pain shot through him, but Josef stayed silent. The Heart was ready when he reached for it, the hilt almost jumping into his hand. With another burst of pain, he stood, and after a few wobbly moments, found his feet again. When he was sure he would not fall down, he crept toward the cabin door and pressed his eye against the crack.

"Oh, no," he groaned. "Not again."

"Liechten!" A horribly familiar voice cut through the thin cabin walls. "Master of the Heart of War! Come and fight!"

Josef steeled his shoulders and opened the door, leaning on the frame for support as he stared at the crowd waiting in the little clearing around the cabin. They were bandits, that much was obvious. A bit better equipped than what he was used to, but Josef dismissed them as soon as he noted their sloppy stances and turned his attention to the real threat, the enormous man standing at the head of the group.

Josef heaved an enormous sigh. "Hello, Sted."

Eli tromped through the woods, kicking the leaves and fallen sticks and whatever else got in his way. This caused the trees around him to rustle uncomfortably, but for once Eli didn't care. He should have known better than to bring this up with Josef. They'd been together on and off almost since the beginning, back when his bounty didn't even warrant its own poster, and though their arrangement had always been one of mutual benefit—he got a swordsman and Josef got to fight as much as he pleased—he'd *thought* they were friends.

Eli gave the rotten stump in front of him a particularly hard kick. Even he knew that was unfair. Josef had stayed with him even when there were no good fights to be had. He might be a stubborn idiot sometimes, but he was a loyal one. But why did the swordsman always have to take Nico's side?

He didn't understand, Eli decided. He wasn't a wizard, he didn't talk to spirits, he didn't really know how horrible demons could be. Of course, Eli thought with a sigh, he was just as bad, letting himself get caught up in Nico's power, forgetting what she really was. Well, the monster on the mountain had cured him of *that* delusion. The demon had made it very clear that the Nico they knew, the Nico Josef defended, she was just a shell. A cracking one, he realized with a shudder. It wasn't a question of whether she would change, but when. When she'd been a normal seed, it had been easy to sweep that little unpleasantness under the table. Now that he knew what she really was, the stakes were different, and the game was getting too rich for his blood.

Eli stared at the woods in front of him, the rolling hills of dappled shade and fragrant evergreens. Thinking about it rationally, he should keep walking. He'd been a thief long enough to know when it was time to cut your losses and get out, but...

Eli stopped in his tracks. First rule of thievery, the *actual* first rule the old Monpress had drilled into him, was never risk what you couldn't afford to lose. He couldn't lose his team, not if he wanted to get his bounty to one million. Over the last year, he'd pushed higher and further than ever, and Nico had been a part of that as much as Josef. Even knowing what he was messing with, he couldn't give that up. Not yet.

He was still standing there, sucking his lip as his better judgment warred with his ambition, when a loud noise, a whistle followed by a thunk, sounded right beside his ear. Eli jumped on instinct, throwing himself sideways into the leaves. He rolled into a crouch, then stopped and looked up. An arrow was quivering in the trunk of the tree he'd been standing beside. Eli stared at it dumbly for a second and then craned his neck, frantically looking for the bowman.

Another arrow slammed into the ground beside him before he even got his head up. Realizing he was still an open target, Eli scrambled to the other side of the tree, madly beating on the trunk as he went.

The tree rustled grumpily. "What do you want?"

"I need to know where that came from," Eli whispered, pointing at the arrow.

"What are you talking about?" the tree said. "I don't feel..." It stopped. "Why is there an arrow in me?"

"That's what I'm asking," Eli said.

"How should I know?" The tree was starting to panic.

"Ask the arrow," Eli said, giving the bark a push. "Quickly, please, if you don't mind."

"Good idea," the tree said, and lapsed into mad rustling.

Eli kept as close to the tree as he could, trying to look everywhere at once. He would have asked the arrow himself, but the tree could get it to talk faster than even he could, short of opening his spirit. But as the seconds stretched on and on, the tree just kept rustling until its leaves were raining down.

"Well?" Eli said.

"Nothing," it answered. "That arrow's dead asleep."

"So wake it up."

"What do you think I was trying to do?" The tree snapped its branches. "Someone put it to sleep."

Eli cursed his luck. "Well, can you see anyone who might have shot it? Another human?"

"I don't see anything that's not always here," the tree said, more confused than ever. "Other than you and the arrow."

Eli was about to offer to pull the arrow out and have a go at it himself when he heard the telltale whistle of fletching, this time from his right. He ducked just in time as another arrow landed in the tree and the wood cried out in surprise and pain.

"Did you see that one?" Eli said, scrambling to get to the other side.

"No!" the tree shouted. "I don't see anything!"

Another whistle screamed through the forest as an arrow struck the ground right beside Eli's foot. This was when he decided to forget finding the archer and just run.

He sprang forward, dashing through the trees. Arrows whistled behind him, each bolt striking his footprint a second after his boot made it. He ran as fast as he could, lungs slamming for air while his brain spun even faster, trying to come up with a plan. The trees were sparse and open, offering little cover. He saw a rocky defile to his left and tried to turn, but the arrows struck the ground in front of him, landing deep in the soil where he would have been if he'd moved a second faster. With an undignified squeak, Eli turned on his heel and kept running, trying the turn again a few dozen feet later only to have the arrows cut him off again. The third time it happened, Eli knew he was being driven. Every time he tried to dodge left or right, the arrows pushed him straight again, forcing him east down a slope toward a wide mountain stream.

It was a trap for sure, Eli realized grimly, but he couldn't stop. Already his feet were sliding on the slippery leaves, forcing him to run even faster or risk going down the hill on his back. He skidded down the bank and landed in the creek with a splash. The mossy rocks slipped under his boots, sending him sprawling face-first into the icy water. He was up instantly, sputtering as he scrambled back to his feet only to slip again. He fell cursing back into the water, flailing around to make himself a harder target. But as he scrambled to get his legs back under him, he realized that the arrows had stopped. He paused, listening, but the forest was silent except for the soft trickle of the water.

Carefully this time, Eli stood up. Maybe he'd gotten out of range of the archer? If that was the case, whoever it was would be coming down after him. He looked over his shoulder, eyeing places on the opposite bank where he could hide and see who had been shooting at him. He spotted a good vantage point and began to quickly, but carefully, pick his way across the slick rocks. He'd made it halfway across the streambed when the water suddenly stopped.

Eli tripped and pitched forward, arms flying out to catch himself, but there was no need. The water, which had been running against his legs, was now hard as baked clay, and he was baked in as well, trapped from the knees down in crystal clear, freezing cold, perfectly still water.

After several moments of desperate tugging proved this wasn't something he could just yank his legs out of, Eli calmed down and took stock of the situation. The water had stopped moving for as far as he could see up and down the creek. Except for the wind overhead, the stream valley was perfectly silent. Experimentally, he tried to wiggle his toes, but even they were trapped, entombed in the water that had flowed into his boots before the freeze. No, freeze was the wrong idea. The water wasn't ice. It was just stopped. Stopped and not talking about it, which meant there was a wizard around.

The moment that realization crossed his mind, he knew who it was. He turned slowly, and there was no shock on his face when he saw a woman with red hair stepping out from behind a tree with an enormous grin on her face.

"Miranda Lyonette," Eli said. "A pleasure, as always."

If possible, the Spiritualist's grin grew even wider. "For once, we agree."

There was a rustle of branches from across the valley, and Eli turned to see her dog loping down the far bank with a grin that matched his mistress's.

"You've outdone yourself," Eli said as Gin joined her. "Caught me flat-footed and unprepared. The arrows were especially nice. Brava, my dear. So what now? Is there a contingent of Spiritualists coming to clap me in irons?"

Miranda shook her head. "No. You showed me how effective irons were back in Gaol. This time I'm using something you can't wiggle out of."

Eli smiled politely. "Which is?"

Miranda stepped into the stream, and Eli swallowed when he saw the still water slide back to make a dry path for her. She walked forward over dry stones, stopping just out of Eli's reach, her smile wider than ever.

"Eli Monpress," she said, her voice deep and joyful, "you are under arrest for crimes against the Spirit Court and the Council of Thrones."

"That's a pretty broad accusation," Eli said. "Can't you be more specific? This *is* my arrest. It would be a shame to gloss over my impressive record."

"Oh, don't worry," Miranda said. "I'm certain they'll read the whole list at your trial." She leaned forward, and, to Eli's enormous surprise, gave him a long, slow wink. "See you on the other side, Eli Monpress."

As she spoke, the stopped water started moving again, but not down the creekbed. It flowed up Eli's body, covering his chest, his shoulders, and finally his head. He struggled and thrashed, but the water simply pushed back, rendering his blows meaningless. He took a deep breath just before the water went over his head, and the last thing he saw was Miranda's face grinning triumphantly before everything went black.

Miranda was almost giggling as she watched Mellinor swallow Eli's head. A trickle of icy water rushed over her feet as Mellinor released control of the creek back to the local spirit, but she wouldn't have cared if she'd been on fire at this point. She'd done it. She'd *actually* caught Eli Monpress.

"Don't smile too hard," Gin said, splashing through the water to join her. "He's not in Zarin yet. I won't feel safe until he's sitting in Banage's office."

"Even Eli Monpress will have a hard time escaping if he's unconscious," Miranda said. "How's he doing?"

"Out cold," Mellinor answered. The pillar of water was floating completely separate from the creek now, with Eli's slumped body cocooned at its center.

Miranda sighed happily. "It's a beautiful sight. How long can you keep him like that?"

"Long enough," Mellinor answered. "Just keep me near a source of water and I should be able to hold him like this all the way to Zarin."

Miranda motioned Gin over. The dog came sullenly, wincing as Mellinor slumped the water-bound thief across his back.

"He's cold," he grumbled, ears back. "And wet."

"It's just for a little bit," Miranda said, adjusting Eli to lie across Gin's haunches. "Buck up."

"We should move," Mellinor said. "The creek is returning."

Miranda looked down. Sure enough, the water was up to her ankles now, and blisteringly cold. She shivered and made her way to the opposite bank as fast as she could. Gin padded along beside her, careful of his precious cargo. The water rose as she went, and by the time they were safely on the other side, her tall boots were soaked.

Miranda looked down with a shrug. Nothing could ruin her mood right now.

"Mission successful, I see," said a voice behind her.

Gin jumped and began to growl deep in his throat. Miranda put a warning hand on his muzzle. Well, she thought, turning around, *almost* nothing. Sparrow stood behind her, leaning against a tree with his bow resting on one shoulder. His gaudy clothes were gone, replaced by a drab brown suit that seemed to shift in and out of the tree shadow, but his smile was smug as ever.

Sparrow glanced at Eli's unconscious, water-bound body, though he was clever enough to stay clear of Gin himself. "I'll hand it to Sara," he said. "She knows how to pick the right person for the job. Well done, Spiritualist. Shall we go back to see how the others are faring?"

"You can go," Miranda said. "I'm still not convinced Izo's fighter can beat Josef Liechten or Nico. I want Eli as secure as possible, as quickly as possible, just in case."

"Caution does you credit," Sparrow said, turning on his heel. "I'll meet you back at the camp."

Miranda watched as the man walked into the trees

without a sound, vanishing into the hills far quicker than any human should.

"I hate how he does that," Gin growled.

"Me too." Miranda sighed.

Gin shook his head in frustration. "No, you don't understand. Before at least he was flickering. Now it's like he's not even there."

Miranda frowned. "What do you mean, 'not even there'?"

"Forget it," Gin said. "I can't even explain it to myself, so I'm not going to bother trying to explain it to you."

Miranda flushed and started to say that she was perfectly capable of understanding if only the dog would take the time to describe things properly, but she shut her mouth at the last moment. Sparrow wasn't worth antagonizing Gin any further. She'd just have to get him to elaborate later. She followed the ghosthound up the bank, watching as Eli bounced on his back. That made her smile. One look at the captured thief was enough to renew the good mood Sparrow had dampened. "Come on," she said, picking up the pace. "Let's get our guest situated."

Gin grumbled, but he matched her speed, and they trotted together up the valley toward where their bandit escort was waiting to bring them back to Izo's hidden city.

CHAPTER
13

Using the Heart as a crutch, Josef limped out of the cabin, keeping his eyes on Sted. The man was even larger than Josef remembered, towering a good foot over the tallest of the ragtag bandits that followed him. He had no black coat this time, and no red sash of trophies. There was no sword at his hip either, no weapon at all from what Josef could see, unless he was hiding something under the ratty black cape that covered his chest, shoulders, and arms.

Sted met Josef's gaze, baring his teeth like a dog. "What is this?" he said. "Are you a cripple now? Stand and fight, if you can."

"I am standing," Josef said flatly. "But even if I couldn't, I could still beat you. After all"——the swordsman smirked—"I've done it before, with worse injuries than these. By the way, how's your arm?"

Sted's eyes flashed with anger. "You'll see soon enough," he growled. He turned to the man beside him, the only one of the group of bruisers who didn't look like he smashed rocks with his face for a living. "This one's mine. Get the girl."

Behind him, Josef felt Nico cower.

"Nico," he said, his voice low. "Run."

"No," she whispered, shaking her head furiously.

"Do it." Josef's voice strained as he lifted his weight off the Heart.

"No," Nico said again.

Josef glared over his shoulder. "Don't be an idiot. I saw what happened up by the mountain. I've seen your arm. If you fight to win here like you are, you could lose everything we've worked for. Run, I'll find you. I promise."

Nico stared at him, clutching the arm she hid beneath her coat, her dark eyes wide. Then, without another word, she turned and ran.

She tore around the cabin, sprinting wildly through the trees. Josef watched her until she vanished over the closest rise, and then he turned back to Sted. As he did so, he noticed that the man Sted had spoken to, the one who didn't look like a bandit, was already gone.

Coldly, slowly, Josef put it out of his mind. He'd done what he could for Nico. If he was going to survive to keep his promise, he'd need all his concentration for the fight ahead.

Sted waved his arm, and the bandits fell back, taking cover in the ring of trees around the cabin. Josef stayed put, conserving his energy. His sword felt heavy as lead in his hands, a sure sign he was at his limit, even with the Heart's help. His only hope was to beat Sted in one blow. His eyes flicked to Sted's covered shoulders. Unless all League men could reform their bodies like the Lord of

Storms, that cape was probably there to hide Sted's missing arm. That is, if Sted was even a League man anymore. Without a coat or a sword, Josef wasn't sure. But he could feel the Heart warning him through the warm metal not to be cocky. League or not, whole or not, Sted was no one to take lightly. He gripped his sword tighter. He'd done this before. One good blow, that was all he needed.

The clearing fell silent as Sted, still seemingly unarmed, took his position. Warily, Josef matched him, keeping the Heart close. Overhead, the treetops danced in the wind. Leather creaked as the bandits eased their weapons into their sheaths, but Sted did not move. Josef's hands grew sweaty against the Heart's hilt. He turned them slowly, keeping his blade even with Sted's chest and his eyes on Sted's feet. The blow would come from Sted's right hand, whipping out from under the cape. He could see it already. All he needed was a hint to when it was coming and this fight would be over. The ground crunched as Sted's heavy boots dug into the dirt. Josef sucked in a breath. This was it.

He stepped forward, bracing the Heart for the blow just as Sted's feet vanished. Josef stumbled, eyes darting frantically. There was no way Sted was that fast, but the man was no longer in front of him. Even as his brain was finishing the thought, the Heart tugged hard in his hands. Josef spun on instinct, raising his sword just in time as the enormous man lunged out of the cabin's shadow.

The Heart met Sted's attack in a horrible squeal of metal, and Josef's knees buckled under the onslaught. His instincts were screaming at him to dodge back, get a better position, but Josef couldn't move. He just stood there, staring, trying to make sense of what his eyes saw.

Sted towered over him, taller than ever. His cape was gone and he was bearing down on the Heart with his arm, his *left* arm, the arm that should not be there. He had no sword, no weapon. He'd stopped the Heart's blade with his *hand*. No, Josef couldn't even call it a hand. It was a claw. An enormous black claw clutching the Heart's cutting edge with five talons curved in a mockery of fingers. Even as Josef realized what he was looking at, the Heart began to buck in his hands.

It was a signal that needed no interpretation. At once, Josef jumped back, wrenching his sword out of Sted's black grip. He danced across the clearing, keeping the Heart close to his chest until he was out of Sted's reach. Only then did he look down. There, on the blade's cutting edge where Sted's hand had touched it, were five shallow notches in the exact shape of Sted's talons. The metal wasn't dented or broken. It was simply gone.

Back by the cabin, Sted straightened up. "What do you think?" he said, spreading his arms wide. "Still feeling cocky?"

It took all of Josef's determination not to look away. There was something incredibly wrong, something vastly inhuman about the black thing growing out of Sted's left shoulder. It hung crooked from his frame, a foot longer than his still-human right arm and twice as large, bulging with muscles that twitched and spasmed. But most horrible of all was the spot where the black arm connected. Just below his shoulder, Sted's pale skin and the black abomination met in a twist of red, raw flesh.

At once, everything came together. The fast movement, jumping through shadows, the arm...Slorn may have thought it was impossible for a nonwizard to become a demonseed, but Josef knew those signs well enough. He looked down at his injured sword. They needed a different strategy.

Straightening up, Josef flipped the Heart in his hands and plunged it point first into the ground. He could feel the metal clinging to his skin, warning him not to do this, but there was nothing else to be done. If Sted was a demon, then fighting him with the Heart would only make him stronger and the Heart weaker. There would be no winning that way, and so Josef let the Heart go. The moment his fingers left the wrapped hilt, he felt his wounds seize up. A tide of pain and dizziness swept over him, and he nearly fell. He planted his feet at the last moment, steadying himself in a fighter's stance, and thrust his hand toward the bandits standing at the edge of the circle.

"Sword. Now."

He heard the bandits shuffle, but he kept his eyes on Sted. The enormous man looked skeptical for a moment, then he nodded, and Josef heard the familiar sound of a blade sliding from a sheath followed by the thunk of metal on the dirt beside him. Without looking, he ducked down, hand sliding across the leaf litter until his fingers found the hilt, and brought his new sword up with a flourish.

Sted's face broke into a cruel smile. "You're going to fight me with that?"

Josef glanced at the sword in his hand. It was pathetically short, more like a long knife than a sword, and dull gray with tarnish.

"It's a blade," Josef said. "That's all a swordsman needs."

"Really?" Sted grinned wide. "Show me."

The words had barely reached Josef's ears before Sted

was on top of him. Josef caught Sted's open claws a second before they landed in his head, digging his feet into the dirt as his poor, dull sword fought to hold the parry inches from Josef's face. Above him, Sted's eyes began to glow like embers, and the dull metal of the sword started to hiss as Sted's claws bit into it. Hiss, and then vanish.

Josef ducked and rolled, breaking the parry and dragging his sword to safety, but Sted didn't let him go. He lashed out, claws digging through Josef's shirt and into the flesh beneath. Josef gasped and rolled away, but it was mostly instinct. His head was getting fuzzy as he scrambled in the dirt, wiggling out of Sted's grip just in time to catch the next swipe on what was left of his sword. But even as he raised his arm, he felt his muscles going slack. The damage from the Lord of Storms that the Heart had been holding back for him was building up again. His vision was dimming until he could barely see Sted break his parry with a sideways swipe. The sword tumbled from his fingers, breaking into pieces as it hit the ground, and Josef would have followed if Sted had not grabbed what was left of his shirt.

"What is this?" Sted's voice roared in his ear. Josef felt his feet leave the ground as Sted lifted him by his collar. "What happened to your back? You're so bloody you can barely stand. Is this how you face me? Is this the best you can offer?"

Josef tried to point out that Sted had been the one bellowing at his door, not the other way around, but all he managed was a choked gurgle. It was very hard to breathe with Sted holding him up by his neck.

Sted dropped him with a disgusted grunt. Josef landed hard on his side, and for a moment all he could think of

was the pain. When his mind at last cleared enough to
focus on things outside his body, he found he was being
lifted up by several of the bandits while Sted's booming
voice shouted out orders.

"Get him to his sword. It's the only thing keeping his
carcass alive. We'll take them both back to camp."

Someone said something Josef couldn't hear, and Sted
roared in anger.

"No, we're not going to kill him! No one is to touch
him without my permission! Josef Liechten is *my fight*,
and I will have it proper and on my terms if I have to kill
every one of you sorry bandit dogs! Now get his sword in
his hand! You'll never lift it otherwise."

Josef felt someone take his hand and thrust it clumsily
forward. A wave of relief washed over him as his fingers
met the Heart's hilt, and he was even able to wrap his
hand around it.

"Good," Sted said. "Take him back to town and get him
to the medics, and don't let him drop that blade. Remember, he is my fight. Keep everyone else away from him,
especially those Council pigs. Anyone who touches him
will answer to me. Go!"

Josef felt the world sway as the bandits hurried to do
Sted's bidding. They carried him strung between two
men like he was a hunting trophy with the Heart dragging
behind them, its hilt tied to Josef's hand with a long strip
of cloth. Sted walked beside him the whole time, enormous and terrible, shoving his cape back over his monstrous arm. When he saw Josef looking, he grinned wide.

"Don't worry," he said. "I'll kill you soon enough, but
on my terms. I didn't sell my soul to slap your beaten carcass around. Rest and enjoy what little life you have left,

Josef Liechten. When you're ready to give me the victory I deserve, we'll face off again. That time, Master of the Heart of War, I won't stop until I have your heart in my hand."

Sted began to laugh at that, a horrible, mad sound. Josef felt himself jerk as the bandits carrying him began to move faster, desperate to put some space between themselves and the mad monster. Josef stayed awake as long as he could, but soon even Sted's laughter faded behind the rush of blood in his ears, and he slipped into unconsciousness.

Nico ran. She shot through the forest, scrambling grace-lessly over fallen logs and gnarled roots with little thought to where she was going. All that mattered was speed, get-ting away, so she ran until her legs burned and her lungs felt like they were going to burst.

You're such a coward, the Master whispered. *Running to save yourself while the swordsman goes to his death. He can't fight in his condition.*

Nico gritted her teeth and ran harder.

You're not even making progress. Look, all that work and you've barely moved.

Nico glanced over her shoulder before she could stop herself. The Master was right. She could still see the thin plume of smoke from the cabin's chimney through the trees. She also saw no sign of pursuit. Nico slowed down, sucking cold, precious air into her burning lungs as she eyed the forest, straining to hear above the thundering of her heart. But the forest was still and empty around her, the sunlight moving in dapples across the leaf litter as the wind tossed the treetops high overhead. Under her coat, clutched against her chest, her transformed arm began to ache.

Pity you didn't take me up on my offer, the Master said. *If your hearing was anything like what it used to be, you would never have stopped.*

Even before the words had faded from her mind, a pair of hard, strong hands grabbed her shoulders from behind.

Nico shrieked and kicked backward, landing a solid strike on whoever was behind her. But the hands on her shoulders didn't even flinch. She scrambled desperately, panic clouding her mind, and all at once, her coat reacted. She felt the black fabric clench around the hands on her shoulder, the stiff cloth growing sharp as needles as it dug into the skin.

The person holding her grunted in pain, and the grip on her shoulders vanished. Nico tumbled to the ground and was up again in an instant, clutching her coat with a whisper of thanks. As soon as her feet hit the ground she was running, pounding flat out into the woods, only to come skidding to a stop a second later.

She hadn't seen anything move, hadn't heard steps on the leaves, yet, somehow, a man in a long brown coat, his hands bleeding from where her coat had stabbed him, was already in front of her, watching her with calm, brown eyes.

"Amazing coat you have there," he said softly, holding up his injured hand. "That wasn't in the briefing. You caught me by surprise, but don't count on doing it again."

As he spoke, the wounds on his hands closed before Nico's eyes. She blinked, then blinked again, but the wounds were still gone, leaving his skin whole and smooth. She'd never seen anything like it outside of demonseeds, but, while she wasn't sure who or what this man was, she knew he wasn't a seed. His skin was too swarthy, his build healthy and whole. She watched, dumbstruck, as the man quietly wiped away what blood was left on a handkerchief. Nico swallowed. Whatever he was, one thing was certain: he was faster than her. Running was out of the question. If she wanted to get away, she'd have to fight.

She planted her feet in a defensive position, keeping her transformed arm close to her chest. It twitched beneath her coat, itching for the chance to lash out, but Nico locked it in place. She might be weak like this, but she didn't need demon strength to take down a larger opponent. Josef had taught her well. All she needed was a lucky break, an open jab at his throat, and she could knock his wind out and get away.

The man watched her take her position with a blank, calm expression, hands in his pockets like he had all the time in the world. Then, faster than Nico's eyes could track, he struck.

A fist hit her hard in the gut. Nico gasped, but before her brain had registered the pain, the man's leg swept around to knock her own out from under her. She reeled and would have fallen, but at the last moment her transformed arm shot out to catch her. Nico stared at the black claw clutching the ground below her, unsure if the arm had moved by her reflexes or on its own. Whichever it was, she didn't have time to worry about it. The man was right in front of her, his fist coming up to catch her jaw. Nico scrambled back, bringing up both arms in defense as the man's fist missed her face by a fraction, leaving his guard open. Seeing her chance, Nico struck, her hand flying for his now unguarded throat.

It was only when her jab entered her field of vision that she realized her mistake. The hand flying for the man's throat was not her pale, white fist, but the black, transformed claw. It struck before she could think to stop it, digging deep into the flesh of the man's neck. Desperately, frantically, she tried to pull back, but it was far too late. Dark, delighted laughter rippled over her mind as the man's spirit roared up inside her, and the demon arm began to eat.

Nico shook uncontrollably as the man flowed through her, past her, and into the thing buried deep inside her. She could feel his soul as it slid by, warm and alive and pulsing with controlled strength, but she could do nothing to stop its flow as the demon ate and ate until the blackness was drowning out her conscious mind.

Then, without warning, it stopped.

The thing inside her roared in frustration, sucking and pulling at the connection through the black arm, but its efforts changed nothing. The flow of the man's spirit had dried up. All at once, the dark weight on her mind began to recede, and Nico cracked her eyes open. She knew already what she would see. She had eaten men before. She would see his body falling from her hand, gray and lifeless, turning into ash as it hit the ground, too empty to even hold its form.

But when she looked up she saw the man, still alive and standing in front of her. Her black claw was still lodged in the flesh of his throat, but though she could feel the demon pulling, trying desperately to get at the life just under the man's skin, nothing was happening. Somehow, the demon could not eat him.

"How?" She didn't know she had spoken until the word was out.

The man pried the black arm from his neck, and Nico saw the gouges from the claws already beginning to close. "I am king of myself," he said simply. "My body is mine alone. Nothing can happen to it that I do not allow."

He dropped his grip on her black wrist and raised his arm. Nico saw the blow coming, but she was too amazed to even move out of the way as his hand came down hard on the back of her neck. The last thing she felt were the man's arms as he caught her, and then everything was gone.

CHAPTER
14

The water over his head parted, and Eli sucked in an enormous breath. He sat there a moment, reveling in the joy of breathing, before Miranda's face dipped down to fill his vision. She grabbed his head, checking his eyes and throat.

"You're right," she said. "He's fine."

Eli thought she was talking to him until he heard the water at his throat bubble in answer.

"Of course I'm right," Mellinor said. "It's my water."

Miranda's mouth twitched in a smile before returning to a stern line as she looked down at Eli.

"Turn him around," she said haughtily. "I'm going to change out of these wet clothes and then we'll see what the plan is."

"Shouldn't you include me in this conversation?" Eli said. "This is my neck you're talking—"

His words cut off with a choke as Mellinor heaved sideways, spinning him dizzily in his watery prison. Eli thrashed, but the water was like cement around him, and all he managed was to get a giant mouthful of cold, salty water down his windpipe as the sea spirit turned him completely around. He coughed loudly and spat out the water on the wall that was now five inches from his nose, filling his vision.

"There's no cause for violence," he said, still hacking.

"If you want to keep enjoying the air, you'll keep your mouth shut," Miranda said, her voice floating from the room behind him. "One more word and I'll let Mellinor put you back underwater. Gin! Do you see Sparrow anywhere around?"

"No." The ghosthound's growl was muffled, and Eli realized he must be outside the small building they were in. Of course, there was no way the hound could fit *inside*.

"Stop him if you see him," Miranda said, her voice dampened by the clothes she must have been pulling over her head. "I want him to ask Izo's men to move us to a better location. I'll need more room to properly contain the thief for tonight."

Eli craned his neck, looking around at the small wooden hut with its low, easily scalable windows looking out onto quiet, sheltered back alleys. "This place looks fine to me."

"Shut up," Miranda and Gin said in unison.

Eli turned sullenly back to the wall.

"I'll send Sparrow your way if I see him," Gin said. "Hurry up, it's already getting dark."

Miranda made an annoyed sound and the room lapsed into silence, broken only by the soft shuffle of clothing.

Eli stared at the wall, listening with interest. From what

he could hear, Miranda was six, maybe seven feet away. Far too short for a break even in the small room, assuming, of course, he could get out of the water spirit, which he couldn't. Kirik would be no use. The lava spirit's burn was waterlogged, and Mellinor was the bigger spirit anyway. The sea would win for sure if it came to a fight.

Eli tried a few experimental movements, then stopped. The water was like a vise, pressing into him so hard he couldn't even wiggle his fingers. He struggled a bit more, just on principle, before flopping down against the water to wait it out.

He'd been like that for only a few moments when he felt something brush his cheek. Eli jumped, lashing his head back in surprise. Or he tried to. All he managed was to wrench his neck into an awful crick. Eli winced and turned to see what had touched him. His eyes widened in surprise. There, standing right next to Mellinor's water, was a man. He was dressed in dull brown with a bow over his shoulder and a quiver of very familiar arrows.

The man put a finger to his lips. "Don't say anything," he whispered. "My name is Sparrow, and I have an offer for the great Eli Monpress."

Eli stared at the man, curious now. He wasn't a Spiritualist, or even a wizard, Eli would wager. Even Great Spirits perked up when a wizard spoke, no matter how used they were to having them around, but Mellinor had remained perfectly still. Still, there was something very odd going on. For one thing, the man had to be standing right behind Miranda, but the soft sounds of her changing hadn't even paused. The Spiritualist could be a little blind at times, but it wasn't like she would just miss something like this. Even stranger, Gin hadn't made a sound either. That made

Eli very cautious. Unless there were two men named Sparrow here, this was the one Miranda had asked the hound to look for, and any person who could sneak past an alert ghosthound was someone to be treated with respect.

Sparrow smiled as he watched Eli's thought process and deftly flicked a card out of his front pocket. "Before you ask," he said softly, slipping the card down Eli's shirt collar, "no, they don't know I'm here." He leaned casually against the wall. "I'm something of an oddity, you see. I've been told I'm the opposite of a wizard, something completely beneath the world's notice, or some such. I don't fully understand it myself, but it's dreadfully useful, especially when sneaking around a girl who relies on spirits to do her watching." He glanced sideways beyond Eli's line of vision to where Miranda was getting ready. "Unless I'm wearing something with some life and color to it, spirits can't see me at all, so I thought I'd take advantage of my current drab attire to have a little chat with you. Of course"—he frowned—"the moment you speak, the jig is up, so things are going to be a little one-sided, I'm afraid. But I'm sure I can count on a man known for his curiosity to keep his mouth shut until he gets an explanation."

Eli gave him a sour look, but nodded.

"Good," Sparrow said. "You should know first that I'm not Spirit Court, and I'm not after your bounty either. I work for the Council of Thrones. Specifically, I work for the Council's Head Wizard, and she's very interested in you."

Eli's eyes went wide as coins, and he mouthed one word.

Sara.

"Who else?" Sparrow said. "I'm afraid things are about

to be very difficult for you, Mr. Monpress. Miranda's on the warpath. I wouldn't be surprised if you were standing trial before Banage within the month. However, it doesn't have to be that way." Sparrow leaned a little closer. "Sara has asked me to assure you that you will always be welcome in her department."

Eli glowered and said nothing. Sparrow shrugged and gave Eli's head a wet pat. "The offer's there, when you're ready," he said, moving silently back toward the open window. "Just remember, the Council's been planning your hanging since your bounty hit twenty thousand. It promises to be quite the event, but even this could be quietly forgotten if Sara wanted it to be. Think on that a bit. I'll be in touch, should you need me." He gave Eli one final smile before slipping quietly through the window, vanishing without a sound into the alley beyond.

Eli was still staring when Mellinor jerked beneath him, whirling him around to face Miranda, who was dressed in one of her standard riding suits, a deep blue one this time, with her red curls pulled up in a severe ponytail and a deep scowl on her face.

She folded her arms over her chest as Eli smiled at her. "What were you looking at just now?"

"Absolutely nothing of consequence," Eli said.

Miranda's look told clearly how much she believed that, but before she could say anything, Gin poked his head in the front door. "Sparrow's headed toward Izo's."

Miranda shook her head and grabbed a handful of Mellinor's water.

"Where are we going now?" Eli said, but Miranda didn't answer. She just dragged him, water and all, out the door and into the dirt street beyond.

• • •

Miranda marched into Izo's hall, leaving a wet trail on the grimy stone as she dragged a water-bound Eli behind her. Sparrow was already waiting for her. His drab clothes were gone, replaced by his usual finery, now a green silk coat covered with a short blue cape that set off his eyes in a way that was obviously planned. He looked impossibly smug, as always, but his expression was somewhat tempered by the sight of their prize being flung around like a wet towel. Miranda paid him no attention. She stopped when she reached the middle of the hall, slamming Eli down on his knees before Izo's empty throne.

Sparrow leaned over. "Miranda, dearest," he whispered. "Perhaps it is not the best idea to bring the object of a negotiation to the negotiation."

"The only spirit I trust him with is Mellinor," Miranda said through gritted teeth. "He's not leaving my sight. And don't call me dearest."

"She can get very touchy," Eli said, his voice somewhat burbled by the watery prison sloshing at his chin.

Sparrow gave him a dashing smile. "The greatest thief in the world. It is quite the honor to meet you, Mr. Monpress."

Eli grinned back. Miranda glowered and snapped her fingers, giving Mellinor a nudge that sent Eli's head back underwater.

"Don't encourage him," she said pointedly.

She let Eli bubble a bit before bringing him up again. "I told you," she said quietly, glaring down at the thief. "You're here because I can't leave you alone, not because we like your company, so keep your big mouth closed." She straightened up, pushing a stray curl out of her face. "Honestly, what part of 'prisoner' don't you understand?"

"Oh, I understand," Eli said with a wet grin. "I've just never been in agreement with the concept."

Miranda rolled her eyes, but before she could retort, or stick him underwater again, the iron gate rattled as Izo entered the room. He was dressed far finer than before, with a scarlet silk jacket over polished chain mail and a black cape edged extravagantly in gold thread. Miranda grimaced. He looked like every tacky minor lord in the Council district of Zarin, which was probably his intent. He was grinning like a cat as he stalked over to his chair, flanked on one side by the thin man in black, Sezri, and on the other by the enormous brawler with the ever-present cape over his shoulders, the man called Sted.

"Well," Izo said, settling down into his throne. "Well, well, well. Let it not be said that Izo doesn't deliver. Monpress kneels before me while his pet swordsman lies unconscious in my infirmary. I hope you understand now, friends, the power of the Bandit King. I have given you the uncatchable thief on a platter, as promised. Now we'll discuss the details of how you mean to hold up your end of the bargain."

Miranda started to point out how they had been the ones doing the actual catching, but Sparrow cut her off.

"Of course," he said, "we could not have asked for a better outcome, and the Council always keeps its bargains. We will leave for Zarin first thing tomorrow, and I will return personally to hand you your invitation to the Council within the month, *King* Izo."

Sparrow looked up, obviously expecting a smile at this new title, but Izo wasn't smiling. He lounged back on his throne, his eyes lidded and dark as he looked Sparrow over.

"No, no, pretty messenger bird," Izo said slowly.

"That's not how this works. I may be king, but I'll always be a bandit, and bandits don't get to be kings by blindly trusting the word of Council dogs. No member of the Monpress party leaves my camp until I have the writ from the Council acknowledging my kingship in my hand."

"My lord," Sparrow said, his voice buttery and soft. "That's simply not possible. It would take two weeks at least for me to return to Zarin. Without Monpress, it could take months to convince the Council to act, even for someone as connected as Sara."

"Then I will keep him for months," Izo said. "But he's not going anywhere until I get my price."

"That's unacceptable," Miranda said. "Every moment the thief spends outside of the Spirit Court's full security is a chance for him to escape. This isn't some cat burglar you can just lock in a cell. This is Eli Monpress we're talking about, the man who broke into, and escaped from, the great citadel of Gaol. Even if I stayed in your camp to guard him, I couldn't promise I could keep him safely bound for months. If he doesn't leave for Zarin immediately, we could all lose."

"Miranda," Eli said gently, "I'm touched. Praise from you is praise indeed."

Miranda waved her hand, and Mellinor's water went over Eli's head again. She held it there until his face was blue. "Shut up," she muttered, keeping her eyes on Izo. The Bandit King was leaning on his throne, scratching his scarred chin thoughtfully.

"I understand your complaint, Spiritualist," he said. "But my terms stand. Monpress goes nowhere until he is paid for. If you want to get him back to Zarin, I suggest you convince your Council to move quickly."

Sparrow smiled. "May I have a moment to discuss this with my colleague?"

Izo shrugged and waved his hand. Sparrow bowed in thanks before grabbing Miranda's arm and dragging her back to the gate.

"I told you to keep your mouth shut," he whispered harshly, though the calm smile never left his face.

"But we have to get Eli out of here," Miranda whispered back.

"Yes," Sparrow said. "And now he knows that. Never give information away, Miranda. Fortunately, the deal he just offered isn't bad. Eli is still only one half of this operation. If you stay to make sure he remains caught, there's a good chance you'll come into contact with Slorn at some point. I'm going to take his deal to Zarin. You and Tesset will stay here. With Tesset doing the hunting, Slorn should be in hand by the time I get back, and then we can all leave together with our missions complete."

"No," Miranda said. "You're not listening. If we wait, Eli *will* escape. I've caught him twice before, Sparrow. He's slipperier than Zarin's bookkeeping. I've put aside too much and worked too hard to accept a risk like this."

"This is a negotiation, Miranda," Sparrow said, and though his pleasant expression never changed, his voice was starting to sound annoyed. "You don't get to just make demands. Sted has most of the cards. We have to compromise. Stay here, keep the thief underwater, look for Slorn, and I'll be back in a month. Everything else is details."

Miranda glared at the floor. He didn't understand that this whole situation was going to fall apart if it depended on keeping Eli caught. But before she could think of another way to explain things, Eli spoke up, his voice ringing loud and clear through the throne room.

"What about my swordsman?"

Eli smiled smugly as everyone turned to look at him. "My head may be worth more than some kings see in a lifetime," he said, "but Josef carries the Heart of War. The Head Wizard of the Council is a collector of oddities, isn't she? She would never forgive you if you let the greatest awakened blade ever created go without a fight."

Sted lurched forward, but Izo's voice stopped him.

"The sword is already spoken for."

Eli's eyebrows shot up in surprise. "Is that so? King Izo, you're a cleverer bargainer than I gave you credit for, keeping the best prize safely off the table."

"Will you *shut up*?" Miranda hissed, knocking Eli down with a wave of water.

"That's because it's not Izo's to give!" Sted roared. "Liechten and the Heart were promised to me!"

"Sted!" Now it was Izo's turn to shout. He glared down from his throne at the enormous man, red-faced with rage. "Everything in my domain is mine to give if I please! I am king here!" He whirled to face Sparrow. "I'll make you another deal. You need the thief out quickly? Fine, I'd rather not wait to be king. I know you have a Relay link on you that allows you to talk directly to your mistress in Zarin. Tell her that she can have everything—Monpress, the Heart of whatever, freedom to hunt down your rogue wizard, *everything*, if Merchant Prince Whitefall himself comes up to welcome me as an equal to the Council by the next full moon."

"Merchant Prince Whitefall?" Miranda almost laughed out loud. "You want the Head of the Council of Thrones,

the Grand Marshal of Zarin, to come *here*? Have you lost
your little bandit mind?"

"No," Izo said coldly. "But you will lose your Spiritualist tongue if you speak to me that way again."

Miranda bristled, but snapped her mouth shut when
Sparrow's hand grabbed and nearly crushed her arm.

"Forgive my companion," Sparrow said, his voice honeyed and dripping with sincerity. "She is a Spiritualist and
a native of Zarin, and as such suffers from an overinflated
sense of importance." Miranda shot him a sharp look, and
the grip on her arm tightened until she could no longer
feel her fingers before he let go.

"It's late," Sparrow said. "Minds are tired and tempers
are running short. I will bring your offer to my mistress
and have an answer for you by morning. Thank you so
much for your generous hospitality, King Izo."

He bowed genteelly and turned on his heel, marching
out of the hall. Miranda followed a second later, dragging
Eli behind her. The thief went with a bemused grin on his
face and a little wink at Sted, who was in the corner turning purple with rage while Sezri held him back. Gin joined
them when they reached the keep stairs and fell in behind
Eli, glaring straight at the thief with his teeth bared. Now
that Gin was looking after their prisoner, Miranda was
free to turn on Sparrow.

"We were just getting into negotiations," she whispered. "Why did you make us leave?"

"Because it was time to leave," Sparrow said. "Or
didn't you see the murder in the big one's eyes?"

Miranda looked over her shoulder. Sure enough, she could
see Sted through the iron gate shouting something at Izo, who
was rising from his throne in red-faced fury as he answered.

"Stop looking," Sparrow said sharply.

Miranda turned back to the torch-lit road. "Whatever you say; one night won't make a difference," she grumbled. "There's no way you're getting Whitefall up here."

Sparrow's grin vanished, and he looked sideways at her with a condescending sneer. "You assume too much, *darling*. There are two pillars that prop up the Council of Thrones. The first is Merchant Prince Whitefall; the second is Sara. If push came to shove she could have the entire Whitefall family up here tomorrow, and for a combination of Slorn, Eli Monpress, and the Heart of War, she just might. She's been talking about that sword for years, but has never been able to find it." His voice softened, and he tilted his head thoughtfully. "Who would have thought its current wielder would be traveling with the thief? Though it makes sense, considering the spectacular feats his group has pulled off."

Eli burst out laughing at that, though the sound turned into a squeak when Gin bit him. Sparrow blithely ignored the entire affair.

"I'm going to check on Tesset," he said. "Then I'll drop by the infirmary to see this Heart of War for myself. You go back to the house and lock the thief down for the night. Tomorrow, I'll answer Izo's demands. You can come along if you promise to keep your mouth shut this time."

"No promises," Miranda said, halting at the door of the house they shared.

Sparrow didn't even stop, he just waved his hand as he walked down the dirt street toward the barracks where the infirmary was set up. Miranda watched him go for a moment and then turned on her heel and stomped off the other way, looking for one of Izo's men to bully into giving her her own building to stay in. Gin stayed close behind her, his eyes pinned on the water-bound Eli as he bumped along behind in his liquid prison.

Back in Izo's hall the air was growing violently tense. Sted stood at the base of the stairs to Izo's seat, held back only by Sezri's slender hand across his chest. "You have no right!" he roared. "Liechten is mine!"

"I have every right!" Izo shouted back, standing before his throne with his hand on his sword. "Everything in this land is mine to do with as I please, and I will not have my rights disputed in front of my guests by one of my own men!"

"I'm none of yours!" Sted bellowed. "I'm no one's servant! I am Berek Sted! I came back from death for this, and I *will* have my rematch with Josef Liechten even if I have to do it on your corpse!"

"Sted!" The demonseed's thin fingers dug into the larger man's cape-covered chest.

"No, Sezri." Izo sneered. "Let the ox bellow. Your Master has been a good ally to me, but I will not be told how to handle my affairs. I rule this land, make no mistake, and I will use its prisoners as I see fit." He sat back down on his throne, drawing his sword and laying it across his lap as he glared at Sted. "Leave. I grow tired of your tantrums. Tomorrow, I'll decide what's to be done with the swordsman. Beg your Master that I don't also decide what's to be done with you."

For a moment, Sted's eyes went wild. He pressed against Sezri until the smaller man began to tilt and it looked like Sted would fall on Izo like a tiger. But then, like a curtain falling over a lamp, the furious light went out. Sted stepped back, turned on his heel, and marched out of the hall, slamming the iron gate as he left. Sezri watched him leave, never moving until Sted's enormous shadow vanished into the night.

"That," he said, turning to look at Izo, "was a very foolish game to play."

Izo waved dismissively. "I've been leading bandits for fifteen years. You think I don't know how to handle men like Sted?"

"Sted isn't one of your thugs." Sezri's voice was sharp with disgust. "Have you forgotten whom he serves?"

"Men like that don't serve anyone but themselves," Izo said, laughing. "Your Master is kidding himself if he thinks otherwise."

"My Master sees all things," Sezri said quietly. "It is by his goodwill alone that you have risen as far as you have. You would do well to keep that in mind."

"He helped," Izo said. "He gave me monsters like you, but I was the one who planned the raids, who beat the other bosses. I was the one who took every two-bit gang from here to the coast and turned them into an army capable of taking on Council cities. True, it would have taken me much longer without your Master's aid, but he has received good payment for what he's given. I've kept my end of the deal. Slaves flow from my camps to the Dead Mountain every day. Now it's his turn. He promised to make me a king of the Council, and I will hold him to his debt."

"And you shall be king," Sezri said. "Offering them the swordsman was nothing but foolish arrogance and impatience."

"Call it what you will," Izo said. "I did what I had to do to make the Council move. If that upsets your Master's deal with Sted, that's not my problem. I'm not about to sit back and give up what I'm owed so your Master can pay another."

Sezri clenched his fist. Izo's arrogance was going too far. Inside him, he could feel the strength of the seed building, ready to lash out, to show this pathetic little man the true power of the Master. But before he could even think the command, the beloved voice filled his head.

Enough, Sezri.

The demonseed closed his eyes, nearly crying as the Master's voice rolled across his mind.

Let the human do as he likes. All will be answered. Now, go and find a spirit you can devour without raising alarm. Your strength will be needed soon.

"Yes, Master," Sezri whispered, bowing his head. "All will be as you command."

The voice chuckled, sliding over his soul like a hand stroking a cat. *Such a good child.*

"What was that?" Izo's voice snapped Sezri from his euphoria, and the demonseed glared in disgust at the tiny, human spirit on his makeshift throne.

"Do as you like," Sezri said, turning on his heel. "King Izo."

There was a scrape behind him as Izo stood up. "I hope you're going to check on Sted."

Sezri didn't answer. He simply stepped into a shadow and vanished, sliding through the dark until all he could feel was the seed inside him and the fading power of the Master's voice on his soul. He stopped when he reached the forest just beyond the city. There, in the dark shadow of the trees, he began to hunt for a spirit that would suit the Master's purpose, unaware of the pair of animal eyes watching him from branches above.

• • •

Nico sat in the dark in the corner of the small house, her coat draped over her head like a funeral shroud. Directly across from her, the tall man in the brown coat sat on a bench by the fire, staring at her. Outside, bandits were laughing and drinking; inside, the room was silent except for the low hissing of the coals. They hadn't spoken a word to each other since the woods.

None of this would have happened if you'd just accept my gifts. The swordsman's dead and it's all your fault. You know that, don't you?

Nico closed her eyes and buried her head in her knees.

Across the tiny room, the door opened, letting in a swirl of cold, smoky air before shutting again. Nico glanced up. A man wearing a green silk coat, green ballooning pants tucked into tall, polished boots, and a short blue cape with silver lining was standing in the entrance. He looked startlingly out of place, but the man sitting by the fire nodded a familiar greeting.

"Sparrow."

"Tesset," the foppish man replied as he bolted the door behind him.

The man in the brown coat, Tesset, waited until Sparrow was finished before asking, "How did it go?"

"The usual way," Sparrow said, unhooking his cape with a shrug. "Wonderfully, then horribly, and finally stopping somewhere just short of acceptable. Izo's no idiot, but he's not subtle enough for politics. He played his hand straight and strong. Unfortunately, though not surprisingly, the Spiritualist and Monpress mucked things up. I had to make some large concessions, but I think we ended up with the better deal in the end."

"What kind of concessions?"

"He wants his welcome to the Council issued by Whitefall himself," Sparrow said, flopping down into a chair beside the fire. "Here, by the end of the month."

Tesset winced. "That's a tall order. Sara will have your skin."

"I don't think she'll care one jot when she hears what she'll be getting in exchange," Sparrow said, grinning wide. "Not just the thief, but the Heart of War. Plus freedom to search for Slorn and all the other little things we'll wring out once Izo's prancing around in his crown like a little girl playing princess."

Nico's head shot up, and she wasn't alone. Even Tesset's eyes went wide.

"The Heart of War?" Tesset said. "You mean the great awakened sword?"

"You know of anything else with such a pretentious name?" Sparrow yawned. "I just got back from having a look for myself. No wonder no one recognizes it. It looks like a piece of junk. Great big dented black metal monstrosity, almost as bad as those Fenzettis Sara made us hunt down last year. It didn't even glow. Even the cheap awakened swords glow, but I didn't see a thing."

"How do you know it's real, then?" Tesset said. "Sara won't be happy if you make her pull strings for a bluff."

"Who do you take me for?" Sparrow scoffed. "I tried to pick it up, but I couldn't even move the hilt. Couldn't even wiggle it. That sword has the weight of a mountain, just like Sara said. Fortunately, its wielder is still breathing or we'd be in real trouble, paying through the nose for a sword we can't move."

"Josef's alive?"

Both men turned to glare at her, but Nico didn't care. Her relief was like a crushing weight on her chest, grinding every other concern into dust. "Is he all right?"

Sparrow considered a moment before answering. "He's alive for now, and less bloody than I'd expect. But seeing as he's under the questionable care of Izo's surgeons, all of whom seem to be bandits no more intelligent or sober than the common rabble, that's all I can say for now."

Nico took a deep breath, and Sparrow chuckled.

"This must be what they call 'loyalty among thieves,'" he said. "Your concern is truly touching, but I suggest you worry less about the swordsman and more about yourself, darling. Of every piece of this expedition, yours is the most expendable. The only reason you're alive right now is because of Slorn."

Nico shrank back into her coat. "Slorn?"

"You're something of a consolation prize," Sparrow said, taking off his boots. "Slorn's research on demonseeds and the corresponding nature of the spirits they inhabit is priceless. However, with the death of his current experimental specimen, my mistress is worried he'll drift out of the field. That's why we're giving him you. Sara has long known of Slorn and Eli's friendship and the coats he makes to hide your...condition. Your job will be to keep Slorn happy, give him something to study once we bring him back to Zarin. Assuming, of course, we can find him at all." Sparrow frowned in annoyance. "He's being very difficult at the moment. But don't fret, darling. If nothing else, we'll trade you in to the League. Sara just loves having Alric owe her favors."

He spoke so fast his words made Nico dizzy. He reminded her of Eli when the thief was making a particular effort to be as difficult as possible. Still, his point was clear enough. She was a payoff, either to Slorn or to the League. That alone gave her leverage, and if Eli had taught her anything, it was that leverage was never something to waste.

"If I cooperate," Nico said slowly, "will you make sure Josef gets what he needs to heal?"

"Of course," Sparrow said. "Considering we need his carcass to haul the Heart of War, he's safer than you. Though don't go getting any ideas. This can be as pleasant as you choose to make it. Sit in your corner like a good girl, don't give Tesset any excuse to do what we pay him to do, and everything will be nice and smooth." He reached into his waist pocket and pulled out something that looked like a blue glass ball on a leather thong, which he proceeded to roll between his fingers. "I've got to report in and get Sara to agree to all this, and then I'm going to bed. Tesset, since you never seem to sleep anyway, you've got night watch."

Tesset nodded, never taking his eyes off Nico as Sparrow stood and climbed the ladderlike stairs into the house's upper loft. There was some commotion as he settled into bed, and then a blue glow flashed in the dark. It shimmered for a moment, cold and watery on the cabin's pointed ceiling, before vanishing as he threw his covers over it. If she strained her ears, Nico could just make out Sparrow's hushed voice speaking as though he were having a conversation. No matter how hard she listened, however, she couldn't make out the words. Eventually, she sat back against the wall and turned her attention to Tesset, who hadn't moved an inch from his seat by the fire.

Unbidden, her eyes went to the smooth, unmarred skin

of his throat, and the black arm she kept buried against her chest began to itch and tremble. How had he done it? She'd felt the connection open, felt the demon as it started to eat him. How had he pushed it back?

Across the room, Tesset's eyes flicked from the fire to meet hers again. "You're wondering how I stopped you?"

Nico froze. Could he read minds as well?

"Go on," he said. "Ask. The first step toward knowledge is a question."

Nico bit her lip. This could be a bluff, a trick to get her to reveal a weakness. But the man across from her didn't seem like the tricky type, and Sparrow had made it perfectly clear she meant little to them. Underneath her coat, her arm was itching more than ever, and she decided to risk it.

"How did you do it?"

"I've already told you," Tesset answered. "Back in the woods. You could not eat me because I did not will it."

"I don't understand," Nico said. "Will stops spirits, not demons."

"And what are you?" Tesset said.

Nico looked down at the floor. "A demonseed."

"Wrong," Tesset snapped. "The demonseed is what's inside you. But you are a human, the greatest spirit of all. The spirit with will, who can control all others."

"That's not true," Nico said. "A wizard can't control another human."

Tesset stood up, pulling his bench closer to Nico's corner until he was almost on top of her. "We have a long night ahead," he said, sitting down. "Let me tell you a story."

"What kind of story?" Nico said, pressing her back to

the wall. This close, it took all of her strength to keep her arm from lashing out again. She kept it pinned behind her, the long demon claws scraping at the back of her coat.

"The best kind," Tesset said, settling in with no care for the danger of being so close to a demonseed. "A true one."

He gave her a knowing smile and began.

"I was born in these mountains, and like all male children born here, I joined a bandit gang as soon as I was old enough to follow orders. I was a hotheaded boy with a small, closed mind and a knack for getting in fights. A good bandit, in other words. I was also a wizard, someone who could listen to the winds and trees passably well. A powerful combination, and one that landed me a nice position in Mel's Red Fist, the largest and most fearsome of the bandit gangs at that time. I loved being in the Red Fist. This was thirty years ago, before the Council of Thrones was around to give bandits a hard time. Pickings were fat, and we were the richest, scariest guys around. That's a heady thing for a kid, and I was deadly loyal to Mel, the man who'd brought it all together and the greatest fighter I'd ever seen.

"The day after I turned seventeen, we returned to our camp to find a man waiting for us. This wasn't unusual. We often had vagabonds and deserters from other bandit gangs show up begging to join the Red Fist, but this man was different. He was the largest man I'd ever seen. He had no weapon, and he was dressed in rags and cast-off furs, but the way he carried himself made other fighters look like bumbling toddlers. He just stood there in the center of camp as we rode in, making our usual ruckus, and when we were quiet, he asked which of us was the boss.

"After a good laugh at the stranger's expense, Mel rode forward and announced that he was the leader of the Red Fist. As soon as he said this, the stranger challenged him to a fight. He'd heard Mel was the strongest of the bandit leaders, having the biggest, strongest gang and a nasty reputation as a dirty fighter, and he wanted to see for himself. Mel said this was all true and accepted the challenge. While Mel got his ax, we stood around laughing and arguing over who would get stuck digging a grave for this idiot who was stupid enough to challenge our boss. The stranger, however, was still unarmed. Mel told the man to draw a weapon, and the stranger replied that he would if he needed one. This made Mel furious, and he charged, meaning to cut the stranger's head off. The next moment, Mel was on the ground in a pool of his own blood and the stranger was walking away."

Tesset shook his head. "None of us saw a thing. One second Mel was charging, the next he was down. He died a few minutes later. Of our entire gang, I was the first to recover, and the first thing I did was run after the stranger. I'd never seen a fight like that. Mel had always been my idol, the ceiling of how far a man could rise. Then this stranger appears and in one blow shows me that the top is further than I could ever imagine. So I caught up with him. He was moving slowly, like he was disappointed. When I reached him, he grabbed me around the throat and asked if I wanted to avenge my boss. I didn't even see his hand move. I told him that I'd never seen a man move like him. Could he teach me, or at least tell me his name?"

"And did he?" Nico asked.

Tesset chuckled. "No. He dropped me on the ground and told me to go home. But Mel was gone, and I had no home to go to. So I kept following him. The man walked day and night, but somehow I stuck to his trail. Every time I caught up, I would ask him to teach me. Looking back, I was desperate. I'd based my whole life around being strong, and in one motion this man had blown away my entire idea of strength. I couldn't let him just walk away. So I made a nuisance of myself and, finally, after a month of eating his dust, the man turned and asked me my name. I told him, and he shook his head. 'That's a weak name,' he said. 'From today, your name is Tesset. If you want to learn from me, I'll give you six months. Anything you learn during that time is yours to keep. After that, we're enemies, and if I ever see you again, I'll kill you.'"

Tesset began to laugh. "I was terrified of course, but I didn't want to look weak. I agreed, calling the man Master. He told me no man was master over anyone but himself, and that I was to call him by his name, Den."

Nico's eyes went wide. "Den the Warlord," she whispered. "The man from the bounty posters?"

Tesset nodded. "Of course, this was before the war, before he betrayed the Council. But he kept his word to me, and for six months he taught me one thing."

"One thing?" Nico said.

"Yes," Tesset said. "It was something I'd always known, what all wizards know, but most will never understand." Tesset placed his hand on his chest. "As a human, a wizard has will. This will is what gives him control over all the world save only the spirits of other humans. However, there is one human spirit a wizard does control." Tesset thumped his hand on his chest. "His own. My body and my soul are subject to my will. Just as an enslaver can make a mountain rise up and walk to the sea if his spirit is strong enough, so can I make my body do impossible things by conquering my soul with my will. Once a man has mastered himself, he has no king, no conqueror, no predator but himself, and that, demonseed, is the answer to your question."

Nico could not believe what she was hearing. "It can't be that simple," she whispered.

"It's not," Tesset said. "But that doesn't make it untrue." Faster than she could react, he lunged forward and grabbed her arm, the demon arm she'd been keeping pressed behind her. She pulled back frantically, but he was stronger than her, stronger than anyone she'd ever fought, and his grip didn't even shake as he pulled her black, clawed hand into his own. The demon hand clawed at Tesset's skin like a hungry beast scenting food, and Nico squeezed her eyes shut, waiting for eating to begin. But nothing happened. There was no roaring connection, no feeling of another spirit pouring into her. Nico cracked her eyes a fraction and then opened them in wonder at the sight of her clawed hand clutched between Tesset's palms, his tan skin whole and sound.

Tesset's dark eyes met hers, and when he spoke, his voice was an iron bell. "There is nothing you or your demon can do to me if I do not will it," he said. "I am master of myself, and nothing can happen to me unless I allow it. Do you understand now?"

Nico stared at their clasped hands. "No," she whispered. "Teach me."

Tesset smiled and released her. "I have already taught you."

Nico gaped at him. "No," she said, grabbing his hand again. "You have to teach me how to do it."

Tesset gripped her fingers so hard they ached. "I taught you as Den taught me," he said. "It is so simple, yet it has taken me over thirty years to get to where I am now. But it is not a matter of strength or training or anything else won by hard work. It is a matter of understanding. A child could master it in one day if only their mind were free enough. To truly become master of yourself, you must be willing to throw everything else away. Fear, anger, doubt; these things undermine your authority. You must become as an enslaver to your own soul. Once you have achieved that, nothing can control or limit you ever again."

Nico stared at him, bewildered. But Tesset just smiled, releasing her hand.

"It helps to find a goal," he said, his gruff voice almost wistful as he leaned back to stare at the fire. "Mastering your soul becomes easier when you're chasing something greater than yourself. Mine is to meet Den one more time before I die and finally fight him as an equal."

"But," Nico said, "he's had that enormous bounty on his head for twenty-five years now with no news. How do you even know he's still alive?"

"He's alive," Tesset said fiercely. "Wherever he is, I know he's alive. Men like Den don't die without the world knowing. One day I will find him, and then I will show him how much I have learned."

Nico looked at Tesset as though she were seeing him for the first time, his brown hair touched with gray, his brown skin warm and dark in the firelight, his hawk-nosed face set with absolute determination, and she believed him. She licked her dry lips, thinking of what she would ask him next about how she could begin down the road to

understanding what he'd told her. But before she could
get the words out, she was cut off by the unmistakable
sound of a door being kicked down, followed immediately by the sound of a dog snarling and a woman's surprised scream.

CHAPTER
15

"There," Miranda said, straightening up. "That should do it."

The house she'd been moved to was smaller than the one she'd shared with Tesset and Sparrow, but far better suited to her purposes. It had been a storage building, and as such it was one large room with a high roof and a pair of double doors wide enough for Gin to squeeze through. He was now lying stretched out against the wall with his head resting on his paws by the front door and his haunches hanging out the back. Next to him, a small wood-burning stove with a roaring fire far larger than it was meant to contain kept out any chill the open back door might have let in. Other than the stove, the building had no furniture. Miranda had made the bandits move it all out to make room for her custom prison.

Everywhere Gin wasn't, a bed of soft, springy moss covered the plank floor in a thick green carpet. At the center of the moss was what could only be described as a stone barrel. The barrel was filled to the brim with impossibly blue water, and sitting in the water up to his chin was Eli, looking extremely nonplussed.

"I'm getting a cramp," he announced, shifting in the water, or trying to. "It's unhealthy to stay still this long. And the water is cold."

"You'll live," Miranda said, leaning against Gin with a smug expression. Eli gave her a pathetic look, and Miranda, after a dramatic eye rolling, waved her hand. All of her rings were glowing like embers, but it was the cloudy emerald taking up the bottom joint of her left thumb that flashed the brightest. A moment later the stone barrel creaked and widened a few inches, giving Eli room to fold his legs.

"Much better," the thief sighed. "Thank you, Durn."

The stone spirit rumbled a warning before settling down into his new shape.

Eli arched his eyebrows and leaned forward. Or he tried to, but the water stopped him before he'd gotten more than an inch. He made himself comfortable as best he could, grinning at Miranda as though this half-forward trapped position was what he had intended all along.

"I've been in a lot of prisons," he said. "But this has to be the most elaborate. How long do you intend to keep this up?"

"As long as I have to," Miranda said. "It's clear we're not getting out of here anytime soon, and I know better than to leave you alone. So until I get you to Zarin and hand you over to Banage himself, I'm not taking my eyes off you."

"What, you're just going to sit there and stare at me?" Eli said. "I'm flattered, don't misunderstand, but aren't you being a bit unreasonable? I mean, I'm just sitting here enjoying the soak while you're keeping every spirit you have on full burn. That's got to take it out of you. How long do you honestly think you can keep it up?"

"I'll worry about that," Miranda said.

There was no reason to tell the thief, but she'd planned out a schedule. Right now, Kirik, her fire spirit in the stove, and Alliana, her moss, were on guard. When they got tired, she'd bring out Eril, her wind spirit, and Allinu, her mountain mist, to take their place. Durn, being stone, could watch forever, and she knew better than to question Mellinor's resolve. Keeping up all these spirits was difficult, but it wasn't like she had anything more important to do. When she did need to sleep or empty her bladder, Gin could keep an eye on things. It wasn't a perfect solution, but since Sparrow was dragging his feet, it would have to do. One thing, however, was certain: She was not going to give the thief a moment of leeway. Not an inch of freedom. She had won; she had him. All she had to do to secure her victory forever was get him back to Zarin. This time, she would make sure that happened, no matter the cost. This time, Eli would not escape.

"Being at the center of so much attention, I feel like I should be more entertaining," the thief said with a grin. "How about this? Free my hands and I'll show you a card trick."

Miranda gave him a stony glare and said nothing.

When he realized this approach wasn't going to work, Eli let out a long sigh and slumped back against Mellinor's restraining water.

"You know, I'm actually very impressed," he said, his voice surprisingly sincere. "That was a neat little trap you pulled off back in the river. Of all the people who've chased me over the years, you're the closest thing I've ever had to a real rival. There've been so many bounty hunters who've come after me, so many traps, and yet no one has come quite as close quite as many times as you, Miranda. Back when I first started this whole million-gold-standard bounty thing, I always envisioned a great rival, some famous bounty hunter who would track me all across the Council Kingdoms and give me a real run for my money. But I never in my life thought it would be a Spiritualist."

Miranda frowned, not sure how to answer. Fortunately, she didn't need to, for Eli kept going.

"I just don't see what you're getting from all this effort," he said. "You've already achieved more than most Spiritualists do in a lifetime. You've got nearly two full hands of rings, position, power, a Great Spirit at your beck and call. You don't seem to care about money or fame, and you're not the type who enjoys the chase for its own sake, so far as I can tell. I keep waiting for you to give up, go home, get a Tower, write some long-winded treatise on spiritual ethics, but you never do. You keep coming after me. Why is that?"

"Is that a trick question?" Miranda asked, keeping her voice carefully flat.

"No," Eli said slowly. "It's a sincere one."

Miranda leaned back, resting her head on Gin's ribs. "Because it is my duty."

"Nonsense," Eli said. "It's the Council's job to catch thieves."

She gave him a long look. "That may be, but the Spirit Court cannot ignore your actions. You go around using spirits to steal kings without even trying to hide it.

Every job you pull is a production, a grand sensation to build your reputation as Eli Monpress, the wizard thief. The Spirit Court exists to promote two goals: the ethical treatment of spirits and building the public's faith in wizardry. In case you've forgotten, wizards used to be seen as tyrants, hated by spirits and people alike for abusing their power. For the last four centuries, the Spirit Court has worked to change that by taking down those who abuse spirits and by holding all wizards accountable to a moral code, whether they want to be held accountable or not."

"You can't force your morals on the whole world," Eli said.

"We don't," Miranda said. "We force them on other wizards, because if we didn't, the bad times would return faster than you could imagine. Spiritualists swear to uphold the Spirit Court's code of ethics precisely so that we never go back to those dark days. That is why, when you decided to abandon those morals, to use your power as a wizard to flout the law for personal gain, it became my duty to stop you. Your actions throw a black shadow on all of us and undo the hard work of a great many good people. It's so much easier to tear down a reputation than to build it, to inspire fear and suspicion rather than trust. That's why I have to stop you, to protect the work of all the Spiritualists who went before me and save the trust they built, which you now take advantage of."

Eli heaved a long, hard sigh. "You remind me very much of someone I used to know when you lecture like that," he said quietly. "How is it Spiritualists can turn anything into a matter of duty?"

"It's called having principles," Miranda said, crossing

her arms over her chest. "Some of us don't have morals as
flexible as yours."

"Well, no one could ever accuse you of flexibility,"
Eli said dryly. "Unfortunately, I fear we will never come
to an agreement. Your world is far too black-and-white
for me."

"There's no agreement to come to," Miranda said
fiercely. "Don't forget who's up to his neck in water."

Eli smirked and started to answer, but he never got a
chance. At that moment, the door exploded.

Miranda screamed in surprise, throwing up her arms
to shield her face as bits of wood shot across the room.
She fell to the ground as Gin slid out from under her, leaping to his feet with a snarl, his patterns swirling madly
as he turned to face the door, ears flat back against his
skull. For a moment, she couldn't even see what he was
growling at through the dust and debris. Then the man
stepped into the room, and Miranda felt her skin grow
cold.

Sted stood in the doorway. He was shirtless, and his
cape was gone. For a moment, Miranda could only stare
in horror at the hideous thing growing out of his shoulder.
The black skin, as hard and polished as scorched glass,
was so alien, so beyond what she expected, that Sted had
walked almost all the way to where Eli was trapped in
the water before she realized it was his arm. With that
realization, everything else fell into place, and she flung
out her hand. At once, Durn threw himself back, sliding
along Allinora's mossy bed to rest beside Miranda, Eli
safely squeezed between the layers of rock and water.
The thief started to protest, but Mellinor's water covered
his head before he could speak. Never taking her eyes off

the intruder, Miranda nodded in thanks. Now was not the time for distractions.

"I knew something was wrong with you," she said, stepping between Sted and Eli, who was bubbling furiously under Mellinor's water. "But I never thought Izo'd actually be stupid enough to employ a demonseed. It must be an idiocy common within the criminal element."

Behind her, Eli made a sound that was half burble, half scoff, and she flicked Durn's ring. There was a loud scrape as the rock closed over Eli's head, trapping him inside a cocoon of stone as well as water. Miranda nodded. Mellinor could give him enough oxygen to keep him from drowning for ten minutes at least, and she was taking no chances.

Sted stood where Durn had been, glaring at her with eyes that were far too bright for the dim room. "I serve no man but myself," he sneered. "I'm here for the thief. Hand him over."

"Never," Miranda said, pulling Allinora's moss back into her ring, away from the monster at the door. "Eli Monpress is under arrest by the authority of the Spirit Court and the Council of Thrones."

"Really?" Sted's voice was slow and sharp, like a knife working through frozen flesh. "And are you ready to die to keep him?"

Gin snarled beside her, and Miranda couldn't help baring her teeth as well. "I couldn't do my duty if I wasn't," she said. "Leave now or I'll call the whole deal off and Izo will never be king."

Sted threw back his head and laughed, a horrible, hollow sound that rattled up from deep in his chest. "Izo?" he cried. "Who cares about Izo? Weren't you listening, girl? I'm here for the thief, preferably alive, but I'll take what

I can get. Your fate I'm far less picky about. Move." He
took a menacing step forward, heavy boots creaking on
the bare plank floor. "*Now.*"

Miranda held her ground, hands clenched in sweaty
fists around her rings. Spiritualists didn't fight demonseeds; it was too risky. But she could not back down. Not
now, not when she had Eli. Her resolve was set, and Gin
must have felt it, for before she could open her mouth to
answer Sted's threat, the ghosthound lunged forward.

It was a tight jump. The little room wasn't large enough
for Gin to turn around in let alone get any momentum for
a flying attack, but Miranda would never have known it.
Gin sprang from a standstill, a shifting blur of claws and
teeth aimed straight for Sted's neck. Sted had nowhere to
dodge and no time to duck before the dog's teeth sank
into his neck and shoulders.

They fell backward, Sted stumbling into the splintered remains of the door with Gin on top of him, the
ghosthound's teeth lodged in his torso. Miranda felt like
cheering. Gin knew as well as she did that the only way
to win this was to take Sted down in one blow, before
he could eat them or terrify her spirits into submission.
From where she stood, it looked like the hound had done
just that. Even demonseeds went down when you ripped
them in half. But then, just when it looked like Sted was
done for, Gin yelped and jumped back, slamming against
the rear wall of the house in a scramble of legs and wild
shifting fur.

"Bastard!" the dog roared.

Gin's muzzle was slick with blood, which wasn't surprising, considering he'd just bitten a man through to the
ribs, but this was too much. Gin coughed, bringing up

more blood as he circled to face Sted again, his head low and cautious, as though he were the one who'd just taken a blow instead of dealt one. Across the room, Sted stood up, a superior grin on his face. Gin's bite draped across his neck and shoulders like a bloody shawl, but the holes were closing as Miranda watched.

"Not fast enough?" she asked quietly.

"No, I got him," Gin snarled, sending blood across the floor. "Bastard let me get him. Let me get in good before he started to eat."

He coughed again, adding more blood to the pool on the floor. "I don't get it," he panted. "I could feel him eating me. It was just like before, with Monpress's girl. But there's no fear."

Gin was right, she realized. Other than her spirits, the room was calm. There was no panic, no overwhelming fear like she'd felt in Mellinor. If Sted wasn't standing there with his monstrous arm, healing right in front of her, she wouldn't have even known he was a demonseed.

Gin growled. Sted was coming forward, a feral grin on his scarred face.

"Is that all?" His voice was thick with laughter. "Is that all you have to throw against me? A pet dog?"

"Miranda," Gin said softly, never taking his orange eyes off Sted. "Take the thief out the back. I'll hold this bastard here while—"

A whoosh of flame cut off his words. The fire in the stove blazed up to the ceiling, and Sted burst into flames. He screamed in pain and began to flail wildly. Gin turned to look at Miranda, who was lowering her hand, Kirik's enormous ruby burning like a bonfire on her thumb.

"No playing hero tonight, mutt," she said, pressing her

fingers against the pendant on her chest. A great wind rose up, and the fire on Sted grew white-hot as Eril, her wind spirit, blasted it like a forge bellow. Sted screamed again, beating the flames, but Kirik clung tight. The blast of heat was enough to blister Miranda's skin, but she didn't step back. Triumph surged up Kirik's connection, and the ring on Miranda's thumb began to almost vibrate with the fire's victorious joy as Sted sank to his knees.

Then, in the space between breaths, the tide turned. The flames were still blazing bright, the smell of burned flesh thick in the air, but Miranda could feel something pulling on the connection that tied her to Kirik. It felt as though the fire spirit was going further and further away from her, fading into the distance. The feeling was so alien that, for a moment, she could only stand dumbly. Then, like a splash of cold water, she realized what was happening.

"Kirik!" Her voice throbbed with power. "Come back now!"

"No!" the fire roared. "I've almost got him!"

"Kirik!" she cried again. She could feel it clearly now, vibrating up their connection. Sted was eating the fire even as it burned him, devouring the spirit's soul. Through the flames, she could see his charred skin mending, growing whole again as he sucked in the fire's essence. But Kirik wasn't stopping. He burned brighter than ever, the heat roaring until the wooden roof began to smoke, but Sted was standing up, his black, clawed hand clutching the fire, drawing it in, and Miranda decided enough was enough.

With a wrench of her spirit she'd never had to use before, she grabbed Kirik and pulled him back. It hurt. The fire burned her control, fighting her, screaming that he had almost won, but Miranda slammed her will down like a forge hammer. Roaring with defeat, the fire fled back to its ring and the ruby's light went out. Dumbstruck by what had just happened, Miranda stared at her ring, her vision wavering as her heart thudded in fear. The red stone was now the color of charred coal, and she could barely feel Kirik at all.

A gust of wind hit her as Eril returned to his pendant, and Miranda forced her attention back to the fight. Sted was on his feet again, standing in a circle of black char. Smoke filled the air, but most of it came from what was left of the roof and the floor. Sted's clothes had been reduced to blackened rags, but his skin was nearly untouched, and what bits of it were still charred were healing before Miranda's eyes.

She cursed under her breath as he turned to face her, his teeth bared in a hateful smile. "Anything else?"

Miranda clenched her fists. All her rings except Kirik's were trembling against her fingers, not with fear, but with anger. They wanted to kill the monster, to stamp Sted out of existence, but Miranda held them back. She raised her hand and gave a silent order. It took a moment for Durn to comply, but eventually the rock spirit opened his stone cocoon, revealing Eli, now unconscious, curled up like a baby in Mellinor's blue globe. The next order was the hardest she'd ever had to give. She reached out to the thick cord connecting her to Mellinor, and the globe of water collapsed. Steam hissed as the cold water ran over the charred wood, washing Eli up in a little heap at Sted's feet.

Sted bent over, scooping the thief up with one arm. "That was the smart choice," he said. "But then, who could expect a woman to give a good fight?"

Miranda shook with rage, but when she spoke, her voice was as cold as Mellinor's water. "If I back down, it is only because I value my spirits more than any prize or pride that thief could bring me. Take him and go, but be warned, Sted." She spat his name. "When we meet again, I'll make you suffer for what you've done."

"Is that so?" Sted said, slinging Eli over his shoulder. "In that case, I'll make a point to eat every one of your little spirits. That is, if I can be bothered to remember."

Gin snarled, but Sted just turned, laughing, and started toward the door. Before his foot hit the ground, he was gone, vanishing into the long shadows. For a moment Miranda just stood there, almost too angry to breathe, then she knelt down beside Gin. "How is it?"

"I'll live," the hound grumbled, licking the blood from his muzzle. He caught her look, and his enormous orange eyes narrowed. "If you're thinking what I think you are, the answer is yes."

"Are you sure?" Miranda said, suddenly hesitant.

"I wouldn't have said anything if I wasn't sure," Gin growled. "If you think for one second I'm going to let that bastard get away with our prize, then you can find yourself another ghosthound. Get on."

Miranda didn't ask again. She pulled Mellinor back into her body and vaulted onto Gin's back. The second she was on they were running, smashing through what was left of the shattered door into the torch-lit street. She caught a glimpse of Sparrow's shocked face, Tesset and Nico standing behind him, but she put them out of her mind. This had gone far beyond Council games and power plays. It was between her and Sted now. Gin thundered through the streets, sending bandits flying when they got in his way. He cleared the last row of buildings in one leap and stopped on the edge of the box canyon that hid Izo's city from the world. He raised his head, holding his nose up to the night air, and took several large sniffs.

"This way," he said, turning north so hard Miranda's neck snapped. She grimaced and bent low on the hound's back, clinging to his fur as they raced through the dark woods, chasing the shadow of Eli's scent on the cold mountain air.

"I don't know how we're getting out of this." Sparrow's voice held none of its usual charm as they stomped through the torch-lit streets toward Izo's fortress. "And that's not a turn of phrase. I really, honestly, do not know how we are going to make this situation into anything other than an unmitigated disaster."

Behind him, Tesset stayed silent, matching Sparrow's frantic pace with his long, ground-eating steps. As the shortest, Nico had to run to keep up or be dragged by the rope Tesset had affixed to her wrists. It was an awkward setup, but Sparrow had refused to see Izo alone and Tesset couldn't leave Nico unguarded, so they had no choice but to face the fallout together.

When they reached the hall, the guards told Sparrow that Izo was waiting for them at the infirmary, though they wouldn't tell him why.

"Probably just wants to save time," Sparrow muttered bitterly.

"If that were the case, he'd have asked us to meet him at the burial pit," Tesset pointed out.

Sparrow shot him a dirty look and kept going, winding his way through the maze of barracks and training grounds until they reached the long, low building that served as Izo's infirmary.

"Looks like they took a pigsty and replaced the pigs with bandits who could tie a bandage," Sparrow muttered, nodding to the boy who opened the door for them. "Remember, let me do the talking."

"That's why you're here," Tesset said calmly.

Sparrow shook his head and walked faster.

The infirmary was a long hall lined with beds. Most were empty, the stained sheets dumped in piles at their feet. Izo was waiting for them at the very end with several men in drab surgeon's smocks. They were all standing around a bed, and Izo was shouting something, his words so slurred together by rage that Nico could barely make them out.

"I don't care if you have to stab him again!" the Bandit King roared. "Wake him up! Now! And where is that Council peacock?"

One of the doctors pointed nervously over Izo's shoulder, and the Bandit King turned, his face going even redder when he caught sight of Sparrow.

"You!" he shouted, grabbing Sparrow by the arm. "You'd better have something to tell me. Where's the wizard girl?"

"I couldn't say for sure," Sparrow said, his voice pinched with pain. "Probably off after your bruiser. You know, the one who stole our thief?"

Izo bared his teeth and jerked Sparrow up until the smaller man was within kissing distance. "You'd better watch that fancy tongue of yours, boy. I'm in no mood to humor Council dogs who can't even keep their downed prey."

He spat in Sparrow's face, then dropped him. Tesset caught him before he could fall, and Sparrow nodded his thanks, pulling an orange silk handkerchief from his pocket to wipe his face with a disgusted grimace. Point made, Izo turned back to the bed.

This time, Nico was close enough to see who was in it, and her heart clenched. There, lying beneath the surgeon's hands, was Josef. His stern face was pale and calm, his eyes closed in sleep. His clothes had been cut away and his wounds rebound, with the exception of the center of his chest. That was where the Heart lay, and from the way Josef's clothing had been cut, it was clear none of the surgeons had tried to move it, not even to get at his wounds. They probably couldn't move it, Nico realized. The Heart never moved unless it wanted to. That thought, along with the steady rise and fall of Josef's chest, made her feel better than she had since she'd first opened her mouth to tell Eli about the Dead Mountain.

After another minute of failed attempts to wake the swordsman, Izo sent the doctors away. They fled as Izo leaned over Josef's sleeping form. He watched the swordsman for a moment and then reached out his hand and slapped Josef hard across the face. Nico lunged forward before she knew what she was doing, catching herself painfully on Tesset's leash, but Izo didn't seem to notice her at all. He lifted his hand and slapped Josef again, but as he pulled back for a third blow, there was a flash of movement from the bed. Whatever it was happened too fast for Nico to see, but one moment Izo was standing over Josef, his hand coming down on the swordsman's cheek, and the next he was on the floor cursing, with Josef's hand locked around the Bandit King's newly broken wrist.

The swordsman opened his eyes and gave Izo a lazy, deadly glare. "Don't ever do that again."

Izo wrenched his hand free with a pained gasp and jumped to his feet—though, to his credit, he paid no attention to his injury. All of his rage was focused on the man lying in front of him.

"You're Josef Liechten?"

"Powers," Josef sighed, slumping back into bed. "If you wanted to know that, there was no reason to wake me up. You could have asked her." His eyes flicked over to Nico. "Are you all right, Nico?"

Nico started to answer, but Izo stepped between them.

"I'm asking the questions," he snarled. "You're the one Sted has this big grudge with, correct?"

"I beat him, if that's what you mean," Josef said. "He's a bad loser."

"That much is obvious," Izo said. "Tell me then what you make of this."

He produced a scrap of paper from his pocket and flung it at Josef. The swordsman caught the paper deftly and studied it with a scowl.

"It's from Sted," Izo said. "He left it on my doorstep sometime after midnight. He's taken Monpress hostage and says he'll bring him back unharmed only if you will answer his challenge. A one-on-one duel in three days' time."

"Well, I'm glad you told me," Josef said, handing the letter back. "Because I could barely make anything out of his writing. I've seen better penmanship from five-year-olds."

"Who cares about his writing?" Izo shouted. "Monpress is worth a kingdom to me! I want him back."

"As he loves to remind people, Eli is worth several kingdoms," Josef said flatly. "What do you want me to do about it?"

"Isn't that obvious?" Izo said. "You're going to give Sted the fight he wants or I'm going to kill you here and now. That clear enough for you?"

Josef looked the bandit up and down. "Ordinarily, I'd say you're welcome to try, but if you just want me to fight Sted, then we have no quarrel. I was going to do that anyway."

"Oh." Izo deflated a bit; he'd obviously been pumping himself up for a fight. "Good then. Makes things easier."

"However," Josef continued, "if I'm going to get Sted to give up Eli, there are a few things you'll need to provide me with."

Izo crossed his arms. "Like what?"

"To start, a place to fight," Josef said, pushing himself up into a semisitting position. "Preferably somewhere people can see him. This is a pride fight, so people need to be there to see him or his pride will not be avenged. Sted doesn't care about Eli. He'll give the thief up easily when he sees he's getting what he wants."

"You can use the arena," Izo said. "That's what I built it for, and Sted was an arena fighter."

"That will work," Josef said, nodding. "I'll also need a few supplies. How many blacksmiths do you keep in your camp?"

Izo frowned. "What kind of a question is that?"

"How many?" Josef said again.

Izo ran a hand through his thinning hair. "Twenty-two, not counting apprentices."

Josef arched his eyebrows, impressed. "Good. Tell

them all to start making swords. I'm going to need a hundred at least, preferably more, made from the blackest, cheapest metal you can give me."

"What game is this?" Izo said. "You've got the greatest awakened sword in the world right there on your chest. Why should I waste my men and resources making you pot-metal blades?"

Josef lay back again. "Those are my terms," he said. "If you don't like them, find someone else to fight Sted."

Izo looked down with a snarl. "All right, a hundred blades. Anything else?"

"Yes," Josef said. "I'm still healing. If you want me in any condition to fight in three days, you'll keep yourself and your doctors away. The only person I want staying with me is Nico. Everyone else will have to leave."

"Done," Izo said, turning to face Tesset. "You don't have a problem leaving the girl here?"

Sparrow opened his mouth to protest, but Tesset was faster. "Not if I am allowed to stay with her as her guard."

Josef looked at Nico, who gave him the thinnest hint of a nod.

"I'm fine with that," Josef said, making himself comfortable again. "Remember, don't touch me for three days or I won't be fit to fight an old man like you, much less a monster like Sted."

Izo seethed with rage, but turned away without a retort. "You," he said, glaring at Tesset. "Keep an eye on both of them. Nothing is to disturb his sleep. If the Council messes this up for me, I'll hang all of you by your own guts, just see if I don't. And you"—he turned to Sparrow—"I hope you talked with your Sara, because the plan is going ahead as agreed."

"Assuming, of course, you hold up your end," Sparrow said.

Izo bared his teeth. "You'll have Monpress, make no mistake. No one steals from Izo."

He made a rude gesture, just for good measure, and then stomped out of the infirmary, shouting for his guards. Sparrow frowned and started speaking with Tesset in a low, hushed voice, but Nico didn't bother to listen. She walked to Josef's bedside, her feet silent on the wooden floor, and sat down on the stool beside him.

She'd thought he was already asleep again, but Josef opened his eyes when she sat down, giving her a weak smile. "Glad you made it," he said softly. "Everything all right?"

"We're prisoners," Nico answered. "And Sted's got Eli."

Josef thought about this for a moment and then gave a tiny, pained shrug. "We've gotten out of worse."

Nico tried to share his certainty, but the angry wounds on his chest made it hard. "Can the Heart really heal you in three days?"

"Oh, I could fight now," Josef said. "The Heart of War is exceptionally experienced at keeping its swordsmen standing. So long as I didn't let go of the Heart, I'd be well enough. But I'm not going to have the Heart, so I need some extra time."

"How will you beat Sted without the Heart?" Nico felt like a traitor even saying the words, but she couldn't imagine how he could win without his sword.

"You'll see when it happens," Josef said, his voice growing soft and sleepy. "Trust me."

Nico nodded and Josef closed his eyes again, sinking

almost instantly into a deep sleep. A minute later, Nico heard Sparrow leaving and what sounded like Tesset pulling up his own stool behind hers, but she didn't turn to see for certain. She just sat there, watching Josef, standing guard beside his bed as the sun began to peek over the mountains.

CHAPTER
16

Eli woke with a start. He was lying on his side, curled in a ball on a cold stone floor with his face pressed against a stone wall. He lifted his head away from the wall and gave his limbs an experimental wiggle. Tied, of course, ankles, legs, arms, and hands. He sighed and flopped his head back down on the stone. This captured thing was becoming depressingly frequent. Still, he wasn't wet anymore, which meant he wasn't with Miranda, and that greatly improved his chances of escape. Spiritualist spirits were so stingy. Of course, if he wasn't with Miranda, where was he?

Slowly, painfully, Eli wiggled against his bindings, turning by fractions until he was on his back. Unfortunately, this only made him more confused. He was in a cave, a high one from the little scrap of sky he could see through the distant opening. A thin, cold breeze blew across him, carrying the smell of snow. He sniffed again, searching for woodsmoke or pine, but he caught nothing but wet stone and frozen water. Wherever he was, he was far away from Izo's camp, far away from anywhere, and that, much more than the ropes, posed a problem.

Eli started wiggling again, turning until his back was to the wall. First rule of thievery, always know what's around you. The cave was quite small, barely six feet across and twice as deep, with a ceiling low enough to make a child claustrophobic. Still, despite the cave's tiny dimensions, it took three look-overs for Eli to realize he wasn't alone.

Sted's enormous shape took up the entire back of the cave, his dull clothes blending perfectly into the dark stone. He was hunched over with his eyes closed, his right arm resting on his knees and his head touching the cave's ceiling even sitting down. His other arm he held cradled against his chest, the black claws twitching. Even in the dark, what little Eli could see of the claw was enough to make him ill. It was simply too alien, too inhuman, the way the black, hard shell met Sted's flesh in that sickening melding at the shoulder...

Eli shuddered and looked away before he really was sick. But as he lay there waiting for his stomach to calm down, he realized something else. With the exception of the place where his hideous arm connected to his body, Sted had been uninjured. Frowning, Eli snuck another glance, just to be sure. It was true. Sted's clothes were blackened in places, ripped in others, but his flesh was whole and uninjured.

Eli bit his lip. Sted was a demonseed, that much was obvious, but even Nico didn't heal instantly. This left two possibilities: Either he'd been out longer than he thought, or Miranda had gone down very quickly. Neither was a possibility he liked to consider.

Sted's eyes were closed, but Eli was sure he wasn't

asleep. Never one to lie in silence, Eli took the opportunity to speak first.

"Congratulations!" he said, lifting his head to grin at Sted. "You've caught—"

"Shut up." Sted's voice was flat and annoyed. He opened his eyes a fraction, revealing the eerie, unnatural glow beneath the heavy lids. "Prisoners who talk too much end up dead."

"That would be some very expensive silence," Eli tsked. "I'm worth much more alive."

"You think I care about money?"

Eli considered. "No. No, I don't think you do."

Sted nodded and lapsed back into silence. After about three minutes, Eli couldn't bear it any longer.

"At the risk of the aforementioned premature death," Eli said in his most charming voice, "would you mind if I ask why you took me from the Spiritualist? Doesn't seem your style, quite frankly."

Sted said nothing. As the minutes stretched on, Eli resigned himself to curiosity. But then, suddenly, Sted answered.

"I took you to force Izo's hand," he said. "That idiot was going to give Josef Liechten to the Council, but now that I have you, all that's changed. Izo will have no choice but to give me my fight."

"Hold on," Eli said, wiggling along the stone floor until he could look at Sted straight on. "You stole me, Eli Monpress, greatest thief in the world, a ninety-eight-thousand gold-standard bounty, just so you could fight Josef?" If his hands hadn't been tied, he would have thrown them up in the air. "*Powers*, man, he'd fight you for free. Just take me back. I'm sure he'll oblige."

"I will," Sted said. "In three days."

Eli frowned. "What happens in three days?"

"I'm letting him heal," Sted said simply. "My victory over the Heart of War and its wielder is not something I want polluted by a handicap. I will fight Leichten when he's at full strength or not at all. You're here to ensure I am not rushed or dictated by the petty ego of that bandit thug. Once I've defeated Josef, I'll set you free."

"Set me free?" Eli said. "Just like that?"

"Or kill you," Sted said, tilting his head. "Depends on how generous I'm feeling and how much trouble you make for me. Whatever happens, you won't be going back to Izo. That bastard deserves nothing, trading away what he'd already promised."

"Well," Eli said, "he *is* a bandit."

Sted gave him a murderous look, and Eli snapped his jaw shut.

When he was sure the thief would stay silent, Sted continued. "In three days, we head back down the mountain. Until then, you're going to sit there and not talk. And don't even think about escaping. I don't sleep much these days, and your dead carcass will still buy me my fight. Am I being clear?"

"Decidedly," Eli said. "But can I ask you one last question?"

Sted frowned. "You can ask."

"You used to be League, or that's what Josef told me after your fight," Eli said. "So why did you kill Nivel? When Pele said you took Nivel's seed, I assumed it was some internal League struggle. But now it's clear that you took Nivel's seed for yourself, even though Josef said you were spirit deaf. So, why? How did it happen? Why did you switch?"

"To fight Josef Liechten," Sted said simply. "I made a deal. A bad one on both sides, as it turned out, but I won't give up until Josef Liechten is lying dead at my feet. He's the only man who ever truly bested me, and if I'm going to die, I'll die undefeated."

Eli's eyebrows shot up. "But—"

He swallowed his words at Sted's glare. Clearly, that was all the answer he'd be getting. Turning away from Sted's uncomfortable, glowing gaze, Eli rolled back toward the wall. He wiggled a bit, trying to find the most comfortable angle, but it was hopeless. Finally, he gave up and flopped on his back, staring up at the low stone ceiling.

It was going to be a very long three days.

Gin crashed through the forest, panting as he jumped over fallen logs and scrambled up slopes slick with fallen leaves. Miranda hunched low on his back, doing her best to avoid looking at the lightening sky or thinking about the fact that they'd already passed that rock formation twice before. But even as she tried to keep hope alive, the ghosthound padded to a stop at the edge of a creek.

"It's no good," he panted. "They're gone. Sted was too fast. I don't even know if we're in the right part of the mountains anymore."

"Just a little farther," Miranda said, clenching her hands in his fur. "We just need a hint of his scent."

"He's gone." Gin snapped the words, then shook his head and lowered his tongue to the swift water, drinking deeply. "I lost him hours ago," he said when he was finished. "We need a different plan."

"Like what?" Miranda said, gritting her teeth. "Go back to the bandits? Wait?"

"We're not going to find him by wandering around," Gin snarled.

His tone stopped her cold, and Miranda leaned back. He'd been running all night; of course he was tired. They were both tired, but the idea of going back to that camp empty-handed, of letting Eli slip through her hands *again*...

She leaned forward, resting her forehead against Gin's neck. She couldn't do it. She couldn't lose again, not like this. But what else was there to do? Saying he couldn't find Eli wasn't something Gin would admit unless he was truly out of options. The forest was huge, and they didn't even know if Sted had continued north or changed direction entirely. No, finding him in the woods would require more luck than she had. She needed to reconsider her options.

Miranda took a deep breath and forced herself to think clearly. There were only two reasons Sted would have taken Eli: the bounty or as a bargaining chip against Izo. That meant he would eventually be headed either toward Zarin or back to Izo's camp. She discarded the bounty idea immediately. If Sted was going to Zarin, then he was already so far ahead of her there was little point in giving chase, and Eli would end up in custody whether she caught him or not. Also, whatever Sted was, he certainly didn't seem like the type to walk into Lord Whitefall's office and ask for a voucher. And there was that display last night. No, Sted was after Izo. She was sure of it, and that meant he'd be heading back to the camp.

Miranda grimaced. As much as the idea of going back to Sparrow empty-handed grated, she had to admit it was the best choice. Also, Josef and Nico were still at the camp. If Eli escaped from Sted, that's where he'd go, and if Sted wanted something from Izo, that's where he'd take the thief.

"All right, mutt," she muttered into Gin's fur. "Take us back to Izo's."

But the ghosthound didn't answer. He was standing still as a statue below her, staring down the stream bank.

Miranda looked around. "What?"

"We're being watched," Gin growled low in his throat, ears going flat against his head.

Miranda pressed herself against his back, mentally nudging her rings awake. She winced when she was forced to skip over Kirik's smoldering ember, but she couldn't think about that now. "Is it Sted?" she whispered, slightly hopeful.

"No." Gin was growling full tilt now. "It's a wizard."

Miranda was about to ask how he could be so sure when a man appeared on the bank a dozen feet downstream. Miranda didn't see where he had come from—he seemed to just appear from the woods—but once she saw him, she could look at nothing else. There, walking toward her, was a large man with a bear's head. She thought it was a mask until she saw the eyes staring at her, intelligent and dark above the sharp-toothed muzzle. Miranda swallowed and began to call her spirits. But even as she reached for the threads of power that tied her to her rings, the bear-headed man stopped and put up his hands.

"I mean no harm, Spiritualist." The voice that came from the bear's mouth was deep and gruff, but undeniably human. "You seem to be lost and in need of some assistance."

"We need no assistance," Miranda said carefully.

"No?" The bear face looked skeptical. "Do you always keep your fire spirit on the brink of flickering out, then?"

Miranda paled, and the bear-headed man smiled. "I thought not," he said. "Miranda Lyonette would never put her spirits in such danger unless things were very grave."

"How do you know my name?"

The bear-headed man laughed, a deep, rumbling sound. "There aren't many Spiritualists who ride ghost-hounds and carry great seas inside their bodies. For those of us who study spirits, you're quite the oddity. I would know, being somewhat of an oddity myself." He touched his muzzle with his hand. "Come," he said, turning. "Let's get your fire stoked before it flickers out. I can hardly bear to look at it."

Gin did not budge an inch, and Miranda made no move to force him. "Who are you?"

The bear-headed man kept walking down the bank. "I'm Heinricht Slorn. Now come."

For a long moment, Gin and Miranda could only stare at his retreating back. Then Miranda looked down at Kirik's dark ruby, and they followed.

The bear-headed man led them up the creek bank to a row of tall bushes, the deep green, waxy-leafed kind that thrive on steep mountain slopes. He pushed the branches gently aside and turned to motion Miranda forward like a well-mannered host inviting guests into his estate. Miranda dismounted stiffly and ducked under the branches. Gin eyed the tiny space with scorn and lay down on the bank. Slorn waited a moment more, and then he turned and followed Miranda into the canopy, letting the branches fall quietly behind him.

Miranda had not gone more than a few steps into the

bushes before she stopped, staring in amazement. Parked at the heart of the little grove was a large wagon. No, that wasn't right. Wagons had wheels. This was shaped like a wooden traveler's wagon, complete with a rounded wooden roof, shuttered windows, a chimney pipe, and a set of folding steps going up to a painted door. But down at the bottom, in the spots where the wheels should have been, were six long, splayed legs. Each leg stuck out from the wagon's body at a right angle and cornered sharply at a knobby joint before reaching the ground on a wide, flat foot with five splayed toes, like a lizard's. Each leg appeared to be newly carved from green wood, bright yellow-white and smelling of sawdust, and they sprang from the cart as though they had grown there. There were no joints, no nails, just the fresh wood of the legs lying flush against the older, stained wood of the wagon's body, molded together as though they'd always been that way. She was still trying to make sense of it when she saw something even stranger. The legs shuffled, adjusting their weight, each one flexing and adjusting its splayed foot so that the cart sat slightly closer to the ground as Slorn came up and flipped down the little stair.

"There," he said, smiling as the red-painted door opened for him of its own accord. "Come in and we'll have a look at your ring."

"How did you do that?" Miranda said, and then bit her tongue. She hadn't meant to blurt it out like a child gawking at a street magician's trick, but Slorn didn't bat an eye.

"I'm a Shaper," he said as he stepped inside, as though that explained everything.

Well, Miranda thought, in a way it did. Even Master

Banage wasn't exactly sure how the Shapers did what they did. One thing was certain, though, the bear-headed man wasn't abusing his spirits. She could practically hear the wood beaming as she gawked at it, the legs shifting to show the cart at its best. That pride made her feel more comfortable than any assurance Slorn could have given, and she hurried up the folding stair after him.

The covered wagon was much more spacious than she would have guessed from the outside. One wall was lined with hinged bins, all neatly latched and labeled. The other was taken up by a folding cot, now stowed away, and a little table that bolted to the floor. Slorn was already sitting on one of the folding seats, his large hands fussing with the small iron stove just large enough to heat a kettle that was built into the wall just above the table.

Slorn unlatched the cold grate and placed a few sticks of wood into the stove's tiny iron belly. "There," he said, leaning back. "Put your ring in."

"Are you sure?" Miranda said, unfolding the chair opposite him and sitting down. "Kirik's a bonfire spirit. I don't want to risk your wagon."

Slorn's bear eyes widened, and he looked at the stove. "What do you think?"

The stove made a scornful sound. "I've never met a fire I couldn't contain," it said, opening its grate wider. "Give him to me."

Miranda blinked in surprise, first that the grate was awake, and second that it was so confident. She slipped Kirik's ring from her finger and placed it with the wood in the stove's belly. The second her hand was clear, the stove snapped shut and a blast of hot air hit her face as the fire crackled to life. A surge of relief radiated up Kirik's connection, and Miranda felt like sobbing with relief herself.

Across the table, Slorn's eyes glowed with pleasure. "My stove is very good with fires," he said. "An hour and your Kirik should be good as new." He reached overhead, taking a shiny copper kettle from a hook on the ceiling. "It would be a shame to waste the heat; may I offer you some tea?"

"Yes, please," Miranda said, still shaking.

Slorn got up and walked over to the water barrel, holding the kettle crooked as the water arced up the spout of its own accord. Impressed as she would have been, Miranda saw none of it. Her eyes were locked on the roaring blaze behind the stove's grate as a great lump of guilt rose up in her throat. She hadn't realized how close she'd come to losing Kirik. Her thoughts went to Gin outside; Gin, who'd run all night for her. Her mind flashed back to the night before, to Gin retreating, blood dripping from his muzzle as he glared at Sted. Was he really all right, or had she been too blind in her pursuit to see? What had she been thinking, fighting a demonseed? She should have tossed Monpress at his head rather than risk her spirits. Miranda clenched her fists. She was becoming as obsessed with him as everyone else seemed to be. What must Slorn think of her, a Spiritualist who nearly killed her fire for a thief? What would Master Banage say?

She jumped as Slorn placed two steaming mugs on the table and looked up to find him staring at her, his dark eyes almost human in the glow from the stove.

"Don't be too hard on yourself," he said. "It's a strong spirit's deepest nature to fight a demon and save the weaker ones from the panic. That you were able to pull the fire back before it was devoured is a sign of the deep bond of trust between you."

Miranda gaped at him. "How did you know?"

"What?" Slorn said. "About the demonseed? What else could do that to a spirit? Also, I've been keeping an eye on Izo's camp for some time." His voice deepened into a growl. "There's a man there I have unfinished business with."

Miranda swallowed, suddenly very aware of Slorn's massive jaw full of sharp, yellow teeth. "Is that why you wrote to Sara for help?"

"At the simplest level, yes," Slorn said, his voice suddenly calm and smooth again. "But Sara and I have been professional colleagues long enough that I knew a simple letter wouldn't be enough to get her to act, at least not in the immediate, large-scale way I needed her to. That's why I made sure my daughter knew how to find Monpress, and that Sara would find out."

"Wait," Miranda said. "You mean that wasn't a leak?"

"Of course not," Slorn said. "At this point, I can afford to leave nothing to chance. I tracked Sted alone as long as I could, but as soon as it became clear he was entering Izo's service, I knew I needed a larger pressure than I could provide myself. I needed the Council, which meant I needed Sara, and if anyone can get that woman to play her cards, it's Eli Monpress."

"Hold on. You're after *Sted*?" Miranda knew she was just repeating things now, but she really could not believe what she was hearing. "*Why?* Demonseeds are League business. Why waste time fussing around with Sara and Eli? Five League members could clear out Izo's entire camp in an hour. You seem to have more connections than

Lord Whitefall himself, so I can't believe you don't have a way to contact the League."

Slorn leaned back, his inhuman face suddenly distant, and Miranda snapped her mouth shut. She'd said too much. She gripped the handle of her mug, waiting for a rebuke, but when the bear-headed man spoke, his voice was gruff and low.

"Can I tell you a story?"

Confused, Miranda nodded.

Slorn took a deep breath. "Ten years ago, my wife, Nivel, disappeared. We were both Shapers then, wizards of the Shaper Mountain. Up there, in the snow, we are always in the shadow of the Dead Mountain. When a wizard disappears, like Nivel did, it usually means only one thing. They were taken by the mountain."

Slorn stopped here, and Miranda watched nervously, unsure if she should offer comfort or simply wait for him to continue. Fortunately, Slorn made the choice for her.

"Because of this, to protect ourselves and our mountain, the Shapers have a law. Any wizard who vanishes is considered dead. Should they be seen again alive, they are to be given to the League as a demonseed. When Nivel vanished, I was prepared to mourn her. But then, suddenly, she came back."

Slorn looked up, dark eyes flashing. "Do you know what it is like, Spiritualist? To see the dead walk again? I expected a monster, but she was the same Nivel I married, my best friend, the mother of my daughter."

"She wasn't taken by the mountain?" Miranda said.

Slorn shook his head. "No," he said darkly. "You misunderstand me. She was what we feared, she was a demonseed. But what I had never been told, what I never prepared for, was that the person would remain unchanged. Nivel had always been strong, always forceful and determined. None of that had changed. She knew what had happened to her. She could feel the seed, but she did not want to give up, and I could not let them take her. So we did the only thing we could do: we ran. We fled the Shapers with our child, and for the last ten years we dedicated our lives to studying demonseeds, how to hide them, how to control them, and, ultimately, how to defeat them. *Ten years*, Spiritualist. Most seeds survive for one if they're quiet, but through constant deals with the League, constant concessions, we held on. And we were making progress, learning so much. But then, a month ago, all of that was ruined. Sted, then just a defeated swordsman, snuck into the valley where my wife was hidden. She was deep in the seed's trance and she could not fight back. He killed her and took her seed into his own body, becoming what before this I would have named impossible, a nonwizard demonseed." Slorn stood up, walking over to gaze out the wagon's tiny window. "I have been tracking him ever since."

"I see," Miranda said softly as his words faded. "You want revenge for your wife. But still, surely the League could help. That's their job, isn't it?"

Slorn began to chuckle, the sound horrible and out of place in his menacing mouth. "Again," he said, turning to look at her, "you misunderstand me. If it was only revenge I desired, I could have had that long ago. I could have called the Lord of Storms down that very day, but it's more complicated than that. Do you know what the League does with demonseeds?"

Miranda shook her head.

"First," Slorn said, "the host body is killed. Demon-possessed spirits are fearsome combatants, which is why all League members must be excellent fighters, but after the fight is when the League's true function becomes clear. When the host body has been defeated, the League member splits it open. Carves it straight down the middle, like a hunter gutting a deer, and takes the seed. Depending on how long the seed was active and how many spirits it ate, the seed can be anywhere from one inch to a foot in length.

"Demonseeds are the product of a seed being placed in a host," Slorn continued. "The host can be killed, but the seeds themselves are not from our sphere and cannot be destroyed by any known method. The best the League can do is lock them away. They have a great vault in their headquarters, a storehouse of every seed they've ever purged. Once a seed enters their possession, it never comes out again."

Slorn looked her straight in the eyes. "Nivel and I both knew it would end eventually," he said. "Maybe not as it did, but still, no one can fight forever. However, the final stage of our research requires the seed itself. There is so much more it can tell us, so many questions to answer. If I let the League get ahold of Sted, then the seed inside him, Nivel's seed, disappears forever into their vault, and ten years of the work my wife suffered for with it. That, Spiritualist, is why I needed Sara, why I needed you and Monpress and this whole farce. I'm fairly certain Sted, being spirit deaf, will never muster enough power to awaken the seed by himself. Already, not being a wizard, he can't generate the kind of fear usually associated with demonseeds, so the League is searching blindly. That gives me a good chance, especially now that he's stolen Monpress."

Miranda started. "How did you know about that?"

Slorn gave her a look. "I told you, I've been watching everything. How else do you think I found you out here?"

Miranda knew she looked petulant, but she couldn't help it. Lately, it seemed she was always the last to know anything.

"Don't worry about your thief," Slorn said, resting his elbows on the table. "Sted is a blunt man who lives only to beat the wielder of the Heart. He cares nothing for Eli's bounty or his true power. He only took the thief to get a hand up on Izo. Now that the prize everybody's after is safely in his possession, Sted is free to demand what he really wants, a rematch with Josef Liechten."

"How can you sound so pleased about it?" Miranda said. "I know Josef has the Heart, but this is a demon-seed." Her mind flitted back to the ruined throne room in Mellinor, to Nico crouching in the dark, her eyes glowing like lanterns while the world screamed around her, and she shivered. If that was a controlled demonseed in a little girl's body, she'd hate to see what a brute like Sted could become.

"I wouldn't worry overmuch about Liechten," Slorn said. "Sted may be a demonseed, but he's a mediocre swordsman. The Heart, on the other hand, doesn't let just anyone swing it around."

Miranda frowned, sipping her tea. She was still turning things over in her mind when a metallic clank nearly startled her out of her seat. Across the table, the oven popped open, spilling out a geyser of blisteringly hot air.

"Ah," Slorn said. "Good work."

Without tongs or mitts, he reached his hand into the roaring stove. Miranda was about to shout a warning when she saw the fire peeling back for him. When he took his hand out again, Kirik's ring was sitting in his open palm, the ruby glowing like a red lamp. Miranda took the ring from his hand. The gold was warm to the touch, but nowhere near as hot as it should have been. Inside, she could feel Kirik sleeping, happy and content and fully himself with no sign of his previous injury.

"I don't know how to thank you," she said, sliding the ring lovingly onto her thumb.

"No need," Slorn said. "I would be a poor wizard indeed if I saw a spirit like that and did nothing."

Miranda sat turning her ring on her finger as Slorn cleaned the embers from the stove and restowed the kettle on its hook. By the time he'd finished tidying up, she'd come to a decision.

"Slorn," she said, sitting up. "Take me with you."

The bear-headed man turned to look at her, curious, and Miranda continued. "I owe Sted a thing or two myself. Let me help you take him down. If I go back to Izo's now, I won't be able to do anything except go along with everyone else's plans. You seem to know everything, but you may not know that Sparrow has orders from Sara to make sure you come back to Zarin with us, whether you want to or not. Take me with you and I'll keep him back long enough for you to get out with the seed."

"A generous offer," Slorn said, scratching his muzzle. "And in return, I suppose, I look the other way while you capture Monpress."

Miranda winced. She wasn't used to people seeing straight through her like this. "I know he's your friend," she started. "But—"

"You misunderstand me again," Slorn said. "I'll gladly

take your help. Monpress reaps what he sows, but he knew that when he decided to become a thief. Besides, I imagine he rather likes having someone as dedicated as yourself on his trail. He would be cross with me if I tried to protect him."

Miranda chuckled. Slorn's words made sense in the twisted, Eli-logic sort of way.

"Well," Slorn said, "if we're going to be working together, the first thing I'll ask is that you get some sleep. You've been riding all night, and I can't have that sort of a liability on my hands. I'm going outside to check up on a few things. You can use my bunk in the meanwhile."

Miranda tried to protest, but Slorn was pulling the folding bed down, its crisp, white sheets already tucked into place. He grabbed a pillow and a blanket from a cabinet beside the door and tossed them on the bed.

"Sleep well," he said. "We'll discuss strategy in a few hours when your mind is awake."

He gave her a polite nod and vanished down the stairs, the red-painted door falling quietly shut behind him. Miranda stood there a minute more before she gave in, flopping down with a loud sigh on the surprisingly soft trundle bed. She had barely kicked her boots off before she was asleep, her head pillowed on the pile of blankets Slorn had left for her.

Slorn heard the growling before he'd reached the wagon's bottom step. He turned to see the Spiritualist's ghost-hound lying at the entrance to the dense bushes, his enormous orange eyes watching Slorn in a way that was far too predatory for comfort.

Slorn stared right back. "She's asleep."

"I can tell that," the ghosthound said. "I presume we're throwing our lot in with you, then?"

"For the time being," Slorn said, nodding. "Is there something you'd like to add?"

"If that's what Miranda says, then that's what we're doing," the ghosthound said with a yawn. "I just wanted to make sure I didn't need to rip your throat out before going to sleep."

Slorn heard the wagon hiss, and he put his hand on the wood, sending out a calming tendril of his spirit. The hound yawned again, showing an impressive line of teeth, and then, almost in the same instant, he was asleep, curled in a ball with his long nose buried in his tail.

Slorn waited until he was sure the ghosthound wasn't bluffing before letting out a long, low sigh. He had no doubt the dog would have killed him if he'd threatened the girl, no questions asked. Slorn shook his head, marveling. Shapers could blend spirits together in ways no other wizard could, but he'd never seen anyone who could match a good Spiritualist for spirit loyalty.

He whispered to the bushes, and they stretched out their branches to cover the dog's sleeping form. It would be awhile before Sted moved again. There was plenty of time to let his guests sleep a bit before moving on. Meanwhile, he would gather more information.

Slorn turned and walked out of his hidden camp, climbing farther up the slope until he reached the crest. They were high up, higher than his own Turning Wood, and the air was cold and swift. Squinting, Slorn looked up and north, following the line of the cliffs until he spotted his wind riding high and bright over the sleeping mountain spirits. He raised his hands, sending a flash toward the wind. It danced a moment longer and then dropped down, spiraling through the trees until it ruffled the fur on his face, making his eyes water.

"The swordsman has agreed to the fight," it whispered. "It was very hard to make out, I hope you know. The spirit deaf are so difficult to focus on."

"I appreciate your efforts," Slorn said. "What about Sted?"

The wind shivered when he said the name. "In the mountains, I think. He's even harder to follow than the others. I can't make out exactly what he is, but I don't like him at all."

Slorn wisely stayed silent on that. "Thank you very much for your help. I won't forget it."

"Don't tell *me* you're happy. Tell the West Wind," the spirit said. "Why else do you think I'm doing this?"

"Of course." Slorn nodded. Even after all these years, spirit politics baffled him, especially winds. "Would you mind going back to the camp?"

"If you like," the wind sighed. "Staying in one place too long makes me ache."

"It won't be for long," Slorn said. "I'll join you there this evening. And I'll be sure to inform the West Wind of the great pains you've taken to help us."

This seemed to please the wind immensely, and it took off with a great whoosh, shaking the thin trees as it flew skyward and turned south, back toward Izo's camp. Slorn watched it go, staring up at the blue dome of the sky until his wind was long gone and replaced by other winds, all moving like great currents through the sky.

He was about to turn back when a flash of movement caught his eye.

As always, something inside him, inside the deep animalistic instincts he'd inherited when he let the bear into his soul, told him to look away, but the stronger part, the curious, purely human side of him, tilted his head upward. There, above the snowy mountaintops, above the winds, something was moving on the dome of the sky itself. It was a subtle motion, one he couldn't have seen at all if he hadn't been looking for it. He'd first noticed it years ago by chance. Now, against his better judgment, he looked whenever he caught a glimpse. High overhead, pressing against the arc of the sky itself like a weight pressed on a taut cloth, was the faint outline of a long, bony, clawed hand. As he watched, the hand scraped slowly downward, running long, sharp grooves in the sky that vanished the moment it passed, only to be replaced by another hand, sometimes smaller, sometimes larger, pressing down again.

Fear like no fear he'd ever felt before began to well up inside him, and a great need stronger than any instinct screamed at him to look away. Even so, he locked his eyes a moment longer, watching the hands scrape across the dome of the sky.

"Slorn?"

He jumped at the voice, whirling around to see the wind waiting, circling him in worried little circles.

"Yes," he said, struggling to keep his voice normal.

"I just came back to let you know the West Wind told me to tell you to be kind to the Spiritualist girl. Who knows why. Spiritualists are busybodies, but Illir's word is law."

"I'll look after her, don't worry," Slorn said, managing a weak smile.

The wind spun again. "Slorn." Its voice was not nearly so certain this time. "What were you looking at?"

"Nothing," Slorn lied. "Nothing at all."

The wind made a frightened wheezing sound. "It's not good to stare at the sky."

"It's nothing," Slorn said again. "Off with you."

The wind held on a moment longer and then whipped away, flying hard and fast between the trees. Slorn waited until it was completely gone before wiping the cold sweat from where the fur met his neck. When his breathing was steady again, he walked down the slope back toward the bushes. He did not look at the sky again.

CHAPTER
17

When the sun rose on the third day, Josef Liechten woke up, took the Heart of War from his chest, and stomped off to his fight. Nico trailed him like a shadow, pulling Tesset behind her so that they made a strange sort of line pushing their way across Izo's camp. The city was packed. Bandits wearing the Bandit King's red and black had come from all across the mountains, abandoning their small camps and outposts for a day of glory.

"What are all these idiots doing here?" Josef growled, glaring as a gaggle of young men, some barely into their teens, made themselves comfortable on a rooftop with a good view of the arena. "This is a duel, not a circus."

"For the men up here, the two are the same," Tesset said. "Sted may have forced Izo to play host, but you're kidding yourself if you think Izo isn't going to get something out of it. The Council's been cracking down and troop morale is low. How better to boost it than a spectacular fight to the death? It's a clever use of a bad situation, but Izo's famous for turning things to his favor. He didn't become king of the bandits for his nobility, you know."

Josef shook his head in disgust. "I just hope he remembered his end of our deal."

"He did," Nico said softly. "They've been hammering for days."

Josef didn't need to ask what she meant by that, for a moment later the arena itself came into view. Lying on the hard-packed sand was a jagged heap of newly forged swords. Some blades were almost black with imperfections, others were actually crooked, lying sideways across the blades beneath them. Still, hundreds of swords in all. Josef grinned and clapped his hands together.

"Perfect."

Izo was standing at the arena's edge with his retinue and the foppish man from the Council, whose finery was looking a little wilted today. They both turned as Josef approached, and Izo brightened visibly, grinning so wide Josef could count his gold crowns.

"The sleeper wakes," he said, laughing. The Bandit King was dressed in silks like a lord and obviously in a fine mood as he stretched out his hand toward the pile of swords. "See, it is all here, as promised. You asked for a spectacle and I delivered."

"The crowd is too much," Josef said. "But Sted will probably like it, so let them stay. Neither of us will be holding back, though, so I can't vouch for your men's safety."

"What bandit looks for safety?" Izo scoffed.

Josef shrugged and stared down at the circular pit of the arena, measuring the wood-braced walls with his eyes. "In that case, get some of your men started putting the swords on the walls. The blades are no good to me piled like that. I need every one of them on a hook, hilt up. I'm guessing that's your seat?" Josef nodded toward the short tower at the edge of the arena topped with a crimson-covered box that held benches, a throne, and a balcony.

"Who else's?" Izo said.

Josef ignored his boastful grin. "I'll need a pillar about the same height directly across from it. There." He pointed. "Just a simple post will do, so long as it's at least a foot thick."

"Easily done," Izo said. "But why?"

"I need a safe place for this." Josef reached over his shoulder and grabbed the Heart's hilt. In one motion, he brought the enormous black blade over his shoulder and plunged it into the ground. The blade sank a foot into the hard dirt before it stopped.

Izo cocked an eyebrow. "As you like, swordsman. But better make it two feet."

He snapped his fingers, and his men ran forward to get their orders. Moments later a small army swarmed into the pit, moving swords and getting the ground ready for the post Josef had requested. While they worked, Josef sat down on the arena's edge, staring at the sandy circle until the men were shadows and all he could see was the field of battle. Behind him, he could feel the Heart's power waiting, but he kept himself apart. As he'd slept, the Heart had been with him, fighting the fight against the Lord of Storms over and over again. Through it all, the sword never spoke, but the underlying message behind the endless fight was as strong and solid as bedrock. In their fight with Sted, Josef and the Heart had taken the first real step toward becoming a swordsman. They had achieved the

unspoken understanding between sword and man. But
that wasn't enough, not for a fight like the Lord of Storms.
To beat a man like that—no, not a man—to beat a force
of nature like the Lord of Storms would take the greatest
swordsman in the world wielding the greatest awakened
sword. He had one part of the equation. Now it was time
to work on the other. He crunched his knuckles together.
Sted may have demanded this fight, but Josef was going
to use it to his fullest advantage.

He heard a soft rustle and turned to see Nico sitting
down beside him, the rope taut across her wrists. Tesset
stood a good five feet away, talking urgently with the foppish man. It was the farthest Josef had seen him stray.

"They're talking about Miranda," Nico said. "She
chased off after Eli and hasn't come back yet."

"Then we know the thief isn't caught," Josef said. "The
Spiritualist girl is a better soldier than most wizards. If
she had caught him, she'd have brought him back to the
chain of command, and for now that seems to be the peacock man."

"Sparrow?" Nico said, wrinkling her nose. "I don't
think she likes him."

"Like has nothing to do with duty," Josef said. "I just
hope Sted doesn't do something stupid. He's never been
someone you could count on for sense."

Nico stayed silent at that, and Josef looked over, taking
note of the haunted look in her eyes, which now seemed
permanently too bright for whatever light they were in.

"I'll beat Sted," he said.

"I know you will," Nico answered. "That's not it." She
paused for a moment, sinking deeper into the dark folds
of her coat. "Sted's a demonseed now. I don't know for

sure how, but if he killed Nivel, then I can guess. He's not a wizard, but he has powers like I used to have."

"I know," Josef said. "I fought him a little back at the hut. He's got speed, shadow jumping, incredible strength, but I've sparred with you, remember? I know what seeds are capable of, and Sted's on a different plain entirely, a lower one. He may be more dangerous now than he was in Gaol, thanks to that arm of his, but it's a brittle kind of strength. He made a bad bargain when he left the League."

Nico pulled herself in tighter, and Josef looked over to see she was clutching her arm under her coat. "Don't underestimate how dangerous he is, Josef," she said quietly.

"I don't," Josef answered. "But I also refuse to underestimate my own abilities. Even the crooked metal pokers down there will strike true if the swordsman wills them to. I know I will beat Sted, Nico. My only worry about this whole business is what happens when I do." He heaved a frustrated sigh. "That part of things was always Eli's job. I'm just here to fight."

Nico looked worried. "I don't think he has a plan this time."

"Don't be so sure," Josef said, leaning back. "Eli's sleeves have more tricks up them than mine have knives. Well"—he shook his empty sleeve—"usually. But I've been with the thief a long time. If there's anything he can pull off, it's an escape. Trust him."

Nico lowered her eyes, leaving a lump of things unsaid in the air. Josef ran a frustrated hand through his short hair. He understood the silence even better than if she'd spoken. She trusted Eli to run, just not to take her with him. Josef gritted his teeth. He didn't blame her for thinking that. It couldn't be easy to trust the thief after the things Eli had said back in the cabin. But as he'd said, he'd known Eli for a long time, and for all his flaws, the thief had never left a companion in the lurch. It took him awhile sometimes, but he always came around. All Josef could do was put it out of his mind, focus on winning, and trust that today wouldn't be the first exception to the rule.

They sat the next half hour in silence, watching as the bandits hung every last one of the shoddy, pot-metal swords on the arena walls. It took a team of ten men to raise the giant log Izo had selected to hold the Heart. When it was fully upright, the log's top was four feet above the arena's edge, but a dozen from the sandy floor, too high for either Sted or Josef to reach. Josef kicked it a few times to make sure it was secure before plunging the Heart deep into the wood. The sword slid in easily, poking out the top of the pole like a trophy in a tournament. Satisfied, Josef returned to his seat beside Nico to wait. Tesset joined them this time, his face neutral as ever, despite his heated discussion with Sparrow.

Neither Josef nor Nico asked him any questions, and he did not volunteer any information. Sparrow, however, had stomped off and was now sitting in Izo's box, swinging a blue jewel on a leather thong and apparently talking to himself. Josef watched him awhile, and then put the fop out of his mind. Even if they were officially prisoners of the Council of Thrones, he had larger problems than Council business. Instead, he jumped down into the arena, circling and getting a feel for the sand, picking out some of the least warped swords to wear at his hips for the opening blows. Overhead, the sun climbed higher into the sky and the bandits began to settle into whatever seats they could find with a good view of the arena. Izo himself was up in his box, talking with the strange, thin man in black who seemed to be constantly at his side, while a bandit poured wine from a barrel into tall glasses. By noon, a hush had fallen over Izo's bandit city. Though no time had been agreed on, everyone was waiting, craning their heads to be the first to catch a glimpse of Berek Sted when he entered the arena.

"I don't understand it," Miranda grumbled, pressing her eye against Slorn's leather-bound glass telescope and shifting her weight so that the root she was lying on would stop digging into her ribs. "And I don't like it."

"What's to understand?" Gin yawned beside her. "It's an arena fight. You humans can be remarkably savage, considering your diet is mostly plants."

"Who lines an arena with swords?" Miranda said. "And *my* diet is mostly plants. I know people who could put your carnivorous ways to shame." She shifted her position again, switching the scope to her other eye. "What's Liechten playing at? There's no way he'll be able to reach the Heart from the arena floor if he leaves it up there."

"The man is a good hunter," Gin said, his voice deep and approving. "If it's up there, he has a reason."

"I just hope Sted doesn't take too much longer," Miranda said, getting up. "I'm going back to report to Slorn. Keep an eye on things."

Gin laid his head on his paws, patterns swirling lazily over his muzzle. "If anything exciting happens, I'll let you know."

Miranda shook her head and started creeping through

the undergrowth. They'd arrived early yesterday morning, setting up camp on the highest part of the rim of the stone canyon that shielded Izo's camp from the outside world. It had been a breathless run. The legs on Slorn's wagon weren't there for show. The thing had scampered through the forest as fast as Gin could run, and Miranda still wasn't sure who had been slowing down for whom. They'd cleared the distance from the mountains back to Izo's in record time, slowing only when they reached the ring of patrols and towers that guarded Izo's home base. There, creeping past lookouts, Slorn had led her to a place on a rocky outcropping both high and out of the way with a good view of Izo's land. From the multiple flattened weeds in the hideout, it was clear he'd camped here before, but what had really shocked Miranda was what he'd left waiting for his return.

It was so out of place up here among the scraggly bushes, she hadn't even noticed it at first. Now it was always the first thing she saw whenever she came back to camp. Behind the bushes where Slorn's wagon crouched was a large...something. It was squat and lumpy, about as tall as she was, and covered in a drab cloth. A line of empty barrels made a sort of makeshift fence around it, keeping her from getting a good look at its shape, but it moved sometimes, and she could just make out the sharp wooden ends of what looked like carved spider legs poking out from the edge of the cloth. Slorn hadn't even mentioned it when they arrived, but something in the bear's eyes kept her from asking, and she'd never found the chance to peek. She did wonder, though.

As usual, Slorn was sitting on the stairs of his wagon, working something in his hands. It was roughly a foot long, round at one end and pointed at the other, vaguely off-white and soapy looking. At first, she'd thought it was the beginning of some Shaper project, an uncarved block he'd turn into something beautiful, but she never heard its voice and its shape never seemed to change. Slorn just kept turning it over in his hands, staring at it like it was the most interesting thing in the world.

He didn't look up from the thing as she entered the clearing, creeping low even though she was well out of sight of the city. "How's it looking?" he asked in his usual gruff voice.

"No sign of Sted yet," Miranda answered, straightening up. "Josef's acting stranger than ever. He's got them lining the arena with swords, really awful-looking ones. I'm no metalworking expert, but I can see the warping from here. Plus, he just put the Heart of War up on a stand like a trophy." She stopped. "You don't think he's wagered it, do you?"

"No," Slorn said. "Josef knows better than anyone it's not his to wager. Still"—he raised a hand to his muzzle, scratching it thoughtfully—"putting down the Heart is a clever plan. I wonder who thought of it, Eli or Josef?"

Miranda gave him a funny look. "How is putting your best weapon out of reach for a hard fight clever?"

"Think, Miranda," Slorn said. "What good is the world's greatest awakened blade when you're fighting a demonseed who cares nothing for what it eats?"

Miranda opened her mouth, and then snapped it closed. "Of course, that explains the awful swords. Metal with so many impurities is bound to have tiny, sleepy spirits, providing no meal for the seed even if he eats dozens of them. He's set up the fight to protect his sword and keep Sted

from getting stronger." She nearly grinned at the simple
cleverness of it. Why hadn't she thought of that?

"Actually, Miranda," Slorn said, looking up at last.
"I've been meaning to ask you a favor. How strong is your
sea spirit?"

Miranda gave him a funny look. "Mellinor's pretty
strong. Depends on how much water is around."

"I see," Slorn said, nodding over her shoulder. "And do
you think Mellinor could fill those?"

Miranda turned, following his gaze to the line of empty
barrels around the cloth-draped shape. "Easily," she said,
turning back. "Why?"

"I'm going to need some water," Slorn said. "I'd been
meaning to talk to a local stream about it, but I've run out
of time. I was hoping your Mellinor could oblige me."

"Sure," Miranda said, grinning. "What do you need us
to do?"

Slorn opened his mouth, but he was cut off by a low
growl from the trees.

"There's Gin," Miranda whispered, dropping her voice
even though there was no chance of being overheard.

Slorn nodded and stood up, carefully placing the white
lump of whatever it was on the wagon steps before coming
over to join her. They crept back through the woods together,
sliding in beside Gin, who was nearly over the cliff edge in
his excitement. One look and Miranda could see why. The
crowd of bandits, who'd been thick as flies over the city for
the last day, were pulling away from a cloaked figure walking in from the north end of town. Even at this range, she
could see Sted clearly, a head taller than anyone else, and
behind him, stumbling through the dust on a rope leash like
a petulant puppy, was a figure she knew even better.

"Eli Monpress," she said, frowning. "He doesn't look good."

"He's fine," Gin growled. "Just making life hard for Sted, which is the most sensible thing I've seen him do."

Miranda nodded and looked over her shoulder for Slorn, but the bear-headed man was staying back, keeping to the trees, his animal eyes large and sharp as he watched Sted drag the thief into the center of town. Down in the valley, a ragged cheer went up.

Josef stood on the arena's edge, eyes squinting against the noonday sun as Sted strutted into the center of town. Bandits scrambled out of his way, whistling and shouting. Josef ignored them, focusing instead on the figure stumbling in Sted's wake. Eli looked tired and disoriented, but unharmed. That was good enough for him, and Josef turned his attention to Sted. The enormous man came to a stop at the opposite side of the arena and grinned a wide, violent grin at Josef like he was the only man in the world.

"Well, Sted," Izo's voice boomed down from his box, "you showed up. Hand over the thief, and the swordsman will fight you on whatever terms you like."

Izo's words hung in the air, but Sted didn't even seem to hear them. He stepped out onto the arena's edge before tossing Eli's rope in the dirt. The thief scampered away as Sted reached up and ripped the threadbare cloak from his shoulders. A great gasp went up from the crowd, and even Josef's breath hitched. Sted's black arm was there, same as ever, but it looked almost natural compared to his chest. The black rot no longer stopped at the shoulder, where the arm connected. It had spread down, spidering across the enormous man's chest in long, inky tendrils. The blackness poured into his scars like tainted water, eating its way across the remnants of his tattoos.

Quick as a flash, Sparrow stepped out from behind Izo's booth to grab Eli's rope, jerking the thief off his feet. He twisted the rope around his hand several times before leading the thief over to the far edge of the arena where Tesset was holding Nico. Sted didn't even seem to notice what happened to his prisoner. He stood on the arena edge, drinking in the fear and revulsion as it rolled off the crowd, grinning at Josef like a wolf that's finally cornered the running stag.

But Josef was too distracted to be intimidated. "Powers, man," he said in a low voice. "What have you done to yourself?"

Sted's smile faltered a moment before it was replaced by a sneer. "Nothing like what I'm going to do to you."

He leaped off the edge, landing on the arena's sandy floor with a thud Josef felt through his boots. Josef cast one last look at Nico and Eli before jumping down as well. Realizing they were about to get the blood they'd come for, the bandits began to cheer, but the sound was very far away. Here in the arena, Sted took up every scrap of Josef's attention, leaving none to spare for roaring crowds.

"I see you're able to stand again," Sted said, walking across the arena. "Finally found your courage, eh?"

Josef's answer was to draw the swords at his hips, swinging the warped blades in a whistling circle before settling into a fighting stance. Sted stared at him, his eager expression turning to one of disbelief.

"What is this?" he roared. "What are those, fire pokers?

Is this some kind of a *joke*?" He looked around, spotting the Heart high on its post. "I didn't call this fight so we could dance, Liechten," he growled, thrusting his clawed arm into the air, curved fingers pointing at the Heart's hilt. "Take your sword and fight me like a man!"

"Why should I?" Josef answered, looking pointedly at Sted's transformed hand. "After all, you could hardly be called a man anymore."

Sted's eyes narrowed. "I'm going to butcher you like a pig for that."

Josef raised his swords, a feral grin coming over his face. "Try it."

Sted clenched his fists with a roar, and then he was gone. Josef waited for the step from the shadows and whirled to his left, catching Sted's clawed hand in his blades.

"I'm not like your coward girl," Sted whispered as his claws began to eat through the steel of Josef's swords. "I don't hold anything back. Take the Heart and fight for real or I'll kill everyone here, starting with you."

Josef glared at him through the quickly vanishing cross of his blades. "You might have always been a monster," he said. "But you were an indifferent brawler and even less of a swordsman. I don't need the Heart to beat you."

"Have it your way," Sted hissed, and brought his demon arm down, ripping Josef's swords in two.

But Josef had dropped the swords before Sted had finished speaking. He jumped nimbly back, hands going out to grab two fresh swords from the arena wall. The crude hilts slid into his hands and he brought the new pair forward just in time. Sted charged with an enraged scream, slamming them both into the arena wall hard enough to knock Josef's breath out, but not hard enough to break his guard. For all its power, it was a sloppy hold, and Josef ducked under Sted's arms with a quick step, his swords flashing in the sun as they raked under the larger man's right shoulder.

Josef turned as soon as he finished the follow-through and was greeted by the beautiful sight of fresh, red blood running from two large gashes across Sted's ribs. Even with his ears ringing from being bashed against the arena wall, he could feel the crowd's roar through the sand. Had he been younger, stupider, he might have raised his arms in triumph, but he settled for a smile as Sted whirled around, hands going to stanch the flow of blood from his wound.

"No more iron skin, I see," Josef said, flicking the blood from his blades onto the sand. "You'll have to be better than that if you don't want me to carve you up, Sted."

He paused, waiting for a comeback, but Sted just smiled, his eyes unsettlingly bright, and removed his hand. Josef blinked. The blood was still there, slick and red against his skin, but the wounds were already gone.

"Yes." Sted chuckled as Josef's eyes widened. "Now you see. If you mean to carve me up, you'll have to hit much harder than that."

Josef started to answer, but Sted was on him before he could open his mouth, claws going for Josef's throat. Josef blocked wildly, losing half his left sword in the process. He blocked again on the broken shard, but Sted was faster than ever. He flitted through the air, feet barely touching the ground thanks to the demon-gifted speed. Josef had no time to square his defense before Sted's right fist, his human fist, slammed into Josef's side. Josef coughed and staggered, but his remaining blade held true, keeping Sted's claws away from him even as they sliced through the discolored metal of the sword. Sted roared and punched again, but this time he hit only air as Josef spun away, abandoning his sword, now skewered on Sted's claws, and lunged for the wall.

The first sword he grabbed came apart in his hands, the hilt sliding off the blade as soon as he touched it. Josef swore and grabbed the next one, spinning just in time to keep from getting pinned against the wall. The second he moved, Sted switched up. Midcharge he turned and kicked off the wall with his legs, launching himself at Josef.

It happened so quickly there was no time to dodge, no time to block, so Josef did the only thing he could. Holding the warped sword with both hands in front of him like a spear, he dug in his heels and met Sted head-on. This time it was Sted who didn't have time to defend. He slammed into Josef, sending them both crashing to the ground. Josef felt his shirt rip, followed by the skin of his shoulders as he skidded across the sand. Sted's weight bore down on him, and he could feel the man's monstrous claw tearing at the ground beside them, trying to stop the momentum and get control back, but Josef's eyes saw only his own hands gripping the now-broken hilt of his sword, the warped, discolored blade of which was now lodged deep in the bloody mess that was Sted's human shoulder.

Ten feet from where they'd started, the slide stopped, and the moment he could raise his arms again, Josef dropped the hilt, clasped his hands in a double fist, and brought them down hard on the broken blade lodged in Sted's shoulder. It worked even better than he'd planned. The sword had landed not in Sted's shoulder blade, but inside the arm socket. Josef's fists hit the sword like a hammer against a wedge, and Sted roared in pain as the blade lurched sideways, disjointing his shoulder with a sickening crack.

Using both boots, Josef kicked himself free, scrambling across the sand before Sted could grab him again. The moment his feet were under him, he was running for the wall. He grabbed two more swords from the endless line and spun to face Sted again, but the enormous man was still on the ground clutching his shoulder. Overhead, the bandits were screaming, a great roaring ocean of throats that drowned out even the pounding blood in Josef's ears. With a deep breath, Josef took a step forward, his eyes narrowing until Sted was all he could see.

It was a sickening, pathetic sight. Sted was thrashing on the ground, struggling to get his clawed arm up to his shoulder to pull out the blade while his human arm dragged on the sand beside him, useless. He finally got it, dragging the blade out with a pained roar. He tossed the broken shard away, glaring at Josef with eyes both too large and too bright.

"Don't look . . . so cocky," he panted, clutching his mangled shoulder. "Our duel isn't anywhere near over."

"Our duel never started," Josef said. "Duels are tests of strength and skill between two equal combatants. This"—he swung his sword, taking in the bloody sand, Sted's limp arm, the roaring crowd pressing in along the arena's edge—"this isn't a duel. This isn't even a fight; it's a slaughter. You're not even a swordsman anymore. You're an animal, an enraged bull wallowing in the dirt." He flipped the flimsy swords in his hands. "I'm glad I couldn't use the Heart on you now," he said. "It would be a disgrace to the blade to waste it on blood like yours."

Sted's face went scarlet, and he began to pant, squeezing his butchered arm until the flesh bulged beneath his grip. "I'll show you a fight," he spat. "You'll eat those words with your blood before the day is through."

As he spoke, a horrible sound spread through the arena. It was an unnatural cracking noise, like hollow bones snapping, underlaid with the wet, sucking sound of something being drawn in. Josef stared at Sted, horrified, as the black stain from his demon arm began to grow. It leached across his chest, sliding under his skin, pouring into the rivulets of his scars like a black, hungry tide. As it spread, the horrible sound grew louder, and Sted's shoulder began to pull together. Muscles sprouted out, bridging the gap between shoulder and arm. Bones pulled together, joints snapping into place as dark skin grew to cover the wound. It happened with blinding speed. One moment his right arm hung limp and useless; the next, Sted was pushing himself up with it, the gaping wound now no more than a patch of discolored flesh over his healthy, functional shoulder.

Sted grinned a horrid, feral grin and raised his fist to thump his chest, which was now completely covered with the black stain. "Slaughter, you said?" His voice had a strange double resonance to it that made Josef's blood run cold. "How do you intend to slaughter a man you can't even wound?"

"The same way you take apart any animal," Josef said slowly. "One limb at a time."

Rage flashed over Sted's face, and he leaped forward with a roar. Josef sidestepped the mad charge in one neat movement, bringing his swords down across Sted's open back. They struck in a clean slice, but Sted didn't even flinch. He dug his feet into the sand and spun around, his clawed arm angled to smash into Josef's face. But again, Josef was too quick. He jumped back, bringing his swords up for another swing. However, just before he struck, Josef stopped, staring at his swords in amazement. The blades were unbroken, but where the cutting edge should have been was a new curve in the exact shape of Sted's back. The edges of the metal were still hissing, as though the blades had melted on contact. For a moment Josef just stared, trying to understand what had happened, and then he heard the hated, hollow sound of Sted's laughter.

"Surprised?" Sted said. He was laughing like a jackal, showing all his teeth as he tilted his shoulders, showing Josef his back.

The moment he turned, Josef understood. Sted's back was the same as his chest, covered in the horrible blackness, including the skin where Josef's strike had landed. The wounds were still there, still open and puckered and smoking slightly, but no blood leaked from the inky flesh, and the muscles flexed beneath it with no sign of pain.

"You see now, don't you?" Sted laughed. "You're right when you say I'm not a swordsman anymore. I'm so much more than that. So much greater than you or any pathetic human could ever be."

"You say that," Josef said, tossing the ruined swords aside. "But what happens when that black stain covers all of you?"

Sted shrugged. "Who knows? You'll be dead long before that happens. After that, I don't care." He dropped into a crouch. "Come then, Josef Liechten. I'll break your little swords until you're forced to use the Heart, and then we'll have a real rematch. Then we'll have the fight I sold my soul for. Come," he said and beckoned. "Give me my victory."

Josef didn't answer. They stood for a moment, sizing each other up. Then, in the same moment, they both moved, Josef dashing for the wall as Sted dashed for him. Josef got to his objective first, grabbing a fresh sword. Sted knocked the blade aside, his claws going through the metal like paper. He struck again and Josef ducked, scrambling out of the larger man's reach. He'd dropped the ruined sword the moment Sted touched it, but he had another in his hand at once. He sprinted for distance, then turned and lobbed the sword with all his strength. The flimsy blade wobbled through the air, horribly off-balance, but it didn't have to fly far. It caught Sted in the thigh, ripping into the flesh. For a moment Sted stumbled, then he was charging again, ignoring the sword in his leg even as Josef saw the black mark spreading beneath the rips in his trousers to surround the wound.

The moment he took to watch nearly cost Josef his head. Sted's figure wavered in the air, and then the larger man was on top of him, raking his claw across Josef's chest. Swordless, Josef did the only thing he could. He kicked Sted hard on his injured thigh, bashing the closing wound with his boot heel again and again. On the second kick the sword fell out, completely dissolved by the black mark that was spreading down Sted's legs. Sted didn't even seem to notice. He clung to Josef like a mad dog, biting and clawing, dragging the swordsman down under his weight. Josef's legs began to buckle. Despite the flurry of clawing, Sted had yet to land a clean hit on him, but Josef could feel the sting from a dozen smaller wounds. Already his shirt was growing warm and damp as the blood trickled down. He had to get out, fast.

Josef dropped to the ground, going totally slack just as his old arms instructor had taught him in the earliest days of his training. It worked perfectly. He slid out of Sted's grip like an eel, touching the sand with his hands for just a moment before ducking between the larger man's legs, leaving Sted stumbling forward under his own weight. As he went down, Josef reached out, grabbed one of the discarded, ruined swords from the sand, and sliced the jagged, broken blade across the still-human skin of Sted's lower back.

Sted bellowed and fell, landing hard in the sand. This time Josef didn't wait for him to get up. He ran straight for the wall, grabbing for the next sword. But as he reached the edge of the arena, he felt a cold claw grab his ankle. He stumbled, slamming against the arena wall just as Sted's fist slammed into his back. Grunting in pain, Josef fumbled for a sword. His fingers closed around the first hilt he found, but he was too slow. The hand on his ankle jerked up, and Josef felt himself lifted into the air. Sted rose from his crouch, holding Josef upside down by his leg, and then, with a great roar, he sent the swordsman flying.

Josef sailed through the air, tucking his feet instinctively toward where he thought the ground was. The world was a blur of sky and sand and the yelling crowd. Then he crashed into the dirt, and everything went black. For a second, Josef thought he was out. Then his breath came thundering back and he retched, coughing the gritty sand out of his mouth. He forced his eyes open, blinking against the enormous black spots that danced over his vision. Across the arena he could see Sted walking forward, kicking broken swords out of his path.

With a gasp that was half sand, half air, Josef forced himself up. His hands raced over the arena floor, searching for his sword. After what felt like a year, his fingers found the warped hilt, and he brought the blade up, holding it between him and Sted as he forced himself to his feet. Overhead, he could see the bandits cheering, see Izo sitting on the edge of his balcony with a worried look on his face, but he couldn't hear anything. The blow had left him temporarily deaf. He took another breath and forced himself to focus, to tighten his vision until there was no more crowd, no more sting from the cuts on his arms, no more tickle of blood dripping down his chest. There was only him, Sted, and the swords. When he had his center again, Josef held the warped blade steady as Sted began to charge.

"Powers," Eli muttered. "Sted's going to carve him into little slices if this keeps up much longer."

"It is a difficult fight," Tesset said. He was standing at the arena's edge just like Nico and Eli, watching the fight with keen interest. "Liechten is the superior combatant, but so long as Sted keeps regenerating, he has the upper hand. Your swordsman will have to land a finishing blow soon or Sted will simply outlast him."

Nico clenched her fists, her eyes glued on Josef as the combatants went around again. Tesset was right; Josef was bleeding freely from a dozen small cuts. His movements were still lightning fast, but Nico had been watching Josef closely since the moment she woke up on the mountain, and she could see the telltale signs of exhaustion creeping in: the way his eyes narrowed even in shadow, the sloping set of his shoulders as he swung his swords, the slight hesitation when he jumped. The two men had been going full tilt for almost twenty minutes at this point, and while Sted seemed as ready as ever, Josef was pushing his limits.

"Let's hope they finish it soon in any case," Sparrow said, swinging Eli's leash from side to side. "Fantastically entertaining as it is to watch two grown men try to kill each other, we've got a schedule to keep. What do you think you're doing?"

This last bit was a shout as Eli suddenly dropped to his knees and reached down into the arena.

"Helping," Eli said, grabbing the shoddy sword on the wall below him. "He'll lose unless he can get a blade that will actually be able to finish Sted, and no one benefits if Josef loses."

"Put that down!" Sparrow shouted, jerking Eli's leash. But the rope unraveled in his hands, slipping off Eli's neck with a snicker.

Eli looked over his shoulder and gave Sparrow a wide grin. "Don't ever forget who you're dealing with, bird boy. Next time, you should listen to Miranda."

"Tesset!" Sparrow shouted. "Grab him!"

"No point," Tesset said. "He'll just get out again. Besides, if he was going to run, he wouldn't have slipped the rope here where he's cornered."

"Excellent observation," Eli said, nodding sagely as he sat down on the arena's edge.

Sparrow had no answer. He just stood there, sputtering, as Eli placed the warped sword in his lap. Nico leaned in to watch as Eli began knocking on the blade with his fist.

"You'd better wake up," he shouted. "You're missing everything!"

For a moment nothing happened. The sword, its uneven surface a mottled mix of gray and black, just lay there. Eli kept knocking, harder now, and shouted again. "You're missing the chance of a lifetime!"

The sword rattled in his hand, and then, very slowly, a tiny voice said, "What?"

"At last," Eli said. "I was beginning to worry you'd sleep right through it."

"Right through what?" the sword said, sounding more alarmed.

"The fight of your life," Eli said. "Look down in that arena. You're going to be in the hands of the greatest swordsman in the world, the Master of the Heart of War itself!"

The sword's anxiety began to wane. "The what?"

Eli rolled his eyes. "The greatest awakened blade ever created. Do you have any idea what an honor you've been selected for?"

He waited for an answer, but the sword remained silent. A second later, Nico realized it had fallen back asleep.

"Damn small spirits," Eli grumbled, whacking the blade against the arena wall. "Come on, wake up."

"What?" the sword said again.

Eli shook his head and tried a different approach.

"Are you ready?" he said, his voice brimming with excitement.

"Ready for what?"

"To fight," Eli said. "You're a sword. It's your purpose."

"I'm a sword?" The sword rolled back and forth in his hand. "Since when?"

"Doesn't matter," Eli said, grabbing the sword by the

hilt. "Now, I want you to go out there and give it your all."

"Powers!" The sword rocked itself toward the arena. "Do you see what's happening down there? Look at all those broken swords!"

"Failures," Eli said. "Listen, everything depends on this. Don't fail me. And don't go back to sleep. You stay together, no matter what it takes, do you hear me?"

"I'm not going down there!" the sword shouted.

"Forget those other swords," Eli shouted back. "They were weak. You're different. You're going to win!"

"I don't want to win!" The sword was vibrating madly in Eli's hand. "Get me out of here! I never asked to be a sword!"

"You have to fight," Nico said. "That man is a demon-seed."

Eli and the sword both turned to stare at her. Nico shrank back, unsure if she'd overstepped her boundaries, but Josef was dying down there. She had to go on.

The sword wobbled uncertainly. "He doesn't look like a demonseed to me."

"He's a special kind of seed," she said, taking the sword from Eli, careful to keep her coat draped over her hands. "One made to hide from spirits and eat them when they're not looking. That's why the League can't find him, and that's why you have to stop it."

"Me?" the sword said. "No, no, no. I don't want to be eaten."

"You'll have a strong ally," Nico said, pointing at Josef. "The greatest swordsman in the world. But he needs a sword. You have to stand up to that demon. You have to fight!"

The sword didn't answer. It sat there, trembling in her hand. Then, all at once, the trembling stopped. "Do it," the sword said, its tiny voice suddenly calm and collected.

Nico stood, shouting Josef's name as she rose. Across the arena, Josef looked up from his struggle against Sted's hold. The moment he did, Nico threw the sword at him. It flew through the air in an unnaturally straight arc, screaming vengeance and death to the demon as it went. Josef caught the blade one-handed and dragged it across Sted's human arm.

The sword cut like a razor, going straight and deep into Sted's elbow. Sted screamed and lost his hold on Josef's shoulder just long enough for the swordsman to spin away. Nico cheered, and beside her, Eli gawked, amazed.

"How did you know that would do it?"

Nico looked at him. "All spirits hate demons," she said quietly. "Normally, the fear keeps all but the strongest of them from fighting. But Sted isn't a wizard. He can't open his spirit, and so the fear isn't broadcast. Without the crippling fear, even small spirits are free to be heroes."

Eli pursed his lips. "That's actually quite brilliant."

"Thank you," Nico said, surprised, but all the good feelings from the compliment faded when she looked back at Josef, who was bracing for Sted's next charge. "It won't be enough, though. Even awake and trying its best, that sword can't become something it's not. It's still pot metal, and Sted is still a demon."

"Then we'll just have to overwhelm him," Eli said, reaching down to grab two more swords from the arena wall. "I'll wake them up; you get them going."

Nico grinned wide. "Right."

They worked quickly. Some swords didn't want to

fight, and Nico set them aside. Others, though, were ready from the moment Nico told them Sted was a demonseed. These she tossed to Josef. He caught each one, sticking it point down in the sand beside him. The first sword they'd thrown him was already whittled down to a sliver, but it was still fighting, slashing Sted like a blade five times its sharpness.

Sted ignored the swords at first, attacking Josef with single-minded purpose. But as the blades began to build up, and the blade in Josef's hands refused to break like all the others, his focus began to shift.

"What?" he shouted, swiping at Josef's head. "You think it matters that your swords aren't snapping like rotten wood anymore?" He thrust his arm into the air, proudly displaying the gash that Josef had made earlier, which was now little more than a red line on his skin. "You can't beat what you can't kill, Liechten! Not without real power. Give up! You don't have a hope without the Heart."

But Josef just smiled, dodging his swipe neatly while catching the next sword Nico threw with one hand. He swung his swords, one fresh, one eaten to nothing but still holding on, and announced in a voice loud enough for everyone to hear, "The day I need the Heart to beat an amateur like you is the day I give up swordsmanship."

Furious, Sted launched into a mad charge, and that was when Josef struck. He jumped out of the way and spun, bringing his swords down on the back of Sted's neck so hard the larger man lurched forward, landing in the sand with a grunt. As soon as he was down, Josef was on top of him, ramming sword after sword into his back. Sted bellowed in pain, but Josef only moved faster. He filled Sted up like a pincushion, using every sword Nico and Eli had woken for him. Nico could hear the blades all the way at the edge of the arena. They screamed at the demon, pressing down with all their might, turning to widen the wounds even as they pinned Sted to the sand.

Plunging the last sword down into Sted's spine, Josef stepped back. He was panting, sweat and blood running down his sides, but his face was triumphant. Sted thrashed on the ground like a speared bull in front of him, the sand turning black as his blood ran down the swords. The blades hissed as he devoured them, but this was too much even for his healing abilities. His struggles grew weaker and weaker, and then, at last, they stopped.

The arena fell silent. The crowd stood still, staring in wonder at what had just happened. Down in the arena, Josef took a careful step forward, nudging Sted's leg with his foot. The demonseed did not move, and a grin spread over Josef's face.

"It's finished," he said, turning to Nico and Eli with his hands raised in victory.

A great cheer went up. Up in the wooden stands and the rooftops, the bandit crowds were falling over one another in their excitement. Money changed hands frantically as wagers were called in, and everyone was smiling, especially Nico. She stood on the edge of the arena, grinning like mad as Josef started toward them. But then, just as she moved to jump down and congratulate him, the Master spoke.

Nothing is over until I say it is.

As the words echoed in her head, a piercing scream shot through the air, and Sted ripped himself up. Josef whirled around and stopped cold, staring in horror as Sted pushed himself to his feet. Blood dripped from his body, sliding in red rivers over skin that was now totally black. He stumbled forward, his head up, his eyes too wide and bright as lanterns. When he opened his mouth, the sound that came out was no longer human at all.

"Not yet," he said. "I will not lose."

Even as the words tumbled from his black lips, Sted began to run. He lurched across the arena, leaving a trail of blood behind him. Despite his wounds, he ran faster with every step until he reached his goal. Sted slammed into the post that held the Heart of War. The wood groaned and crumpled under the demonseed's pressure, and the Heart tumbled down, landing with a great crash on the sand below. Even before it hit, Josef was running toward his blade, but he was too late. Grinning around teeth that were suddenly too large and too sharp for any human mouth, Sted laid his hands, now both transformed into claws, on the blade, and the Heart of War began to scream.

CHAPTER
18

The Heart's scream reverberated through the air. Nico fell to her knees, slamming her hands over her ears as it hit her. Eli was down as well. She could see his lips moving as he shouted something, but she couldn't hear anything except the enormous roar of the Heart of War as Sted's claws dug into the black metal. Then, as quickly as it started, the sound stopped.

Nico looked up just in time to catch Sted's surprised expression before the Heart of War erupted in a blinding flash of light. The blade did not change. It was still the same black, dented metal, and yet it shone like noon sun on fresh snow. Even as she saw the light, Nico heard another sound, like a whip snapping, and Sted flew backward. He rocketed through the air, blown backward by the Heart's will, and landed with a bone-cracking crunch on the edge of the arena. The Heart was blown backward as well. It flipped through the air, whistling gracefully, its light fading to a warm glow as it landed perfectly in Josef's outstretched hand.

The second the Heart was in his grip, Josef rushed at Sted, who was still lying stunned at the arena's edge. He moved so fast Nico's eyes could barely keep pace, but when he struck, Sted was no longer there. Josef stopped his blow and whirled around just as Sted crawled out of the shadows on the other side of the arena. Nico held her breath. She couldn't even call the thing on the ground Sted anymore. Sted had been human, at least in form. This was something that did not belong in the world. Its skin was pure black, but deeper. Looking at the thing was like staring into a void, like the shape on the ground was a hole in the world rather than the remnants of a man. What had been human arms were now sickeningly long, thin as beanpoles, and triple jointed, bending to completely circle Sted's body. Its legs were long and powerful, tipped with claws that had sliced through what was left of Sted's boots. But worst of all was his face. His face was a black nothing, too black to look at. The only thing Nico could make out were the rows of sharp, uneven teeth, and the eyes. Sted's eyes floated in the void that was left of his face, enormous and golden yellow. Shapes moved behind them, horrible clawed shadows that made Nico's skin crawl, but she could not look away. She could only watch as the creature opened its mouth in sickening slow motion, its long, black tongue sliding hungrily across its jagged, black teeth.

The demon panic hit her like a stone wall. She felt Eli seize up beside her, and even Tesset stumbled. For a moment they sat there, paralyzed, and then the world went crazy. All around them, spirits began to panic. The ground was shrieking, the sand was shrieking, the wooden arena walls were shrieking, even the blunt swords were shrieking in terrified horror. Behind them, Nico could hear the wooden buildings weeping in fear, followed by the surprised shouts of bandits as the rooftops and balconies began to twist and pull against their supports in a desperate attempt to flee. This started a human panic, and the arena crowd dissolved into pure chaos in a matter of seconds. Bandits were pouring out of collapsing buildings, crying in terror as the ground under their feet tried to run with them. Nico could hear Izo shouting from his box, but his orders were drowned out in the panic. None of the bandits so much as looked at him as they fought and clawed their way down the packed-dirt street toward the gates.

But even as the screaming bandits jostled past her, Nico didn't look away from the arena. Despite the fear, Josef was still advancing, the Heart rock-solid and steady in his hands. The demon hissed and sank to the sand, its triple-jointed arms reaching out, claws spread, ready to strike. Josef turned the Heart to a defensive position, but the blow never came. Instead, the demon just grinned, a sickening spread of teeth, and plunged its clawed hands down into the arena sand.

The ground lurched with a horrific scream that soared above all the others. Each tiny grain of sand cried in mortal terror before snuffing out in a silence that was even more horrible as a black circle began to grow from the demon's claws.

"Josef!" Nico screamed, lurching forward until she was almost falling into the arena. "It's eating the spirits! You have to strike now!"

But she never knew if he heard her, for at that moment the ground erupted. Nico's coat seized around her shoulders, yanking her back just in time as enormous stone spikes stabbed up from the arena floor. Great swords of stone charged upward with a vengeful scream, scattering sand everywhere as the awoken, angry, deep spirits of the bedrock lurched forward to crush the demon.

The creature dodged effortlessly. It slipped through the shadows faster than even Nico had once been able to, snickering as the stone spikes crashed and broke when they tried to give chase. But Nico wasn't even watching the demon anymore. Her eyes were glued to the tiny figure flying through the air, launched upward when the ground exploded below his feet.

"*JOSEF!*"

Josef tumbled as he flew, his body going slack. Nico sucked in a breath as the Heart left his hand. He landed with a crash in a building two blocks away from the arena. The roof shattered when he hit, sending wood raining down through the hole he left behind. The Heart landed in the next building over, crashing through a shuttered window like a sledgehammer through paper.

The crash rang out over the din of the panicked spirits, and Nico shot up before she knew what she was doing. But as she started to run to Josef, she was yanked off her feet. Her breath slammed out of her as she landed on her back. She coughed and retched, staring hatefully at Tesset, who was standing over her, holding the rope that was tied to the manacle at her neck.

She bared her teeth at him like an animal. "Let me go!"

Tesset gave her a dry look and opened his mouth.

But whatever he was going to say, he never got it out, for at that moment something extraordinary happened. All around the arena, white lines began to appear. They cut down through empty space, first five, then ten, then twenty, all shining the same brilliant white. The lines hung in the air, shimmering for a split second, and then men in black coats began to step through.

They came out with swords drawn, surrounding the arena in a loose circle. The moment their feet were on the ground, half of them opened their spirits, pressing the panicking landscape into submission. The other half kept their focus on Sted, who was clinging to the edge of one of the stone spikes with his claws. The demon hissed and dug its claws into the screaming stone, ready to pounce, when another white line opened in the air not a foot from Nico's head. Nico scrambled sideways just before a man stepped through. He was dressed in the same black coat as all the others, but he had an undeniable air of competence and command. He had a thin, intelligent face and a slender, golden-hilted sword that, unlike the others, was still sheathed. Though he'd nearly stepped on her, he didn't even look at Nico. He simply walked to the edge of the arena and held out his hand, his long fingers pointing directly at Sted.

Don't move.

The words slammed down like a boulder. Nico could feel the weight of them pressing on every inch of skin that wasn't protected by her coat, but for Sted, things were much worse. The moment the man spoke, the demon howled and fell. It toppled from the stone spikes and slammed into what was left of the arena floor below, shrieking in that horrible dual-tone voice as it fought against the weight.

Nodding, the man lowered his arm and glanced over his shoulder, looking straight at Nico. She shrank into her coat, clutching her transformed arm against her chest. But the man said nothing. After several awkward seconds, Sparrow broke the silence.

"Hello, Alric," he said, dusting himself off. "Fantastic timing."

Alric gave him a blistering look. "Shut up, Sparrow. I don't have time for whatever games your mistress is playing." He reached down and grabbed Nico's rope, dragging her to her feet. Once she was up, he turned and grabbed Eli before the thief could object, nearly throwing him into Sparrow. "I have no idea how you caught Eli Monpress," he said. "Frankly, I don't care. If he's stupid enough to get himself caught, then that's none of my affair, but I want these two out of here now."

Sparrow arched an eyebrow. "But you seem to have the situation well—"

He was cut off by an enormous roar as Sted began to thrash. Several League members threw out their hands, shouting commands to the spirits as the demon fought to get to its feet.

"*Go!*" Alric shouted, his hand going for his sword as he jumped down into the arena.

"You heard the man," Sparrow said, grabbing Eli.

Eli pried Sparrow's hands off him. "Now wait just a—"

His words cut off as Sparrow grabbed the length of rope Eli had slipped out of earlier and flung it around the thief's neck. "Let's go," he said, yanking the rope so tight Eli's face began to turn red.

Tesset nodded. He reached down and scooped Nico up, tossing her over his shoulder like an oat sack.

"No!" Nico screamed, writhing against his grasp. "We can't leave Josef! He'll die without the Heart!"

But the two men kept going, Tesset carrying her, Sparrow dragging Eli, who was digging in his heels as best he could with a rope crushing his windpipe. They ran through the collapsing city. Bandits were good at running away, and the dirt streets were nearly empty now, save for a few stragglers and those unfortunate enough to have been trampled in the panic. The buildings groaned and twitched around them, collapsing as they watched, and Sparrow began to push them faster, cursing loudly as he fought to drag a still-struggling Eli behind him.

"Want me to knock him out?" Tesset said, looking over his shoulder.

"No," Sparrow grunted, yanking the rope tighter. "Sara would kill us if we injured him. What is it about this damn thief, anyway? First Sara goes crazy for him, and now the great Alric himself stoops to giving me the time of day just to tell me to get him out of town?"

Tesset shrugged and got a tighter hold on Nico, who was trying to claw his face while kicking him in the chest as hard as she could. It did no good, of course. Hitting Tesset was like trying to beat a rock into submission. But she kept trying. Dumped over his shoulder as she was, she could see the great cloud of dust rising from the arena as Sted's roar echoed through the box canyon. Nico bared her teeth and fought harder. She couldn't even see the roof Josef had crashed through anymore, but she was certain he wasn't up yet, not without the Heart. He was defenseless, unconscious, and alone. If the panicked spirits didn't kill Josef on accident, Sted would for sure. She had to get to him.

"Stop it," Tesset said, thwacking her across the back. "You're slowing us down."

"Then leave me!" she shouted.

"Calm down," he said softly. "You can't win. Don't make me hurt you."

"No!" Nico shrieked. She bent her neck back as far as it would go, staring him in the eyes. "If he dies, I can never repay him. He gave me my life as I know it. He taught me everything. If that story you told me was true, then you know what it's like to owe your rebirth to someone. I can't just let him die. *You have to let me go!*"

"Don't be stupid," Sparrow said. "That's the League back there, sweetheart. Have you forgotten what you are? I don't know why Alric spared you, but I wouldn't count on him to do it again. You go back, and they'll have two seeds to bring home to Papa Storm instead of one. You're much better off going home to Sara and seeing what she can make of you. I'm sure she'd like a demonseed of her own."

Nico beat her human fist uselessly against Tesset's back as the arena fell farther and farther behind. Hot, frustrated tears streamed down her cheeks. Josef was dying, and she could do nothing. She'd never felt so useless in her entire life.

That's because you are useless. The Master's voice was nearly cackling with laughter. *Sted didn't even have a proper transformation, the deaf idiot, and he's got nearly twenty League men fighting tooth and nail just to contain him. You can't even beat one man to save your precious swordsman's life.*

"No." Nico sobbed.

Yes, the Master said. *And you have no one to blame but yourself, you miserable, pathetic failure.*

Nico slumped against Tesset's shoulder. The Master was right; he was always right. It didn't matter how hard she tried or how much she fought, she was weak. Weak and pathetic and worthless and untrustworthy and a failure and—

Her thoughts stopped as something brushed against her cheek. She looked up in alarm before she saw it was her coat. The black fabric had wrapped itself up nearly to her head, coiling itself like a snake ready to strike. It knew she was upset, she realized, and it was reacting to her, trying to protect her just as Slorn had told it to. Suddenly, she had an idea.

She bent her head down and pressed her lips into the fabric. In all her life, even the parts she couldn't remember, she was sure she'd never tried what she was about to do, but at this point, she didn't care.

I wouldn't try it, the Master said sadly. *It won't work. Failures like you shouldn't waste other people's time on wild shots.*

So what, she thought fiercely. *It's not like I have anything left to lose.*

The voice laughed and said something back, but Nico didn't hear it. All she could hear was the memory of Josef's voice in her ears telling her that even if she failed, she could not stop trying. You were only a failure once you stopped trying.

Holding his voice in her mind, she took a deep breath, and, for the first time in her life, began to talk to the spirit of her coat not as a seed, but as a wizard.

Tesset stopped running, slamming his feet into the hard-packed dirt. Sparrow skidded to a stop a second later, turning just in time to see Tesset whip Nico off his shoulder and hold her out in front of him like an ill-behaved child.

"What are you doing?" he said. "You've been muttering for nearly a minute now."

Nico just stared at him, her lips drawn tight.

"Powers, Tesset!" Sparrow said, bracing himself against Eli, who was now blue, but still kicking. "You stopped us for some muttering? Knock her out and let's go."

Sparrow reached to bash Nico across the back of her head, but his hand hit nothing but air. At that moment, Nico's coat unraveled, and she dropped out of Tesset's hands.

Tesset grabbed for her as she fell, but the threads of the coat wrapped around his arms, spoiling his aim. Nico landed on her feet and rolled away, coming up just out of reach with her arms out, ready to block whatever came next.

But nothing came. Tesset just stood there, watching her as he calmly tested the massive tangle of black thread that tied his arms together. He was alone in his calm, however. Beside him, Eli and Sparrow were staring at her like she'd grown another head.

"Powers, child," Sparrow said. "What happened to your arm?"

Nico lowered her eyes, carefully avoiding Eli's horrified stare. "None of your business. Give me the thief."

Sparrow started to laugh. "Are you joking? If you're going to run, then run. I'm sick of your trouble, but the thief stays. There is no way I'm leaving this bollixed-up pit empty-handed."

Nico shifted her stance. Without her coat, she could

feel the spirits around her, already awake and on the verge of panic, start to lose control. The voice in her head was silent, but she could feel him waiting, watching in anticipation. "Give Eli to me, or else," she said.

"Or else what?" Sparrow rolled his eyes. "This is taking too long. Tesset, let's go."

Tesset looked at him. "You sure? Alric said to get her to safety."

"Hang Alric!" Sparrow said, pulling Eli's rope taut. "Since when are we League? There isn't enough cash in the world to make me put up with this."

As he spoke, Nico flexed her demon claw. She couldn't take Tesset, but Sparrow was another story. She tried one last time. "Let him go."

Sparrow sneered and started to turn away. Nico raised her claw with a snarl, but just as she launched herself forward, an enormous whistling scream cut through the air as something shot overhead. It exploded through the buildings, including the one right next to them, and landed with an enormous crash in the arena behind them.

For one long second, everything seemed to stop. Tesset's mouth opened, shouting a warning that he never quite got out. Beside him, Sparrow was staring up as the enormous wall of the building above them, broken by whatever it was that had crashed through the town, broke free of its supports and began to fall forward. Even Eli had stopped struggling. He was also watching the wall as it fell toward them, his bound hands coming up to cover his head. And in that long, slow moment, Nico decided what she would do.

She spun in midair, turning the demon arm away from Sparrow. The creature inside her snarled in frustration, but Nico ignored it, focusing all of her attention on her other fist, her striking fist, just as Josef had taught her. Sparrow was wide open as Nico's human fist slammed into his jaw, knocking him back. He stumbled in surprise, and his hands let go of the rope around Eli's neck just as Nico caught the thief's shoulder. The moment she had him, Nico changed directions, kicking off the ground and throwing herself toward the collapsing wall. She glanced up and found what she was looking for, a glass window. She stepped into position and forced Eli down, covering him with her body as the wall crashed around them.

The glass broke over her shoulders, and Nico grunted in pain as the shards sliced her skin. The ground shook under her feet as the wall landed, and then, quickly as it had happened, it was over. Nico cracked her eyes open. She was standing perfectly in the center of the window, surrounded by broken glass. Eli was choking and panting beneath her, grabbing his throat, which was bright red where the rope had cut in. Right beside his knee, buried by the broken glass, she could see Tesset's hand, still wrapped in the threads of her coat. The rest of him was lost beneath the collapsed wooden beams.

She reached down and helped Eli to his feet. "Are you all right?"

"No." Eli coughed. "I'm bruised, beaten, and bloody... and alive, thanks to you."

Nico smiled and bent over, reaching down for the thread of her coat. It woke when she brushed it, sliding up her arm like a snake. She winced when she touched Tesset's skin. His hand was still warm, and she felt a twinge of guilt. For all that he'd been her captor, he'd been a good man. Too good to die like this. But she couldn't think about that now. She kept her arm down, letting her coat reweave itself across her body until she was completely covered again.

"Let's go get Josef," she said, standing up.

"Right," Eli said, rubbing his neck as he looked around at the wreckage. "I don't suppose you know what that was just now."

"No," Nico said, picking her way quickly through the debris. "And I don't care. All I want to do is get to Josef."

"Fair enough," Eli muttered, starting after her.

Their building wasn't the only one that had collapsed. The dirt roads were now more like tunnels through great piles of broken timber, and they had to change direction several times when the way was blocked. The air was filled with horrible sounds, mostly the demon's horrible screaming mixed with explosions and the sound of buildings collapsing, though at this point Nico was surprised there was anything still left to collapse. But despite the horrible noises, she pressed on, letting the sounds lead her toward the center of town, where Josef was.

They were almost there when Eli broke the silence.

"Nico," he said, quickening his pace until he was walking beside her. "Why did you do that?"

His voice was soft, but Nico flinched anyway. "What?"

"Save me."

She took a deep breath, pushing a fallen beam out of the way. "Because Josef would have saved you. And because we're a team." She stopped to look at him. "Comrades don't leave each other in the lurch. Aren't those your words?"

Eli nodded, but his face was closed and expressionless,

just as it had been during those awful three days in the cabin. Nico looked away, blinking back tears.

Did you really expect anything to change?

Nico shook her head. But then, just as she reached out to knock a broken beam out of the way, Eli grabbed her human hand. She froze, but he didn't let her go.

"Thank you," he said, squeezing her hand in his.

Nico looked up in surprise.

He gave her a wide, genuine smile before letting her go. Nico didn't move. She just stood there, staring as Eli walked past her and started pulling at a fallen window frame that blocked their way.

"Are you coming?" he said, looking over his shoulder.

Grinning wide, Nico ran to help Eli tear down the last bits of debris between them and the building where Josef had landed.

The outer edges of Izo's bandit town were completely destroyed. Great piles of wood and broken glass lay over the once orderly streets, and those buildings that were standing were little more than skeletons teetering on supports that still occasionally twitched in terror. But down on what had been the road to the canyon's southern exit, the rubble was stirring.

Glass slid crashing to the ground as Tesset pushed himself up with a groan, tossing the splintered wood beams aside with one hand. His other hand was still on the ground, fingers dug into the dirt where he'd braced himself to make a shelter of his own body for Sparrow, who was curled in a ball on the ground, coughing and clutching his bleeding nose.

"Do you see them?" he choked out.

"No," Tesset said, surveying the wreckage.

Sparrow began to curse loudly, tearing off his ruined coat and using the silk lining to wipe the layer of dust from his face. "This is just bleeding brilliant. No thief, no demonseed, no legendary sword, and no missing Shaper wizard. Let's just quit now, before Sara sticks us on file duty for the rest of our lives, how about?"

"No need for that quite yet," Tesset said. "We know where they're going."

"The swordsman?" Sparrow said. He wiggled his tongue around before spitting the dirt out of his mouth. "There's no way we can beat them there, and I'm not sure I want to. Just listen."

He hardly needed to point it out. The demon's scream was everywhere. It reverberated through the air, horrible and unnatural. Despite his years of training to master such a basic human weakness as fear, Tesset couldn't help the cold shudder that ran down his spine. Still, his face was bored and impassive as he stared down at Sparrow. "Do you want to be the one who explains to Sara why we're coming back empty-handed?"

Sparrow heaved an enormous sigh and held out his hands. Tesset yanked him up, and they began to clear their way toward the arena, now hidden behind the toppled buildings.

Benehime crouched by her sphere, a wild look in her white eyes as she watched her darling boy run through the panicked city.

Just one word, she murmured, clenching her fingers against the pulse of demon-born fear reverberating through the world. *Just one plea.* She smiled as she saw

Eli trip. *Things will only get worse, darling. How much farther can you go on your own? How much more can you suffer for your pride?* She pressed her lips against her orb. *All you have to do is say you need me. Submit, and all the world will be yours, darling star.*

But as she watched him, something blurred her vision. She blinked several times, but it was no use. A great wind was circling at the top of her sphere, deliberately obscuring her view. Scowling, Benehime crooked her little finger. The wind vanished instantly, reappearing in the nothingness beside her.

Illir, she said coldly. *You had better have a good reason for making a nuisance of yourself.*

The West Wind bowed deeply before her. "All apologies, Shepherdess. I knew of no other way to get your attention."

Benehime frowned. *And why does a wind need my attention?*

"With all respect, White Lady," Illir said, his enormous voice shrunk to a shaking whisper, "my winds are in a demon-driven panic. I would never presume to question your judgment, Lady, but it is hard to quiet them while you keep our protector, the Lord of Storms, blowing on the southern coasts."

Benehime's eyes flicked to the tropical sea where the Lord of Storms was still raging, just as she'd left him.

He disobeyed me, she said. *I will not interrupt his punishment for something as small as this. Tell your winds the League will handle it.*

"The winds see much, Lady," Illir said, trembling. "It is hard to put them at ease when Alric and the spirits who have come to his aid are so clearly in over their heads."

The Shepherdess's hand shot out, grabbing the wind at its center. Illir screamed and began to thrash, but she held the wind tight, pulling him close until his breeze ruffled her white hair.

You are the Great Wind, she said slowly. *Find a way to keep your subordinates in line, or I will find another wind who can. Understand?*

"Yes, Lady," Illir panted.

Good. Her grip tightened. *Any other complaints?*

"Yes, actually," Illir said.

Benehime's eyes widened. *This had better be important.*

"It is the most important question I've ever asked," Illir said. "Several days ago, an old, old friend and one of your strongest spirits, the great bear, Gredit, vanished. I ordered my winds to look everywhere, but they found no trace of him, not even his body. You would be within your rights to kill me for this impertinence, Lady, but if my years of loyal service have ever pleased you, answer my question before you do. What happened to my friend?"

A slow smile spread across the Lady's white face. She opened her hand, and the wind fell from her fingers, shuddering with relief.

You are very bold, Illir, she said. *I like that. You are also loyal, and I like that even more. If you want to know, I will tell you. Gredit was an old spirit, far past his prime, given to fits of hysteria and insubordination. Even so, he was one of my flock, and so I tolerated his behavior. But then, in his delusions, he threatened one of my stars, my own favorite.* Benehime grew very grave. *This I could not forgive. I am a lenient mistress. I set very few rules. However, there is no place in my sphere for spirits who disobey. Am I making myself clear, West Wind?*

"Very, my Lady," Illir said. "I will go and calm my winds now. I apologize for wasting your time."

Benehime nodded and went back to her sphere, sending the wind away with a flick of her finger. *Don't let it happen again.*

The wind vanished, spinning back down to the world below. She watched for a moment, and then smiled when she saw him fall back down to reassure the lower winds. Illir was a smart spirit. He knew the limits of his place, unlike the bear. Still, she had not known they were friends, and she made a note to keep a closer eye on the wind. Satisfied, she went back to watching Eli crawl across the ruined city. She'd let things go very far this time, but it would be worth it. This time for sure, he would call her. He would fall crying into her arms, pleading for rescue, and then everything would be as she wished. She need only be patient and wait for him to beg.

Benehime smiled at this, running her white fingers gently across her sphere. Behind her, the claws began to press more fiercely on the walls of her world while, down on the ground, the demon grew larger.

CHAPTER
19

"Sir!" one of the League men shouted, grabbing Alric by the sleeve. "It's no good, sir. We can't hold him down."

Alric didn't need to be told. He had his will on the demon as well, and he could feel for himself just how useless it was. The ability to command the spirits to hold down a demon regardless of their own safety was a power the Shepherdess herself granted to the League, but its weakness was that the command was only as strong as the spirits who obeyed it. Here, even with the bedrock spirits helping, it wasn't enough, not for this demon.

Down in the spike pit that had been the arena, the demon roared and batted at the League men who sliced at it. Whenever it touched their swords, large chunks disappeared from the blades, and the demon grew larger. Already, the monster was close to twelve feet tall and showed no sign of stopping. Alric sighed in frustration, shoving his own sword back into its sheath.

"Stop attacking!" he shouted. "It's no good. We're only wasting our swords."

The League stopped its attack at once, forming a loose circle around the demon, who, now that it was no longer being attacked, turned and began to eat the bedrock spikes.

"Sir!" One of his lieutenants ran over. "We have to do something. If it keeps eating like this, the demon will soon be too large to contain."

"It's already too large to contain," Alric said, watching the stone writhe as the monster bit into it. Rage washed over him. He'd faced hundreds of awakened seeds in his long years with the League, but this one was different. Different and familiar.

"This isn't a normal takedown," Alric said. "This is the seed that was in Slorn's wife. I'd know it anywhere."

His lieutenant grimaced. "I thought Slorn's wife was contained."

"Apparently even the world's greatest Shaper couldn't contain a demon indefinitely," Alric said dryly. "What I want to know is what it's doing *here*, and why it's in Sted's body."

"Sted?" His lieutenant recoiled. "Berek Sted?"

"Who else?" Alric said. "Stop panicking and you can feel his soul clear as day, what's left of it anyway."

"But Sted was spirit deaf. How—"

"I don't know," Alric snapped. "But it's thanks to his not being a wizard that this situation isn't any worse than it is. Though his being here with Nivel's seed nicely explains what happened to our missing swordsmith." He sincerely hoped Slorn wasn't dead. Artisans like him were impossible to replace.

"All right," Alric said. "We're dealing with a seed that spent ten years germinating inside the body of a powerful wizard, but is now trapped inside a spirit-deaf shell. That is our only advantage. The devouring force is already too strong for awakened blades or spirit commands, and because the seed is lodged in a human, directly commanding the host spirit is out of the question." *As always*, he thought with a sigh.

"We need the Lord of Storms," his lieutenant muttered, his face pale as he watched the demon finish the stone pillar and leap to the next one. "Where in blazes is he?"

Alric wanted to know the same thing. The Lord of Storms had left in a hurry a week ago and hadn't been heard from since. This happened sometimes, but never for this long, and never without a message. Still, Alric kept his mouth shut. Things were bad enough without panicking his men.

"We can handle this," he said, clapping his lieutenant on the shoulder. "We are the chosen protectors of the world, blessed by the Shepherdess herself. She would not have given us our gifts if we were not able to handle whatever situation arose."

"Yes, sir," the man said, gripping his sword with renewed determination.

Alric smiled and released his grip, hoping he hadn't just told the biggest lie of his career.

"Spread out," he ordered. "We're going to take the creature down in one strike, before it can eat our swords. I will deal the cutting blow to the chest that frees the seed. The rest of you focus on its joints. Try to take off the limbs, just like in drill."

"Yes, sir!" the men shouted, fanning out in a circle.

Alric positioned himself at point, directly in front of

the demon, who was still feeding with little attention to its attackers.

Alric drew his sword with a crisp metallic scrape. It lay heavy and perfect in his hands, impossibly long and slender, the cutting edge glowing with its own golden light. He looked at it sadly. His beautiful Dunelle, Last Sunlight, his partner and treasure. If this strike succeeded, it would probably be her last. From the way the hilt pressed into his palm, she knew it. But she shone as brightly as ever, urging him to strike the blow. Alric tightened his grip. She had been his best sword; he owed her a valorous death.

Sensing danger, the demon stopped eating. It coiled itself on what was left of the sandy arena floor, enormous claws flexed and ready, its jaw open and drooling around its horrible, ragged teeth.

"On my mark," Alric said, raising his glowing blade. "Three. Two. One—"

As the word left his mouth, a whistling scream drowned out his voice. He threw his head back just in time to see something white crashing through the buildings behind him. It flew screeching over his head and into the arena, striking the demon square in the chest.

The demon's scream ripped through Alric's mind as the ground rocked under his feet. The shock wave hit him a second later, knocking him over. Alric's hands went instinctively to cover his face as he landed hard on his side, buried instantly by the wave of dirt, rocks, and broken swords that flew out from the impact. For a moment, he lay there, stunned, and then he began to thrash, kicking himself to his feet and scrubbing the dirt from his eyes just in time to see something enormous, white, and sharp-toothed running across the ruined city toward him.

"Alric, isn't it?" said a familiar, female voice. "Are you all right?"

Alric looked up to see a ghosthound staring down at him, and on its back was a redheaded woman with a concerned expression on her face.

"Miranda Lyonette," he said, coughing. "What are you doing here?"

"Saving your neck, League man," the ghosthound growled, nodding toward the center of the arena.

Alric turned to look. The place where the demon had been crouching seconds earlier was now nothing but an enormous crater. He stared at it for a second, not quite believing what he saw.

"What did that?"

Miranda grinned and pointed behind him. Slowly, Alric turned around and his eyes went wide. Standing on the rim of the canyon that surrounded the bandit city was Heinricht Slorn. He was crouched on one knee, holding something on his shoulder that Alric didn't have a name for. Nearly as long as Slorn was tall, it was metal and hollow, like a tube. It had two legs in front that dug into the ground at Slorn's feet to brace its weight, but its back was a nest of piping that hooked to an enormous wagon, which was absolutely covered with water. Even at this distance, Alric could see the blue water arcing in and out of a dozen different containers, moving against gravity and glowing with its own watery light.

Alric shook his head and sheathed his sword. Of course Slorn was here. He should have known it would all come together. At the canyon's edge, Slorn lowered the metal tube from his shoulder and hopped into the water-filled cart. The cart began to move as soon as he was in, climbing down into the valley on spindly spider legs. It picked its way over the wreckage and came to a stop at the arena's edge. The cart knelt and Slorn climbed down, landing stiffly beside Miranda.

"Well," the Shaper said, staring at the crater. "That worked rather well."

"Quite," Alric said. "Mind telling me what you did?"

Slorn reached into the bag slung across his chest and took out a white object. It was the size of a small melon, slightly longer than it was round, and sharpened to a rough point at one end. Its surface was smooth, like carved soap, and from the way Slorn held it, Alric could tell it must be very heavy indeed.

"What is it?"

"Bone metal," Slorn said. "Rather amazing stuff, really."

"And inedible by demons," Alric finished. "Very clever. But how did you do that?" He pointed at the destroyed buildings.

Slorn gave him an astonished look. "Water pressure," he said, like it should be obvious. "Spiritualist Lyonette was kind enough to lend me the use of her sea."

Alric glanced at the blue water that was still flowing in great arcs from barrel to barrel and smiled. "You made a bone-metal shot for a water cannon powered by a sea?"

"Can you think of a better way to take down a demon as powerful as Sted?" Slorn said.

"Yes," Alric said. "But in the absence of the Lord of Storms, I'll take your solution. In the future, though, Heinricht, I'd appreciate it if you left League business to the League, or at least told us what you meant to do before you did it."

Slorn had the good grace to look abashed at that, and Alric stood up to survey the damage. The other League men were getting up as well, many slowly, some clutching broken bones. But they obeyed instantly when Alric motioned for them to form a perimeter around the crater. Once his men were in position, Alric moved forward, keeping his hand on his sword as he crawled up the crater's edge to peek into the hole Slorn's cannon had left.

The demon lay sprawled at the bottom of the crater, motionless. Its long, unnatural arms were flung spread-eagle, the left one shattered below the second elbow. The demon's head was bent backward at a hideous angle and surrounded by broken teeth while its chest was caved in completely, the shell-like skin shattered around the bone-metal slug, which had passed straight through the ribs to lodge in the creature's spine.

Alric was still studying the damage when he heard a scrape on the dirt. He turned to see Miranda lying next to him, staring wide-eyed into the crater.

"Is it dead?" she whispered.

"A demon is never dead until you take its seed, Spiritualist," Alric said. "You can watch if you like, but do not interfere."

He could see her starting to ask what he meant, but Alric gave her no chance. He stood up and signaled to his men. They nodded, and the League members began to move slowly down into the crater. When they were in arm's reach of the demon, Alric drew his sword. He could see the seed's edge through the demon's shattered chest, a black, wet, oblong shape just below the heart, wrapped in bloody tissue. Alric cursed under his breath. Most seeds were a few inches long, never more than six. If his eyes weren't deceiving him, this seed was over a foot. No wonder the demon had given them so much trouble. He didn't even want to think about what would have happened if this seed had awakened in a wizard instead of a spirit-deaf lug like Sted. Seeing the reality of the situation, Alric began to regret all the times he'd championed Slorn's research. If he'd known that something like this was living inside Nivel, he would have killed the woman himself.

He held his sword out, slipping the point deftly inside the demon's shattered chest. But just as he was about to press his blade against the sinew connecting the seed to the host body, he heard the faint sound of a sucked-in breath.

Alric threw himself back, snatching his sword out just in time to block the enormous black claw before it landed in his head. The demon launched itself up with a earth-shaking roar, its shattered arm flopping helpless at its side as its good claw pulled on Alric's blade. Alric tried to yank his sword free, but the creature slid its claws down the blade to grab Alric's arm. The claws dug into his flesh, and the monster lifted him clean off the ground. He barely had time to kick before it threw him as hard as it could.

Alric tucked and rolled, landing on his feet at the edge of the crater. But even as he caught his balance, he heard a hideous crunching as the demon grabbed one of his men and shoved him, sword and all, into its mouth. The other League members cried out and charged, hacking at the demon with their screaming swords. The demon ignored them. It simply kept eating, pushing Alric's lieutenant between its broken teeth as it devoured the man whole.

"The head!" Alric shouted, charging back down the crater. "Take off the head!"

But it was too late. The moment the lieutenant vanished down the monster's throat, its wounds began to heal. Its broken arm snapped itself back together with a hideous cracking of bones, and the gaping hole in its chest began to knit together. The League men were still attacking, but the sword wounds closed as soon as they were made, and each new strike injured the sword more than the monster it struck.

"Fall back!" Alric shouted, grabbing the nearest soldier.

His men scrambled back, and the demon rolled to its feet, screaming as a fresh wave of demon panic washed out of the crater.

"Alric!" Slorn shouted.

Alric whirled around to see Slorn back atop his wagon with the long metal cannon on his shoulder again, and this time, Miranda was beside him.

"Hold it down!" the bear-headed man bellowed.

He didn't need to say anything else. Alric threw out his hand and opened his spirit until the entire panicking world was roaring in his ears. He grabbed everything, every weeping spirit, every terrified spec of dust he could touch, and forced them all into one command.

DON'T MOVE.

The world froze, and the demon fell to its knees. It threw its head backward, roaring in defiance as it fought the command, but Alric held it firm. It took everything he had. He could feel the sweat pouring down his face, feel everything in the town fighting his hold in the panic to escape the demon, but he did not let go. With every second that passed, he fought to hold it just a second more, hoping it would be enough.

"Do it!" he shouted. "Do it now!"

On the edge of his vision, he saw Slorn slam the bone-metal slug into his cannon. Behind him, Miranda raised her arms. The spider-legged wagon began to shake as the impossibly blue water raced across it, picking up speed as it flowed from barrel to barrel in an endless loop. Slorn mouthed a command, and the cannon's metal legs uncurled, anchoring the Shaper on the wagon's top just as the Spiritualist thrust her hands forward. The second her hands moved, the water followed, blasting itself into the piping at the cannon's back. There was an enormous crack as the water hit the bone metal, and then the sea's triumphant roar. The bone-metal slug shot out of the cannon faster than Alric could see, nearly turning the wagon over with its force. It split the air with a whistling scream, flying right past Alric's ear to land square in the demon's neck.

The shock wave blasted Alric into the air. He landed on his back in the dirt, but was on his feet in an instant, waving his hands in a desperate attempt to see what had happened. The crater was thick with blown-out dirt. He could hear Slorn's wagon scrambling behind him, probably trying to right itself after the cannon's kick, but he couldn't see anything but yellow, billowing dust.

He'd taken two blind steps when the demon's claws lashed out of the dust cloud and hit him hard in the shoulder. Alric went down with a shout, raising his sword instinctively to block the next blow. But the claws went right over him, thrashing wildly through the air.

Alric rolled clear, gripping his bleeding shoulder as the dust began to settle. The first thing he noticed was that several of his men were down, knocked over by the blast wave or taken out by the demon, he didn't know. The cratered arena they'd been fighting in was now twice as deep, and he could see the outline of the demon at its center, still madly lashing out. Alric wiped the dust from his eyes with a bloody hand. How could it still be standing? Had the shot missed? But as his vision cleared, he saw the truth. The demon's head was gone, blasted clean off, but the body was still fighting. It struck blindly, the claws stabbing out. As he watched, one of the random blows landed in the back of one of his downed men.

Alric shouted, but it was too late. The man screamed as the claw skewered him, and the demon stopped thrashing to lunge at its kill, dragging the man toward its ruined body as its claws began to eat his flesh right then and there, drinking in his power to heal its wounds.

"Shoot it again!" Alric shouted, scrambling up the edge of the crater. "Damn it, Slorn, shoot it again! Now!"

Miranda jumped down from the scrambling wagon, landing on her waiting ghosthound. The water followed her, sliding over her shoulders like a mantle as the hound cleared the distance to Alric in one jump.

"There aren't any more shots," she said as Gin slid to a stop. "We only had two."

Alric gritted his teeth. "Then we do this the hard way."

Miranda jumped down. "What do you mean the har— Wait!"

But Alric was already gone. He charged through the dust cloud, picking up speed as he ran down the crater toward the demon, who was still eating its victim.

He launched himself off the slope, drawing his sword in a golden flash. Hungry and blind, the demon didn't raise a claw to defend itself. Alric's blow sliced into its back, his golden blade peeling through the demon's shell and into its spine. The creature screamed, and the demon panic hammered Alric's mind. But he was further than fear could reach. He pressed the blow, cutting down through the demon's torso. It dropped the soldier and reached backward, clawing wildly at Alric, but it was too late. With a shout of triumph, Alric turned his sword and sliced up through the tissue that connected the seed to its host.

The demon howled. Claws ripped into Alric's back and threw him down. He landed under the demon's clawed feet. There was no time to dodge; the thrashing demon's claws landed right on top of him. He closed his eyes, bracing for the explosion of pain as the demon's foot ripped into his chest, but he felt nothing. He opened them again, staring up in amazement. The demon's foot was on his chest, but there was no weight to it. The monster was still thrashing, but with every movement, bits of it were breaking away. The demon was crumbling like ash, breaking apart and floating away. Already, the fear was receding as the demon crumpled in on itself. By the time Alric managed to sit up, it was nothing more than a pile of black dust around a long, black seed.

Alric took a deep, pained breath. It was over. The demon was dead. He looked around, doing a quick count of his men. Two dead for certain, three more lying motionless, but the rest were pushing themselves up. Not bad considering what they'd faced without the Lord of Storms' backup. But there was one loss he felt more than the others.

Alric looked down at the sword in his hands. The long, slender blade still glowed faintly with its own golden light, but the cutting edge was ravaged. Enormous chunks were missing, leaving great gaps all the way to the core of the blade.

"Dunelle," he whispered. "My Last Sunlight. I'm sorry. I'm so sorry."

"You did what had to be done." His sword's ringing voice was warped and muffled with pain, but the pride in the words stood bold and clear. "It has been an honor to serve you, sir."

The golden light grew dimmer as it spoke, and Alric felt tears in his eyes for the first time in a century. "The honor has been mine," he whispered, laying the destroyed blade across his knees.

He heard the crunch of boots behind him, but he did not take his eyes from the blade until the last of the golden light faded out completely.

"A noble sword," Slorn said, his voice soft by Alric's ear. "One of the finest I ever made."

Alric nodded, but said nothing. Slorn knelt down beside him. "I know it will be no replacement, but I can make you another blade."

"I don't need another blade," Alric said, sliding his ravaged sword back into its sheath.

Slorn left it at that. "You should see to your wounds."

"What," Alric said, "and leave the seed to you?"

Slorn stiffened. "That is not what I meant, but it is Nivel's seed." He turned his bear head, staring at the long, black shape lying in the demon's dusty remains. "It is all I have left of our work together, of our lives. If I was ever kind to you, Alric, if our work ever opened a door of thought in your mind, you will let me study it a moment before you lock it away."

Alric heaved a deep sigh and waved him on. Slorn stood with a murmur of thanks and walked over to kneel by the seed, staring at it with an intensity Alric had never seen.

"You really should do something about that shoulder," said a voice behind him. "You're bleeding everywhere."

He looked back to see Miranda hovering at the edge of the crater.

"Thank you for your concern, Spiritualist," he said, pushing himself up. "But your worry is wasted. I am very hard to kill. It is my gift."

Miranda frowned. "Your gift?"

Alric smiled. It was refreshing to meet someone who didn't know all the secrets for once. "The League requires great sacrifices of its members. To counterbalance this, the Lord of Storms bestows gifts upon us. Some men choose power, others choose invulnerability. I chose eternal life."

"You mean you can't be killed?" Miranda said, impressed.

Alric frowned. "There is a wide difference between eternal life and invulnerability to death. I can be killed just like any other man, given enough damage, but over the years I've gotten fairly good at staying alive. Don't worry, it will take more than this to kill me."

He left her pondering that and walked off to gather what was left of his men. There was much to clean up before the day was done.

"Eternal life," Miranda said, shaking her head. "No wonder he's always so smug. I'd be smug too if I knew I was going to survive most anything."

"Well, I don't like it," Mellinor said. "The only defense

most spirits have against humans is your short lives. No matter how bad it gets, we can always outlast you. An immortal wizard sounds like a disaster to me. Thank goodness he's working for the League and not trying to rule some spirit domain somewhere."

Miranda was slightly insulted by that train of logic, but she held her tongue, turning instead to see how Gin was faring.

"Find anything?"

"I've got Eli's scent," Gin said, running his nose along the ground. "No trail yet, though." A little dust cloud rose up as he spoke, and Gin sneezed several times. "This is a horrible place to be looking," he snorted. "The dirt's so jumpy it's flinging itself up my nose. We'll have to wait until the League calms things down before I can get a good fix."

Miranda sighed in frustration. "The trail will be stone cold by then."

"Even I can't work miracles," Gin said, lashing his tail.

"Sorry, sorry," Miranda grumbled. "It's just that every single time I get close to catching Eli, something horrendous happens, and it's getting really old."

"Don't worry, we'll catch him," Gin said. "Sparrow had him last, remember? Much as I can't stand him, the bird boy is just as sly as the thief. It'll all work itself out."

"I hope so," Miranda said. "Because if I have to go back to Zarin empty-handed one more time, I think I'll cry."

Gin whimpered sympathetically and went back to sniffing. Miranda strolled along beside him, searching the destroyed town for a clue, any clue, the thief might have left behind.

CHAPTER
20

Nico and Eli found Josef buried beneath a collapsed house. He was unconscious and bleeding badly, but miraculously unbroken.

"Probably because he was out before he hit," Eli said, grabbing the swordsman by his arms. "Going limp saves your bones, though I can't vouch for the rest of him."

Nico nodded, pushing a beam off the Heart, which was lying in a crater of its own about ten feet away. When she had the path clear, she grabbed Josef's feet and they hauled him over to his sword.

"There," Eli said, folding Josef's fingers around the hilt. "Now let's get out of here."

Nico couldn't agree more. They couldn't see the fighting from where they were, but the sounds coming from the crater that had been the arena were horrible enough that she didn't want to. Using Josef's arm for leverage, they got the Heart on his chest, and Eli tied it down using a strip of Josef's shredded shirt. When the swordsman was secure, Eli grabbed his shoulders while Nico got his legs and together they carried him out of the wreckage to the road.

It was slow going. Josef was amazingly heavy and the road was constantly blocked by toppled buildings, forcing them to retrace their steps and go around. They kept to the side streets as much as possible, but even when they had to use the large main roads, they saw no one. Except for the League men at the arena, the city was empty. The bandits were long gone, and Nico didn't blame them one bit. She would have run too if she could have.

Yes, you're very good at running.

Nico closed her mind and focused on keeping up with Eli's grueling pace.

By the time they reached the canyon wall that separated the bandit city from the surrounding forest, her knees were ready to buckle. Josef's body seemed to grow heavier with every step. Her arms ached with the strain of holding him. Sweat dripped into her eyes, making them burn, but worst of all was her transformed hand. Though she'd wrapped her demon claw in her coat as best she could, she could still feel Josef's flesh through the cloth, feel the life in him calling out. The claws twitched in anticipation. The raw hunger she felt every time her transformed fingers brushed Josef's skin made her ill, but she could not let him go.

You're only having this problem because you refuse to accept yourself, the Master said with a sigh. *How many times have you carried the swordsman's unconscious carcass? Fifty? A hundred? More? You never had problems helping him then. Now look at you, ready to fall over after a quarter mile.*

Nico tightened her grip. Unfortunately, it only made her hand itch worse as she pressed it into the flesh of Josef's calf.

If you would only accept reality, everything would be so much simpler. For the first time that she could remember, the Master's voice sounded earnest. *I can help you control the hunger. I can even help you remember what you've forgotten. I can make you a god among insects, Nico. A power Eli Monpress would treasure above all others and a companion Josef Liechten would never abandon. I can make you everything you want to become. All you have to do is stop being stubborn. You are my child, my dearest daughter. I know more than anyone what it is like to be outcast. You don't have to struggle on alone. Let me help you.*

The words were so sweet, so sincere, that for a stumbling moment, Nico almost gave in. But then Nivel's words, words, she realized with a stab of sadness, she would never hear her speak again, sounded loud and clear in her mind.

Never trust the voice.

What? The voice was sneering now, all sincerity gone. *You're still listening to that woman? That pathetic creature? Did you know she died without lifting a finger to save herself? Defeated by Sted, the one-armed, spirit-deaf, League reject? She died like a dog, whimpering and crying for her precious bear-headed freak of a husband. Is that the kind of strength you want?*

The voice began to laugh, but Nico cut it off.

"You said she died without a fight," she whispered fiercely. "But you said nothing about her giving in. She didn't, did she? She died with her soul intact."

I ate her soul and gave her seed to Sted, the Master said.

"No," Nico said, eyes wide as the revelations tumbled through her mind, snapping into place one by one. "That would make her less powerful. You would never accept a weaker servant when you could have a stronger one. She beat you, didn't she? Nivel died human. That's why you had to give Sted her seed." She stopped midstep, causing Eli to stumble.

"Nico?" Eli said, looking back. "What's wrong? What are you muttering about?"

"She was the master of herself," Nico said, her voice trembling with wonder. "You couldn't take her."

Eli gave her a nervous look. "Take who where?"

Don't get cocky, the Master snarled. *I've been very, very patient with you, Nico, but this is your last chance.* An image invaded her mind, a long-fingered hand outstretched in the dark. *Take it. Take it now and I promise you'll never feel pain again.*

Nico stared at the outstretched palm and, slowly and deliberately, spoke one word.

"No."

The image vanished.

That is the last mistake you'll ever make.

"Nico?" Eli put Josef's shoulders down and hurried to her side. "What in the world are you—"

Before he could get the last word out, a figure stepped out of the shadows behind him and clubbed Eli across the back of his head. It happened so quickly Nico didn't even have time to drop Josef's legs before Eli was knocked sprawling onto the leaf-covered ground.

"Eli!" Nico rushed to his side, but before she'd taken two steps, the figure from the shadows grabbed her arms and wrenched them behind her. She screamed in pain and twisted her neck back to see a tall man with pale skin holding her down, his eyes glowing with that horrible light.

"Excellent work, Sezri."

Nico turned to see Izo, his lordly silks torn and filthy, step out of the trees. The Bandit King didn't even look at her. He walked over to where Eli was groaning on the ground and jerked the thief to his feet.

"Do you mind?" Eli said. "I'm getting pretty tired of being dragged around like a prize at the fair."

"Too bad," Izo said, sliding a long knife against Eli's throat. "That's what you are. What you made yourself when you decided to court your bounty rather than mitigate it like any sensible criminal. But you shouldn't complain. It's precisely because you're the prize everyone wants that you're still alive. Though how long you'll stay that way is entirely up to you. The posters do say 'Dead or Alive.'"

Eli leaned nonchalantly against the knife's edge. "I'm worth more alive."

"That may be, but the extra gold is offset by the trouble you cause. Corpses are far less of a liability." Izo lowered his knife. "Don't forget that."

Eli's smile faltered just a hair. "Consider it remembered. So, what now? Are you going to chop me into bits and mail me to the Council?"

"Not yet," Izo said. "First, I regroup my army, administer some needed discipline, and then I'm going to hold the Council to its bargain."

"Oh, yes," Eli said. "Me for a throne. It's a bad deal, you know. I'm worth more than—"

The knife returned to his throat, cutting Eli off midsentence.

"That's better," Izo said. He gave the thief a push, and they began walking northward, into the woods, away from Nico and Sezri.

"You know, Monpress," Izo said, "I can see now why my bounty is higher than yours. You're nothing but a fraud, a little thief with a pathological need for attention. You don't know what it means to have real ambition."

Eli gave him a nasty look, but kept his mouth shut. Izo just smiled and looked back over his shoulder. "Sezri," he said, "now that we've found the thief, we've no need for the girl. Kill her, and the swordsman. I don't want any more liabilities."

Nico's eyes went wide, and Eli started to protest, but Sezri didn't move. He just stood there, holding Nico's arms in a lock against her back, staring into the distance like he was listening to something.

"Sezri!" Izo shouted, shutting Eli up with another jerk of his knife.

The demonseed ignored him. He tilted his head down to stare at Nico, his free hand moving up to grip her jaw.

"Did you think you could run?" he whispered. "The Master always knows where his children are." The hand on her jaw tightened. "You don't deserve this," Sezri hissed. "He gave you everything and you threw it in his face. But I serve the Master in life and death with all my soul. I will show you what it means to be a child of the Mountain."

"Sezri!" Izo roared, but the name was lost in Nico's scream. With incredible strength, the demonseed forced her jaw open and pressed his mouth to hers. Nico's eyes went wide as the connection exploded open, and Sezri began to pour into her. She writhed against him, beating him with her fists while her mind recoiled from the wrongness of the man's flowing into her. This couldn't be happening. Demonseeds couldn't eat other seeds.

No. The Master's voice was hard as iron. *But you're not eating him. He's feeding you every spirit I told him to eat into you.* The Master chuckled. *Such a good, obedient child.*

A look of bliss spread over Sezri's face as the Master praised him, and the flow of devoured spirits sped up. Nico choked and gasped, trying to pull away, but her transformed arm shot up of its own accord, ripping into Sezri's chest to gorge on the spirits inside him. The flow of spirits doubled, and blackness washed over her mind. Nico felt her control slipping as the tide of power poured into her. She fought to hold on, to close her mind, but it was too late. The blackness was everywhere, eating her thoughts, her fear, her control until there was nothing left to hold on to.

I told you, the Master said, *I always win.*

And then even his voice vanished as Nico fell into the dark.

A piercing scream ripped through the air above Izo's destroyed city, followed by a pulse of fear that sent Miranda to her knees. She gasped for breath, clutching her rings as her spirits began to panic. Gin was on the ground beside her, whimpering, and even Mellinor was shaking. One by one, she got control again, calming her spirits with an iron will. When they were as steady as she could hope to make them, Miranda looked around. She was clearly not the only one who'd been caught off-guard. The League men had stopped in their tracks, and even

Slorn was on his feet, staring into the distance. Alric stood beside him, his calm, severe face distorted in a look very close to sheer terror.

"No," Alric said. "Not now."

Realizing she would probably regret it, Miranda turned to look as well. There, past the northern edge of the bandit city, something horrible and black was rising above the trees. As she saw it, Miranda felt her spirits start to panic again. She wanted to join them. The thing was like nothing she'd ever seen, awake or asleep. As she watched, two more enormous black things rose beside the first, unfolding in hideous slow motion. After a terrible moment, she realized they were wings. Enormous wings, taller than the trees, reaching up with their hideous clawed talons toward the sky.

The thing jerked, and the scream sounded again, bringing with it a blast of fear even stronger than the first that turned her bones to jelly. When Miranda could move again, she looked frantically for Alric. Whatever that thing was, it was surely a demon. That meant the League could make it stop. But Alric wasn't there anymore. The spot where he'd been standing seconds before was now empty, save for the telltale glimmer of a cut in the air as it vanished.

"He abandoned us!" Gin howled.

Miranda didn't think that was the case, but she couldn't even get the words out. All she could do was hang on as the waves of fear broke over her.

Izo had dropped his hold on Eli when Nico's transformed arm had ripped through Sezri's chest, but neither the thief nor the bandit had moved. They just stood there, frozen, unable to look away.

For a few seconds, the two demonseeds stood as close as lovers, and then Nico pushed him away. The thin man fell like a tree. His body shattered when it hit the ground, and he turned to black dust that seemed to vanish even as Eli watched. When it was finished, all that was left of Sezri was a small, black seed, about the size of Eli's middle finger, that fell to the ground like a stone.

Nico, however, stayed perfectly still. Eli began to fidget. The way she was standing, he couldn't see her face, but it couldn't be good. He took a hesitant step forward.

"Nico—"

Nico threw back her head, and a scream like he had never heard blasted through the air. Eli slammed his hands over his ears, but it was no use. The scream went straight to his soul. But worse, far worse, was the wave of fear that followed. For a moment, Eli was drowning in pure, abject terror before he got his mind back under control. Behind him he heard Izo screaming, and then a loud crash as the Bandit King fell, but he didn't turn to see where or why. His eyes were trapped by what was happening in front of him.

Still screaming, Nico threw out her arms, human and demon claw. The manacles on her wrists were going mad, beating themselves against her skin. With a horrible wrenching of flesh, toothed mouths appeared on Nico's arms. They gnashed their horrible, spiny teeth and bit deep into the manacles. The metal screamed and shattered, wailing as the demon mouths ate the pieces. The same thing happened to the collar at her neck and the shackles on her ankles.

When the last shred of metal vanished into the hideous mouths, Nico's coat, which had clung faithfully to her the

entire time, tore down the middle. The cloth cried as it
ripped, the threads still reaching out for one another even
as they snapped, but it wasn't enough. The coat fell in a
shredded pile at Nico's feet. Without the coat, Eli could
see that her skin was now the same horrible black shell as
Sted's, but even as he wrapped his brain around what that
meant, the shell began to crack. Liquid black oozed from
the lesions, and Nico began to grow.

At that moment, all trace of humanity vanished. Blackness ripped from Nico's body, forming long, clawed arms
reaching out from a shape that was like nothing he'd ever
seen. It was long and spindly and full of sharp angles, or
that was the impression he got. He couldn't look at it for
very long before the terror overwhelmed his mind. He
caught glimpses of eyes in the blackness, great glowing yellow orbs, and not just two. There were hundreds
scattered across the unspeakable expanse of the demon's
body. They clustered on the demon's long head, gathering at the edges of its great, fanged jaw, which opened
slowly, dripping black bile as it screamed again. Its black
body convulsed as a pair of wings, black as coal and as
sharp as knives, burst from its back. The creature stumbled forward at the impact, and the new wings flapped
awkwardly, stretching for the sky with clawed talons. Its
enormous, clawed feet ripped into the forest floor for balance, tearing up great mounds of roots and stone in the
process. These turned to black dust as Eli watched, their
souls devoured by the creature's touch.

Unable to tear his eyes away, Eli would have watched
until he too was eaten. But then, just before Nico's deadly
skin reached him, a rough hand grabbed him by the collar
and tugged him sideways. Eli felt the strange whooshing

sensation that came with traveling through a cut in the world before landing on his face on the ground twenty feet from where he'd been standing. Izo was there too, still staring dumbly into the distance, but that was all Eli could make out before the hand on his collar dragged him up until he was inches from Alric's enraged face. Even so, it took Eli a few seconds to realize that the vibrations coming from Alric's frantically moving mouth were words.

"I said you have to do something!" Alric shouted, shaking Eli until the thief saw spots. "The Lord of Storms is missing and I can't contact the Shepherdess on my own. She'll listen to you. You have to make her do something or our world will be devoured!"

Eli's poor brain had a hard time keeping up with that. "What do you mean?"

Alric's grip on his collar tightened until Eli thought he was going to choke. "Look at it!" the League man shouted, forcing Eli's head until the thief had no choice but to look where Alric wanted. "This isn't some errant seed grown out of control. It's the *Daughter of the Dead Mountain*!"

The demon was nearly twenty feet tall now. It reached out, dragging its hands along the ground, leaving great, blackened rents in the forest wherever it touched. Its enormous mouth devoured the trees whole, and the air was full of the screams of dying spirits.

"I can't stop it," Alric said. "The whole League can't stop it, not without the Lord of Storms. Even then, he took its head off last time and it still didn't die."

"What do you want me to do?" Eli shouted. "The Shepherdess is the guardian of all spirits. If she won't leave her little white world for *this*"—he pointed at the demon—"what's my opinion matter?"

Alric jerked him. "Oh, come off it! You're her favorite little pet. She'll do anything you want, even her *job*."

Eli started trying to pry Alric's fingers off his collar. "That's a low blow," he muttered. "Even for you."

Alric's eyes narrowed. "I do what I have to, favorite. Now, will you do it, or do I have to kill you to get her attention?" He dropped Eli and drew his sword, pressing the ruined edge against Eli's chest.

Eli swallowed, eyes flicking from sword to swordsman. He did not doubt for a moment that the League man would do it. Alric had never been the idle-threat type. But . . .

"Forget it," Eli said, crossing his arms over his chest. "Groveling to Benehime for help is on the same level as dying, so far as I'm concerned. You'll have to think up a better threat."

Alric stared at him for a moment, and then he drew his fist back and punched Eli square across the jaw. Eli fell backward, flailing to catch himself, but Alric was there first, grabbing him around the throat.

"*Do you think this is a game?*" Alric's fingers pressed tighter on Eli's windpipe with every word. "Do you have *any* idea *what is at stake?*"

"More than you do," Eli choked out. He wrenched himself from Alric's grasp, rubbing his bruised throat. "You think the Shepherdess isn't watching this right now? She could fix everything with a single word, but she won't. Not while there's a chance of forcing me to ask for it. That's what she's like. It's all a game to her. She's trying to corner me, to make me act how she wants me to act. But I'm no one's dog, Alric. Not hers, and not yours."

Alric screamed his answer, but the words were lost as the ground began to erupt. Great shards of stone shot from the ground as the great sleeping spirits of the mountains woke and began trying to fight the threat. Eli, Alric, and the still-staring Izo fell as the ground rolled like a bucking bull beneath them. Alric was back on his feet at once, bracing his legs against the moving ground like a sailor on a storm-pitched ship. Eli stood more slowly, gripping a screaming tree for support, watching wide-eyed as the valley began to tear itself apart.

The spirit's fight was over as soon as it had begun. The demon ate the stone spikes even as they struck home, absorbing the screaming spirits into its growing body until there was nothing left but black dust falling down on the valley like snow. Even so, blind and desperate with panic, the spirits kept attacking. With nothing left to lose, the ground tore itself open beneath the demon's feet, screaming vengeance as great stone hands reached out to pull it down and crush it beneath the bedrock. The creature stumbled, grabbing hold of the fissure with its long claws. Scenting victory, another fissure opened in the other direction, trying to spoil the demon's hold. The creature screamed and began kicking with its claws, cracking the fissures and collapsing them in on themselves even as it ate the stone. Eli watched in horrified silence, unable to speak until he saw something horribly familiar on the edge of the collapsing cliff. After everything he'd just seen, it took him a few seconds to realize he was looking at Josef's unconscious body, still lying where they'd left it when Alric had pulled them to safety.

"Josef!" Eli shouted. But it was too late. The ground collapsed beneath the swordsman, sending him falling into the abyss.

"*Josef!*"

As Eli screamed Josef's name, the demon moved. With horrifying speed, it caught the falling swordsman between its claws. The demon climbed out of the collapsing fissure, carrying Josef and the Heart, which Josef still held clutched against his chest, in its palm. When it reached a stretch of unbroken ground, the demon gently laid the swordsman down. It hovered over him a moment, staring at him with its hundreds of yellow, glowing eyes. Then, with a horrible scream, it turned and began to attack the forest more violently than ever.

Eli ran to Josef and pressed his fingers against the swordsman's neck. He heaved a huge sigh of relief when he felt his friend's strong, steady heartbeat. Despite what the demon had done to everything else it touched, Josef was unharmed.

"She's still in there," he said, looking up at the rampaging demon with a sort of wonder.

His thoughts were interrupted by Alric as the League man yanked him around.

"Now do you get it?" Alric shouted, shaking him. "There's nothing we can do, humans or spirits, to stop that thing. We need the Shepherdess, and you're going to get her." He swung his ruined sword up, the broken gold glinting in the dusty sunlight. "Last chance, favorite. I'm ready to die to do what I have to do, and I have absolutely no qualms about taking you with me. Call her down or die for your pride. Either way, this ends now."

Eli flinched away, his brain madly trying to think of a way out. But before he could even open his mouth, a deep, deep voice he'd never heard before spoke over the roar.

"Leave him, League man. Even if she does come down, we will suffer for it."

Alric and Eli both turned. On Josef's chest, the battered blade of the Heart of War began to glow.

"If you call down the Shepherdess, she will deal with this one as she did the last," the Heart said. "She will bury it under a mountain, and we will have twice the problems we have now."

"No," Alric said. "The Daughter of the Dead Mountain is still not a hundredth the size of the original. All we need is—"

"Demonseeds are shards of the great demon," the Heart said. "Fractures small enough to escape its prison and move freely through the world. Yet each tiny piece has the same attributes of the whole. Think. The League, the Shepherdess's arm in this world, can't even destroy those small seeds, only cut them off from their human hosts and store them in starvation. What, then, can the Shepherdess do with a demon this size except what she did with the original? Mark me, Alric, she will do what she did before. She will seal it beneath a mountain. But this time there is only one remaining mountain spirit strong enough to hold a shard of the demon that large in check, and I very much doubt the Shaper Mountain would be willing to spend the rest of eternity as a sword."

"Wait," Eli said. "You mean you..."

"Yes," the Heart answered. "At the beginning of this world, I willingly gave my body as a prison for the demon. In return, the Shepherdess let me choose my new form. I chose to be a sword. It has been a hard, lonely journey, but I have never regretted my choice. However, I will not let another be forced to it, least of all my brother, who has dedicated his life to guiding his Shapers."

"Wait," Eli said. "The Shaper Mountain is your brother?"

"All mountains are my brothers," the Heart said. "But

the Shaper Mountain, Durain, is my twin. We two were birthed from the will of the Creator at the dawn of the world to stand as guard and guide to the lesser mountains. We were the greatest of the Great Spirits of stone, and we can never be replaced. The Shepherdess is not the Creator. She can only guide and order the spirits, not form new ones. When the demon first came, I gave up my body to serve as a prison because I knew my brother would watch in my stead. But now, history repeats itself. My brother is the only mountain strong enough to hold the creature Nico has become. If you call the Shepherdess down now, she will have no choice but to use the only tool she has left, and the last of the great mountains will be gone."

"That's a fine sentiment," Alric said through gritted teeth. "But we have no choice. I cannot sit here and watch that thing eat the world."

"But we do have a choice," the Heart said. "The thief saw it himself. Inside that monster is one of our own."

"The girl is gone," Alric said. "Don't kid yourself. Human spirits are the first consumed on awakening."

"Then why did it save Josef?" Eli asked.

Alric's eyes narrowed. "How should I know?"

"Nico is still alive," the Heart said. "She is a survivor. I had my doubts as well at first. Since the morning Josef took her naked from the crater, I have come close to killing her myself on several occasions. Every time, I thought the demon had won, but every time she fought back. I think that this time will be no different. That thing may not look like Nico, but it is still her body. So long as there is some shred of her soul left, so long as she still has will, she is still a wizard. So long as she has will, she has the weight of a mountain, and there is still hope."

Alric shook his head, but Eli stared past him, watching the demon with an uncharacteristically serious expression on his face.

"Alric," he said quietly, "I'll make you a deal."

Alric sneered. "This isn't the time for tricks."

"No," Eli said. "No tricks, just a clean proposition. We may not have always gotten along, but Nico is still my companion. I take only the best into my line of work, and she's no exception. The sword is right. The demon never beat her before, and I'm willing to bet my life and my pride that it hasn't beaten her now." He held up his hand, fingers splayed wide. "Five minutes. If she doesn't beat her seed in five minutes, then I'll do anything you want. I'll call Benehime down here to dance with you, if you like. Do we have a deal?"

Alric considered for a moment, and then released his death grip on Eli's shirt. "You do realize that in five minutes there may not be anything left to save." He looked at the demon, then at the Heart, and then at Eli. "All right," he said, sheathing his sword. "Five minutes."

Eli nodded and stepped over Josef's splayed body. He ran to the edge of the ruined fissure, parts of which were still collapsing and, cupping his hands to his mouth, shouted as loud as he could.

"Nico!" he cried, layering just enough power into the words to make sure they would cut through everything else. "Listen! Me, Josef, the Heart of War, we're betting it all on you! You've got five minutes to turn this around before Alric and the League get their way, but I think you can do it. I'm sorry about before. I was stupid. I admit it. Come back to us, Nico, and everything will be like it was, only better. Just you, me, Josef, and anything in the world we want to steal. All you have to do is kick that demon out and come home. Five minutes. We'll be here waiting for you."

His voice echoed through the hills, and the spirit panic dimmed to listen. On the other side of the fissure, the demon paused its eating. It stood there, listening for one long moment. Then, with an angry scream, it began to eat again.

Panting, Eli sat down on the crumbling stone, rubbing his hands over his dusty face and hoping on whatever luck he still had that he'd made the right choice.

CHAPTER
21

Nico raised her head. She could have sworn she'd heard someone calling her, but now, no matter how she strained her ears, all she heard was silence. She was alone, sitting on a cold floor of smooth black stone. It went on forever in all directions, an endless, endless darkness of the kind she'd seen only once before.

"Yes," a deep, smooth voice whispered behind her. "When you were with me."

Nico spun around, sliding back on the stone. A man was standing behind her where there had been no one a second before. He was tall and broad shouldered, dressed in a simple black shirt and dark trousers tucked into tall boots, just like Josef's. He looked a lot like Josef too, and a little bit like Eli, but the cruel look in his golden eyes belonged to only one person.

"Master." Her whisper was little more than a breath.

"At last you remember." The man smiled.

Nico did remember. She remembered the slave pens.

How she'd been taken from them. How the cult members had held her down, their dead white faces leering beneath their cowls. She remembered the hideous feeling of the seed, then barely larger than a grape pit, being shoved down her choking throat. But more than that, she remembered the unadulterated joy of the Master's good opinion. The absolute pleasure that came from being a good child who pleased her father. The warmth, the understanding, the acceptance that no one outside could give her.

The Master opened his arms, and she ran to him, flinging herself against his chest with a sob. Joy and belonging like she'd never felt washed over her, but even as she savored the feelings, there was something wrong about them. Something alien, almost sticky in her mind. Slowly, painfully, she released her grip and stepped back.

"You're making me feel this, aren't you?" she whispered.

"Of course," the Master said, stroking her hair. "You're home now. It's only right you should share in my happiness." He ran his hand under her chin, tilting her head up until their eyes met. "You are mine again, every bit of you. My greatest weapon is back in my command, and she'll never escape again. Is that not cause for joy?"

Nico ducked out of his grasp, or tried to, but her body would not move. The Master just smiled and kept petting her, stroking her hair like a huntsman petting his prize hound.

"Now, now," he tsked. "You lost, Nico. You don't get to play keep-away anymore. It's over; take it gracefully. If this works out the way I expect, a new Dead Mountain will be born. I'll be twice as powerful as I am now, and it's all thanks to you. That's why I'm being so generous, despite everything you've done. If you were any other seed, I would have crushed you and left you to die the moment you disobeyed me, but I didn't. I stayed with you, despite your defiance. I never abandoned you."

He slid his hand up to cup her cheek before stepping back.

"You should be grateful," he said. "I have given you everything. Made you the ground for my greatest creation. Yet even now you stand there staring at me like you're some kind of victim." His smile grew impossibly cruel. "I have done nothing to you that you did not deserve. It is I who have suffered the most, suffered as you denied me over and over again, despite everything I've done for you. Have you nothing to say?"

"No, Master." Nico lowered her head. "I am sorry, Master."

The Master's arms slid around her shoulders, pulling her against him as the sticky, alien joy flooded her mind. "There, there," he said. "I forgive you. It's over now. You've lost. You don't have to think anymore. You don't have to try. I'll take care of everything. Just let it go. There's a good girl."

Nico let herself slump into his arms. She couldn't even remember why she'd been fighting, only that she'd been trying so hard for so long. But the Master was here now, and he would take care of everything. All she had to do was be good, do as he said, and nothing would ever hurt again.

But as that thought circled round and round in her mind, a tiny, lingering doubt nagged at her. She felt like she was forgetting something terribly important.

"Wait," she said. "Where's Josef?"

"Gone," the Master said. "Abandoned you, along with

that no-account thief. Everyone has abandoned you, except me. They see you as a monster. They're probably trying to kill you right now."

"No!" Nico said, looking up at him. "Josef would never abandon me."

The Master slapped her hard across the face. Nico stumbled and fell without a cry, landing hard on the cold stone floor.

"Never speak back to me," he said, his voice colder than the stone. He walked to where she had fallen, his steps fading off into the endless nothing. Nico gasped as he grabbed her hair, yanking her up until her feet were a foot off the ground. He grabbed her chin with his other hand, pressing so hard she thought her jaw would break as he turned her face to his.

"Your body is my body now," he said slowly. "Your soul, your power, everything. It is all mine. You are only here because I wish it." He dropped her, and she crumpled. The moment she was down, he kicked her in the ribs, sending her tumbling across the floor. She slid to a stop several feet away, panting against the cold stone. When she looked up again, the Master was standing over her, looking down on her like she was a piece of trash in his way.

"Never defy me again," he said. "I am your Master. You live by my generosity alone. Never, ever forget that."

Nico pressed her head down onto the stone. Desperate, sobbing apologies and promises of obedience filled her mind. She wanted to shout that she would never disobey again, that she had no master but him, but for some reason her mouth would not open. She could not speak the words.

Pain exploded through her as the Master kicked her again, and she flew across the endless chamber, landing so hard she saw stars.

"Do you think you're too good for this?" he shouted. "Or do you not understand the very simple words I am speaking? Has being a weak, pathetic, stupid creature for so long also made you mute?"

Nico began to hyperventilate. She moved her mouth desperately, but no sound came out. She could hear the Master coming toward her, and her body seized up in preparation for the kick she knew was coming. Why couldn't she say it? Why couldn't she swear that his will was the only will she knew?

Because it's not true.

Nico stopped cold. The voice spoke in her head like the Master's had so many times, but it was not his. It sounded like Nivel, like Eli, like Josef, like Miranda, like Tesset. Like everyone who'd ever said, in one way or another, what the voice said next.

The only human soul a wizard can control is their own.

At last, her lips parted, but the whispered word that slipped out was not what she had meant to say.

"Why?"

The answer came a heartbeat later. *Because a wizard has no master but herself.*

As the last word faded, Nico recognized the voice. It was her own. All at once, she understood. She understood everything, and she knew what she had to do.

She caught the Master's kick right before it landed in her side. He stumbled and nearly fell. He caught his balance at once and stomped down as hard as he could on her fingers, but Nico did not let go.

"I know what you're doing," she said, turning her bruised face to stare at him. "You're trying to intimidate me. To get me to surrender."

"Get you to..." The Master thew back his head and laughed. "Why would I waste my time on someone so stupid? You need power to surrender. You have nothing."

"No," Nico said. "You forced me to awaken, but you didn't beat me. I never surrendered my will. This is still my body."

"So what?" the Master sneered. "You're too far gone to go back now. You've eaten thousands of spirits. You nearly ate Josef and that horrible sword of his. Everyone's seen what you are. There's nothing for you out there. You belong here, with me. You've always belonged here. That life out there was a joke, a dream. Even if I'd done nothing, the end would have been the same."

"No," Nico said again. "Only if I'd let it. This is still my body, my soul." Her crushed fingers tightened on the Master's boot. "I am king here."

She stood up in a fluid motion, throwing the Master back. He flickered in the air, landing perfectly several feet away, but the look on his face, the mix of rage and disbelief, was as good as if he'd stumbled. Nico pushed herself up, wincing as her muscles protested. She ran her hands over her body, wishing she had enough light to see the damage.

The moment she wished it, light appeared. A beautiful shaft of yellow sunlight shot down from the air above her head, creating a wide circle around her. Nico looked at herself in the sudden brightness, examining her broken fingers and the bruises on her ribs and knees. She closed her eyes. When she opened them again, the bruises were gone. Her fingers were straight again, and the pain had vanished. She realized with a shock that it had never really been there to begin with. This was her soul, her world; everything that happened here, including pain, only happened because she allowed it.

She looked up at the Master. No, she scowled. Not Master, not anymore. The demon was looking at her cautiously now, circling just on the edge of the sunlight. Now that she had light on her side, she could see the thing behind his human form. A great, black shape lurking in the dark with a mouthful of jagged, glistening teeth.

Fear began to creep in and Nico tore her eyes away from the demon's true self, forcing herself to focus on his human face as she said the two words she'd wanted to say her whole life.

"Get out."

"Ah." The demon chuckled. "You think that now that you've had a little revelation about the nature of the soul you can do the impossible? Sorry, princess, it doesn't go that way. This might be your soul, but you're still a demonseed. So long as there's a piece of me in your body, you can't kick me out."

Nico narrowed her eyes. "You always lie. Why should I trust you now?"

The demon crossed his arms and gave her a sly smile. "If it were that easy, Nivel would have been free of me her first year. She was much smarter than you, and more determined. She had something to go home to. What have you got? Eli? Josef? You think they'll take you back after what you did?"

"I don't know," Nico said. "But I'm going to let them decide that. You don't get to say anything anymore."

"Don't I?" the demon said with a smirk. "Just because you know the rules of the fight doesn't mean it gets any easier. You're still the Daughter of the Dead Mountain. My mountain, my daughter. Your powers are my powers, and the more you use them, the stronger my presence becomes. You may have retaken control today, but you will never, ever be free of me."

"Then I'll have to live with you in a way I can handle," Nico said.

She closed her eyes and pictured what she wanted. When she opened them, everything was just as she'd imagined. She was standing in a wide-open field, like the ones around Home. Noon sunlight blasted down from the clear blue sky, banishing every shadow, except for one. In front of her, the demon stood in a pit. The pit alone was still black, shaded from the sun by the boulder balanced on its end above it.

The demon stood at the edge of the light, staring up at her with a smug smile. "You can't lock me away forever, Nico. The moment you are weak, the moment your control wavers, I'll be back. And you will be weak. The longer we fight, the stronger I'll become, while your power will only diminish. No matter how hard you struggle or for how long, the end will be the same. After all, you're just a human. I, on the other hand, have all the time in the world. Sooner or later, you'll be just like Nivel, alone and helpless in the dark. When that happens, I'll be there, and you will crawl on your knees begging for what you just threw away."

"That may be," Nico said. "But Nivel died with her soul intact." She reached out and put her hand on the boulder. "And so will I."

With that, she gave the boulder a push. It rolled sideways with a slow scrape and fell into the pit. The demon kept eye contact the entire time, smiling even as the boulder came down.

See you soon.

Then the boulder landed with a solid thunk, cutting him off completely.

Nico closed her eyes, feeling the warm sunlight on her skin, the wind against her bare shoulders, listening to the perfect silence of her world without the demon. She stood like that for a long moment, drinking it in. Then, with a deep breath, she turned her back on the boulder and began to walk across the plains, back toward the real world and the people who were waiting there for her, for good or ill.

CHAPTER
22

"Time's almost up," Alric said.

Eli nodded, but didn't say anything. It had been four minutes since he'd shouted at the demon, and about two minutes since it had suddenly stopped moving. Now it was just standing there, staring stupidly at the sky with its hundreds of horrible eyes while its wings flapped slowly. Eli wasn't sure if this was a good development or a bad one in the long term, but at least it wasn't screaming anymore.

"Time," Alric said. "All right, Monpress, do it. Call the Shepherdess."

"No need," the Heart rumbled. "Look."

Eli and Alric both stepped backward as the demon, now grown twice as tall as even the tallest tree, began to dissolve. The hideous body broke apart, collapsing like a dried-out sandcastle to the destroyed forest floor. The darkness became simple black as the glowing eyes winked out one by one. Once it began to fall apart, the demon was gone in less than a minute, and everywhere it had touched, the valley began to grow back. A great torrent of dirt filled the sundered ground. Broken rocks repaired themselves, and though the toppled trees could not be righted again, new growth instantly began to spring up from the felled trunks.

The last to dissolve was the demon's head. It fell with a shudder, the jagged teeth breaking free before dissolving like everything else until only one part remained. Nico landed gently on the new grass where the demon had been standing only moments before. She was naked, but something moved to cover her as Eli watched, snaking over her body so quickly his eyes could barely keep up. It had covered half of her before he realized it was her coat stitching itself back together.

He started to laugh and ran to her, dropping to the ground just as she opened her eyes, which were no longer even slightly yellow, but a deep, deep brown.

She stared at him, confused. "Is Josef okay?"

"Yes," Eli said, grabbing her hand. "Are you okay?"

"Yes," Nico answered, smiling. "More than okay."

"So I see," Eli said. "You'll have to tell us how you did it later. Right now, it's time to collect. You just won a very nice bet for me."

Nico frowned. "I did?"

Eli just grinned and stood up, turning to Alric, who was still walking over.

"Well," Eli said, "I believe I just saved your bacon."

"What?" Alric stopped and crossed his arms. "You put all of our lives on the line for a long shot and I'm supposed to fall over myself thanking you?"

"I never said anything about a thank-you," Eli said. "I'm

a thief, remember? I can't use thank-yous. No, we made a deal, Alric, Mr. Deputy Commander. I held up my end, but we never set down what you would pay if I won."

Alric gave him a dirty look. "And an uneaten world is not payment enough?"

"Of course not," Eli said. "Who do you think you're talking to?"

"Look," Alric said. "I don't think—"

Eli rolled over him. "There's also the little matter of you threatening to kill me earlier. Considering you're not even supposed to go near me, I think you should be more open to bargaining."

Alric started to say something, then he looked away. "What do you want?"

"Oh," Eli said, "just a tiny favor. Itsy-bitsy, won't take but ten minutes of your time."

"What?" Alric said, glowering.

Eli grinned from ear to ear and began to lay out his plan. By the time he was finished, Alric was ready to revisit the option of killing him.

Miranda sat on the edge of a broken building with Gin's head in her lap. She kept her mind perfectly blank, letting her calm be an anchor for her terrified spirits. The demon had stopped screaming ten minutes ago, but it took longer than that to bring her spirits out of their panic after something like this. Deep inside, however, Miranda couldn't help shuddering. She could still see the thing in her mind's eye, the hideous wings reaching up to claw the sky. If that's what it had looked like to her blind human eyes, she dreaded to think what her spirits had seen.

She had heard horrible stories of demons all her life,

but not even in the most terrifying had there been anything like what she'd seen today. How could something like that even exist? Wasn't the League supposed to keep this sort of thing from happening?

When her spirits were finally calm again, Miranda opened her eyes. The League men were moving around her, putting things back together, just as they had in Mellinor. They worked in pairs, walking down the destroyed streets putting buildings back together with a few hushed words and a wave of their hands. Slorn was still down in the crater working on Nivel's seed with a pair of League men standing guard over him. Alric, however, was conspicuously absent. That bothered Miranda, but the League men didn't seem worried. Maybe he was still dealing with the other demon? She bit her lip. That seemed like a lot for one man to handle. She looked north, studying the trees where the enormous creature had been scarcely an hour ago. The forest was deathly still now, but she could still see the monster's shape above the trees, an aftervision burned into her eyes even when she closed them. Miranda sighed. She'd just have to deal with it for now. Things like this took time to fade away.

Anxious to be moving, Miranda left Gin where he was and walked over toward Slorn. The bear-headed man was handing the seed to the League men, who took it with gloved hands. One of them made one of their cuts in reality while the other put the seed in a black sack. When it was secure, they stepped through the portal, vanishing instantly. Slorn watched the space where they had been, his face distant as Miranda walked up to him.

"Did they make you give it up?" she asked.

"They would have," Slorn answered. "But I handed the

seed over of my own volition. I had learned all I could hope to learn from it." He looked up, staring off at the snowcapped mountains. "That thing was never a part of my wife," he said quietly. "Nivel's soul has already been reborn. All I can do now is work to make this world a place that is worthy of her."

He reached into his pocket and pulled out a sealed letter. It was quite fat, several pages, and sealed with a large smear of wax. Slorn hefted it in his hand, and then tossed it high into the air. It spun a few times, and then took off like a bird, soaring through the air south and a little east.

Miranda whistled, impressed. "What was that?"

"A letter for my daughter," Slorn said. "Explaining where I went and why I'm not coming home. I'm not sure where she is, but the letter will find her sooner or later. Preferably later. I don't want her trying to follow me."

Miranda frowned. "You're not going home?"

"No," Slorn said, walking past her toward his wagon. "I stayed in isolation for Nivel. Now that she's gone, there is much for me to do. The world is changing, Spiritualist, and not for the better. A great demon eats an entire forest and the Shepherdess doesn't even send the Lord of Storms to deal with it." Slorn snorted as he pushed his spent cannon under the now dry and empty barrels. "I've dedicated ten years of my life to studying demonseeds, and yet the League has never asked for my findings, nor welcomed them when I forced the subject. Their Shepherdess has no interest in how to make things better. She only cares to keep things as they are, even as her world crumbles around her. So I'm taking my work to someone who will care."

"Who?" Miranda said.

"The Shaper Mountain," Slorn said, climbing into the wagon seat.

Miranda's eyes widened. She'd heard stories about the awakened mountain, but she'd never been there. No one had, except Shaper wizards. It was rumored they knew more about spirits than anyone, and if Slorn was an example, she believed it.

"Take me with you," she said.

He looked down at her, confused. "Why do you want to go?"

"Because I hate working for the Council with jerks like Sparrow," she said. "Because I'm sick of going back to Zarin empty-handed, and because I'm sworn to protect the Spirit World." She looked north again, tracing the outline of the demon that was still burned into her eyes. "After this afternoon, catching Eli Monpress to save the Spirit Court's pride feels almost petty." She turned back to Slorn. "Let's just say my priorities have taken a pretty significant shift in the right direction. If you're taking your knowledge of demonseeds to the Shapers to make sure things like that don't happen again, then I'm going with you."

Slorn leaned back. "And what of your orders? What about Sara and the Council?"

Miranda rolled her eyes. "The Council can choke on its paperwork for all I care, and Sara can go back to her menagerie. The only command I follow is Master Banage's, and he would tell me to go."

Slorn smiled, showing his sharp, yellow teeth. "Yes, I believe he would. Very well, you can come if you like. I warn you, we'll be moving quickly over hard terrain. I hope you're ready."

"Travel we can do," Miranda said. "Just say the word."

Slorn's spider-legged wagon stood up with a creak, and he turned it back toward the cliff where his other wagon waited. Gin was already up by the time Miranda reached him, his long body pulled in a great bowing stretch.

"So we're tossing our lot in with the bear," he said. "Good. I like him much better than the idiot bird."

"Glad you feel that way," Miranda said, jumping onto his back. "Because we're in deep now."

"Like we ever do anything halfway." Gin snorted.

Miranda gave him a friendly kick, and he bounded forward, hopping over the destroyed city after Slorn.

"There they go," Tesset said, watching the ghosthound through a hole in the wreckage.

"You see?" Sparrow said. "I told you she would turn traitor."

Tesset looked over his shoulder, but Sparrow wasn't talking to him. He was talking to the ball of blue glowing glass in his palm.

"She *is* Banage's little pet." Sara's voice pulsed through the orb. "I'd hardly expect her to do otherwise."

"Well, what do you want us to do about it?" Sparrow said. "Eli's gone, the Heart is gone, and now Slorn's off to who knows where. Even if the Spiritualist hadn't run off, this whole bloody mission would still be a disaster. I say we cut our losses and head back to Zarin before Izo finds us and sends our skins to Whitefall's office as a warning."

There was a huff over the orb that Tesset recognized as Sara blowing a stream of smoke into the air. "There's no call for such drama," she said. "And there's no call for scrapping the mission. Honestly, you just got up there. Coming back now would be a waste. I want to know what

Slorn is up to and what kind of mission he found to inspire Banage's girl wonder. Follow them."

"Sara!" Sparrow cried.

"Do it," she snapped. "I'm cutting off now. Whitefall just sent a page. I have to go to some sort of emergency meeting in ten minutes and it will take me at least that long to get up to the hearing room. I'll check in tomorrow to see how you're doing, and I don't want to hear any complaints, Sparrow. Don't forget, there's still a nice-sized bounty on your head I could turn in to Whitefall any time I like, and they don't hand out prison sentences for what you've done."

"How could I forget," Sparrow grumbled, but the orb had already gone dim. He glared at it for a moment more and then shoved the Relay into the pocket of his ruined silk jacket. "Well, isn't this just lovely?"

"It is," Tesset said. "It's been awhile since I had a good old-fashioned hunt."

Sparrow harrumphed and ran his fingers through his dusty hair.

Tesset watched him, frowning. "Why didn't you tell her about the demons?"

"Because I'm trying to get out of here, remember?" Sparrow said. "If I'd told her, she would have asked us to investigate that as well, and I'd rather her hand me to the bounty office on a platter than go anywhere near that place."

"She'll find out," Tesset said. "And she's going to be mad."

"We'll worry about that when it comes," Sparrow said, giving up on trying to tame the dusty mess on his head. "Come on, let's get this over with."

Tesset nodded and followed him out of the maze of broken buildings. He was grinning. A hunt, and a fine quarry too. Just what he needed to combat the city softness he'd been sinking into. He needed something to push him forward, because he wasn't getting any younger. Somewhere out there, Den was waiting for him. When they met again, Tesset knew he would have only one chance to show his master that his lesson had been well learned. He had to be ready.

Clenching his fists, Tesset started jogging toward where they'd last seen the ghosthound. Sparrow stumbled along behind him, sending a stream of curses into the late-afternoon breeze.

Sara marched up the stairs of the fourth and largest of the Council Citadel's seven towers. Servants in flawless white pressed themselves against the walls as she passed, peeking at her curiously from under their lowered lashes. She bit her pipe and kept walking.

The meeting room was already full when she got there. Council officials milled beside the catering table, enjoying the array of little sandwiches, cheese plates, and brandy aperitifs that the Council demanded even for its emergency meetings. Sara pushed right past them, going straight for a tall man with close-cropped silver hair holding court by the picture windows, the only person in the room who actually mattered.

"Whitefall," she said, nodding as the crowd parted to let her through. "I'm extremely busy. What's this all about?"

Merchant Prince Alber Whitefall, Lord Protector and Grand Marshal of Zarin, gave her a politician's bright smile. "I was hoping you could tell me, Sara dear." He touched her shoulder, guiding her in beside him. "I received an urgent message from the League of Storms. Normally, they fall under your jurisdiction, but this time the message was addressed specifically to me. Very odd. Haven't I asked you not to smoke in here?"

Sara took a pointedly long draw from her pipe. "What does the League want with you?"

"I don't know, the reasons were quite vague, but the letter specifically said that I was to call a meeting with you, Phillipe, and all the upper Council. And since you've always stressed that the League of Storms is never to be ignored, I did."

"Phillipe?" Sara gave him a skeptical look. "The bounty office windbag? What does the League want with him?"

"I'm sure I don't know," Whitefall said. "But that's my cousin you're talking about. Only I get to call him a windbag." He waved and smiled. Across the room, the topic of their conversation jumped, and then hesitantly waved back before returning to his plate of sandwiches.

Sara rolled her eyes. "Well, since we're all here, can we get this mystery meeting under way? I have work to do."

"Not quite yet," Whitefall said, adjusting the lapels of his black dinner suit. "We're still missing the representative from the Spirit Court. And, of course, whomever the League is sending to enlighten us."

"Spirit Court?" Sara said as the doors opened. She looked over her shoulder just in time to see Etmon Banage himself sweep into the room.

"Powers," she muttered, smoking furiously.

Etmon saw her as well, but to his credit the only change

was a slight hardening of his eyes as he approached to pay his respects to the Merchant Prince.

"Lord Whitefall," he said with a nod. "What is the emergency?"

"I think we're about to find out," Whitefall said, glancing toward the far wall. Sara and Banage both turned to see a thin white line dropping down through the air. When it reached the floor, a man stepped through. Sara winced. Alric looked furious. He also looked worse for wear. His face was badly bruised, and he walked with a limp. Of course, in his line of work, that wasn't unusual. What was unusual was the man he was dragging behind him.

By the time the white doorway closed, the room was silent. Everyone was watching the Deputy Commander of the League of Storms and the man dragging on the floor behind him. When he was sure he had everyone's attention, Alric tossed the man forward. He fell sprawling, leaving thick smears of dirt on the silk carpet.

"Ladies and gentlemen of the Council of Thrones," Alric said through gritted teeth. "I bring you Izo Barns, also known as Izo the Bandit King, wanted by the Council for one hundred and fifty thousand gold standards."

The man on the floor curled into a ball, moaning softly to himself with his eyes wide open like a horrified child. Alric just stood there with his arms crossed over his chest.

It was Sara who recovered first. "What's wrong with him?"

"Nothing," Alric said. "He's just had a bit of a fright. But it doesn't matter. His bounty is good whether he's dead or alive, correct?"

This question was directed at Phillipe Whitefall,

though it took a few moments for the bounty office director to realize that.

"Yes," he said, his voice trembling as he bent over for a closer look at Izo's terror-stricken face. "Izo, scourge of the north, wanted dead or alive for one hundred and fifty thousand. But how did you catch him?"

Alric closed his eyes and took a deep, calming breath. "I didn't. Izo the Bandit King was captured by Eli Monpress. I'm only here to deliver him."

There was a collective gasp around the room, and then everyone started talking at once.

"Hold on!" Banage's voice rose over all others. "What right does a wanted criminal and enemy of the Council have to a bounty?"

"Well," Phillipe Whitefall said, wiping his brow with his handkerchief. "There's no rule about who can turn in bounties. Keeping them open to lawbreakers actually encourages derision within the criminal element."

"That's all well and good," Sara said. "But how does Eli intend to claim his hundred and fifty thousand? Is he coming to Zarin to collect it himself?"

"Of course not," Alric said with a long-suffering sneer. "Monpress wishes for the reward to be added to his own bounty."

This time the room went silent.

Merchant Prince Whitefall stepped forward. "You want us to add a hundred fifty thousand to Monpress's bounty? But that would bring it to..." He looked at his cousin.

"Two hundred and forty-eight thousand, your grace," Phillipe answered.

"Two hundred and forty-eight thousand," Whitefall said, jabbing his drink at Alric. "A number like that is on the level of nations. We can't pin that sort of power on a thief. What kind of fools do you take us for?"

"I am only the messenger," Alric said. "Will you combine the bounties or not?"

"It's not like we have much of a choice," Whitefall said. "If we deny him, we break our own laws. I'm not about to set a nonpayment precedent that will jeopardize our highly successful bounty system."

"I take no more joy than you in this," Alric said. "Monpress will be watching for his new posters. If they do not show up within the month, the world will know that the Council does not pay its debts."

"No need for threats," Whitefall said, sipping his drink. "The bounty will be adjusted, may the Powers save us all."

Alric nodded and turned around. The white slit in the air opened immediately, and he stepped through into what looked like a destroyed town. Sara got a glimpse of shattered buildings and mountains in the distance before it closed again. She frowned and made a note to check with Sparrow to see if he'd heard anything about demons in the north.

By this point, guards had been called in to apprehend the man on the carpet, but it was hardly necessary. Izo was limp as a rag doll, his face still frozen in a mask of fear. Sara watched as the guards dragged him away, then turned to find Whitefall deep in conversation with Phillipe and half a dozen representatives from the major Council Kingdoms. It wasn't worth the political capital to butt in, so Sara turned, walked to the window, and looked out over Zarin as the white buildings turned golden under the setting sun.

"Can you believe this?" a familiar, angry voice said behind her.

She turned as Etmon Banage stepped in beside her, his sharp face scowling as he stared at the city below.

"What?" she said. "Our being forced to see each other more than once a year?"

Banage's glare could have melted the glass. "That's not what I meant, and you know it."

Sara took a long draw off her pipe before answering his question properly. "I thought it was a fairly clever plan."

Banage bristled. "It's a disgrace to the Council and the entire bounty system."

"Good thing you don't care about the Council, then."

"The Council speaks for us all," Banage growled. "I'm in it whether I want to be or not. What I don't understand is how the boy did it. I can't even get the League of Storms to give my Spirit Court the time of day, and here's Eli with Alric himself on a string."

Sara smiled. "Impressive, isn't it?"

Banage stared at her. "How can you think that?"

"How can you not?" Sara snapped. "He's your son too, Etmon."

She whirled around and stomped toward the door, sending officials scrambling to get out of her way. Banage stared after her, shocked beyond retort. When he came to enough to realize he was being stared at, he turned back to the window and glowered out over the city as the lamplighters began their rounds.

Benehime sat in her white nothing, staring, as always, at her orb when a man appeared in front of her. There was no opening portal, no door in the air. One moment there was nothing, and the next he was standing there, glaring down at her.

Shepherdess.

Benehime's white eyes narrowed, and she pushed her orb aside. The man's white face was that of an old but active man with a pure-white beard that fell to his knees. His hair was the same, a snowy cascade that hung around him like a robe. His white hands were folded in front of him, the white fingers long and skilled, and his eyes were the same white as her own.

Weaver, she said. *You're out of your element.*

You left me no choice. The Weaver's deep voice filled the air. *Not when you take such risks.* He looked at the orb. Benehime followed his gaze to the ruined valley where the demon had woken.

I had everything under control.

Did you? The Weaver's beard did nothing to hide his frown. *It didn't look that way from where I stood.*

It is not your place to be looking at all, Benehime said fiercely. *Your place is to tend the shell. The sphere and everything inside is my domain.*

So it is, the Weaver said. *But when your risks threaten the shell, they become mine as well. What were you thinking, letting a demonseed grow that large? You put everything in danger, and not for the first time, I hear. Your spirits have been complaining to me. They say you ignore your duty, that you play favorites to the point of exclusion. Have you forgotten why you are here?*

I forget nothing! Benehime shouted. *It is you who has forgotten his place, Benehin! Now get out. You have no right to order me around.*

And you have no power to make me leave, the Weaver said. *We three, Shepherdess, Weaver, and Hunter, are the children of the Creator, equals in all things. There is no power you can wield that I cannot counter. You may force your spirits to grovel at your feet, but you cannot touch so much as a hair on my beard.*

Benehime stood up, eye to white eye with the Weaver. *This is still my sphere. It is by my will alone that you can exist at all in this place, and I am done listening to the hysterical ravings of a cowardly old man. Leave, now, before I force you out.*

The Weaver stayed perfectly still.

Eyes still locked with hers, he stretched out his white hand and laid it against the edge of her domain. As if in answer, the dim shapes of clawed hands began to gather, their edges pressing hard against the wall, scraping at the fabric that separated her world from theirs. Far in the distance, the screaming grew louder.

The shell is a delicate thing, the Weaver said, stroking the thin barrier as the claws scraped against his hand. *I can maintain it against assault from without, but not from within as well.* He glared hard at her. *Remember that the Hunter has his day of rest in one year's time. When that happens, it will be two against one. I suggest you think very carefully about what happened today, Benehime. We have served together for a long, long time. I would hate to lose you over something as petty as a favorite, sister.*

I forget nothing, Benehime whispered. *Get out.*

As silently and suddenly as he had appeared, the Weaver vanished. Benehime stared at the place where he had been for a long time. Eventually, her white eyes drifted past it, to the edge of her domain and the long, clawed hands still clustering where the Weaver's hand had rested. With a furious snarl, she turned back to her sphere and buried herself in her world.

Acknowledgments

Thank you to Peggy, Steve, Judith, and Rob. This book would not exist without everything you do.

extras

orbit

meet the author

Rachel Aaron was born in Atlanta, Georgia. After a lovely, geeky childhood full of books and public television, and then an adolescence spent feeling awkward about it, she went to the University of Georgia to pursue English literature with an eye toward getting her PhD. Upper-division coursework cured her of this delusion, and she graduated in 2004 with a BA and a job, which was enough to make her mother happy. She currently lives in a 1970s house of the future in Athens, Georgia, with her loving husband, an overgrown library, and a small, brown dog.

Find out more about her at www.rachelaaron.net.

introducing

If you enjoyed THE SPIRIT EATER,

look out for

THE SPIRIT WAR

The Legend of Eli Monpress Book 4

by Rachel Aaron

The Perod bounty office was packed with the usual riffraff. Dozens of men (and a few scowling women) lounged on long benches stolen from the tavern across the street, polishing a startling variety of weaponry and trying to look bored and not like they were waiting. It was a farce, of course. It was criminally early on a Monday morning, and the only reason bounty hunters ever came into a regional office before noon was to get their hands on the weekly bounty update from Zarin.

The only person who didn't try to hide his anticipation was a young man toward the back of the crowd. He stood on his bench, hopping from foot to foot and ignoring his dour-faced companion's constant attempts to pull him back down, an anxious scowl marring the boyish face that everyone should have recognized but no one did.

"Honestly," Eli huffed as Josef finally managed to drag him down. "Are they walking from Zarin?"

"It's not even eight," Josef said, his voice low and annoyed as he nudged the wrapped Heart of War farther under the bench with his foot. "The post isn't due until eight fifteen. And can you at least pretend to be discrete? I love a good fight, but we walked all night to get here. I'd like some breakfast and a few hours of shut-eye before I have to put down an entire room of bounty hunters, if it's all the same to you."

Eli made a disgusted sound. "Go ahead. I could wear a name tag on my forehead and these idiots still wouldn't notice. No bounty hunter worth his sword goes to a regional office for his tips. There's not a soul here who's good enough to see what they don't expect." He slouched on the bench. "Sometimes I think there's no pride in the profession anymore, Josef. You were the last of the bounty hunters worth the name, and even you got so bored you took up with the enemy."

"Not bored," Josef said. "You just gave me better fights. And Coriano was quite decent. And what about that man who attacked you at the hotel? Gave you quite a scramble for a dying profession, didn't he?"

Beside him, Nico did her best to stifle a laugh, but her coat gave her away, moving in long, midnight waves as her shoulders shook. Eli rolled his eyes at both of them.

"Well, too bad you killed them both, then," he said with a sniff. "Knocking over the best of a dying breed without even leaving a calling card. It's such a waste. No wonder your bounty's only ten thousand."

Josef shrugged. "I see no need to define myself by an arbitrary number, unlike some people I could mention."

Eli bristled. "Arbitrary? I earned every gold standard of that bounty! You should know. You were there for most of it. My bounty is a reflection of our immense skill; you should take some pride in it. After all"—he grinned painfully wide—"I'm now the most wanted man in the Council Kingdoms. Two hundred and forty-eight thousand gold standards! That puts even Nico's number to shame. My head is worth more than a kingdom—no, two kingdoms! And to think, just last year I was struggling to break thirty thousand. This is an achievement no one else in the world can touch, my friends. You are sitting beside a *national power*. Tell you what, the moment the Zarin post arrives with my new posters, I'll sign them for you. How's that?"

Josef looked decidedly unimpressed, and made no comment.

"It *is* a large number," Nico said after the uncomfortable silence had gone on long enough. "But you're not the highest. There's still Den the Warlord with five hundred thousand."

"Den doesn't count," Eli snapped. "He was the first bounty, made right after the war. The Council hadn't even decided on a valuation for its currency yet. If they'd made the bounty properly with pledges from offended kingdoms rather than just letting old Council Daddy Whitefall pull some grossly large number out of his feathered helmet, Den would never have gotten that high. Anyway, it doesn't matter. I'll be passing him soon enough. Just you watch. This time next year I'll be at a million, and see if I offer to autograph your poster then."

"I'll take my chances," Josef grumbled, eyeing the crowd. "Look lively, I think the post is here."

Eli was on his feet in an instant, elbowing his way through the crowd that was no longer even pretending to look bored. The hunters thronged around the door as a sleepy-eyed bounty officer and two harried men in Council uniforms with piles of paper under their arms attempted to push their way in.

"No shoving!" the officer shouted. "Stand back! Individual posters can be purchased after the official notices are hung!"

The crowd took a grudging step back as the Council postmen began tacking up the latest posters under the bounty officer's direction. First, they hung up the small-fry, lists of names with tiny descriptions and even tinier numbers beside them. Next came the ranking bounties, criminals with a thousand or more on their heads whose notoriety had earned them a sketch and a small poster of their own. These were all posted between the floor and waist level. The top of the wall was reserved for the big money. Here, the Council men hung the famous names.

Izo was gone. The men stripped his old poster down with minimal fanfare, moving those bounties below him up a notch. The old, yellowed poster offering two hundred thousand for the Daughter of the Dead Mountain was left untouched, as was Den's large poster at the top of the board. Between these, however, the men tacked up a fresh, large sheet featuring a familiar face grinning above a rather astonishingly large number.

Eli stopped shoving the men in front of him and gazed up at his poster, his eyes glowing with pride. "It's even more beautiful than I imagined," he whispered. "Two hundred and forty-eight thousand gold standards."

Josef pressed his palm to his forehead in frustration as Eli began shoving his way forward. Thankfully, no one else seemed to have heard the thief's remark. The bounty hunters were all loudly clamoring for copies, shouting over one another while the bounty officer tried to shout over everyone that no one was getting posters until the official copies were up.

Eli vanished into the fray only to reappear moments later with a scroll tucked under his arm. Josef raised his eyebrows and began easing the knives out of his sleeves, just in case, but the bounty officer was too busy screaming at the bounty hunters to get in line to notice one of his carefully protected posters was already missing.

"They get better with every likeness," Eli said, proudly unrolling his poster for Josef and Nico to appreciate. "If it wasn't black and white, I'd say I was looking in a mirror."

Nico nodded appreciatively, but Josef wasn't even looking. Eli turned to berate his swordsman for his shocking lack of attentiveness, but Josef was just standing there, staring at the bounty board like he'd seen a ghost. Eli followed his gaze, glancing over his shoulder at the bounty wall where the Council men were hanging one last poster, just below Den's and just ahead of Eli's. As the Council men tacked the poster's corners up, a familiar stern face glared down at the room, and below it, in tall blocky letters, was the following:

JOSEF LIECHTEN THERESON ESINLOWE.
WANTED ALIVE, 250,000 GOLD STANDARDS.

"Josef," Eli said, very quietly. "Why is your number larger than mine?"

Josef didn't answer. He just stood there, staring. Then, without a word, he turned, pushed his way through the crowd to their bench, grabbed his bag and his wrapped sword, and stomped out the back door.

Eli and Nico exchanged a look and ran after him.

"Josef," Eli said, running to keep up with the swordsman's ground-eating strides. "Josef! Stop! What's this about? Where are you going?"

Josef kept walking.

"Look," Eli said, jogging beside him. "If you're worried I'm upset that you have a higher bounty than I do, you shouldn't be. I mean, I am upset, but you shouldn't be worried. I'm sure it's just a mistake. If you'll stop walking for just a second, I can go nick your poster and we'll take a closer look. Maybe they added an extra zero by accident or—"

"I don't need a closer look."

Eli stumbled a little. Josef's voice was taut with rage. Quick as he'd taken off, Josef stopped and turned to face them. Eli shrank back at the cold, white anger on his face, nearly stumbling into Nico.

Josef's eyes flicked from thief to girl. "It's no mistake," he said. "That bounty is her last card. I can't let her do this."

"Her who?" Eli said.

"Queen Theresa."

"I see," Eli said, though he didn't. "Well, if it's not a

mistake, then I'm stumped. What did you do to this queen to earn a number like that?"

The side of Josef's mouth twitched. "I lived."

Eli crossed his arms. "Could you try being a little less cryptic?"

"No." Josef pulled his bag off his shoulder and tossed it to Nico. "I have to go away for a while. There's food enough for the next day in there. Nico, I'm counting on you to keep Eli from doing anything stupid. I realize it's a tall order, but do your best."

Nico glared at him and tossed the bag back. "I'm going with you," she said.

"And I'm with her," Eli said, straightening up. "You can't just walk out on us now."

Josef raised an eyebrow. "And I suppose my opinion in this doesn't matter?"

Eli crossed his arms over his chest. "Not in the least. Where are we going?"

For a moment, Josef almost smiled. "The port at Sanche. We can catch a ferry from there to Osera."

"Osera?" Eli made a face. "You mean the island with the carnivorous yaks, endless rain, and zero-tolerance policy toward thieves? Why?"

"Because," Josef said, setting off down the road, "I've been called home."

Nico fell in behind him, her feet kicking up little clouds of yellow dust as she hurried to catch up. Eli stared at their backs a moment longer, and then, cursing under his breath, he shoved his new poster into his bag and ran down the road after them.